His Date With Fate

Wesley Thomas

First Edition Design Publishing
Sarasota, Florida USA

His Date With Fate
Copyright ©2020 Wesley Thomas

ISBN 978-1506-908-27-4 PBK
ISBN 978-1506-909-09-7 EBK

LCCN 2019906202

April 2020

Published and Distributed by
First Edition Design Publishing, Inc.
P.O. Box 17646, Sarasota, FL 34276-3217
www.firsteditiondesignpublishing.com

For you.

CHAPTER 1

January eighth, two thousand and whatever. I hate this time of year as I've already rescinded on my new year's resolutions. Although, to be honest, when I made them I kinda knew I wouldn't follow through. I have no discipline whatsoever and have given up feeling bad about shit like this.

Every morning I lay in bed just staring at the grey, patchy ceiling while cynical thoughts about life plague my mind. Or I drift off wishing I've invented something cool that changed the world and made me rich. It's either extreme pleasure or extreme pain that enters my mind upon awakening, and lately the ratio has been a lot more of the latter.

My life is hardly a Hollywood movie; I live in a regular house in a regular neighborhood, with a fat wife and an Attention Deficit Disordered child who plays video games for about eight hours a day.

I recently celebrated another digit added to my chronological age, although I shouldn't exactly call it a celebration; there was nothing to be happy or thankful for. My annual bornday celebration used to be a great joy for me, now they are nothing but a cruel reminder of how everything is going downhill from here. Yep, these forty-one years that I've been on this planet have whizzed by in what seems like a blink; I haven't exactly been living it to the max. Each year my belly gets fatter, my skin gets droopier, I'm getting little grey sprouts in my hair, and I've officially grown some man-boobs which are embarrassing and disturbing to say the least. I'm at the heaviest I've ever been—three-twenty-five and growing. I get awful stomach pangs from a recent peptic ulcer I've developed, probably from all the stress I'm going through and I'm having major trouble digesting foods.

My energy is at an all-time low, as is my sex drive towards my wife. On the rare times when we rock the casbah, I usually just drift off and think of wrestling. I'm too easily distracted, that's my problem. No matter what's going on in my life I never stop to enjoy the moment because I always have fifty million things going on in my damn head. It just doesn't stop, I have no peace or zen whatsoever, which is what I really yearn for. Instead, I usually just numb myself with beer and television for hours, watching endless amounts of crap including a new reality show called *Geeks, Freaks and Butt Cheeks…* Yeah, really.

I often think how did I end up here? Is this all there fucking is to life? Every day seems to be the same monotonous bullshit — minutes turn into hours, hours turn into days, and then years go by until you realize what the hell did I do with my life?

"Morning, honey," my wife, Sherri, murmurs half asleep.

I don't even want to tilt my head in her direction — she looks like a troll in the morning — but of course, I would never say that out loud.

"What do you think of this?" I say, staring at the ceiling. "A cleaning product that smells like a cologne or perfume so when you clean the kitchen, for instance, it smells of Versace or Gucci instead of foul toxins." I turn in her direction and notice little whiskers popping out her upper lip. "Think about it: why don't name brand cosmetic companies have cleaning products that make the house smell like their high-end fragrances?"

"I don't know," she says. "What made you come up with that?"

I reveal a quick tale from yesterday when I spilled a bottle of Calvin Klein on the bathroom floor. "After wiping it up the whole bathroom smelt of CK1, that's when I had the light bulb moment because it smelt so much better than those bland poisonous chemicals."

"Did it smash?" she questions tilting her head towards me.

I admit it did but this is not enough. She grills me making sure I swept up every last particle.

"Relax, I got it all. It was a miniature so there wasn't much glass. Why do you always have to be so cynical, woman?"

This doesn't sit well with her, I guess I did come off a little curt but defend my point by proclaiming I've potentially come up with a million-dollar idea that could change the whole cleaning industry, but she's more concerned with some stupid little glass particles.

"I just wanted to make sure, that's all," she says, rolling closer to me.

"So what do you think?"

"I think you better get up for work."

"You just don't get me. You never believe in me." I roll away from her, stuffing my head in the pillow, making no attempt to leave my cozy Tempur-Pedic haven.

"What I get is, it's 8:20, if you don't get out of bed you're going to be rushing around and stressed for work."

She's right but I'm not trying to hear that right now. It seems like we go through an idiotic rigmarole every single morning. My enthusiasm to get up is about as low is my desire to go down on her.

She then proceeds to beat me with a pillow to motivate my ass. "Get your fat ass up!"

That's rich coming from the sloth that is my wife. I mean, the nerve of her calling me fat, what a freaking hypocrite! She's small, dumpy and round like a bowling ball with legs. In fact, she's got more of a pear shape figure like Earthquake from the World Wrestling Federation in the nineties.

"Come on, Mr. Grumpy. Those legs ain't gonna move themselves now."

"Alright, pumpkin-head, enough already!" I hurl, stopping the assault. "I'll jump in the shower double-quick. Have the pancakes and coffee ready in ten." I reluctantly roll out of bed and waddle to the bathroom.

"I can't!" she squeals before telling me she's got too much to do, including driving our daughter Max to the doctor.

"Just make it happen!"

The nerve of the woman, trying to worm her way out of making my breakfast! It only takes a minute or so to microwave some damn pancakes and make coffee. I'm not falling for her slimy tactics today.

The crisp water hits my face full force, giving me a much needed wake-me-up while I smear aloe veda shower gel across my Buddha belly. Man, I'm really getting tubby, I can't even see my dick anymore because of all this flab. It's so embarrassing that I don't even want to focus on it. All I can think about is the asinine day that lies ahead of me. Oh, how I loathe these mornings.

I arrive downstairs to my coffee and pancakes, which were not made with any love. Jeez, this place is a fucking tip. Unkempt would be a vast understatement as I witness piles of magazines, boxes and discarded kiddy toys haphazardly around the dining area. And one thing that really irks me is uneaten food left rotting on the table, especially when it starts to putrefy. This is some foul shit. To make matters worse, I spot a baby cockroach crawling out the woodwork in the corner.

"Dammit, Sherri, another roach! Will you please keep on top of this? Remember that word: *cleanliness*, this shit is disgusting."

No verbal response which is no surprise at all. I kill the damn bug with one whack of my shoe and plop myself at the breakfast table, informing her she forgot the syrup.

Without saying a word, Earthquake opens the fridge, grabs the maple syrup and slams it in front of me. Boy, is she looking dumpy. What a turn off. I might have to start choking the chicken in the shower every morning unless she loses that churro flab. I'm not kidding.

I soon notice her staring at me as I chow down my poorly prepared breakfast.

"What happened to you? You didn't use to be like this."

"Like what?" I sneer in between chewing the stodge.

"Like *this*. You snap at the drop of a hat, you're mean to me all the time, we don't do anything fun anymore and we barely spend any quality time together as a family."

I freeze up as this attack catches me off guard and she has no problem giving me more by telling me I neglect this family, I barely even smile anymore and I'm just not emotionally present with her (whatever that means). "This is not the man I fell in love with."

Her face is now flushed with a pinkish hue, she's bitter and scorned but remains somewhat composed.

"I'm under a lot of stress at work!" I defend. "I'm putting in long hours to meet quotas I must hit." (A complete lie, but hey, I'm an expert at that). "It's not like you're pitching in or bringing anything to the table. Remember, this is my house, my kitchen, my table and my fucking plates! All this shit was bought with my money!" I stab into the last soggy pancake and devour it like a caveman.

Earthquake turns irate. I sense fire about to blow out her mouth.

"How dare you say that?! I'm the mother of your child! I work twenty-four-seven, three-sixty-five, but who's fucking counting?"

Oh boy, I've opened up a can of worms now; this could be a big one on the Richter scale. She demands to know how can I say that as she does *everything for this family.*

"Look, I haven't got time for this right now," I stand up. "I'm gonna be late."

I leave the kitchen without looking back at her menacing face. Steam is probably coming out of her ears.

See what I mean? This is not a zen-like way to start the day. Ugh, welcome to the world of Bobby James Jannetty.

CHAPTER 2

Trees sway in the gusty wind as I march down the street on this dull, miserable morning. I got the hell out of there without even brushing my teeth, I just had to. I can't let her mess with my emotions before work. I need to be clear-headed and anxiety-free.

I walk to work every day to save money and because it's fairly close, which is not by fluke, I deliberately chose a house in close proximity to my store. Who wants to be stuck in traffic in this concrete jungle to earn a living every day? Too much stress. This shitty city has gone downhill being overpopulated with morons who can't drive, so I made a conscious choice to avoid the hustle and bustle by commuting to work on foot which is about the only exercise I get these days.

Oh shit, I'm so inside my head I've totally forgot to cross the road. I make it a priority to avoid my neighbor's monotonous conversations, especially Mrs. Wienerschnitzel, an elderly crow-faced dame that reminds me of the Wicked Witch of the West. She always wears her hood up for reasons I'll never know, and never changes her foul smelling old-lady perfume. I think she takes pleasure in delaying me when I'm trying to get from A to B.

"Bobby, how are you?" she says with her notorious croaky dialect.

"Morning, Waylene. How's that little hot-dog of yours?"

"Bungle's had a little boo-boo but she's getting better now. Here, let me get her for you."

Yes, her fucking dog is called Bungle! I keep walking at a brisk pace. I ain't getting suckered into her horse shit today.

"Sorry, Mrs. W, I'm gonna be late. I'll catch that ghastly little beast another time."

Without looking back I march away with my briefcase in hand. In case you're wondering what's inside, it's nothing of great importance. It just makes me feel more professional carrying it around. All that's in there today is miscellaneous junk foods like potato chips, Nutella and Gummy Bears, this month's edition of *Inventions Today* and a 1988 WWF sticker album. Yep, I'm far from a big shot CEO or entrepreneur, more like a *wanttrepreneur*.

I turn a corner.

"Excuse me, sir, my name is Barry Bockwinkel and I'm homeless. Any money you can spare would be greatly appreciated. It would mean the world to me."

The frail voice belongs to a tramp who's gotten way too up, close and personal for my liking. He looks like a complete disaster: his teeth are brown not yellow, and he smells of wine, piss and Kentucky Fried Chicken. Who introduces themselves using their full name when begging in the street? This has to be a hustle from a slick conniver or something. I don't have time to be chit-chatting to some bum, I'm running late as it is, but I can't resist cutting a quick promo to let him know where I stand.

"You, pal, are what's wrong with this country. You've got it way too soft here and you think pestering people for money is an acceptable behavior, and that, my friend disgusts me. My grandfather came here with nothing but a dream and a desire to work hard. He couldn't even get a working visa for months, and let me tell you something; he never stole, cheated or begged people for money—he simply worked low paid, shitty 'wetback' jobs until his papers came through." I scrunch my face up like a bulldog to convey my lack of pity. "So what's your fucking excuse? You have a social security number, don't you?"

Nothing. He just gawks like a perv at a peep show.

"I said you have a social security number, right?"

"Yeah…"

"And judging by your voice you are an American, are you not?"

His eyes look down to his raggedy shoes before admitting that he is.

"Then what's your fucking excuse, man? Or more precisely, what's your justification? You can get a job. People come here from all over the world to build something great and become a proud American citizen. That's what the *American Dream* is all about. And here you are begging on the corner like a piece-of-shit bum. They should ship you off to Ethiopia where you'll see what real poverty looks like and see how long you'll survive out there."

I'm on a roll and it feels good. He just takes it full force and stutters with a response so I strike again.

"No matter how bad your circumstances have gotten, the absolute lowest resort should be trying to extract money from strangers. I mean, come on, man, step your game up! I'll become a corpse before I'll become a bum!"

My statement leaves him looking shell-shocked as I attempt to depart before I really let him have it.

"Please, sir, I'm just trying to get something warm to eat."

I stop in my tracks and exhaustedly turn back to him. His little sob story ain't gonna work on me. "People like you make me sick to my stomach. How can you let yourself get like this, you're a grown man for Christ's sake!"

No reaction once again, he's softer than a bowl of soggy cornflakes so I can't resist giving him more:

"You're a fucking disgrace! A disgrace to yourself and a disgrace to this great country. If you can stand on a corner all day asking people for money, then you can stand behind a counter and say *'Welcome to McDonald's, can I take your order?'* It doesn't matter that you're forty-eight or however old you are, working at Micky D's at forty-eight is still better than scrounging in the streets like a scumbag! So do yourself a favor and go do something constructive with your life, capiche?!"

Beads of sweat have formed on the fibers of his scraggly beard as he just stands there like he's been zapped in the ass with a cattle prod. I don't think he knows what hit him, so I wind up for the final blow:

"The next time I see you, it better be at the drive-through, so practice these words: *'Do you want fries with that?'* Now get the fuck out of my face before you make me late for work!"

CHAPTER 3

So here's my life: a fucking sales manager at a lame mattress outlet, Box Spring Boogie. This job has about as much excitement as a WNBA game. My office is in complete shambles with unfinished projects scattered everywhere cluttering up my shit, but I'm too lazy and distracted to do anything about it. I've quite frankly come to the point of not caring.

It's fair to say I work with morons all day long, both staff and customers. This is not me being mean or judgemental; I'm merely stating a fact. You wouldn't believe the kind of riff-raff we get in here. One guy last week came in saying he wasn't interested in buying anything, he just likes to roll around on different mattresses for fun. Un-fucking-believable. And don't get me started with the staff.

First, you have Candi; voluptuous with bright red hair like the Little Mermaid, with about as much knowledge of this industry as a damn Ding Dong. I guess David hired her because of her good looks and crudely nick-named her *Eye Candi*. How corny can you get?

Then you have Johnny who wants everyone to call him *Johnny Ace*, another freaking dimwit. If he had half a brain, it would be three quarters too much. Two Saturdays ago, he asked me if it's alright to leave early to participate in a milkshake drinking contest. I'm telling ya, you can't make this stuff up.

Finally, you have Billie, who's a little sweetheart but couldn't close a fucking door. Her previous job was working in a cafe, thus she has no real sales experience and is way too nice to be working in this industry. She should stick to being a latte girl because she won't cut it here long term in my opinion, but the girl makes a mean cappuccino, I'll give her that.

My daily routine is notoriously hiding in my office to avoid the animals before they bombard me with ridiculous questions. Today's objective is to try and do as little as I possibly can, then tomorrow, outdo myself by doing even less. It's become a game of beating my slothfulness from the day before. I bet you're thinking I'm a real go-getter, right? A real asset to the company? Well, I wasn't always like this, I was once a dynamite realtor producing ten to fifteen stacks a month if you can believe it. That was until the company went belly-up when the economy went to shit, and I've been stuck here ever since.

My level of caring and compassion has been AWOL for so long that most of my time is spent drifting off in my office surfing the World Wide Web to distract myself with porn, eighties wrestling or documentaries about Edison, Tesla or Leonardo da Vinci. I love anything on inventions and the geniuses that created them. That's what I should be doing with my life, inventing something of value for mankind, something that could impact the world. Yeah, that's what I need to do instead of being stuck in here with these sorry sacks of excrement.

A sudden knock interrupts my inner rant.

"Whatever you want I'm not interested until eight fifty-five," I hurl back at the door.

"Bobby, my boy, I've got something for ya. Why is the door locked? Is everything copacetic?"

That zany voice behind the door could only belong to one man: David, my freaking boss. What the hell is he doing here? He only spends about twenty minutes per week at this location and is usually a stickler for calling first. I hope I'm not in trouble for all this goofing off. If one of those slithery snakes has snitched on me, they will regret the day they were born!

"Gimme two seconds," I reply.

David is a pretty good guy to work for to be honest, even though he's a bit eccentric; always sipping bright colored smoothies and preaching about his California vegan lifestyle. I've never met a happier business owner than him. He's like a boisterous child trapped inside a seventy-two year old's body, probably because every month he beds a different blonde between the ages of nineteen and thirty-five. I think he's trying to be the Hugh Hefner of the mattress industry; testing out different springs with chicks a third of his age or less. He often brags that he's popped more viagra than I've had hotdogs — which is a lot as you can imagine.

"Bob-Bee, what's percolating? I hope you're practicing those rejuvenating breathing techniques that I showed you."

Just listening to him babble gives me an aneurysm and makes me want to take an immediate nap. If you ask this guy what time it is he'll tell you how to assemble the damn watch.

"Sorry, David," I unlock the door. "Wasn't expecting you today."

"It's quite alright, partner," he says, gliding into my office sporting an Armani suit that must have set him back a few Gs. "Thought I'd just swing by to inject some ju-ju-juice up here so we can get shaking and baking."

See what I mean? He's a manchild.

"My boy," he parks himself on my rickety chair, "I've been going over the facts and figures and they've been on the decline for a couple of months now. Not too much to be super-concerned, but enough to give you a good old kick up the wazhoo."

He cocks his leg out and bursts into laughter. Even when he reprimands people, he does it with a ridiculous smile plastered across his tanned leathery face. I don't know whether to laugh or cry.

I agree and tell him in all honesty I've been too soft lately and haven't been motivating the team as well as I should.

"Forget the numbers a minute, Bobby; I'm more concerned with this."

"With what?"

"This —" he motions to my appearance. "You look ill and over-acidic."

"Well…"

"And I see you're holding your stomach like you're in pain."

"It's just a mild peptic ulcer, no biggie."

He babbles on and on about holistic remedies for the next ten minutes which makes me tune out. I resist informing him I'm taking pills and antacids as that would be an additional fifteen minutes of him chewing me out about the evils of prescription drugs.

"What's been going on? You've gotten more chubby than Checker and your waistline has turned into a damn waste-mine. Let me ask you something: every time you put on weight and your pants no longer fit, what do you do?"

"What do you mean, *what do I do?*" I shrug. "I buy new pants."

"Hmmm, evidently you do," he presses, "but think about this for a second: the moment you bought bigger pants was the moment you lost because you accepted a lower standard. You should have remained in your old pants as a painful reminder to slim back down so they fit again. Does that make sense?"

I've got to admit, the old dog has cornered me. I don't think about this stuff all that much. I'm an unconscious snacker, that's my problem. I once went through a whole box of cookies before I realized they were gluten-free dog biscuits.

"What have you been eating to blow up like this?"

I remain vague and tell him pizzas and stuff.

"Oh, so it's pizza's fault you're fat?"

"No, David, it's mine."

"That's right. Remember that saying: *GIGO — Garbage In, Garbage Out.* If you put in junk you'll significantly shorten your life by clogging up your arteries, and this ain't no practice run, is it? We have to make the absolute most of it by WRENCHING THE NECK OF LIFE AND SQUEEZING OUT EVERY

LAST FUCKING DROP!"

His over-the-top statement almost makes me startle as it was delivered with so must zest and enthusiasm that his face turned beetroot red. I hate it when he goes off like this.

He composes himself and opens up his oversized briefcase that looks more like a mini science lab with test tubes, beakers, multi-colored liquids, powders and supplements. He pulls out a couple of twenty-ounce glass containers filled with a foul looking green liquid that can only resemble swamp juice.

"This, Bobby is your new best friend. I call it my *chlorophyll elixir* as it's predominantly made from wheatgrass but actually contains over fifty-two other grasses: lemongrass, kamut, barley…"

He doesn't expect me to actually drink this shit, does he?

"Oatgrass, shavegrass, broccoli sprouts…"

My head is spinning and it has nothing to do with the six-pack of Old Milwaukee I had last night.

"Boy, pay attention! You're drifting off! If you drink four quarts of this every day, you'll turn into a God damn highly-charged sexual intellectual, just like me!"

"Four quarts?" I gasp.

He instructs me to start with baby steps. "It's the best way to start the day. *Breakfast* literally means to *break* your *fast* so you need to give your body proper nourishment, not hickory-smoked bacon and eggs! Not Froot Loops drowned in cow's milk! Not coffee and frickin' donuts! That's what's been happening to you, Bobby; you've lost your drive because you haven't been taking care of what's going in your gut. I know you've got a fire inside your belly, but it's been extinguished from all that coffee and cinnamon buns, so the time has come to get back to the house of health."

He unscrews the lid of his swamp juice and gestures for me to do the same.

"Uhh, what does it taste like?" I ask with great caution.

"Tastes like grass! It's phenomenal!" He stands up raising his glass of grass. "Here's to being happy, healthy and horny."

He remains standing with his glass held high waiting for me to join this barbaric ritual.

I cave.

I stand up, unscrew the lid and grimace at the ghastly foreign liquid. It smells like Yokozuna's jockstrap.

"Let's go on three," he instructs.

Of course, I'm still stalling. I have to treat it like a Jägerbomb, which I can't stand either, but sometimes I get forced to ride the *Jäger-train* with some drunk neanderthals. This though is a sixteen-ounce glass. Still, I have to use the same strategy—down in one quick gulp.

"Three!"

Before I can worm my way out, he knocks his back with one big mouthful. I have to follow suit, can't back out now. I've gotta show him I can play ball. Fuck it, let's get this over with.

I guzzle it down as quickly as humanly possible. As I wipe my lips from excess sludge he notions me to vent my opinion.

"It wasn't as bad as I thought," I say, lying through my fucking teeth. It tastes like ass, not grass! The second he leaves I think I'll hurl it back up, which I'm praying will be soon.

"Here's a six month supply," he says, handing me a tub of this shit.

Supergreens, it says on the container. It should be renamed: *Superpuke.*

"I spent a pretty penny on this for you because I know it will cleanse you from the inside out and you'll start performing again."

I nod and remain mute. I want to get off this subject as quick as possible.

"I brought you a book too: *Think and Grow Rich.* Doesn't that title intrigue you? It's a classic. *Think and Grow Rich* by Napoleon Hill. I'm not going to tell you anything about it, just treat this book as a gold mine."

Yeah, yeah whatever, David. Please go away.

"I'll check it out," I mumble.

"Don't merely check it out, you ignoramus! You must heed this priceless information and take action on the instructions! It very well may change your life like it did mine and so many others. Anyway, time is ticking, let's assemble the team for a good old team talk."

Ugh, will this shit ever end?

CHAPTER 4

Our motley crew of a sales team gather in the showroom as David stands at the helm like Adolf Hitler addressing his troops:

"Let me say a few words about why I'm so passionate about this industry. We are not just selling a mere bed, we are selling relaxation. We are selling comfort. We are selling joy, pleasure, peace of mind. We are selling better sleep, better sex, we are selling a better quality of life!" He flings is arms in the air like an opera conductor. "If you sleep better, you feel and perform better — thus you become better. Healthy sleep is absolutely paramount to the quality of your life."

His speech is making me drift off to sleep, I'll tell you that…

"In fact, the CIA discovered one of the most powerful ways to extract information from prisoners is to keep them continually awake. After three or four days of sleep depravity it becomes so unbearable they have no choice but to start coughing up info."

"I did not know that," says Johnny, all impressed.

"When a new prospect comes through those doors, don't just jump straight into bed with them—" he elbows Candi who lets out a girlie giggle "—begin by getting to know them as your brother, your sister and ask if they're sleeping well on a regular basis. Look in their eyes and heal their pain with the finest quality bed that they can afford. That's when you strike! It's a hurt 'em and heal 'em business."

Johnny raises his hand like a little schoolboy. "What if they say they can't justify spending thousands on a Divan Divine and get a cheaper deal elsewhere?"

"Johnny, my boy," he says rubbing his hands together, "you have to raise the value of our brands in the mind of the customer. You say: '*Sir, you're absolutely correct, you can get cheaper deals elsewhere, but that's exactly what you'll get: a cheap bed, a cheap quality of sleep and ultimately a cheap quality of life! Not to mention cheap sex! Do you and your wife want a cheap thrill every time you do the hanky-panky?*'"

Everyone laughs.

"All because you decided to skimp a few bucks on something of this importance?' Then you wait for their response and hit them with the shoe analogy."

"What's the shoe analogy?" asks Billie.

"You tell them you should never skimp on shoes or a bed because you're always gonna be in one or the other. Ain't that something?"

David seems pleased with his slick response. I've been using that one for years.

"Beds are not something to pinch pennies on, we're going to be using them eight hours per day, for a minimum of ten years, *'so doesn't it make sense to purchase the finest one available, sir?'* That's how you handle resistance. Are you guys getting this?"

Everybody nods like a bunch of hypnotized robots.

"We have to raise the value of our luxurious beds in the customers' minds and trust me; they will have no problem spending a little extra dough on such a quality product which improves their life massively. Does that make sense to y'all?"

"Sure does to me!" says the now pumped-up Johnny Ace.

"Selling doesn't have to be a battle. It can be more like making love. I don't know about you guys, but I'm feeling pretty sexual today."

The whole squad giggles once again. I've heard this stuff a thousand times so I drift off like I normally do and find my eyes wandering to Candi's cleavage.

"So give it your all today, team! Get your mind into a peak sexual state and use that undeniable charisma that every one of you possesses and let's go-go get 'em!"

He jumps up hi-fiving everybody like we're at a pep rally.

This zesty old bastard sure has a way with words, but oh my God, how over-the-top can you get? I'm counting the seconds until he leaves so I can finally goof off in peace.

CHAPTER 5

I leave for lunch early as I can no longer suppress my hunger pangs. All morning I've had a giant, high-def image of mouth-watering meatballs melting on my tongue. I'm a fast-food fiend so I'm gonna order about twenty-five bucks of that shit when I get there. Why? Because I'm just in one of those moods, plain and simple.

I arrive at the *convenience* restaurant (as they're now called) excited to get my indulgence on. Unfortunately, there's a horrendous sea of people lined up out the door, but it's worth the wait as I've sampled everything on the menu twice already and it's only been open a few weeks. As soon as I heard about a Swedish meatball fast-food franchise I knew it would be a big hit around this country. Fat ass Americans love their junk food as long as it's fast, cheap and unhealthy.

At last, only one lady in front of me, who has way too much junk in her trunk — wouldn't like to be stuck next to her on an airplane. As the delicious smell of the deep fat fryer wafts in my direction, my right leg starts to bob up and down from the anticipation of stuffing my fat fucking face.

"Hello, sir. Welcome to Meaty-Alright where it's our treat to feed you meat." The voice belongs to a bubbly little Hispanic girl who can barely see over the counter.

"Cute. They make you say that, don't they?" I smile rubbing my hands together. "Let me get three large Meaty-Alright specials with no onions, no peppers, and definitely no pineapple, let's keep it simple. Also, I'll have the frozen yogurt, the Kladdkaka Kake, and a large root beer please."

"Certainly, sir," she returns with a typical robot response. "Will that be all?"

I wonder if she's judging me knowing this food is all mine. Whatever, who cares? Her BMI is probably in the same bracket as mine.

"I think if I order anymore I'll end up like Elvis in the mid-seventies. Did you know that Elvis used to eat deep-fried banana sandwiches for breakfast? Pretty crazy, huh?"

She turns a tad startled from my random knowledge and tells me that's kinda gross.

"And get this: Elvis was a natural blonde, but he dyed his hair black to look cooler and sell more records. Not a lot of people know that..."

Her face makes a strange gesture that's pretty hard to describe, basically a frown, a nod and a scrunch all in one. I think it's safe to say I've weirded this chick out. Or maybe she doesn't believe me as many people don't when I hit them with unknown facts about *The King*.

"It's a hundred percent true. But anyway, I digress. Yes, my dear, that will be all."

I pay the transaction, stand off to the side and feel my right leg convulse again as I watch the pimple-faced teenagers make up my cholesterol clogging order.

Hurrah, here it is—fifteen-hundred calories of bliss. However, after further inspection, I notice my three sandwiches are laced with all the shit I specifically said I didn't want: onions, peppers and pineapple! What kind of imbecile invented putting pineapples on meatballs or pizza anyway? Disgusting! I can feel my blood boil as I turn to the little fat girl who took my order.

"I can't believe you fucked up a simple order of bread and meat, you useless fat fuck!"

As those venomous words eject from my potty mouth, I can feel all eyes on me from everybody in my radius. She's on the brink of tears and apologizes sincerely, but I ain't trying to hear that. I have no sympathy for incompetence.

"You know what, I can believe it. Nobody in these places can ever process a simple order, that's why you're a jobber in this shitty establishment! Imbeciles!"

I have a short fuse and their ineptitude has triggered it big time.

"Again, I'm sorry, sir," she hushes. "I will fix it for you—"

"Don't fucking bother!" I snap, grabbing the tray. "It will just waste more time. Time I haven't got! You go back to fucking up people's orders and I'll fix this shit myself. Have a nice day!"

I couldn't have been more condescending as I depart from the counter. I can feel the evil stares of the staff and surrounding customers as I hunt for an open table in this packed out meat market.

"Hey, Bobby," calls a voice from a direction that I can't quite locate. "Over here, jackass."

Oh, that's who it is; Cam aka the Fireman. He's not actually a fireman; we used to work together back in the day. Now he's a slick-talking insurance spokesman who works down the block at the most prestigious firm in the city. They gave him that nickname because he puts out the firm's fires like no other. And I can attest to that, I've actually witnessed him influence a room full of healthcare professionals that smoking cigarettes are not that dangerous for one's health. He's a real piece of work.

"What's going on, broski?" he says wiping his mouth with a pink doily. This dude reminds me of a human version of Dick Dastardly, but for all his devilish attributes there's a lot to admire about this guy. "Pull up a seat."

"Don't mind if I do, Mr. Spin-Doctor. This place is more packed than a forty man Battle Royal." I join him at his well-organized banquet and waste no time tucking into mine. "Did you bring your own doily? You know they have napkins here."

He pouts telling me it's a fifty dollar silk handkerchief from Europe and doesn't trust cheap fast-food napkins. He then points out that I look a little rough around the edges.

"Yeah I know, I've been pretty stressed and haven't been sleeping well at all. I keep having these reoccurring nightmares where the Nasty Boys have me stuck in the *Pit Stop* for like six straight hours."

He laughs, calling me a jackass again, knowing I love that word.

"How's things at work?" I ask as I pick out the gross little peppers and pineapples.

"I just got a bonus added to my bonus. *'My shoes cost more than your house!'*" he says doing a great Ric Flair impression which cracks me up every time. "How's things over at Boogie-Woogie?"

His question kills my Nature Boy high, directing focus to my bleak reality. "Same monotonous bullshit." I chomp into sandwich number two like a piglet. "After working there for so long I can finally understand why people who work boring jobs for years start getting the urge to shoot the place up…"

Judging by his surprised look my remark has thrown him off.

"… It's because they're doing the exact same repetitive shit every single day like fucking robots and don't feel any sense of variety, significance, or joy, so they devise a plan to take it out on strangers. After years of wrestling with evil thoughts they can no longer take it, so they buy a pump-action shotgun, shell that shit up to the max and blow everybody's fucking brains out!"

I pause to inhale more meatballs into my gullet while Cam looks a tad freaked (which is predictable when you drop psycho shit on them). It's that built-up tension inside me again.

"Damn, bro, you got issues. That was intense. You need to get laid or something."

17

He's right on the money so I reveal how long it's been since I've even got my fingers wet (which I probably said too loudly).

"*#SexualFrustration,*" he grins.

"Guilty."

"Hmmm, I have an idea," he waves his index in the air and tells me he's got just what I need and pulls out a little baggie of white powder from his blazer. "Bam!"

Is this guy fucking crazy? He knows I'm not into drugs of any kind.

"What the fuck is that? Coke?" I ask (being ninety percent sure, although you never know with him).

"Exact-a-mondo, Amigo. Coke is back like the NWA and this is the finest snow on the streets. This is what you need to help you forget your troubles and drift off into oblivion."

I stare at him blankly like he's lost his mind.

"Are you gonna grab it, Bobby? I'm not trying to announce it to the whole place, bro."

"You know I don't mess around with that shit. I'm not some punk college freshman."

"Come on, don't be a lameo. It's not like I'm trying to make money out of you, it's on the house, brother."

I reject his offer once again as I dig around my pockets for my *prescribed* drugs.

"Fair enough. But you don't know what you're missing out on," he slips it back in his suit then informs me about a launch party tonight at a new spot called The Blackout. "Open bar from eight 'till late. It's gonna be a banger."

He observes my unenthused face before washing down multiple pills with my root beer.

"What are they?"

"These are for my ulcer, and these are for acid reflux."

"You alright?"

"Yeah, it's no biggie, just a little stomach thing. The worst part is how they taste, these shits are nasty."

He stands up, giving me a full view of his expensive attire that glistens under the low hanging IKEA bulbs. Maybe he wasn't joking after all, his outfit probably costs more than my damn house, lucky bastard.

"So come on, man, it's gonna be a lot more fun than that shitty Duck Dive you spend way too much time in."

"Maybe. I'll think about it." I say with absolutely no intention of attending.

"*Maybe* is for slackers who can't make simple decisions. If you wanna get out of that rut and have some fun, you know my digits. Laters."

CHAPTER 6

Back at work, the clock seems to be moving at a damn snail's pace. Boredom has completely hijacked my mind like an evil plague, making this afternoon more torturous than a Mexican soap opera marathon. I'm so jaded I could eat sixteen Babybels back to back just for the hell of it. I must stop binging like a savage, it's playing hell with my stomach and I'm popping more acid tablets than a hippie at Coachella.

Pretty much like every day, monotony has once again got me in a choke-hold, so I decide to lock my office and surf the net for porn sites; particularly muscle porn. I seem to gravitate towards muscular men pounding skinny blondes with oversized fake breasts. I'm not sure why it gets me off; it's probably a sense of power that I'm lacking in my life.

Here we go: *abs&slags.com*. Hmmm, this should be interesting. Every time I see these jacked-up dudes flexing their pelvic muscles into a hot bitch's vag, it becomes a harsh reminder how fat and overgrown I've become, and it angers me why I'm still not doing anything about it. I can feel my health slipping away on a daily basis. I hate to admit it but David's right; I've got to get control or I'll be in major jeopardy down the line.

It only takes me three point five minutes to clean the pipes and throw away the Kleenex but now what? I can't be bothered to deal with any humans so I decide to avoid the floor, I'll leave that for the subordinates. Oh God, I'm so bored. Somebody put me out my misery. I guess I'll just fuck around on YouTube to kill a couple more hours and sneak in a nap before five.

After work I have no intention of going straight home, I feel like a few beers in my local dark and dingy watering hole: The Duck Dive. This place is stuck in the eighties; old rickety tables, wobbly bar stools that you have to put coasters underneath, dated TVs with no high-def and ghastly toilets which seem to have permanent shit stains on. It's no wonder nobody new comes in here. It used to be popping back in the day, now it just seems to attract the same sweaty old drunks with halitosis and foul body odor.

Despite the flaws, it does have character. It's *our* bar, the beer is cheap and they have the sound on when they show sports, which is the way it should be. I loathe those modern sports bars that play music instead of having the commentary on when it's game time. It totally ruins the experience of sports entertainment in my opinion because the commentary keeps you engaged, along with the ruckus fans, players and whatnot.

Growing up, I had a little clique of friends that were just as obsessed with wrestling as I. When I say *obsessed* I mean we'd sometimes rewatch a match in slow motion and break down each high-spot like forensic experts in the JFK assassination. I'll never forget this one time we decided to watch the opening match of *Prime Time Wrestling* with the sound off and unanimously came to the conclusion that it ruined ninety percent of the fun. It just seemed like a bunch of muscled up men in trunks pretending to hit each other. It's when you add the over-the-top color commentary, the entrance music and crowd to the mix, that's what makes wrestling so much more entertaining.

As I sit alone at the bar finishing the dregs of my first adult beverage, in struts one of the funny regulars, Jolly Jim. He's a tall, slender bag of bones but definitely can hold his beer, he is British after all. He always speaks that funny cockney slang that most of us have to google just to understand, and can light up the room with his wit, even though most his material revolves around gays or him being so brilliant.

"Hey, fat boy, how's it going?" Jolly says in that thick London accent of his. "Fancy a Joe Swale?" (Meaning *beer* or *ale* to be precise).

"I'm not gonna say no to that, pal."

"Fack me, Bobby, what's up with you? Did you just get out of bed or sumfing? You look like a right fackin' gypo, my son."

"Well excuse me; I didn't realize we're at the Ritz, Jol."

"It doesn't matter where you're at, Bob, you gotta have some class about ya when ya out in public. A fackin' dog wouldn't lick that mug!" he points with his rolled-up copy of the *Wall Street Journal* that he notoriously carries everywhere.

I shrug him off and tell him I love him too.

Despite the fact he's just walked in, and basically nobody else is here, he still acts all impatient for a pint to Mitch the bartender.

"Come on, Mitch, I've been stood here for *donkey's* dying of fackin' thirst. Get us a couple of frosty ones on the yanger's tab, will ya?"

He then tells me to '*get it down my Gregory Peck*' and clips me around the ear with the *Wall Street Journal*. I have no arsenal against him, and if I did he just turns it around and uses my material right back at me. I usually just laugh and let him do the entertaining.

"Always a pleasure, Jol," says Mitch as he hands us a couple of cold frothy beverages.

"Cheers, big ears," he says as we clang the drafts together. "Hey; what do you call a deer with no eyes?"

Mitch and I look at each other clueless.

"*No idea!*" he says with more cheese than a Papa Johns stuffed crust. I can't help but laugh, it's his delivery. Mitch smiles and walks away to serve old man Sam at the other end.

"You're too much. Happy hump day, funny man."

"Owwwe, that's a cold beer!" he says wiping the creamy froth from his mouth. He then starts sniffing the air around us. "Faww, what's that smell? It smells like fackin' coconuts or something."

"Oh yeah," I say realizing it's me. "I was bored earlier in my office and got this great idea for a hand cream made from coconut oil, aloe vera, black African soap and ethanol."

"Ethanol?"

"Yeah ya know, pure alcohol."

"I know what ethanol is, you silly puff. Are you right in the fackin' head? You smell like a West Hollywood massage parlor, you queer cunt."

I burst into laughter and can't rebuttal for the life of me.

"I thought you worked at that mattress place? Not the fackin' gay cosmetic outlet. Have you got something you wanna tell me, fluffer boy?"

"You may mock, but there's a lot of money to be made with cosmetics and toiletries."

I knew it wouldn't go over well with him, he oozes too much machismo, not exactly my target consumer. I switch subjects before he unloads on me more and ask what he's been up to lately.

"Mate, you have no idea; in the past month I've had more adventures than the chicks in those Tampax commercials! One minute I'm jumping out a *Michael Caine*, then I'm scuba diving down the *Hurricane Katrina*, and the week before last I was skiing down in Tahoe, frigging off all the birds on the ski lift!"

He delivers lines like a well-rehearsed comedian. Now I really am Googling his lingo. *Michael Caine* evidently means airplane and *Hurricane Katrina* means the marina.

"And you ain't gonna believe what happened at the weekend, this is the yarn of all yarns, I tell ya…" He goes on to tell me how he won two grand against some *soppy septic cunts* playing poker, broke up a big fight at the pub, ended up at a titty bar with some Hollywood producer dude and brought back a bunch of strippers to the Jol-Radisson.

"You're a piece of work, my friend," I say, shaking my head. "A wild weekend for me is a case of Buds, a takeout and binge-watching a full season of *Total Divas.*"

"What can I say, some people are cut out for greatness while others just haven't got the swag." And with that, he guzzles down the rest of his beer and wipes his mouth.

"I'll get the next round in," I say, even though I still have half a pint left.

"Nah I'm good, geezer, I gotta take off."

"Already? Stay for another," I plead.

"I ain't got time to be drinking in fackin' pubs all day, I got business to take care of and birds that need a good rogering. I'll catch you next time, Bobby Boo."

He tosses a twenty on the bar and struts towards the door. "Oh, and, Bobby," he turns back, "what do you call a deer with no eyes and no legs?"

Once again I can't think of the punchline so he helps me out.

"*Still no idea!*" and glides out the door taking all the fun with him.

What a character. I wish I had the gift to light up a room the way he does.

I better head home and face the music, or shall I stay for one more? Hmmm, decisions, decisions…

CHAPTER 7

Yep, I procrastinated remaining glued to the bar stool for another five innings of baseball until I finally get my act together and stumble home.

I'm dreading the encounter with Earthquake, but what can I do? I have to face her at some point so I might as well get it over with. I really can't be bothered with confrontation but I doubt that I'll be that lucky.

I quietly insert the house key and enter, but before I've even hung my jacket Sherri swarms me in the hallway.

"Where the hell have you been and why is your phone off?!" she screeches.

You can just feel the tension and hostility suffocate this house, it's palpable. "I was working late again, then went to the Duck for a couple of beers. Jesus, relax, woman."

"But why is your phone off?"

"The battery ran out."

I lie so much it's become an art for me, the art of congruency. I've become so good at it, I often forget when I'm lying or telling the truth. "Why are you always on my case? It's the last thing I need after a long day at work."

My little seven year old, Maxine comes running up to greet Daddy with a hug. Maybe she can rescue me?

"You don't care what you put me through! You could have easily contacted me from another phone to say you're going to be late. That's what a normal husband would do."

I notice a little beetle creep into the house and use it as a perfect pivot from her hostile interrogation.

"Look, a beetle!"

I raise my leg about to strike, but Max interjects:

"—No, Daddy. Don't send it to buggy heaven!"

SPLAT!

Too late. I squish the little critter with so much force that yellow puss squirts out its body like a crater faced virgin popping zits before the prom.

"You didn't have to kill it, Daddy. Now bad things are gonna happen to you." Max continues giving me the third degree about karma before running away, leaving me exposed to more verbal combat with you know who.

"You don't do anything constructive anymore. You're drowning your priorities in beer."

All I hear is nag nag nag, doing my best to tune out as I try squeezing past her wide load so I can raid the fridge. But she stands her ground like a linebacker, blocking my path to escape.

"Everything is so negative with you, Bobby. I can't remember the last time you laughed or smiled even. It's like you've lost your smile."

"Lost my smile?" I question. "What kinda shit is that? I work hard every day to put food on the fucking table and this is how you twist shit as if it's my fault?!"

We square off nose to nose like we're about to spar.

"You're never *here* anymore."

"What are you talking about?"

"You're never present with me," she says more calmly. "You may be physically here, but you're never actually present with me. You just slouch around like a bum and I'm losing more and more respect for you."

Damn, she isn't holding anything back, but I know her tactics. I bite my tongue and react with a blank stare.

"In fact, I'm becoming less in love with you every day it seems like."

Now she's welled up with tears. I don't buy it. This is a test to see if I'll cave. The longer I stay here, the longer I'm susceptible to her trap. I can't deal with this right now.

CHAPTER 8

"So wait a minute," Cam presses, sipping his tall cocktail with about twenty-eight ice cubes, "you never noticed all the racial connotations from DiBiase hiring Virgil as his bodyguard, doing all his dirty work?"

"That angle would have worked just as well if he had a white bodyguard," I challenge.

"I couldn't disagree more. It was a race angle. Didn't you notice all the slavery implications?"

"I guess I never thought about it that deeply before," I shrug.

"What about the vignettes where Ted made Virgil clean his toes, shine his shoes and other degrading stuff before *SummerSlam '91?* You didn't click that it was the rich white man flaunting his wealth and power over his negro bodyguard?"

"Well, maybe, but I also figured where they were going with it. I knew one day Virgil would get sweet revenge."

"But you never figured it was like a slave rising up and defeating his master? Come on, Bobby, what's wrong with you?"

"I was like twelve, bro."

He blows me off.

"Hold on a second, Cam, if Ted was an all-out racist he would never have hired a black bodyguard in the first place. A true racist wouldn't ever be associated with any blacks, let alone being accompanied to the squared circle with one."

"You're missing the point, jackass. He hired the black man to flaunt his supremacy, then degraded him in front of everybody!"

"Nah, I don't buy that. Granted it ended up that way and Virgil won the Million Dollar Championship, but before all that Ted employed a black man, put clothes on his back and food on his table, when he could have easily hired a white man. That's the facts."

Cam shrugs me off again and gulps down more rum.

So I decided to take Cam up on that promotional night at this lounge I've never been to: The Blackout. It's a posh venue attracting the upper echelons of society, way too classy for a guy like me, plus I'm well under-dressed for this occasion but I don't care, anything's better than that hell-hole I call home. This is not my scene at all, I like dive bars where the Miller Lite is three bucks and they have free peanuts; this place is way too extravagant. It has a huge fireplace that could fit three Santa Claus and a sculpture made from un-meltable ice—which I'm still trying to figure how it works (the stingy waiters won't reveal the secret).

They must have spent a pretty penny doing all this fancy bullshit, that's for sure. I never did get all this over the top restaurant/lounge stuff; I mean, you sit down and have a guy in a tuxedo kiss your ass all night, who pushes you to get the filet mignon, or chateau cabaret or some other shit that's ludicrously overpriced. Then they bring out a teeny steak with two potatoes, while some other suit plays lift music on a piano and then the bill comes and it's a hundred-and-fifty-two-fucking-dollars before tax and tip. No thank you. I'd rather get a KFC and a six-pack any day of the week.

"So tonight is a launch of a new rum called *Rum's Away,*" says Cam. "I got invited by the HMIC."

"The what?"

"The Head Man In Charge. He doesn't like the traditional title of Chairman or CEO, so he insists on being called the HMIC. He's a real piece of work."

"He sounds it," I laugh.

"You'll see later when I introduce you. He's actually an alright guy, but when he's had a few too many, he gets all up in your grill and tries to out-alpha you, especially in front of women. He's like the special guest referee: he always has to get involved."

"Ha, nice analogy," I guzzle the rest of my rum. "Let's go get another free refill."

"Free refill? Where are we, Taco Bell?"

We hit the rum and coke like a couple of drunken sailors, taking full advantage of this free promo. We basically keep ourselves to ourselves, apart from a few phonies that cross our path with asinine meet and greets. Cam loves this networking bullshit while I can't stand pointless small talk.

"Hey, is this a good time or what?" chirps Cam with his smug mug. "Beats that shitty dive bar of yours."

"It's alright, I love any night that's on the house," I finish another one. "Honestly though, I'm kinda bored. These are not the kind of people I associate with. Everybody's so uppity in here. To them, I must stand out like motherfucking Papa Shango."

Cam cracks up. "Well then let's mingle with the cool folk then. Look around, man: top-notch pussy galore."

"Yeah I know, but it's not right talking to women when you're a married man. I know I've been arguing with Sherri a lot lately but I'm not gonna try and commit adultery."

"Come on, B, how's she gonna find out? Tell me you don't wanna eat that pussy," he points discreetly to a stunning brunette in a sleek cocktail dress.

"Ugh, you eat pussy?"

"Only if it's well-manicured, and I mean really manicured like a high-end golf course."

I laugh at his stupidity as he throws it back to me asking if I eat pussy.

"Nah, man, my wife is fat as fuck. Not to mention sweaty."

"I bet you would eat *her* out," he points to the hottie again, "if she showed you her U.S. Open."

I turn to him in a serious manner. "I would eat that bitch out after a sixty-minute gang-bang from a bunch of AIDS infested Sumo Wrestlers!"

We laugh until the moment passes and I turn serious. "I've never cheated on my wife, I couldn't go through with it. Although I have been having thoughts towards other women lately."

Damn, I'm opening up like he's my shrink or something. This is unusual for me, must be the Puerto Rican rum.

"I think you should go with your intuition. All the big shots have a little chicky on the side."

"Bro, I'm a mattress store manager! I'm hardly Mark Cuban, Elon Musk or Sean motherfucking McGuire! I'm not that guy anymore, he died a long time ago."

"You've still got it, man. So what you've had a little snag in your career, you're still one of us. I see greatness in you. You'll get back on top."

If only he knew that I spend most my days goofing off watching muscle porn and eighties wrestling. I ponder on his statement though, he always knows how to make me feel good about myself, I have to admit.

I thank him for the compliment and tell him I don't have the confidence to interact with these people, especially hot women. I'm beneath them.

"That's horse shit, man, you ain't beneath anybody! Even the Brooklyn Brawler got laid and he was a garbage man."

I smirk for a second and shake my head.

"I've never heard you talk like this. You would have never said this back in the day."

"You're right, but things have changed since then, Cam, I was brimming with confidence because I was young and successful, now I'm just an over the hill loser. If someone here asks me what I do for a living I'll feel embarrassed telling them the truth."

"So lie then."

"No because just my luck they'll one day walk into the store and see me in my cheap paisley suit."

Cam's adamant in not allowing my shit to bring me down and hits me with the truth. "You've lost your drive because you stay at home in your little fucking safe zone playing X-Box, drinking shitty Bud Lights. You need to spice it up, bruh."

"What do you mean *spice it up*?"

"What you're doing obviously isn't working, I've never seen you this down in all the years I've known you."

"You're right, man. I'm in a permanent rut and have lost all self-worth." I look down at my scuffed Payless loafers.

"Like I told you, I got something that will turn you back to the old you." He discreetly pulls out the baggie of cocaine that he waved around in the meatball place.

"Not this again, Cam. I told you I'm not into putting shit up my nose. It's stupid and a waste of money."

"You're hearing me but you're not listening, chico. This will help you forget all your problems and give you pep like you won't believe."

He's such a smug bastard like he's pushing a late-night infomercial product. I return with an evil glare and tell him drugs are nothing but Bad News Brown.

"You don't know what you're missing, Bob. This stuff will give you confidence like you wouldn't believe. The last five presentations I knocked out the park thanks to my secret weapon."

I cut him off right there.

"Whoa whoa, wait a minute: you do this during work?!"

His face lights up like a Christmas tree. "Oh, Bobby, Bobby, of course! That's what I've been trying to tell you. You will sell a shit load of beds if you hit this bad boy at work. All the big-shot players do blow throughout the day. Haven't you seen *The Wolf of Wall Street?* That shit is real."

"Doing blow to get through the day is called *addiction*, dude, I'm not down with that."

"You're getting way ahead of yourself, Bob. I'm not trying to turn you into Razor Ramon, it's just a little magic powder to get you out your rut."

He's in ultimate slickster mode—I know his tricks. But he has got me thinking. Maybe this will help kill the cynical voices in my head.

"You don't know what you're missing out…"

He always says that. I ignore him the best I can and wrestle with my inner thoughts.

"Come on, bro, you'll never know unless you try it."

I look around at everybody else having fun and remain mute.

"This is what you need, I gar-ran-tee!"

"Alright, enough!" I blurt. "But I ain't paying for this shit."

"I told you it's on the house, partner. What kinda guy do you think I am?" He grooms his oily Gordon Gekko-esque hair with his comb. "Come on, hotshot, let's go powder our noses."

We soon find ourselves sharing a disabled bathroom stall. Now I'm paranoid that some MoFo in a wheelchair will roll up on us and be pissed, plus we have to whisper in case people with legs enter the men's room as well.

He pulls out the baggie and sprinkles a couple of lines on the toilet top.

"You do it off there?" I whisper. "That's foul, man."

He's obviously done this before and tells me this is how everybody does it in the john. I shake my head thinking what the hell am I doing here.

"This shit is rocket fuel, it will give you balls of steel and make you think you're B. A. Baracus!"

"I'm more of a Hannibal Smith guy."

"Well, him too. Now watch and learn." He chops up the lines like a well-trained sous-chef with his American Express. "You do it in one easy swoop like this." He wastes no time in demonstrating like the human vacuum he is. Up the nose it goes, dilating his eyeballs and giving him that oomph. He now looks like Brock Lesnar about to enter the ring. "Oh yeah, that's the shit! Okay, your turn."

We switch positions as I lean over and examine the powder like a mad scientist. All I can think is I can't believe I'm actually gonna do this…

I must have been about twenty when I first encountered this thing called 'peer pressure.' Man, I was in shape back then, it seems like a lifetime ago that I was once labeled a jock. My frat boys and I would hit the gym hard at least five times a week. It was the MET-Rx / Creatine / Hot Wings era — the cornerstone of a steady jock diet. Some of the guys took it real serious and became obsessed with Arnold and Lou in *Pumping Iron* watching it every night it seemed like.

Then, at the other end of the spectrum, came the naughty stuff. Our close circle of bros and I would get wasted on cheap booze every Friday afternoon as if it was a religion. It was our pregame ritual where lots of ribbing and shenanigans would go down like Dave W masturbating into Leeroy's protein shake. How gross can you get? The funny thing was Leeroy wasn't all that mad when he found out, he just shrugged it off saying it's only a little semen.

With all the testosterone floating around soon the drugs followed, which is something I just didn't get. I mean, some of these dudes were so strict with their diets and used to meticulously read every food label at the supermarket to see the protein, fat and sugar contents, but thought nothing about sniffing copious amounts of powder every weekend which fucked up their training regime.

"Come on, Bobby, stop being a faggot! Take a little bump," Big Bryan would say.

"You can call me what you want, I'm not into this shit." I would defend to him and the whole group. "The amount of cash you suckers waste on this shit, you could be all up in the club popping bottles like Puff Daddy."

Everybody who knew me eventually stopped offering me drugs, and I never once felt like I was missing out. I went to the same parties as everyone, I just went to bed at three instead of staying up until seven like a zombie. I had life by the tail back then because it was all about fun. Man those were the days—no cares, no drama and no responsibilities. I guess that's why everybody recalls their prime years as *the good old days* because you lived so loose and free when you're young. I didn't care about grades or my shitty job at the bowling alley, I just wanted to drink, watch sports and raise hell like Biff Tannen and his cronies.

Throughout my four years of college, I never once got tempted by coke. The peer pressure thing never affected me at all, yet every single one of my friends had at least tried it, along with ecstasy, ludes, ketamine, pot, molly, speed and some even tried crack and smack, now here I am at age forty-one about to put this shit up my nose for the very first time...

I snap out of my little trip down memory lane and put the rolled-up hundred-dollar bill into my nostril and just stare. Mixed feelings come into play making me hesitate: Shall I, or shall I not? That is the question. It feels like I have a devil and an angel on each shoulder chirping in my ears... Fuck it, the devil has won! I give in and take one big sniff.

WOW.

That rush feeling hits me instantly as I straighten up and gaze in the mirror. My eyeballs have become all white like the Undertaker. Freaky! It's a head-rush unlike anything I've had before. I'd be lying if I said I didn't like it.

"Whoa. This is new." I say, not quite knowing how to express the feeling.

Cam looks on with his patented sinister smile. "You learn quick, young Padawan. The force is strong with this one. Come on, let's go party like it's 1982."

"1982?"

"That's the year Prince released *1999!*"

The rest of the night turned pretty manic. We hit the bar and chugged more rum like a couple of frat boys, while intermittently going to the bathroom to sniff more 'ya-yo' as Cam calls it. We probably hit the bathroom five times in two hours. The more we sniffed, the more we drank.

Despite being toxy from all the free rum, the coke gave me a feeling of control and power that I've never felt before, it was strange. I was very conscious of my actions and didn't slur my speech at all. I even drove home perfectly fine. Obviously, if a cop had stopped me I most definitely would have failed the breathalyzer test and been locked up. Pretty stupid I know, but all sanity went out the window.

I had to take a sick day the following morning — my head and stomach were killing me. But even worse; I had a nagging wife throwing jabs at me all day calling me a *'worthless fucking slob who's not there for his family.'* Much of what she said is the truth so I just took it on the chin and remained pacifistic.

Taking verbal beatdowns have become an everyday occurrence, I've almost become immune to her acid tongue and do my best to ignore her.

Weeks go by like this, I'd drink after work, come home to venomous arguments and fall asleep on the sofa watching *Baywatch*. Can't remember the last time we had sex. What a travesty. Our marriage is spiraling out of control and I barely make any effort to try and save it.

Not only did my drinking escalate, along with my big Buddha belly, but my coke habit too. I find myself hanging with Cam a lot more regularly to go 'skiing' so I can numb myself from all the arduous shit going on in my life and the irony is I don't actually like coke, I just like the way it smells.

CHAPTER 9

I've come to loathe going to work all week and now I've even started to hate my days off as it means spending more time with Earthquake. It feels like I'm in a lose-lose situation no matter how I look at my life. On this rare Saturday that I'm off Sherri guilts me into having a family day at the spring fair. I'm usually pretty good at worming my way out but because it's the final weekend I'm locked in like the Cobra Clutch and have no choice but to obey.

The weather is just right — a ham-and-egger if you ever saw one, with little white spring clouds casting shadows on the freeway. It takes us a while to arrive at the fair because of the congested traffic, and as expected it's completely packed from tent to tent and stall to stall making this family day even more hot, humid and unbearable. I freaking hate crowds especially if I'm hungover, which seems to be a daily occurrence these days, and I can already feel my clothes sticking to me. It feels like the whole city is crammed in this damn field, and to make things ten times worse an old nemesis that I usually do anything and everything to avoid are scattered around here — clowns.

Growing up, I was petrified of clowns. They've always freaked me out, especially if they get close to me. The hair, the makeup, the red nose, the bow tie, all looks so wrong to me and sends shivers down my spine. My friend Molly from down my street had a bad phobia with them too, and always had to cover her eyes whenever Doink came on TV, but that was back when we were about nine. A grown man having similar fears to a little girl is beyond embarrassing.

Not only that, I also envisioned them having ulterior motives towards children like they're secretly child predators wanting to kidnap the young and do sick things to them. I find myself gripping Max's hand tighter when we get within a hundred feet of those fuckers. And I'm pretty sure I know where the fear stemmed from as well.

When I was eleven I went to Rodney Stark's bornday party where he had a creepy-looking clown performing in his backyard. He picked me out from the crowd to participate in his bullshit but I really didn't want to because I was terrified. He was as close to Krusty from *The Simpsons* as you'll ever get. I felt everybody's eyes glued to me as fear and intimidation consumed my body turning me bright red. It got worse as he got close to me, I couldn't stand it, his breath smelt of Jim Beam and jalapeños which made me want to puke. Sweating profusely, I just couldn't take it anymore so I ran away, not just from the scene, from the whole party altogether.

The following Monday at school was a nightmare. The news spread like locker room gossip, all my friends made fun of me for running away from a children's entertainer. I never forgave that tipsy, halitosis ridden motherfucker and now today in their proximity my physiology thrusts into fight or flight mode. I usually just eject from the situation to save myself catching a case and getting sued by a silly kook in a green afro. I have to stop myself from even focusing like this because my mind starts raging like a psychopath.

"Daddy, let's go to the Merry-Go-Round!" says my little girl, breaking my ill trance.

Yes! Anything to get away from those sickos. There's a freak show next door too, how cool—I just love me some freaks. I know what you're thinking; freaks are okay but clowns are not? Exactly. That's how my bizarre brain is wired. Down with the clown!

I suggest the idea of the freak show but of course, it gets shot down by the big fat party pooper.

"Oh come on, Sherri, look there's a man who staples five-dollar bills to his body and the bearded lady is always fun."

"I want the Merry-Go-Round!" pleads little Max.

"A freak show is no place for a young girl. It will give her nightmares. We're going to the Merry-Go-Round. End of story."

The ladies have spoken.

We walk towards the Merry-Go-Round through a sea of people who mope about like clueless lemmings frustrating the shit out of me. Having said that, scattered around this over-populated fairground is a plethora of fully-developed teenage chicks and some yummy mummies pushing around baby strollers. I've been having more and more sexual thoughts towards other women lately and masturbating vigorously about three or four times a day. I yearn for a woman that's in shape, I mean really in shape with a six-pack, silicone titties and a voluptuous frame like Torrie Wilson in her prime, not some dumpy hippo that snores like a donkey on Prozac.

I once read in a magazine that *attraction is not a choice*, it's ingrained in our nervous system and you cannot help but feel it once it's been triggered. It's oh so true. I literally cannot stop these vivid thoughts of debauchery towards hot chicks and within seconds my dick gets harder than Haku. This is the first time since being with Sherri that I've had these kinds of thoughts with the notion of acting upon them.

Right on cue, a fine young specimen with brown mousey hair emerges from the crowd heading towards us. It feels like she's coming directly towards me, ready to embrace me with open arms. My whole reality disappears in this very moment. All that matters is her—her and her stunning beauty. She sparkles in the sun like a glacier with a perfectly shaped hourglass figure and big melon-esque breasts, juicy as a Sunkist. All this seems to happen in slow motion as she transitions past with her hair blowing in the wind and gone from me forever. All I can do is fantasize about mounting her behind the hotdog stand, screaming my name.

"Honey, you're walking the wrong way," says Earthquake, interrupting my wet dream. "It's this way."

I snap out of it as we turn a corner only to see a little man-boy with a clipboard blocking our path.

"Hello, friends, I'm Clive with *Paws, Jaws and Claws,*" he smiles, tightening his Bob Backlund-like bow tie. "We believe that animal cruelty is one of the most devastating afflictions in society today—"

"Whoa-whoa, hold your horses, sonny."

I just hate these space invader type assholes who think it's okay to disturb people and use guilt tactics to donate to their campaign. I have a strong fucking urge to knock those jam jar glasses off his silly little head.

"Whatever you're trying to push on me, I'm not interested, alright! I can't stand aggressive intruders when I'm trying to enjoy a nice day out with my family."

"Sir, we're just trying to raise awareness to help animals."

"Sounds like a fucking scam to me, pal."

"Honey, don't curse in front of the kids." Sherri tugs my arm.

I make it very clear to Sherri, Max, this A-Hole and anyone around us that wants to listen that I've never respected this method of conducting business. They're just as bad as those pieces of shit who beg for money in the street because they're too fucking lazy to get off their ass and work for a living, so they leach off the rest of us who do. The only difference here is a title and a name badge.

He begins to sweat and loosens up his collar from my unapologetic tirade.

"At the end of the day whatever your spiel is, buster, I know you want me to make a financial contribution to your 'precious fucking cause' and that's how you get paid! I heard it a thousand times before, so there's no way you're getting a red cent of my hard-earned fucking money."

My machine gun mouth is out and it feels great as Sherri continues tugging at me to move on.

"Sir, I assure you we are a non-profit—"

"What you need to do is go back to your organization, sit down with your team and brainstorm more respectful ways to raise awareness instead of begging in public gatherings like bums. Nobody likes to be hassled by some jerk with a clipboard so my advice to you is to rethink your whole operation without annoying people like me. So please, with all due respect, get the fuck outta my face."

I fantasize having a crowd around me cheering at my heroics because everyone I know hates to be approached by hawkers in public, but unfortunately, this is not the case. I just have a rather embarrassed wife leading me away before I escalate any further.

A few people look on probably thinking I'm an angry fat fuck but I don't care; I don't know these people. I have more in my arsenal and have no problem giving it to him or anybody else. I hold on to too much inner rage so sometimes it feels good to go off like Jim Cornette at Dairy Queen.

CHAPTER 10

The highlight of my day thus far is lunch. Not only can I pig the fuck out on some USDA brawn, I'm gonna have a few frosty beers to boot. There's a strip of nice places to eat outside the fair where we find ourselves but the problem (as always) is deciding which one to go to. Even making simple decisions like this has become debilitating between us.

"Who's ready for some deep-fried salty goodness?" I say in my happy camper voice.

"Come on, honey," whines Sherri, "you know I've been trying to eat better. Not to mention *you* need to as well. I want to go to the salad bar."

She hits me with her puppy dog look so I tell her she knows I hate those places and I'll just be hungry again in an hour. She comes back with her vegetable defense, then I counter with my meat offense, she then comes back with ugh…you know what? I can't be bothered to explain. We go round and round like this until I finally break the cycle.

"How about we let our little snickerdoodle decide. What do you say, Maxie? Do you want to go to a boring salad bar or a big juicy burger house where you can have burgers, fries and your favorite Reese's Pieces butter cup milkshake?"

I'm such a conniver I know, but a lot is on the line. The king salesman inside me cannot accept defeat.

"I wanna go here," she says, pointing to the salad bar, "because fatty food makes you fat and being fat makes you die."

Sherri and I just look at each other shell-shocked.

There it is, I have nothing. I can't argue with that. My little angel speaks the truth. I've always admired that about kids, they rarely sugarcoat things. If you've got a booger in your nose, they will just come out and tell you with no beating around the bush. They are that direct. And they are master persuaders; have you ever told a kid that they cannot have an ice-cream but they just keep coming at you over and over until you break down and give them what they want just to shut them up? Tremendous! I admire the art of persistence.

"Well…" says Sherri.

I wave the white flag. The King has been dethroned.

We walk into this God-forsaken veggie place which is full of nerdy hipsters and other Venice Beach type health freaks who munch on avocado lettuce wraps and sip herbal tea from large ceramic cups. This is not my cup of tea at all. I'd sooner prefer a good old steak house to smell that burning meat aroma. It's my favorite smell in the world and honestly think it should be bottled up and sold as a cologne. I'm not joking. I think it would be a big hit around this country. People would love to smell like they've just came from a BBQ. When I walk into a good chicken joint or even McDonald's, it turns me on and puts me in a ravenous state that makes me want to gorge. I once heard that when you walk down Main Street, USA in Disney World they have underground pipes that emit certain food scents. This triggers people into powerful states of hunger—luring them into their ridiculously overpriced eateries. Talk about a fiendish avenue of manipulation.

In this salad bar, however, I receive no olfactory buzz, it just smells like foliage and bell peppers as we are led to a booth by a bonnie little broad. All that's on my mind is some tall, ice-cold Heinekens to make it through this fretting ordeal.

"I'm thirsty. Can we order some drinks right away please?" I notion to the little lady.

"I'm sorry, sir, I'm the host, but I'll notify your server to come take your order right away."

I've recently developed a ritual to order two beers up front as I get very impatient if my server has disappeared somewhere after I've guzzled my first and I'm just sat around craving my next. So one day a light bulb goes off: all I need to do is order two beers up front, so I'm not left high and dry. Talk about the elusive obvious.

"Hello, folks, welcome to Fresh & Leafy. I'm Caroline and I'll be looking after you today," beams the jazzy waitress that still has teenage acne. Much good those vegetables have done her skin.

"Hello, Caroline," I rub my hands together. "I would like to start with two of your finest, coldest drafts of Heineken, please."

"Wait a minute," Sherri interjects with that look on her face, "I thought you were going to wait until tonight to drink?"

Oh shit, I did say that earlier, but I can't not drink in a place like this; it's my only salvation amongst the green leafy vegetables.

"I did, but you and I both know that what I said had no merit whatsoever. And besides, you get to eat in this God-forsaken tree-hugging place. No offense," I notion to Caroline meaning no ill will. "I'm the one paying, Sherri, so that means

I can purchase anything I want. Why that's the American way after all. Isn't that right, Caroline?"

Caroline looks a little perplexed making that "errr" sound, so I continue.

"So, to reiterate; I've got that Friday feeling on this Saturday afternoon, I would like to begin with two ice-cold Heinie's and a Big Mac Meal with a batch of Chicken McNuggets on the side." I hit her with the cheesiest of grins.

"I'm sorry, sir."

"Oh, Caroline, I was joking about the Big Mac. The beers will do fine thanks."

"Ermm…" says the timid waitress with disappointment flooding her face, "…usually that would not be a problem, but last night a gentleman was served alcohol who turned out to be underage in the presence of an off duty police officer, so our alcohol license has been temporarily suspended." She grits her teeth like she can sense my reaction will not be a good one.

"Well that's it then. We're out of here."

"Don't be stupid, Bobby. You already said you weren't going to drink until tonight, now you can actually live up to something you've said for once."

I stand up completely ignoring my wife's statement. "Grab your things, both of you; we're leaving for that burger place across the street."

"You can't be serious, Bobby."

"Deadly serious," I eyeball her. "Don't make me cause a scene in here, Sherri."

"I'll be over there if you decide to stay," murmurs the innocent waitress caught in the crossfire as she ejects from our tension-filled booth.

"You are unbelievably f-ing selfish, Bobby! Here we are trying to get some good nutrition into our lives and you can't resist ruining it with beer."

"No, you're the one being selfish, Sherri. How could I possibly stand a place like this without beer?"

"You need help with your drinking."

"Actually I think I'm pretty good at it by myself," I smile trying to ease the tension. It didn't work. She's seething at me like a hound from hell. I must deflect. "Look, let's not make a big deal out of this. We just have to take it as a sign from the universe that eating in this salad bar on this day was not meant to be."

"No, it's the opposite. It's a direct sign from the universe saying eat here and make some sort of attempt to become healthy instead of ordering a greasy burger with five beers."

"Daddy," Max whines, "I wanna stay."

"No, I'm putting my foot down; it smells like kale and yoga in here. We're off to that burger joint across the street. Grab your things. This conversation is over!"

I let out a satisfactory belch after consuming my fourth beer and double cheeseburger inside this delicious smelling steak house. I'm worse than the late great George 'The Animal' Steele when eating in public and make no apologies for my slob-like behavior. I feel we earn the right to eat like a piglet if we're the ones paying.

The food here is awesome and it's surprisingly quiet for a Saturday afternoon, and you'd think we'd have a waitress that could take care of us efficiently, but sadly we don't. The whole meal was basically plagued with an awkward silence aside from me complaining about our slow, incompetent waitress Linda.

When Sherri and I go at it like this it affects her whole day. She makes little things become huge and then the volcano erupts and that's when I like to be somewhere else. I find it a lot easier to run away from conflicting interests than to face the music in the moment.

"Thanks, guys. Here's your check," says Linda as she drops it off and tends to another table.

I waste no time scribing the following on the rating card inside:

There will be no financial gratuity today as I cannot possibly reward an incompetent server for poor service. My tip to you, Miss Linda, is to step your game up and pay more attention to your tables, if you do that, I will quite happily tip you graciously. However, seeing that I'm a nice guy I've enclosed two coupons for Chuck E. Cheese for you to enjoy at your leisure.

As I drop the exact cash and coupons inside the bill-holder, Sherri questions what am I doing.

"I added a couple of coupons in the bill."

"Coupons? Coupons for what?"

"Chuck E. Cheese."

"Why on Earth did you put coupons in there?"

"They're for Linda."

"They're for Linda?" she frowns. "I don't follow."

"You don't follow what?"

"I don't follow why you put them in there."

"I didn't tip her because she didn't deserve it."

"Hold on, you didn't tip her so you left her *coupons* instead?"

I decide not to respond. I remain mute and just stare back at her mean mug.

"Are you freaking kidding, Bobby? You're seriously going to leave her coupons for Chuck E. Cheese as a tip for bringing you all those beers and taking care of us?"

"She's lucky she's getting anything. I could have been a real dick."

"You *are* being a real dick! I've never heard of such ridiculousness in all my life. If somebody pulled that shit on me when I was a server, I would have punched them in the face."

"Ah, but you busted your butt and deserved good tips. You know I tip well when someone deserves it, but this girl on a quiet day took way too long to bring me my third beer, she was nowhere to be found when I needed more BBQ sauce and she messed up my dessert order by giving me caramel instead of cream. The only thing she brought quickly was the damn bill."

"Oh come on, Bobby, she wasn't that bad. You're being a snob."

"I'm sorry, that's just how I feel and I'm the one paying."

She shakes her head in disgust. I see it in her dragon-like eyes.

"If word spread that we tipped her with coupons we're gonna be the laughing stock of the whole town."

"I don't care."

"Well I care, Bobby. Here, give me the bill and I'll leave the damn tip."

"Not a chance."

"What?"

"I can't let you do it."

"Oh yes you will!"

"Sherri, if you tip her she's A: being rewarded for incompetent service and B: she'll never learn from her slacker-daisical ways."

"I don't care. You cannot tip that girl with a damn coupon! Now give me the bill!"

"No. I'm putting my foot down!"

"No, Bobby, I'm putting my foot down! You will totally regret it if you don't give me that bill right now!"

Silence.

It appears we've reached a stalemate.

"I cannot believe you'd do that, Bobby, I'm getting sick to my stomach just looking at your face."

Earthquake is on the verge of erupting, but I keep a poker face as I unscrew my antacid bottle and wash a couple down with the last of my beer. Even Max looks intimidated. I wonder what's going through her little head as she watches her parents fight over principles and coupons. I decide not to call her bluff because I'm damn sure she isn't bluffing.

I've noticed over the years that if you're dining with somebody who's in (or used to be in) the service industry and you don't tip up to their standards, they'll often chew you out because it's like you're disrespecting one of their own. I've never worked in that industry so I have no emotional connection when it comes to tipping. I simply reward good service with a fair tip and punish bad service with no tip, along with advice to why there's no tip so they learn not to do it again. Is that so unreasonable? I guess Sherri is extra mad with me for demanding we go to this burger joint in the first place. Anyway, I'm tired of this asinine shit, I'll let her have her way on this occasion but not without a little lesson not to fuck with me.

"You know what, Sherri? Fine. If you want to reward this lady's poor service be my guest, but not only can you take care of the tip, you can take care of the entire fucking bill. I'll be outside."

I retract my cash and coupons, sling the bill across the booth and depart from the scene in a huff.

CHAPTER 11

By nightfall, I use my manipulation skills to worm my way out of staying in with Earthquake. I feel perfectly justified as I spent all day with her on my only day off. She's still mad about the whole coupon incident, which soured her for the rest of the day. When I told her I'm going over to Cam's house for a quiet drink she put up no resistance and said she doesn't care what I do, so it is what it is. The old me would have fallen for her reverse psychology but I don't care at this point. Those old tricks don't work on me anymore. Our marriage has entered a new low.

So yes, I lied and arranged a bender at the casino with Cam the Man, and his new confidant Benny B who's allegedly been killing it with the ladies. People who are good at attracting the opposite sex have always intrigued me. It's just another form of sales if you think about it: instead of demonstrating a product by highlighting the benefits. With attraction, the product is you, so you're essentially selling yourself by conveying all the benefits they will receive by developing a relationship with you. It's a fascinating subject that I sucked at all through high school and college and basically settled for Sherri ever since.

Cam thought this kid would be an interesting injection of energy tonight as he's about fourteen years our junior and seems like a know-it-all. Apparently, after studying some pick-up gurus, Benny turned himself from dud to stud by diligent research from books, seminars and mentors, along with a daily practice of approaching women in bars, restaurants and clubs.

Inside the sixty-thousand square foot casino is a bar called Pyro, where, if the gambler wins at one of the machines, pyrotechnics go off creating all this hoopla and attention, and this is where we chose to sit — go figure.

We shoot the shit at a table in the middle of all the rah-rah sipping seventeen dollar mojitos while Benny B eyes up every server in our proximity. His term for servers is *hired guns*—women hired for their beauty to keep the marks liquored up and gambling. Whatever you call them; these eye-candy waitresses in their six-inch stilettos and oh so perfect figures have got me harder than Stephen Hawking's homework. I can't help myself from gawking at them as they wiggle past delivering fancy cocktails. Man, look at that one; what I would give to exchange bodily fluids with her. After sleeping next to Earthquake for about twenty years what do you expect? They are everywhere, scattering around this casino like roaches and making good money too, after all, big tits equals big tips, it doesn't take a guru to work that out.

When I'm in the presence of women of a particular grandeur I get so engulfed by their beauty I freeze up, even if it's just a bartender wanting to take my order. I can't help it. It's like an overwhelming pang in the pit of my stomach which immobilizes me. It's the strangest thing like my body has detected a threat, but of course, I'd never admit this to the boys.

"...so then I said," (Benny finishing a cheesy joke), "my mother is half-Irish and my father is half-Russian, so I guess that makes me half-drunk!"

It's hard to swallow what Cam had told me about this kid, on the surface he seems way more of a Screech than a Zak, so I can't help but scrutinize him from head to toe. I mean, this kid oozes dorkiness; he's not easy on the eyes and far from optimal condition, podgy gut, bumpy face, spiky ginger hair and is like five foot five in Timberlands. He looks like a cross between a redheaded Sonic the Hedgehog and a character from *South Park*. To me, it seems like he's trying too hard to stand out. He's well-groomed and whatnot, but he's wearing too many cheap accessories like an oversized hip-hop watch he calls *Big Ben* and two fake diamond earrings he calls *Lemon Heads*.

Despite my cynical preconceived notions, I'm actually enjoying listening to this kid preach his game to us.

"Guys, it's a system," Benny recites with a high pitched intensity, "a step by step formula to systematically trigger a woman's hard-wired attraction circuitry."

"Whoa-whoa," I interject, "that was a mouthful. What was that again?"

"Listen carefully, my friend. I was the world's most lovable loser when it came to seduction. Women had been my Achilles heel throughout my teenage years until one day I found out there's a step by step methodology to attract women so they'll sleep with you within four to ten hours from your initial encounter."

"Didn't I tell you he was something?" Cam jumps in.

"Of course there are no definite time frames and this is not an absolute law. You can technically sleep with a woman within minutes after meeting her if you're in the right place at the right time or if she's pissy drunk, but we call that *fool's mate* and is not solid game."

"Interesting," I say, sipping my sugary mojito. "So how did you come across all this stuff again?"

"Well, let me give you a little back story so you know where I'm coming from."

Benny cracks his knuckles and begins to tell us a good friend of his returned from a six month trip around the southern hem — Australia, Cambodia, Vietnam, Argentina, Brazil and everywhere in between. "Out of all of them Brazil was his favorite because he put up legendary stats; bedding twelve different chicks in the twelve nights he was there!"

The more this kid speaks the more animated he gets.

"That's some incredible numbers," I muse.

Benny goes on to tell us that Mighty King David (as he calls him) was a complete natural who's never studied *The Art of Seduction* or anything like that. "When I tried picking his brain to find out his secrets he didn't know. He said he just goes out with the boys, has a few drinks and starts chatting up the chicks. So I developed the belief that some people are cut out to be lover-boys and some just aren't and it frustrated the fuck outta me."

Benny is reliving his pain a little, I can see it in his wandering eyes. People with a chip on their shoulder can often turn it into drive, which I'm guessing is the case in his story.

I ask him how did he make the shift into being confident with women.

"I needed help, big-time, so I started surfing the web and stumbled across a quote by a brilliant Canadian author and master Venusian Artist called Mystery."

"*Mystery?*" repeats Cam.

"It's a pseudonym, his real name is Erik."

"Oh. Can you remember that quote that blew you away?"

"Of course!" booms Benny. "I remember so clearly it got etched in my brain…"

"So what is it?" Cam asks almost frustratingly.

"*'Nature will unapologetically weed your genes out of existence if you don't take action and learn how to attract women now.'*

"It frazzled my brain because I kept thinking I'll be weeded out of existence unless I do something about it immediately. I got so sick of feeling unworthy and sorry for myself that I hit a threshold and just snapped. I went out on a quest to study the pickup arts like an obsessed madman, sometimes for as much as eighteen hours per day."

Benny continues steamrolling, telling us he got totally immersed with any information that could help him become better with women, "and luckily I found the book of all books which totally changed my life!"

"What book was that?"

"It's called: *Boy Wonder: My Life in Tights* by Burt Ward."

"Wait a minute," says Cam. "Are you talking about Burt Ward who played Robin in the sixties Batman show?"

"Correct-a-mondo! Give the man the prize!" says Benny rewarding him with a hi-five.

"He wrote a book?" I frown. "What's it about?"

"Pimpology 101, my friend. Pimping ass morning, noon and night. It's so inspirational!"

"Get the fuck outta here," says Cam. "The Boy Wonder wrote a book about picking up chicks in the sixties? That's fucking hysterical!"

Benny goes on to say that Robin and his sidekick Batman were straight-up pimps, having bedded more chicks than Wilt Chamberlain, Joe Namath and Bill Clinton combined.

This is some unexpected and fascinating shit, to say the least.

"I wanted so bad to be just like them," Benny continues, "and knew if I didn't dive head-first into the seduction community and make women my number one priority then I'd regret it when I'm old in a rocking chair with saggy balls and a wrinkly winky."

I can't help but laugh at and with him. This kid is more effervescent than Jimmy Hart, you have no choice but to be drawn in, but I still have my doubts to whether he's good at pulling chicks.

"So going back to what you said a minute ago," I say, "how do you trigger attraction in a woman if you're not rich, good looking or whatever?"

He tells us that despite what we've all been led to believe, women aren't really attracted to looks, they just think they are. "Women are more inclined by status than physical appearance."

"Is that actually true?" I ask, playing the doubting Thomas.

"Just look at me, Bobby, let's call a spade a spade. I'm no A.C. Slater or Jonathan Rambo. How do you think I'm crushing it? Once I learned this stuff it changed my whole outlook and I've been winning ever since." Benny turns to Cam for another hi-five.

"That's what I'm talking about," returns Cam. "To get what you've never had before you have to do what you've never done before."

"True that," agrees Benny, raising his glass. "Did you guys ever hear the story about burning the boats to take the island?"

Cam and I shake our heads. He proceeds to tell us an in-depth story about a great warrior who, when arrived on enemy land, ordered his soldiers to burn the ships that had carried them across so there was no turning back. "When the soldiers saw their boats go up in flames it became an absolute must that they conquer the enemy. They couldn't retreat, it was win or die trying and they ended up defeating the enemy and conquered the island because they were more driven to succeed."

"That's an interesting fable, but how is this related to women?"

"Well, when I first read that story I thought I'd try a similar proposition in Pimpology."

"How so?" Cam smirks. "You sailed to an island and burnt your boat?"

"No, you dumb-dumb. I started experimenting with chicks out of town where there was no turning back. I'd hop on the train to an unfamiliar town where I didn't know anyone and I'd only bring thirty bucks for drinks, but obviously not enough for a hotel so I was forced to game chicks and convince one to take me home. I sure as hell didn't want to stay out in the cold all night."

"I gotta be honest, that's a ballsy fucking move, bro. Did it work?"

"Damn right. I've done it six times in six different towns now and have a hundred percent success rate, and with some cuties too."

"Much respect, man," I say. "I certainly wouldn't have the cohones to do that."

"I tried harder because I *had* to. The thought of being stuck all night in a random town with no way of getting back is way scarier than spitting some pimp shit to a few chicks in a bar. If you burn the boat to take the island, it becomes a MUST that you succeed!" He leans back, sipping more liquor.

I've got to admit I'm beginning to be won over. Gotta respect his balls. "Cam, where did you find this kid? This is some interesting shit, dude."

"What can I say," remarks Cam. "I only hang out with high value alpha males."

"It's funny you say that, Cam, because I still don't feel very alpha, but I know how to convey it. Once I learned that status can be manipulated if you embed DHV's within your gambits, it was an absolute game changer."

"What the hell is a DHV?" I ask. My head is starting to spin now.

"A Demonstration of High Value. You have to demonstrate or convey that you're a high value male without sounding like you're bragging. How you ask? By covertly embedding DHVs into your stories. This is what turned me from an AFC to a PUA in six months!"

I'm getting confused with all these silly acronyms although I'm pretty sure PUA means Pick-Up Artist. I feel like I'm around a couple of kids who've just discovered their first porno mag. It sure is entertaining though, better than a boring night at the Duck talking about Ice Hockey or government conspiracies that's for sure. I want to see him work his magic, not recite some silly acronyms and terminology.

"Don't take this the wrong way, Benny, but I'm all about seeing is believing. Are you telling me that a tubby little fuck like you can bag one of these stunning cocktail servers?"

I can tell he's not insulted by my remark, which was not my intention; I'm just cynical about him being successful with one of these hotties.

"Be patient, my friend. You're about to be wowed!"

"Oh yeah?" I challenge.

"Once you master this amazing power you become like Keanu Reeves in *The Matrix*. You start out flirting and then you end up squirting — it don't get much better than that, boys!" He leans back all cocky sipping the last of his fruity cocktail. "But you're right, Bobby, why should you believe me? Seeing is believing, right? Gentleman, observe…"

And with that Benny flags down the delicious waitress who's been working our section.

"Hey, guys," she smiles warmly. "Ready for another round?"

"Listen, lady, will you stop following me around. I'm not going home with you tonight! What kind of guy do you think I am?"

I did not see that coming. He's got some balls, this kid.

"Very funny, trouble," she plays along.

This girl is so exquisite, like a human version of Jessica Rabbit, red hair, voluptuous, milky white teeth and a rack that is oh so tremendous (as is everything else about her). I think my body has detected a threat again—a threat of horniness.

"I've met a million girls like you before, I know your type; you're only after one thing."

"You've met a server before, that's here to take your drinks?"

Her deadpan delivery was fucking legendary. I love this bitch.

"That's cute, toots," Benny says holding his ground. "You're only here to get me drunk and take full advantage of me. I'll tell you what guys: you can dress this one up, but you can't take her anywhere."

That gets a chuckle as Benny wastes no time by going into another routine or gambit or whatever the hell he calls it.

"And who you calling *trouble*? I've heard all about you, Miss *Thing*. You know that bartender over there?" he notions to a tall brunette working the bar.

"Of course, that's my girl Lou-Lou."

"I really don't think she likes you, honey, she talks about you behind your back."

"What?"

This definitely gets her attention.

"Yup. She told me you're like a man trapped inside a woman's body. You're a slob, you constantly fart and burp and curse like a redneck truck driver…"

Her mouth just hangs open.

"… She even made fun of your bingo wings…"

If I was sipping my drink I would have spat it out from pure shock like in the movies. I could not believe he just fucking said that. The audacity of this kid! This near-perfect specimen doesn't have a shred of fat on her, yet it still made her blush and examine her triceps. This is incredible. My dick is getting excited from watching this madness!

Benny then grabs her arm and inspects her triceps before telling her she needs to try harder in the gym in a playful, cocky way. This kid has Giant González balls. She still has her mouth open from all this playful insulting and seems to be tongue-tied.

"Anyway, toots, we have some affairs to discuss right now. You see, business never stops when you're an entrepreneur, right, guys?" Benny turns to us. "These two gentlemen accompanying me are two of the finest businessmen I've ever been affiliated with. I'll tell you more later, but for right now we'll take another round of mojitos and stick them on the house tab, we're special guests of Mandi Mack."

This kid is smoother than the Fonz on his best day and she is just eating it up.

"You're too much," she glows. "What kind of business are you guys involved in?"

"It's too soon for that, you little Nosy-Nora. There's plenty of time for personal affairs later if you play your cards right."

"Whatever. And what might your name be?"

"They call me Benny B."

"What does the B stand for?"

"That's classified information, babe, just call me by my code-name: *Jack the Stripper*."

Benny is on fire. She playfully clips him and tells him to stop, even though she's loving every minute of it.

"I'll be right back with your drinks, fellas."

"And watch where you swing those bingo wings, girlfriend!" Benny says as she wiggles away.

"You are a ballsy fucking madman, my friend," I say, hand-slapping him.

"Listen, chicks like that get hit on all the time by morons telling them how beautiful they are and '*can I buy you a drink?*' and a bunch of other amateur hour shit. I had to playfully insult her with a bunch of *negs* to lower her value while simultaneously raising mine. Plus I had to do it quickly because she's a server so there's an obvious time constraint. You probably noticed how fast I was talking."

"You always talk fast," remarks Cam.

"That I do. But this is just the tip of the iceberg. Later on, in isolation, I'll switch tactics and behave a little more cool, calm and collected because I'll be at a different phase of the game." Benny looks all smug and cocky now. "I'm telling you guys, this shit works if you take a little time to learn a script or routine and practice it in the field over and over. And when you start to reap the results it can become like a drug. I'm so confident right now I carry my toothbrush everywhere I go..."

Cam and I look at each other puzzled.

"Because each night I go out I never know where I'm gonna end up."

We all laugh and make a toast. My brain is fried, but I'm a believer now. I honestly didn't think a little nerd like him could get that kind of reaction from such a stunning specimen. Attraction was definitely sparked. I can see why Cam took a shine to this kid; he certainly can talk the talk.

I'm fascinated by this underground movement he keeps alluding to: The Seduction Community, where men teach men one of the biggest mysteries of the entire universe — women. Cracking the woman's code by entering her mind as well as her soft moist vagina. I can't wait to see more.

CHAPTER 12

Thanks to Cam's connections we get ushered to the club inside the casino and receive high roller's treatment like we're The Fabulous Freebirds. Believe it or not, there's actually a dentist's chair in the VIP section. The gimmick is you sit down, get strapped in and recline back, then three big-bosomed shooter girls pour multiple liquors down your throat for a minimum of ten seconds. I know I can last at least twenty, but I'm too preoccupied to indulge in the shenanigans tonight and I'm definitely not going on the dance floor as my moves are about as goofy as Mean Gene when he danced with the Gobbledy Gooker. Instead, I'll just stick to my little white powder.

Cam and I hit the ya-yo with a vengeance, while Benny just sticks to mojitos and champagne. I'm in the mood to go hard tonight like a beast has taken over my faculties. I want to be like this Benny B kid around women, so I make my lines extra thick and vacuum them up like a DustBuster thinking this will give me confidence. Benny tells me it took him about six months to become a pro at picking up chicks after he discovered the community. It took me half that time to become a pro at sniffing coke. In fact, not that long ago, Cam and I ended up at a swanky after-party in the 'burbs with some of his associates, and I out-sniffed the whole party. Cam actually started bragging to everybody, saying how quickly I've turned into Charlie Sheen and I should be crowned the new coke-sniffing heavyweight champ. I've just got one of those bodies that can tolerate a lot of abuse, probably because of my excess flab. I can out-eat anybody when it comes to food, and no matter who I'm drinking with, I notoriously drink more than them. I'm a well-conditioned athlete when it comes to this shit.

One time, I got pulled over on my way back to work by this animated cop who got all in my face about people who run stop signs are the scum of the Earth. I felt like a naughty schoolboy and started smirking because he was so over-the-top and reminded me of Sheriff John Bunnell from that old cop show. He smelt beer and made me blow into the breathalyzer which made me shit myself because I'd just power-drank four drafts in my lunch break. I really thought I was gonna get pinched, but surprisingly I passed the test, blowing a zero point three. My body can absorb anything in record time including my new love: cocaine. And because of my high tolerance, this has turned into an expensive recreational pastime.

I hate spending a lot of money on it, but it feels so good which makes me not care about the money, which is not like me at all. Tonight though, I really don't care how much money goes up my nose. I feel so alive again hanging out with these two, and this is the first time since being with Sherri that I'm seriously considering committing adultery. In all honesty, I'd fuck anything with two legs and a pair of titties right now. I'm high, I'm horny and have friends with the same interest. And I'm especially excited to be a wing-man with Benny B to see if I can get any spill-offs. The sober me wouldn't even entertain the thought of being cocky and conceited towards women, but drunk Bobby is all for it.

I sit back, marveling at Benny in action. Just like I can tell when one of my staff is about to close a sale, I can tell this kid is gonna close tonight and I'm not talking about selling a damn Zenhaven spring mattress. He brings a unique presence to our booth where we find ourselves laughing, cheering and toasting with ridiculously overpriced champagne that Cam insists he'll take care of.

Benny instructs that we must become the flame of the party by creating an ambiance of fun and curiosity to our table, like moths to a flame. With this VIP treatment and bottle service, it doesn't take long for them to start hovering, and let me tell you — these chicks are far from moths.

"Hey, guys…" Benny says to three cuties who are lingering in our proximity. "Did you know that ninety-three percent of women admit that they play with themselves in the shower, and the other seven percent sing?"

The girls smile in unison.

"Do you know what they sing?" Benny says directed at the brunette.

"What?"

"If you don't know what they sing then I guess you're one of the ones that like to play with yourself…"

Everybody laughs. I can't front, that ice-breaker went over well.

Wasting no time, Benny stacks into another routine: "Check this out:" Benny pulls out a tiny cologne bottle and sprays his neck, then signals them to lean in and smell him. "Pretty sweet, right? It's called Mone. You can figure out why for yourselves."

"It's nice," says the black-haired girl whose arms are covered with sexy sleeve tats. "why is it called Mone?"

"I guess you're the learning disabled one of the bunch, sweetie… It's short for Pheromone which comes from an ancient Egyptian Pharaoh that used special scents to lure women into his boudoir and make them moan. *Pharaoh-Moan,* get it?"

"Oh… Now I get it," she says, taking the bait.

All looks and no brains, evidently.

"You are my official new best friend, doll-face," he smiles. "I can tell you are the leader of your tribe. These bitches worship you!"

They chuckle like little girl scouts as Benny continues. "And get this: not only is it an alluring cologne, it also doubles as a moose repellent. Ladies observe…"

He sprays the cologne around us and starts counting down: "Five, four, three, two, one. Look around, quick, look everywhere…"

The girls look all around the vicinity. I have to admit, I do too.

"…do you see any moose…?" Benny leans back.

Once again everybody laughs. I fucking love this kid.

The clock spins a complete cipher so most of us are now a little tipsy as the drinks continue to flow in mass. The arrangement has been perfectly orchestrated by Benny B which he drew out on a napkin when the girls went to the bathroom. I'm sat with the redheaded girl at the left corner of our booth, so from this position external interruptions are limited. Benny is back to back with me so we can discreetly communicate while still keeping each of our girls engaged, while Cam and his tattooed cutie are at the far end of the booth which is a healthy distance from us, thus limiting any interruptions from our end.

The beauty is everyone can see each other having a good time which is very important. The last thing we want to do is bring them down or make them feel unsafe in any way. Benny calls this 'mini isolation' — they're separated from each other because of the way us boys are strategically positioned, but yet they're still together because they are all sat around the same table having fun. He's a mad scientist I tell ya, and the science is how to get these chicks back to the room for a fuck.

"So right now I'm doing my major in business studies," says the mousey brown-haired chick Jesse that's next to me. She's twenty-freaking-one, which makes her twenty years my junior. There's no way in the world that she'd be talking to me if I wasn't with these guys or the free champagne. I've got nothing going for me, I know that but at least I'm dressed somewhat decent tonight in my best suit, so Benny suggested earlier that I play the role of a nightclub owner. I have that look apparently, so that's my angle tonight; I own a nightclub. God knows where or which one, but he said not to worry about the specifics, just keep it vague and say my new club is in development across town. It's funny because I think I've got more of a Larry the Cable Guy look instead of a nightclub owner.

I don't know what these guys see in me, but I feel better about myself than I have in years. Cam's always good at picking my spirits up because he knew the younger, more driven version of me from our real estate days and strives to bring it out of me every time we get together.

"That's cool," I say, lost in her plump purple lips, "so what do you want to be when you grow up?"

"Hmmm. I always wanted to run a little French patisserie."

"I thought you were going to say you want to be a Princess or something."

"You mean you didn't know that I'm Princess Jess of New Jersey?" She brushes her shoulders with a little panache. The game is on.

"Oh, Princess, please forgive me," I refill her glass. "More champagne, your highness?"

"Why thank you, squire."

We clink our glasses together.

"So, Jesse, what do you think of this as an idea for a ladies shampoo: An organic essential oils based shampoo, which—and here's the twist—leaves your hair smelling like mushroom soup?"

Silence.

An awkward silence if you want to be more precise, along with an all-around look of befuddlement.

"I could brand it as Mushroom Head! What do you think?" I say raising my hopeful eyebrows.

"Well…" she grits her teeth.

Reality hits me, she doesn't like it. Maybe I should switch it to potato soup and brand it as Mrs. Potato Head…

"Neg her, then kino escalate," whispers a sneaky voice from behind that could only belong to one Benny B. What the hell is he talking about?

"Huh?"

"Playfully tease her about her nails or something then start lightly touching her, but keep it subtle, don't grope her obviously."

I have no idea what to do, especially with all the drugs and alcohol swimming around in my brain. I have to think of something though; she's checking her phone which could be a sign of boredom.

"And then stack forward by telling her you like her ELF."

"Her ELF?" I question. Once again, what the fuck?

"Her Eyes, Lips and Face. Then you move in for the kiss close."

"Stop confusing me, bro. I'm getting overwhelmed by all this shit! I'm losing it!"

"No you're not, hang in there, soldier! Stop talking to me and reengage."

I've gone blank and Benny knows it. I've got to dive back in especially now she's put her phone away.

"Wow, I just noticed those killer calves you have there," I say squeezing them. "Did you grow them yourself?"

This throws her a little but she plays along. "Yes, I did. Both of them as a matter of fact."

"Love those dynamite stilettos too, they're hot. They compliment your chubby ankles…"

I turn away and sip the bubbly trying to act cool and cocky like the Honky Tonk Man. I can't believe those words actually came from me—the guy who can't find his dick in a shower. But it fucking worked!

She drops her jaw temporarily until a radiant glow illuminates her face. What a relief! She innocently defends that she does not have chubby ankles then chops my chest like a homage to Wahoo McDaniel until I grab her and pull her closer. I guess this is what they call flirting. Benny is a fucking genius.

Now I have a little moxie I sling my arm around her shoulders and she's receptive. Fuck yeah!

"You're in there now, champ," whispers Benny. "Pimp that shit like the Boy Wonder! POW!"

CHAPTER 13

An hour or so later and about four more drinks down the hatch, the party is in full swing. Everybody is getting along fabulously; the scene is almost too perfect.

I lean into Jesse who seems very comfortable being close to me. "I've got a secret for you, Princess Jess."

"Oh, do tell."

"Do you party?"

"What do you mean?"

I stare at her thinking *you know what I mean, silly.*

"I can do the robot if that's what you're getting at." She breaks out doing the robot dance right there in her seat.

"Touché. I think your scholastic mind can figure out what I'm getting at. I know you've seen *Blow* and *Scarface*," I say, raising my eyebrows.

"Yes and hell yes. Two classics."

"Soooo, what do you think?" I raise my eyebrows again.

Hint, hint, Jessica...

"I've never done it before. What's it like?"

"It's a fucking rush, baby, you have no idea. Are you down?"

"Ahhh yeahhh," she says sounding like a California surfer girl.

"We've got a room upstairs if you wanna come check out the sample sale."

She reacts with a slight nod and a half-smile but says nothing. Does that mean she'll come to the room with me? I'm supposed to be good at reading people but now I'm not sure. What shall I do? Ugh, I'm totally overthinking this. Focus, you dickface, she's giving you a green light, she just said she's down. But then she gave me a half-assed nod. Stop fucking overanalyzing, you incessant fuck and go with your gut.

"Cool," I say trying to keep my composure, I think my dick is about to burst out my pants. "Let's duck out for a quick ten."

Perfect, that was pretty smooth and this time I don't look nor analyze her reaction, instead I lean into Benny B and recite our code phrase for: *I'm bouncing her to the room:* "shake, rattle and roll."

Benny leans into Cam and very slyly obtains the key-card, which he hands to me without Jesse's friends getting wise. They're pretty tipsy drinking our champagne anyway, but I don't want any cock-blocks if I can help it.

I slide the key-card into my suit pocket and stand up holding Jessica's hand. "Hey, guys," I address the table. "I'm gonna go teach Jesse how to play Blackjack. We'll be back in fifteen with more WINNINGS than Charlie Sheen!"

"Have fun," the brunette with Benny says.

Yes! Greenlight!

With no time to waste we walk out of the club arm in arm and back into the casino. Her body is just scrumptious, curvy like barbecued ribs. I can barely contain my excitement and nor can she.

"Thanks for not telling my friends what we're really up to. They're pretty square, they don't even smoke pot."

"It sucks being square," I say through a sly fox grin. "They don't know what they're missing."

"I can't wait to do this! I bet it's gonna be wild."

"It is. I remember my first time, doesn't seem that long ago…"

We walk right past the Blackjack tables, towards the elevators. Of course, I have no intention of really hitting the tables, more like hitting that ass. Besides, I rarely gamble because I don't like to waste money. Except on drugs, although, I don't really view it as a waste. Nights out with the boys are what's keeping me going right now.

That's how I've been rationalizing spending all this money on coke; it's my way of dealing with all the shit going on in my life. Some people read self-help books; others go to church or see shrinks or whatever, my new thing is this little white powder. I've been living in a rut for years and now I feel alive again — and yes I know it's a false way to feel good but so fucking what.

Ever since my first taste I fall for it every time, just like when I'm stressed I'll binge on a whole tub of Ben & Jerry's cookie dough ice-cream in one sitting. I know I'll feel bad later from an upset stomach, but I still do it because it feels good in the moment. I'm an instant gratification fiend, plain and simple.

We ascend in the elevator as the only two riding and for some reason I can't think of anything to say. I have nothing and no Benny B to bail me out. I'm fucking frozen. I hope these annoying bright lights don't give her sobering thoughts like *'what the hell am I doing here with this fat guy?'*

The awkward silence envelops this elevator worse than a smelly fart. It's so uncomfortable because we just came from a loud club and now it's deadly silent—

where's Kenny-fucking-G when you need him? I don't know what to do or say. Now she's doodling on her phone again, a clear indicator of boredom. I bet she doesn't even have a signal in here. Fuck! I've blown it! I have a chronic case of paralysis from analysis. Just relax, you fucking idiot and talk about something interesting... Nah I'm not gonna bring up wrestling... Think, dammit think!

"Hey," I blurt, "did you know you can actually cook lobster in a dishwasher?"

"What? That can't be true."

"That's what I thought but it is, you should watch it on YouTube sometime, it's pretty crazy..."

And we're back in silence. I couldn't have sounded more nerdy. Oh my God, this elevator is taking forever, come on, come on come on...

Finally, I got something: "What do you think of this as an idea? I was thinking the other day that nobody likes taking their medication, right? Especially the really old or the really young, so why not make prescription drugs flavorful and re-brand them with cooler sounding names like 'Tasty' Tylenol or 'Appetizing' Advil, and have a large variety of flavors like chocolate, raspberry, coffee, chicken..."

"Chicken flavored Advil?" she grimaces.

"Or better yet, how about it's laced within the food already? So when you eat your favorite muffin or flapjack, you simultaneously get rid of your headache. It's win-win! And you could do this with any drug basically: carrot cake laced with Ritalin. Chocolate pudding spiked with Ibuprofen. This is a hot idea, especially with kids who don't like taking their meds. They wouldn't even know if their parents didn't want them to."

"Hmmm, I don't know. Sounds kind of...ya know..."

My phone starts to ring as we approach our floor. This is surprising because my Motorola is more dated than the Beverly Brothers and usually doesn't receive any signal in confined spaces. I take a quick look and see that it's Earthquake. Shit! There's no way I'm answering. I'm not trying to think about her saggy, cellulite ass right now. I have an opportunity with a cutie and I'm not going to let anything get in the way so I cancel the call and power down the cellular.

"Who was that?" she says as we step out to the hallway.

"Somebody I don't wanna talk to right now."

We arrive at door 5858 and like the nervous fat, klutz that I am; I drop the key-card on the floor. My hands are literally shaking as I pick it up and attentively stick it in the slider. Get a fucking grip, you faggot! This is a golden chance that I cannot fuck up!

We enter, flip on the lights and look at each other for a brief second. I feel a spark between us but I don't want to maul her or think I'm a creep by making a move right away. Her comfort levels have to be kept intact, so I suggest we go out to the balcony to check out the spectacular view of the city.

This suite is so sweet, it has all the luxuries one could need for seduction thanks to Cam the Man. Cam always pays extra for the finer things in life, like first-class flights, two-seater sports cars and gourmet mayonnaise.

"We've got Goose in the fridge. Shall I whip up a couple of screwdrivers?"

"Sounds good to me."

You don't have to tell me twice. I fix up a couple of drinks quicker than Tom Cruise in *Cocktail* and join her back out on the balcony.

"What a view," she says as I hand her an extra-large vodka OJ and sling my arm around her. She's so petite compared to me, with the frame of a little Mexican girl and an ass like a black girl. I feel so fucking lucky at this moment. I just keep thinking I'm gonna fuck it up. Gotta kill these thoughts!

"One day this will all be ours," I say with the cheesiest of grins.

She gleams and asks with a little more detail how coke makes you feel.

"Well, for one thing, it makes you pretty horny."

The words came out my mouth but I don't exactly know how. That was my inner voice talking. The rational sober me would never have the panache to say that, but I did and judging by her warm glow it went over well.

"Really? Keep talking."

I take that as an obvious green light and move in for the kiss.

She reciprocates.

Yes! I can't believe it!

She swirls her tongue around my mouth like she's licking a McFlurry container completely dry. She's quite the strange kisser, almost forceful, and then suddenly breaks it.

Oh fuck, what did I do? She's got cold feet, I fucking know it. "You okay?" I gasp.

"You gotta gimme more tongue."

"Oh," I say relieved. "You like it aggressive, huh?"

"A-huh."

We resume lip-locking.

It's funny noticing the differences from kissing someone new as I haven't made-out with anyone else since meeting Sherri all those years ago. This girl kisses with a lot of passion, probably from all that alcohol. Oh how I praise ye olde alcohol. I seriously doubt this cute college chick would be in a hotel room with my fat ass if it wasn't for the wonderful invention of alcohol. God bless whoever it was for inventing this glorious substance thousands of years ago. I wish I could invent something as cool and impactful as alcohol to really leave a mark in this world and become a legend.

Anyway, I'm getting side-tracked — back to the smooching. I can taste the champagne and cigarettes as she whizzes around my mouth. I usually can't stand the taste of cigarettes but because of this little cutie I feel like I'm licking a divine ashtray. And of course, my dick has responded accordingly — he's standing at full attention, you better believe.

"That was pretty passionate. I'll give you an eight."

"Just an eight?" she pouts with her hands on her hips.

"There's always time to improve."

I'm trembling on the inside but have to remain witty and cocky like Benny B emphasized earlier. I pull out the bag of sniff and suggest that we hit the slopes.

I lead her back inside and get comfortable on the plush, Savoir bed. I'm fighting the urge to seduce her right here, right now but think it's wise to just stick to the plan. I dump a little powder on the bedside table and chop it up while reassuring her it will be fine.

"Watch and learn." I roll up a twenty-dollar bill and VOOM! I vacuum up the skinny line like an aardvark sucking up a small army of ants. "Easy-peasy, see?"

"Yeap."

"Are you ready, baby?"

"Oh, I'm ready."

She seems very congruent (quite unlike my first time) and with no hesitation she grabs the twenty and goes to town. She's cool, calm and collected, sniffing that shit up with ease. Her eyes turn huge like Garfield and have that wow look.

"How was it?" I grin.

"Ohhh what a rush… I feel like I wanna expand." She lays back and stretches out like a starfish.

I follow suit by cuddling up next to her in hopes of taking full advantage. Affirmative! She starts swallowing my mouth again. I'm so fucking honored to be here right now. Thank you, baby Jesus! I escalate quickly by running my hands over her erogenous zones to turn her on.

My hands stay busy inspecting her voluptuous frame, I can't stop myself, it feels that freaking good. I have to nickname her Jesse 'The Body'—it's so apropos. I still can't believe I've got a hot college chick in bed with me and she isn't getting cold feet. I'm sure any minute now she'll come to her senses. I better take it to the point of no return like burning the boat to take the vagina.

I hit the lights above the bed, enveloping us in darkness; I don't want her to get freaked out by my deposits of fatty acid. She slips out her silk blue dress in one swift motion while leaving her heels on. Wow! Her silhouette is amazing. I think I might bust a nut before I even stick it in. Time is an obvious factor so I undress quickly, slinging my suit to the floor and slip under the covers. We resume kissing passionately for some time, I still can't believe how much she's into this! Is she fucking blind? No, stop that! Get a fucking grip! I can't waste time with cynical thoughts, I have to stick it in and start pumping like a soldier. I remove her thong and begin finger banging to get the juices flowing. It works. She's so into this; making funny noises and tossing her head around like Al Snow.

There's no exchange of dialogue between us about protection, it's all happening so quick. I just stick it in without entertaining the thought of wearing a raincoat. I'm too paranoid about any last-minute resistance, although I'm pretty sure that she actually does want me, God knows why but she does.

I start thrusting inside her — *pump pump pump* working my pelvis like Ravishing Rick Rude. She moans more and starts yelling "yes yes yes! Fuck me, daddy, fuck me, fuck me, fuck meeeeee!"

Amazing! Talk about the heat of passion! I've never been a dirty talker in bed but have to play along, so I start making huffing sounds like The Berserker. She's really digging it which makes me feel out of this world. I guess this is what animalistic sex feels like.

I step it up a notch and start grinding because I know I won't last long. She takes it like a veteran, loving every minute that I'm long-dicking her. She keeps telling me to fuck her harder and harder—you better believe I comply! The orgasm is oh so approaching and she tells me she wants it all in her mouth. I keep thinking I'm going to be jerking off over this for months! This will be my go-to place. I'm not delusional enough to think this kind of wild sexual escapade is going to happen every time I hit the town with the boys. I won't need to be messing around with muscle porn for a while because I'll have a vivid memory of this to fondle myself to.

"Here we go, baby!"

BOOM!!

There it is. My massive ejaculate all over her mouth and chin, dangling like saliva from a retard. She licks up the last of my man-goo as if it's a hot fudge Sundae and collapses with me on the bed.

Wow! That was a more satisfying climax than when Hogan slammed Andre at *WrestleMania III*! I even tongue kiss her and can taste my babies around her mouth. I don't know what compelled me to do that, I guess I'm saying thank you for making me feel like the fucking King Of The Ring! That's some nasty shit I know, but I've never felt like this before.

I want to keep the high going by doing more coke, but don't want to rush out of bed in case she thinks *he's got what he wanted so he's leaving,* so I snuggle up and caress her.

"Baby, that was amazing."

"I know, right? I've got a thing for older guys, ya know. Most guys my age are brain-dead from Snapchat and Miranda Sings."

"Is that right?" I move in for another kiss. "Shall we keep the party going with more narcotics?"

"Fuck yeah."

I jump up and slip into my suit, then hit the lamp and gaze at her wearing nothing but heels and a thong as she makes the drinks. She's absolutely spectacular and I get hard again even though I just busted King Kong Bundy balls like three minutes ago.

We do another line and sip more Grey Goose, while I keep wishing for this to never end, but her phone keeps blowing up as we've been gone way too long so the time has come to leave. I just want to savor this magic moment a little while longer...

CHAPTER 14

I once heard that human beings and pigeons are the only two species in the world that have an in-built homing mechanism in their brains. Apparently, you can take a pigeon out his coop, place him in a box, drive a thousand miles north, east, south or west and let him free. He will then fly up into the air, circle three times where his homing mechanism kicks in and the bird will fly back to his coop with a precise sense of direction.

A human's homing mechanism is somewhat similar, no matter how drunk we get we can always make it home. At least I can anyway. I'm not proud of what I did last night but there's nothing I can do about it now. No, I'm not referring to Princess Jess, I'm talking about driving home drunk as a punk. I got in the car like a real moron after even more drinks following my epic conquest. What went through my mind was pure drunken stupidity and it's a miracle I didn't kill somebody on my ride home. It's also a miracle I'm going into work today.

When I enter the house wrestling a devastating hangover, I find Sherri in bed emotionless. Being emotionless on the outside is an obvious sign of being deeply emotional on the inside. I'm pretty sure she can sense something wrong, either that or she's pissed that I stayed out all night, or the fact I cut her call or a million other fucking things I've done lately.

I use time as an ally to divert from having a senseless argument. Of course, I really am running late and don't pause to acknowledge her. I just keep moving and bullshit her by saying I passed out at Cam's around midnight. She doesn't buy it. Didn't think she would, but I can't stop to face her wrath so I duck out after a quick Puerto Rican shower and a change of clothes. No breakfast, no coffee, just a much-needed shot of mouthwash to freshen me up.

I can't even see straight on the short walk to work but luckily make it on time with seconds to spare.

I inform Johnny Ace that I'm not feeling well so he'll have to man the floor for a bit while I sleep in my office, (I didn't mention the latter as that would be unprofessional). He's happy to oblige and man the floor like the trooper he is as long as I buy the Whoppers, fries and shakes for lunch. Done, done and done.

Speaking of shakes, I literally collapse shaking in my futon after silencing all phones and dream about the shenanigans of last night. Maybe it was a dream because it was freaking unreal.

I'm out for hours until I wake up in time for my lunch break — I know, I'm worse than Homer Simpson. The problem is I'm not at all hungry even though I haven't eaten in hours. Coffee won't do anything for me right now; I need something stronger.

"Wait a sec…"

I dig deep in my wallet and pull out an emergency bag of yay, dice it up rapidly like Paula Deen with a Ginsu and up the nasal cavity it goes. Instant stimulation! I've never done coke in the day before. I wonder if I've just crossed the line from recreational user to addict. Nah, not me. I just need a little pep in my step to get me through this God awful hangover. I'm not used to not sleeping. Mix that with hard drugs and alcohol and you have a nightmare day upon the horizon. The coke did the trick, though, now I feel like I can actually go out there and face humans.

Witnessing me coked up selling mattresses must have been a strange sight to see. I was on fire talking a mile a minute and surprisingly making sense. You'd think I'd be babbling incoherently like Nikolai Volkoff — not so. Johnny was in awe and told me whatever I'm on he wants some. I just laughed and said I had too much coffee.

Over the next couple of hours I felt like a young success again. I usually let my team do the selling because they get commissions, but with only me and Johnny in today I thought I'd help the kid out and actually be some form of value for the company. It felt good to get my mojo back. I'm still riding high from making the best sale of my career. When I really contemplate what I did, I don't at all feel bad about cheating, it's the opposite. I feel rejuvenated, like the real me is back because that guy has been dead for a long time and it took Cam, Benny and Jesse 'The Body' to resurrect me.

CHAPTER 15

"You're a fucking disgrace!" screams Earthquake as soon as I get through the door. "You stay out all night without calling and drive home drunk! What the hell were you thinking?"

"Err, excuse me. Didn't you say you don't care what I do?"

"I was worried sick!"

"Look, I'm sorry, alright, I just lost track of time because we were having so much fun."

That statement did not go down well. She gets testy and tells me she knew that I never fell asleep at Cameron's place and demands to know what really happened. I've learned over the years if a woman's mad at you and you say you were having a good time without her, they always react with hostility like you're rubbing it in their face. But this is part of my strategy; I'm going to be honest for once (with the exception of the chicks and the drugs).

"So you want me to tell you what really happened, huh?" I stare into her inquisitive eyes as I lean against the sofa which will probably be my bed tonight.

"Yes."

"Alright then. Cam was super excited from hitting his bonus and wanted to celebrate by treating us to a night at the casino. What was I supposed to say? 'Sorry, guys, I want to stay in and watch *Shotgun Saturday Night*.'? It was impossible to say no and I'm so glad I didn't because we had the most amazing time."

If I could read her mind it would probably say *'did you really just say that, asshole?'* But I know what I'm doing.

"I'd be lying if I told you any different, Sherri. It was literally the best night I've had in the last twenty years, that's the God honest truth. Would you like to know why?"

She scrunches up her face and tells me to enlighten her.

"Benny B..."

"Benny B?"

"Yes. Cam brought this kid along who's just full of zest and spunk. Do you know what's great about this guy? He looks a little geeky, but he's well-read and has studied some fascinating subjects like social dynamics, persuasion engineering — all that self-help stuff. This kid has an amazing ability to gain rapport with anyone and make them feel good about themselves."

I pause for a quick breather and add a little emotion to my delivery.

"Honestly, Sherri, one of my problems is I just haven't been feeling good about myself lately, hence all the late-night drinking. So yes, I'm sorry, not just for last night but for the last few months. I'm sorry for not being there for you…"

It's just rolling off my tongue like a freestyle rap as I plow on before she can intervene.

"And you know something else? This kid saw something in me which made me feel freaking outstanding. I know it sounds strange like it ought to be the other way around, but he and Cam brought something out of me last night and made me feel like I'm in my prime again. So I got a little excited. The vibe was awesome, the free drinks kept flowing and we just had a barrel of laughs all night long. I didn't want it to end. I didn't want to come back here and argue. I didn't want to come back to reality and break down like I'm having a midlife crisis, 'cause that's what I've been feeling like lately."

A lot of this has been on my chest for so long, but instead of venting I usually just repress my anguish. This is stuff we never talk about in the open, she knows she's married to an emotional robot, but opening up actually feels good.

I don't think she's buying it as she remains dead still, looking on with such exasperation. I can almost see wicked thoughts oozing out of her, so I continue my defense reiterating what she already knows — I'm not good at facing problems, I just run away and drown them in alcohol.

"You can't use that as an excuse to drive drunk!" she shrieks, pointing her chubby digit in my face. "You could have killed somebody, including yourself!"

"I know. That was the stupid part. And for that, I have no rational explanation at all, other than I had to make it to work on time. I should have taken a cab. But it's not often I get so loaded like that. I was drinking these funny mojitos and expensive champagne, you should have been there, it was unbelievable."

That last part I should not have said. Hatred is still written all over her droopy face.

Lately, we've been binge-watching those true crime docs on Netflix that notoriously revolve around domestic homicides and the fascinating ways they figure out how to solve them. Now I'm paranoid that she'll grab the iron poker from the fireplace and beat me to death with it while taking the necessary precautions to prevent getting caught by a blood-spatter analyst. Luckily this is not the case right now, she just shakes her head and questions me about my midlife crisis.

Before responding I gaze down at the floor an open up a little more. "I'm ashamed to admit it, but yeah, that's what I feel like."

"Why didn't you come to me?" she asks with a little more empathy.

I explain in all honesty I didn't want to burden her with my problems as she's got enough on her plate as it is. Plus it's embarrassing and unmanly, that's why I keep my shit to myself.

"Do you think you should go talk to someone about it?"

"Nah, not really. Except maybe Benny or Cam, I guess."

"Ugh, you're such an imbecile! I mean a professional therapist to help you."

"No, I don't. I'm not into all that therapy stuff."

"Well, do you think we should see a couple's therapist for our issues?"

"No, and here's why: the solution is not you and I having counseling to air out our differences because you are not the problem, Sherri, it's me. I need to do more things that make me feel good about myself and in turn, I'll be a better husband and father."

"That's your big solution, is it? It's just that simple, Bobby?"

"It really is. That has been my problem all along. I've been feeling so down lately, I've been running away and satiating myself with booze and junk food but I'll change, I promise."

This is one of those instances where I'm not sure if I'm telling the truth or it's a facade that I'm making up.

"Look, our problems are way deeper than that—"

"I'm telling you they're not," I intervene. "You want me to be honest, so I'm being honest. Our problems have stemmed from me focusing on how shitty my life is and how life isn't fair and all this other crap swimming around in my head. I need to stop putting my attention on what I haven't got and focus on all the wonderful things I have like you and Max and this house and whatnot. Thus: therein lies the solution: Me. It was never to do with you or us. I just turn into an asshole that doesn't handle problems well, so I take them out on you and my subordinates at work. We don't need to go to therapy to figure that out."

"This is not as simple as you're making it out to be, Bobby."

She looks puzzled but I think I'm making sense.

"I know I'm right about this but if you need a second opinion; fine, let's get Benny B on the phone and see what he thinks." I pull out my cell.

"Look! I'm sick of hearing about this stupid Benny fucking B! Is he your toy-boy now, or something?"

Anger has definitely settled in. Her face has turned to an inflamed red and she keeps making nervous, jittery movements with her hands.

"He's a smart kid and a great analyst. I can't wait for you to meet him but listen, after a long night and even longer day at work I need to go to bed."

I walk past and climb the stairs without waiting for any retaliation. Before reaching the top I stop and turn to her.

"My intuition tells me you're not convinced with my theory, Sherri. Well, while I'm asleep, I want you to think deep down about the solutions to our problems. And when you rack your brain and can't think of any, you will come to the conclusion that if I'm feeling better about myself then everything else will fall into place. I'm the source of our marital problems and thus, I am the solution. Many times the best solution is the simplest one."

I ascend the remaining stairs feeling like a great thespian leaving the stage after a dramatic crescendo. I wonder if she's buying any of this? I'm not sure if I do. All I know is I'm tapped the fuck out, I need sleep for about nineteen straight hours starting right now.

CHAPTER 16

The next few months are like a precarious rollercoaster at home. Sure, we make some subtle improvements and even some okay sex, but I slipped back into my cowardly ways again by running away and drowning myself in drink and drugs and even doing something I'd never thought I'd bring myself to—

"Ready for another, Bobby?" says Mitch, interrupting my sad inner reflections.

"A-huh," is about all I can be bothered to muster.

So here I am again at the Duck Dive like the loveless, lonesome, loser that I am — drinking myself numb, not wanting to face my abysmal life. I keep thinking about that night at the casino, I knew it was a one in a million. I wish Benny B lived in town but he resides way out in Madison and Cam is away on business for a few days.

I've spent the last hour or so lost in my head thinking about another idea for an invention. Sometimes great ideas pop into my brain when I'm inebriated, the hard part is acting upon them. I got this great idea when my coffee turned cold the other day, if only I could put together a prototype… Ugh, who am I to think I can actually put something together and launch it into the market?

I get all excited about a project then get distracted with work, family problems or boozing. It's hard to make something tangible from the intangible, I might as well not even bother putting energy into my ideas and just stick to what I'm good at: drinking…

Fuck, I've gotta get out of my head.

"Hey, Mitch, what do you think of this as an idea?" I motion as he hands me a fresh beer. "A self-heating coffee to-go flask that reheats your coffee without needing a stove, pan or microwave."

"Hmmm," he contemplates, but tells me it's flawed and doubts that such a thing can be made.

"Oh I think you're sadly mistaken. If they can invent a portable charging case for cell phones then this definitely can be done."

"How are you going to power the damn thing?"

"I'm thinking lithium batteries."

He shrugs me off again saying he thinks it's silly when you can just make a fresh pot or reheat it in a microwave.

"You're missing the point. What happens if you're out fishing for hours and your coffee has gone cold? Imagine at the bottom of your flask there was a tiny electrical ring so you could reheat it whenever you wanted."

He shakes his head telling me it will never work and goes to the cellar to change a barrel.

Closed-minded prick.

Jeez, I'm so jaded. To my left is a hairy old man who reminds me of a skinny version of Santa Claus with a bronze tan. I wonder what he'll think of my re-heatable coffee flask... Nah, fuck it, I can't be bothered to ask him his opinion. This dude is like sixty wearing ridiculous little short-shorts that should not be allowed out in public.

He picks up on me smirking at his tanned wrinkly legs and asks if I'm okay.

"I'm sorry, friend. I was just thinking that your beard is longer than James Harden's and your shorts are shorter than John Stockton's."

"Oh yeah?"

"It tickled me. How long have you had a ducktail beard?"

"Since *Happy Days* was a hit show."

"I've gotta be honest, I've never quite understood why men grow long beards. I've always thought they look icky. I could never pull one off, I know that. Plus, I'd get annoyed every time I'd eat a bowl of Campbell's Chunky Chicken Corn Chowder."

Now he's the one laughing, telling me I'm quite forward. I guess he's right. That was the type of thing I'd usually say in my head.

I scoot two stools over and exchange formalities. He is Fritz, originally from Norman, Oklahoma—the home of the greatest BBQ sauce on the planet, he proudly informs me. I find myself strangely intrigued by him and don't really know why.

"Fritz, I would like to buy you your next Guinness. This may sound a little strange but I want to know how's your life going, and wondered if I can pick your brain."

Silence.

I think he's a little startled, that was a bit of a waffle after all.

"I'm not a weirdo, I'm just going through some life and wife problems and need to get out of my head. These voices are driving me nuts."

"It's okay," he mutters, "you get those voices too? I don't think you're a weirdo, you're just very forward but it's quite alright." He takes a big gulp of stout and asks what do I want to know.

"I don't know," I shrug spotting his wedding ring. "Life, marriage, family, I guess."

"Hmmm," he leans back. "You know something; as I look back at my fifty-nine years, I think I can give you a little sage about marriage. I messed the first one up, you see."

I question him on how (I want the juicy details).

"Everything was fine for the first twenty years. When I changed industries, that's when everything went pear-shaped."

He continues by telling me he's been a chef his whole working life, but about eleven years ago he felt the need to spice things up so he landed a job as the head-chef on a private yacht. "I figured it would be a fun way to get paid and see the world, but it was not a good idea for a married man, believe you me." Beaches, bitches, bikinis, bongs, booze and bonking — that's what it's like when you get sucked into the yachting industry he goes on telling me. "It's a blessing and a curse."

"Shit, I'm in the wrong industry," I chuckle.

"*Yachties* as we're referred to in the community, don't live a healthy or normal life. We were always away from home, busting our ass on a boat, but the money can be pretty lucrative, plus it's tax-free."

"Tax-free? How come?"

He tells me the industry is not properly regulated and a lot of the time they work in international waters which complicates things for Uncle Sam. "You know that saying, there's only two promises in the world — death and taxes? It's not quite accurate in the yachting industry," he snickers sipping more suds. "On the downside, we could be working sixteen hours a day for a twenty-two-day stretch. So when the guests and owners would leave, we'd get our break and have crazy blowouts because we felt like we deserved it."

"I guess that's when all the fun goes down," I remark. "Work hard, play hard."

"Right. And nearly everyone was single, except me. On most boats there's usually a higher ratio of women to men, so when it came time to party we'd end up fraternizing with each other more often than not." He sips more of his pint and looks down into it. "And that's where the conflict arose. When I'd come home to my wife the spark just wasn't there anymore. It messed me up because I was riddled with guilt. And my wife could sense it too. They've got a sixth sense, them broads."

"Shit, I know all about that," I slur, patting his back.

It didn't take long until his wife left him, he tells me as he stares into his drink. "I knew I had to quit the industry if I met someone special because I'd no doubt repeat the same process. So when I hit fifty, which was not long after, I made the decision to jump ship and become an architect."

"Architect, really?"

"Yep. It's a passion of mine, like a young Adolf Hitler."

"Hitler was an architect?"

"He studied it in his early days but never had what it took to make it, so he was more of a wannabe," he says downing the last of his Guinness. "So my plan was to invest my earnings into architecture courses so I could land a cushy nine-to-five gig. Everything was going to plan until I got side-tracked."

As I question what he means by that, I order a round of brew, no Guinness for me though (turns my shit black).

"I landed a job on a boat that sailed to Thailand. Ever been there, Bobby?"

"Sadly no. Just Thai Town, Los Angeles."

"First off, being a white man is a big deal over there," Fritz continues as our new drinks appear, "even for an old bastard like me. In fact, being old is a sign of high value as it is in many Asian cultures. The young actually envy the old, because age represents wisdom, wealth, and knowledge. Quite unlike this God damn country."

"That's a pretty interesting contrast between east and west. They value old people, what a concept."

"You're telling me. I'm an opulent old stud to them Asians, they treat me like a damn savant." He cracks up. "As soon as I arrived, I immediately fell in love with the place. Here I was, fifty years old, recently divorced and now I had twenty-two year olds throwing themselves at me. Probably because I'm rich, at least in *their* eyes I am. So it didn't take me long to shack up with a young gal in Hat Yai, and let me tell ya: they will do anything and everything with zero complaints. And I'm not just talking under the sheets either, I'm talking about mundane shit like cleaning the gutters or painting the fence. All you have to do is put in the request and it's as good as done. They are the most loyal humans on the face of this Earth."

"I bet."

After being there not even a year, he ended up marrying a twenty-eight year old and was totally smitten, he informs me. But long story short, her cousin came to stay with them and old Fritz—the sly dog—got caught in bed with her. "I swore to myself after ruining my first marriage to never be a cheating asshole again. But I slipped up. I felt terrible and couldn't blame it on being drunk or stuck at sea — it was ten o'clock in the morning while my wife was out catching fish."

"How did she take it?"

"You ain't going to believe this, but I'll tell you anyway. She actually reacted with gratitude."

I can hardly believe my drunken ears. "Gratitude?"

"My wife was so grateful for taking them both in, that sex with her cousin wasn't a big deal. Her only concern was, was she going to be replaced and kicked out. After I assured her this was not the case, she said if having another woman around makes me happy then so be it."

Smugness now appears across his seasoned leathery face — awe and jealously across mine. This is nuts! I have to double-check that he's not yanking my chain. He presses he's not and tells me they live together as one big sexual family.

"So let me get this straight," I press with no malicious intent, "an old fart like you who looks like a tanned version of Santa Claus lives it up in Thailand with two women who are about twenty-five years your junior?"

"Three," he coyly replies displaying three fingers.

"Three fucking chicks?" I clamor. "Come on, man, you've gotta be ribbing me."

"That's what everyone says but I got nothing to prove."

"Where does the third one come into the picture?"

"I got greedy again. After being with the same two girls for a couple of years, I figured adding one more couldn't hurt. And you know what their only concern was?"

"What?"

"That once again they are not going to be replaced and kicked out on the streets. So I reassured them everything will remain the same, except there's one more girl thrown into the mix."

I'm shocked. This is better than a freaking fairy tale.

"It is kind of unfathomable, I know, but if you understand their culture it's not that uncommon."

I laugh to myself and look off to the distance with more thoughts of envy. Why can't shit like this ever happen to me?

"So your daily routine is waking up with three women more than half your age who do whatever you want?"

"Yep. It's almost like I'm their master. They do anything I say whether it's feeding me, scrubbing the floor, cutting the grass, massages, orgies—anything I want."

I'm getting hard just listening to this. "Brother, you have it made. So what are you doing here in the States?"

"I'm just here on a boat for the next three weeks and then it's back home. I know I told you I was gonna quit the yachting industry but I re-evaluated from my original plan. I now work six weeks out the year on a boat in the US. That six weeks of hard work allows me to pay for me and my three girls to live comfortably for the next eleven months over there. It's a great set up."

I have to agree and ask to see pictures of them. He rummages around in his pocket and pulls out his phone to show me a selfie with his three little sex slaves. He looks like their grandfather and they look like clones: slim, petite, straight black hair and light-skinned. I don't know how he tells them apart.

"Wow. I'm in complete awe of your life, Fritz."

"It's very not bad."

"What's it like waking up with three chicks in your bed every day?"

"What happens in Hat Yai, stays in Hat Yai," he grins while patting me on the back.

"Come on, Fritz. Don't be a stinge. Can I get a little snippet of the bedroom scene? Pleeeze?"

"Well, I'm pretty accustomed to it now; one makes my coffee, the other brings my breakfast while the other tongues my balls—sometimes all at once," he shoots me a cheeky wink.

"You're living the Hugh Hefner life over there it sounds like."

"Ha. I don't know if I'm quite like that but it is kind of crazy. The only way a regular Joe could live like me in the states is by paying hookers, but that's all fake and it wouldn't be the same. These girls truly love me, the real me—warts and all. It's beyond my wildest dreams."

I press (like the curious perv I am) to hear more about the orgies.

"Well, my friend, at first I used to be embarrassed about them seeing me with the lights on; I've got a saggy, cottage cheese ass and my balls look like shriveled-up prunes but I don't care anymore, they do anything I want, and I do mean *anything*. You get the picture." He looks at his watch. "Man, I gotta go. Nice talking to ya, Bob." He swallows the last of his draft and leaves me in a trance of jealousy.

73

CHAPTER 17

As I consume more beer into the late night thoughts of envy towards old Fritz inundate my mind. I just can't shake those Thai bitches out my head. A great sense of gloom washes over me because I'll never experience anything like that in my lifetime. Unless I can sneak off to Thailand somehow… No, no, that's ludicrous — too much moolah.

"Hey, Mitch, let me ask you something."

"Shoot," spouts the bald barman looking up from his newspaper.

"What do you think of Asian women? Have you ever been into them?"

"Nah, not my cup of tea. They've never really done it for me."

"Yeah, me neither."

"It's funny you mention that, Bob because I know this kid, Victor that has 'yellow fever' like no other and I tease him about it whenever he comes in here."

"Have I met him? What does he look like?"

"You may have, he comes in here from time to time. He's a big brolic MoFo, like six-three, two fifty-five, who looks Spanish, dresses like he's black but speaks like he's white."

"That's quite unusual," I snicker.

"He's a real New York mutt, always talking that criminal slang. Do you wanna hear my theory to why he's got the 'fever' so bad?"

"Sure," I tell him while he pulls me a fresh draft as my current one is getting dangerously low.

"You've probably heard the rumor and innuendo that Asian men have peewee sized dicks."

"I've heard that," I chuckle.

"Well, just like their male counterparts; Asian broads apparently are known to have the tightest pussies on God's Green Earth."

"Don't you mean God's *Blue* Earth?"

He looks at me gone-out, so I feel the need to enlighten the bald bastard that the Earth is approximately seventy-five percent water, thus, it's a lot more blue than green.

"But nobody says that, Bobby. The saying is *God's Green Earth*."

"Well, they should change it to blue. It's more accurate."

He tightens his face and asks me if I'm feeling alright. "*Re-heatable coffee flasks* and *God's Blue Earth?* I think you're a few cans short of a six-pack, son."

I blow him off.

"So anyway, back to the tight coochies, you got me all off track here," he vents, passing me my pint. "I think Victor gets off on them Asians purely because of the principle of contrast. You see, once he gets down to the hanky-panky his average size *Johnson* suddenly seems like a *Black Mamba*, because of their petits pois size pussies, but really it's an illusion."

His hypothesis cracks me up. "And when you told him your theory what did he say?"

"He denied all prospect, claiming Asian women are so classy and elegant but I know his M.O., he loves their tight little minkies."

I chuckle once again as Mitch goes off to serve someone else. I wonder if I slept with an Asian chick would my dick seem bigger than normal? Hmmm. Something to think about...

The night seems to just drag on and on, and there's nothing going on here. I still cannot shake the images that a regular old man can live this kind of orgy lifestyle with three chicks more than half his age. It's killing me. I think I've been bitten by the Beijing virus. I'm green with envy and yellow with fever, I have to get me a taste somehow...

When Fritz said the only way a regular Joe can live like him is with hookers it struck something inside me. I've never contemplated messing around with a prostitute even before I met Sherri. Most of my friends back in college did but not me. I always figured they were dirty and diseased and would do anything for money so I didn't see the fun in that. I can't believe that I'm actually entertaining the thought of soliciting a prostitute. An Asian prostitute... Wait a minute, do they even have Asian ones? Of course they do, dummy. I can't bring myself to do that...can I? Man, this must be the booze talking, I've gotta get a grip.

CHAPTER 18

As the clock spins another round, I consume another two. I'm pretty inebriated now as a blowout hockey game broadcasts in the background failing to hold my attention. I'm constantly interrupted by little Asian girls calling my name, luring me into their wild orgy — that's what broadcasts in my mind. I feel like I've been deprived of all my favorite foods like Philly cheesesteaks and New York cheesecakes and now I want them more than anything. Forbidden fruit like a motherfucker.

I cave.

Despite being probably twice over the legal limit to drive, I stumble from the barstool and get behind the wheel like a fucking idiot and head to the part of the city I never go. The part where crime, drugs and prostitution are rampant.

It only takes me fifteen minutes or so and I arrive in the ghettos of the southside. All I see through my impaired vision is creepy looking characters of many races: men, women and some teenagers lingering on street corners where the boarded-up stores are. Whatever they're up to it can't be good. Many gape at me as I cruise slowly through their hood scanning the perimeter as cautious as can be. My shitty little Civic usually attracts zero attention, but it's not the car people are looking at—it's the clueless fat white guy that looks so out of place searching for a lady of the night.

Bingo, here we go! That wasn't as long as I thought. But she isn't Asian. Bummer! She's a curvy black chick with hair like Rick James and looks feisty with a capital F. She wiggles towards my car rocking white thigh-highs and too much pink lipstick accentuating her DSLs.

"You looking fo' some action, baby boy?" she says while chewing gum in an oh so slutty manner.

"Hello, ma'am," I say, putting the car in park. "I was wondering if you could help me with some directions?"

"Directions? Shit. I ain't no good with directions, but I can suck a dick like a fucking champion."

"Is that right?"

"A-huh. Around here they call me the Brain Surgeon. I can make your eyeballs pop out! Whuddaya say, cutie pie?"

"Well, to be honest, I've never done this before and I'm kinda looking for an Asian lady tonight."

"Ain't no Kung Pao bitches around here. And those skinny hos don't know how to work the thang-thang. Once you go black, you'll never go back, Jack!"

"But I'm—"

"I'm telling y'all, can't nobody get down like me — I'm the baddest bitchy that fucks like Lionel Richie!"

"Lionel Richie?"

"A-huh, I can give it to you *All Night Long!* If you gots the dime, Daddy, I gots the time! How 'bout it?"

I thank her for the proposition but politely decline and ask for help.

"Help you with what?" she says before blowing a bubble with her Juicy Fruit gum.

"Do you know any Asian ladies in the same line of work as you?"

"I know me some Asian hoes, just not around here."

"Where can I find them?"

"What's it worth to you, Jack?" she blows a bubble again and makes it pop trying to fuck with me.

"I'll give you twenty bucks if you tell me where I need to go."

"Tell you what; I'll do you one better. For forty, I'll call my girl across town and see if she's available—and I got a picture too. Wanna see?" She pulls out her phone and soon reveals a pic of a cute little Asian girl with pigtails, in a silk grey negligee.

"You can hook me up with her tonight?" I gawk, trying to contain my excitement.

"A-huh unless she be busy or she dun turned herself over to Korean Jesus or somethin'. We ain't dun speak in a minute."

"Okay, you broker the deal and have her meet me close by."

"Broker? What you talkin' 'bout?"

"Broker, ya know; you arrange the deal and I'll pay you thirty bucks for the hook-up."

"Forty and we got a deal."

I reluctantly shake her hand before she walks away, dialing her phone.

Paranoia starts to hit me now as she speaks into her burner. What the fuck am I doing here? What if a cop pulls up and arrests me for soliciting a ho, possession of coke and drink driving? I'm fucked! I better get outta here now. Or what if this is all a big set up and her pimp mugs me or jacks my Honda? I try my best to block out my paranoia, then do a little bump to keep my head together.

Finally, I see her childbearing hips wiggle back towards my car.

"You in luck, mister," she pops her gum again. "She can meet you in like twenty-five if you down to jive. You got my money?"

I hand her two twenties with no resistance or negotiation.

"Flamingo Inn, Johnson BLVD, China Town. Meet in the car park."

"China Town. Of course, that's where the Asian hookers are!" I say wanting to slap myself.

"Duh!" She stuffs my money into her breasts.

Why didn't I think to try China Town, you fucking grade A idiot! She must have seen the word *imbecile* scribed across my forehead when I pulled up.

"And we ain't hookers, white boy, we're *entertainers*. Now make like my legs and split!"

CHAPTER 19

I get to China Town in less than twenty minutes and pull up in the Flamingo Inn car park. This place is seedy and poorly lit because of the smashed street lights, it's also pretty quiet as it's late, so I leave the engine running just in case this is some kind of setup.

Then it hits me: *what the fuck am I doing here?* I smell a rat and start to contemplate that I've been conned. I bet that fucking black bitch had just made the whole thing up just to get my forty bucks. How could I have been so fucking stupid?

I pull out my coke and do another quick bump to keep my wits at bay. Something feels off. There's nothing going on here at all, and nobody in sight. All I see is an abandoned mattress off to the side and a newspaper blowing in the wind.

But suddenly I see a silhouette of somebody walking through the car park. It must be her. Holy shit, it is! I feel like I've spotted an oasis in the desert. Well, I'll be damned, she wasn't bullshitting after all.

I flash my lights a couple of times and she approaches my window where tell her that I was with her friend across town. This cute Asian reminds me of an attractive version of Bjork, and I mean really attractive — pigtails, nose ring, rocking a schoolgirl uniform with knee-high socks. Bonus!

"You looking for fun too-night, misssster?" she says with her stereotypical broken English.

"That I am." I kill the engine. "So how does this work exactly?"

"We go hotel an hav sex."

Her retort was so deadpan and direct it caught me off guard.

"That simple, is it? What's the price structure?"

"Prrrice struct-suuure?" she frowns, obviously puzzled.

What a fuckhead! Why did I say that? I'm not purchasing a fucking life insurance policy. She's a whore!

"Sorry, honey. How much money do you charge for your services?"

"Oh monnie. It's fifftee for sucky-sucky. One hunndrod for sex. One fifftee for sucky-sucky, plus sex. Two hunndrod for evvythin', plus anal. Two fiffftee for evvythin', plus anal, plus tossed salad…"

Damn, that was a mouthful, she *does* have a price structure.

"And five hunndrod for Lionel Richie."

I start laughing hysterically. That's the last thing I'd ever expect from an Asian hooker with poor English. And she said it perfectly too. I guess Lionel Richie is ubiquitous among ladies of the night. I can barely compose myself before replying.

"So for five hundred bucks you'll fuck me *All Night Long,*" I say, imitating that classic 80's hit. "That's what you're saying, right?"

"Yesss."

"Alrighty then. And when do I pay?"

"You pay affter, silly. Are you virgin?"

"I guess I am," I open the door. "Let's go pop my cherry."

I must have weighed three times as much as her in mass which was an embarrassment in itself, it's the irresistible force meeting the immovable object, but once we got naked, she knew all the right things to do to get me off.

I plowed into the little broad like Big Van Vader throwing potatoes, dicking her down long, deep and hard with her yellow legs spread wide like the Golden Arches. Her pussy was real wet and sloppy just how I like it, and the strangest high pitched screams came out her mouth which sounded like Tatanka's war cry. Guess I've still got it…

Initially, I only wanted to pay a couple of hundred, but she up-sold me to the *Lionel Richie Package* like the master closer she is, (although, I didn't exactly give her a lot of sales resistance). She did it first by sticking her tongue in my asshole and swirling it around like Mr. Whippy. My lame-ass wife has never done anything even close to that—she barely even gives me head. Bjork, however, is a real pro and I can tell she takes pride in delivering an extraordinary life remembering experience, like a tour guide at Magic Kingdom. She brought a kind of fantasy aspect to the whole night, making me feel justified spending this kind of bread.

Six hours of absolute bliss.

I used to have a hard time parting with cash, (I come from a family of accountants after all,) but this was money well spent with no buyer's remorse. That's what's great about this country, you can do anything you want providing you have the right amount of green. I must invest in more things that bring me peak levels of happiness.

I drove home still a little buzzed and deliberately took the windy, picturesque route. The hills had never looked so beautiful as the sun rose in the east. I felt rejuvenated like I'm coming home from a spa, despite my bloodshot eyes and numb face. I might have to get back into real estate so I can afford to have this much fun every weekend.

CHAPTER 20

I wake up on the sofa to an annoying fucking Motorola ringing in my ear. Nobody is in sight so I guess I'm safe. Holy shit, it's Jolly Jim. In all the years that I've known him, we must have only spoke on the phone like twice. He usually just sends funny texts involving puffters or priests. Why on Earth would he be calling me this early in the morning?

"Hello?" I say softly into the phone, wiping my mouth from sleep drool.

"I'm just checking you're alright, shagrat," he says in that funny British accent of his. "I hoped to God you didn't fackin' drive anywhere last night."

"What are you talking about?"

"I knew you wouldn't remember, you silly wank stain. I popped in the boozer last night to drop some coin off to Stubsy, and believe you me, I've never seen you in a two and eight like that before."

"A two and eight?"

"A *state*, you donut!"

"Really?"

"Yeah, geez really. You were fackin' plastered like the Sistine Chapel. Was you on drugs or something, you silly cunt?"

"I had a little," I admit. "I'm just going through some shit with the wife."

"You're not a fackin' bag-head are ya?"

"No no, nothing like that, Jol, just a little sniff." I keep my voice discreet in case the wife's around.

"Well listen 'ear, Bobby fackin' Boo, I facked about doing shit like that back in the day in Ibiza—"

"Ibiza, really?"

"Don't cut me off, you nonce! There's a lot about me you don't know, sonny boy. While you were still watching *Baywatch*, jerking off to the Hoff, I was living it up in San Antonio with Fat Face Freddy — finger blasting all the gash and riding the white horse all fackin' summer, so I ain't pointing no fackin' fingers! But I thought I'd warn ya I've seen that powder turn people into degenerates time after time, that's why I knocked it on the head."

His Sergeant Slaughter-like splutter echoes through the phone making me jolt.

"You better get your shit together, you big fat bender! You've got a wife and little girl to take care of."

He hits a nerve but I don't let out. I stay brief and agree he's right.

"I know I'm fackin' right. You better take this shit seriously or it will ruin ya!"

"I know, I know. And I appreciate you looking out for me like this, Jol."

"Remember; drugs are for fackin' mugs. Don't be a queer, just stick to the beer. Know what I mean? And don't mention what I just told you to nobody, alright. I've lived about twelve lifetimes back to back, my son, so I got a few goblins in my closet that only a select few know about."

"Understood."

"Right, I gotta go. I'm installing some fackin' wetback's decking across town and I can't be late. Can you believe it; seventeen years this nob-head has been in the country and he don't speak one word of English! What a proper cunt!"

The call ends as I stare at the backdrop picture of Max and Sherry on my home screen. Shit, look at the time, I'm gonna be late for work!

The rest of the day went south. I felt worn out from my debaucherous night of drinking, drugs and ravenous sex while dreading coming home to another twelve rounds with Balboa. Instead, I directed my focus towards my little fantasy girl Bjork. I may be delusional thinking I'm special because she gave me her number in case I wanted another midnight liaison, and she, quote: 'doesn't do this with her other clientele.' Yeah, I know that was probably a bullshit line but I'm smitten. She has an uncanny ability to make me feel like a man, so of course, I take her up on another late-night rendezvous the following night as a matter of fact.

The affair goes on for weeks. It even gets to the point of kissing and cuddling with in-depth conversations about zen, life, and deep shit like Copernicus and the universe. She's smart as a whip and schools me how the Earth evolved after four billion years. That's some sexy shit.

After many nights of wild, animalistic sex, we'd also talk about the principles of influence, compliance and persuasion engineering. She put me onto a book called *Buy-ology* by Martin Lindstrom; the psychology behind why people buy. We'd compare our industries on how we both up-sell and cross-sell products and services. I'd tell her once we've sold a mattress we try to up-sell the customer with bed sheets, duvets, and extended warranties and whatnot. Her version of up-selling is doing anal, rusty trombones and swallowing sperm. The girl is a hustler through and through and knows exactly how to stack paper, both street smart and book smart. She even has a Yelp account where tricks can review her performance. I couldn't believe it — a hooker on Yelp! She's amazing at getting guy's off just the way they like it and never worried about receiving bad reviews. You can't argue with results — she gets nothing less than five stars from fat, sweaty, truck drivers who love to empty their bags after a long day behind the wheel.

Inevitably, our relationship got redundant as time went on, so I ventured towards other Asian entertainers to spice it up a little. It basically became an addiction, doing it in every possible way invented. Soon once a day wasn't enough so I kept coming back for more. Then I got into doing freaky shit like using toys, then having two girls at once, then two girls with toys and then three, and things getting more and more bizarre. Each time wanting to top the last and live *the dream* like old man Fritz in Thailand.

I started to venture into escorts of all races just to meet my variety need; Chinese, Japanese, Vietnamese, Korean, Cuban, Mexican, Malaysian, black, white and everything in between — treating prostitutes like my very own Baskin & Robbins Thirty-One Flavors and having the time of my life.

Jolly Jim once told me an old quote by a soccer star from England who I believe was called George Best: *'I spent most of my money on booze, birds and fast cars. The rest I just squandered.'*

At first, I thought that was pretty irresponsible but now I can totally relate where he's coming from. This is what life's all about! This is where the juice is! I cannot fathom how much money I must have channeled into my secret life over the past few months. I don't dwell on it too much and certainly don't have any regrets.

Although at times I do try to curb my spending by encasing my bank cards in a block of ice in the garage freezer. The method behind my madness was whenever I get the urge to get my rocks off, I'd have to wait at least thirty minutes for the ice to melt before my card could draw cash from an ATM, (you probably know that prostitutes don't accept plastic), so hopefully, by that time I will have let the urge subside. But sadly it never works because after thirty minutes of waiting, I'm just as horny as before, so to speed up the process I'd melt the ice with a hairdryer then sneak off to get my dick sucked.

I eventually abolish the idea of trying to curb my libido. Spending my hard-earned savings on a service of this quality is a good thing because it makes me happy. It's far more satisfying spending money on pussy than buying a new lawnmower, that's for sure.

The fact that I kept this a big secret is probably another delusion of mine. The whole atmosphere in the house has become drab and dreary and I can tell she senses something amiss from all the late nights and my out-of-control drinking, but like me I think she's tired of arguing and knows she can't control me anyway. And sex between us is basically non-existent, she's the most vanilla motherfucker under the bedsheets and I make no attempts trying to turn her Cookies & Cream.

Ever heard this joke? *A married couple are in bed trying to get it on but nothing is going right, so the man says "what's wrong? Can't you think of anybody else either?"* That's basically how it is with us. When I attempt to make love to my wife my mental stimulation is just not there anymore. I have problems getting it up because all I see is a fat lump of unhappiness laying beneath me, so I continue on with my scum-bag antics completely oblivious of the repercussions.

CHAPTER 21

Today is my little girl's bornday. Can't believe she's eight already. She's such a sweet, innocent angel, the complete opposite of me. We throw a party in our recently rejuvenated back-yard and make it a clown-free zone. We do have Twister, a piñata and a bouncy house or bouncy castle—whatever the hell you call them— plus a ton of food that Sherri and I spent all morning preparing.

The weather is perfect especially for mid-October and the turnout is pretty good, so everything's clicking on all cylinders — everything except my destructive, self-sabotaging brain. For months now I've felt hollow inside and today is no different despite the fact I'm supposed to be celebrating. I feel like everything I do around my family is a complete facade and it's weighing on me.

Every time I focus on all the sins of my life I feel so down in the dumps that it makes me want to numb myself with drink, drugs and hookers; which in turn makes me feel even worse but I still continue. And it isn't just the drugs and boozing (and my dozen other vices), it's like I have a deep psychological scar that I just can't heal. I'm popping pills every morning just to function (which is new for me) and I'm so constipated every time I take a shit I feel like I'm gonna croak on the crapper like the late great Elvis Aaron Presley.

And just like *The King*, my eating habits have really gotten out of control. I once read that Elvis would gorge on junk food so vehemently that his assistant had to literally piggy-back him to the bathroom. That's the direction I'm moving toward if I don't break this ill cycle of destruction (although I doubt many people could piggy-back my fat ass).

I've begun to crave pies and pudding for breakfast now and strange things like deep-fried Nutella sandwiches and key lime pie flavored milkshakes. I even bought a mini-refrigerator for the bedroom because I'm too lazy to walk to the kitchen when I get a late-night snack-attack.

Every time I look in the mirror I seem uglier and fatter than the day before which makes me paranoid, so I'll eat some more to try to feel good but it only makes things worse. I wake up in cold sweats thinking my heart is about to thump out my chest like Sylvester the Cat when he sees Pepé Le Pew. It beats rapidly one minute and slow the next. I freak-out walking down the street thinking everyone's staring at me as if I'm some kind of hideous beast like Kamala.

I've almost convinced myself that prostitutes will to reject me from my ugliness, but I continue to solicit them in my clandestine life to try and feel some kind of love and connection. But it doesn't work, I still feel hollow inside. I've messed around with so many prostitutes now that the buzz is not the same. It's moments like this that I really feel like—

"Hey, Bobby, good to see you, buddy!" says an overzealous mingler breaking my inner rant. "Love that potato salad! I'm going in for round two. Don't you go nowhere!"

"Right on, Brad," I mimic his corny enthusiasm.

Man, this is all so phony. I sit back and observe the parents playing with the kids, laughing and enjoying the festivities and suddenly become envious of them. They seem so happy and content doing nothing except acting childlike around the young. Why can't I be like that? I have a great family and a million other reasons to be happy, but if I join them I think I'll feel like a charlatan. I can't even relax in social situations like this anymore.

Every forty-five minutes I've been sneaking off to the bathroom for a little bump of ya-yo, (yeah, even at a children's party in the middle of the day!) How the fuck did I end up so low?

"Bobby, my man," says cowboy Bruce, our loud-mouth neighbor who's here with his kid Julie. "How's life treating y'all?"

"What can I say, Bruce? Living the dream."

"Dang, boy, I haven't seen you in some time but errr, do you consider me a straight shooter?"

"Yes, sir."

"So I can be perfectly honest with y'all?"

"I wouldn't expect anything less from you, cowboy," I say, washing down a Pepcin AC with my Yuengling.

"You know when you ain't seen somebody in a while you notice how they've changed? For instance, I haven't seen Max in a few months so I notice how much she's grown, but take my Julie; because I see her every day, I don't realize how much she's grown."

"Sure, I notice how much Julie's grown and you notice the same with Max. So what?" I stomp out a small army of pesky ants by my feet.

"Well, I gotta shoot straight from the hip, partner. You're packing on the pounds like a hog in humping season."

What can I say? I can't disagree. But who is this tubby fuck to say anything?

He's hardly a conditioned athlete himself.

"Hell, I'm hardly conditioned athlete myself," he says coincidently, "so when I point fingers at you, I'm pointing three back at myself. I just noticed how much personal growth you've accumulated since the last time I saw y'all, that's all."

"It's okay, cowboy, I don't take offense. I've have been neglecting my health along with other things to be quite frank. You know what my problem is? No matter how stuffed I get, I can always find room for pudding."

"Daddy!" hails little Julie bursting into our conversation, "we're gonna hit the piñata! Come watch me."

"Yes, sweetie, in a second. Have you said hi to Mr. J yet?"

"Yes. Hi, Mr. J!"

"It's *Bobby* and hi again, little legs."

She looks adorable with her tiny pigtails as she runs over to the piñata that I filled earlier with Dollar Tree candy.

"Yeah, I hear ya, partner," Bruce continues. "I've been pretty slacker-daisical too lately. There's so much confusion around this diet business. One minute you have an expert who says eating a lot of lean meat is good for you, then you read somebody else who says eating meat clogs you up. Then you read another dang magazine that says drinking milk is good for your teeth and bones and everything, and then you watch a show about how milk makes you lactose intolerant! Then you hear about eggs being a good brain food but then some other dang dietician saying eating eggs are bad because of the cholesterol. It's all so confusing."

"You're preaching to the choir, my friend. I often think *what's the point* and go stuff my face with turkey bacon until my insides hurt. I've gotta stop doing this to myself."

"You should, son because you look like the south end of a northbound mule. No offense," he adjusts his belt. "Any-hoo, I'm gonna hit the grill before those Jimmy Deans go AWOL." He tilts his cowboy hat and excuses himself.

These are the kind of social interactions that drain me mentally. I might have to sneak off for another quick belter to make it through the next few hours.

CHAPTER 22

"HAPPY BORNDAY TO YOU. HAPPY BORNDAY TO YOU. HAPPY BORNDAY DEAR, MAXINE. HAPPY BORNDAY TO YOU!"

The garden crowd sing in unison as Sherri brings out the triple-layered Belgian chocolate cake with eight lit candles dancing in the wind. I'm tipsier and more emotional now as I stare at my precious little darling with all her friends surrounding her like she's queen of the castle. Sometimes I can't fathom how this little angel actually came from me—from my nut-sack.

"Now close your eyes and make a wish," Sherri says, placing the cake in front of her.

"What shall I wish for, Mommy?"

"You can wish for anything you want. And remember, close your eyes and then blow out the candles."

Max closes her eyes and waits, then opens them and looks boggled. "Mommy I don't know what to wish for."

"Well," says Sherri, "what do you want more than anything in the whole wide world?"

Max looks up to the heavens, gathering her thoughts in that little brain of hers. Then something hits her where she can barely contain herself. "I know—I know!" she screeches before locking eyes with me for the longest three seconds of my life and then blows out the candles.

As everybody cheers in celebration, Max remains glued on me like a little creep from *Children of the Corn* before I break the trance by grabbing another beer.

"Daddy, come bounce with me," says my little snickerdoodle with a face full of cake.

"No, honey, Daddy's too chubby for a bouncy castle," says my unapologetic wife in front of everyone. "We don't want it to collapse."

That's rich coming from that fat-Albert-fuck. When she throws jabs at me like this, I have to retaliate. Maybe I'll stick it to her by doing my old party trick from college: guzzling back to back bottles of beer in six seconds or less. She made me promise that I'll drink responsibly today. Well, that plan just went straight out the window.

"What did you just say?" I crack open a cold one and chug the whole thing right in front of her.

"Come on, Bobby, you promised."

I knew this would work, she's already regretting fucking with me. It serves her right. I make fun of my fat ass all the time in private or with the boys, but I'm sensitive about my belly with a crowd like this. There are hot single moms here for Christ's sake.

"Why don't you go to the kitchen and grab more beers for our guests. I'm gonna go bounce with the kids."

"Oh no you're not, Bobby" she hurls. "It will collapse! It's designed for five to ten year olds. Plus you're too drunk despite your so-called promise."

Shots fired. I have to retaliate.

"What are you talking about, *collapse*? Maybe if *you* jumped on it it would."

"Bobby, I've watched you drink at least ten beers in the last two hours, you can't go on there."

"I can handle ten beers for breakfast, woman, especially after your cooking. Now outta my way."

I drunkenly shove her aside but she adamantly doesn't back down. "No, Bobby! It will collapse! The manual says it can only withstand a maximum of two hundred and fifty pounds. You wish you weighed two-fifty!"

"Oh come on," I slur. "Don't talk shit. You worry too much that's your problem. This is supposed to be a party and you're being a big fat party pooper. Now get out of my way!"

"No!"

She stands her ground.

This has become a joust.

We stare pupil to dilated pupil as I lower my voice to emphasize my seriousness. "Sherri, I'm going to bounce with my daughter. I will not tell you again! Fuck off!" I physically shove her out the way. God knows what the onlookers think of this. There's definitely tension in the air.

"Go ahead, Bobby, be a reckless drunk around young children!"

Max looks up at me like a deer in the headlights as I lead her away from the angry Earthquake.

We remove our shoes and join the bouncing fun with the other younglings. I stare at Sherri making *"weeeeeee"* sounds just to fuck with her. She always makes me out to be the heel in front of her friends, but I'm not putting up with that shit anymore. Today I'm the babyface and I'm gonna win over this crowd with my awesomeness.

After bouncing for a couple of minutes I begin to feel funny. It's probably all that beer, cocaine and jerk chicken swishing around my breadbasket. This can't be good.

Then, all of a sudden the unthinkable happens.

POP.

The fucking bouncy castle collapses!

Me, along with four kids and the bornday queen hit the deck as the castle caves in on us like the WWF ring at the 1991 Albert Hall Battle Royal. The kids wail in unison. Max screams something about her leg. I lay in shell shock, on the brink of throwing up all this light beer. I have to remain still for a minute. Oh, God, here comes the angry Earthquake.

"Are you satisfied now, you fat fucking drunk? You've ruined the party! I hate you, I hate your fucking guts!"

Sherri has to be restrained by her friend Carol. But not for long, she breaks free and starts slapping me while I'm grounded and helpless. She then gets pulled away by two others as Carol grabs Max and helps her out the deflated rubber.

Then when you think it can't get any worse, nausea hits me like a motherfucker:

BLAHHH!

I projectile vomit everywhere like I'm the Creature from the Black Lagoon. The stuff just keeps coming out of me, I'm talking real nasty shit — big chunks of partially digested corn and pink slime. Needless to say, it goes everywhere including my damn T-shirt. I must look so ghastly to the entire party. This is so humiliating! I'll never show my face in public again.

"Are you alright, Bobby?" asks Brad.

I don't answer. I remain TKO-ed like I've been hit with a DDT. I can't take this embarrassment any longer, I'm outta here, and have no intention of doing anything rational. The only thing I can do is what I do best: run away.

I pull myself up and wait for my equilibrium to balance out. I can't bring myself to look anyone in the eye, I just walk through the whole cluster of guests who part like the red sea and exit out the side gate.

CHAPTER 23

"I can't believe you did it again, you son-of-a-bitch!" said my stocky co-worker Carl upon entering my pristine office unannounced. "How the hell did you get those newlyweds to invest in that dump on Flack Street?"

"Hey, you know me, Carl," I winked. "I could sell SlimFast in Ethiopia if I had to."

"You probably could, Bob. You know you're in the leading position to win the London trip."

"Oh, I'm well aware of that, big boy. It's in the bag. I can't wait to taste their fish and chips with a tall pint of Carling."

"Carling?" he frowned.

"Black label. It's supposed to be the best and most popular beer over there. I've done my research."

"Ahh, well, you deserve it. When you're locked in like this, we might as well tell everyone else to stay in bed."

"That's right, big C, keep feeding my ego. I won't lie and tell ya I don't like it. I've got to stay laser-focused. I'm dead set on winning the year-end bonus too. How many days have we got left? What's the date today?"

"What do you mean, *what's the date*? It's the eve of Christmas Eve, you mad man."

"It is?"

"In less than nine days it will be 2005 and you're the only one alive! It's a wrap, finito, the fat lady is eating and singing. You have nothing to worry about."

"Well, I'm not gonna let anybody come close and risk taking away my bonus. Vince McMahon once said: *You've got to grab your competition by the throat and squeeze the life right out of your competition!*"

"You and your silly fake wrestling," Carl smirked. "Anyway, I have to go set up the party. It's gonna be a big night. Be there at six, sharp."

"I donno, man. I still got a lot of work to cover."

"You're addicted to this place, Bob, I swear. It's Christmas, you should be with your family. Remember we work to live, not live to work."

I smiled and turned my attention back to my computer screen and told him he is my family.

"Just be there at six."

"Yeah, yeah. Sherri and I will be fashionably late around eight-thirty."

"Seven at the latest, but that's it."

"Alright. I can just about squeeze that if I wasn't so distracted around here."

"That's more like it," he said, heading out the door.

"And don't you be calling wrestling fake!" I yelled. "Santa Claus is fake, wrestling is real…"

Reality snaps back into focus as I scrape bits of regurgitated food from my T-shirt while halted at a stoplight in my Civic. I often drift off back to my heydays in real estate and get reminded that it's all downhill from here. I wonder if that's why I have the constant need to numb myself with booze and drugs because I'm a mere shell of the former me…

I soon arrive outside my local watering hole and take a couple of shots of mouthwash with a few splashes of Mone that I keep in the glove compartment. I make a quick change into a semi-clean T-shirt that I luckily find discarded on my backseat so now I'm some-what presentable to be out in public. I still look horrendous but I have to try and make chicken salad out of chicken shit.

Speaking of shots, I order drinks like I'm a one-man frat party; Fireball, Kamikaze, Rolling Rock and a new rum called Wild Child. It doesn't take long for the room to start spinning. I also purchase a Cuban cigar which is a new thing for me that Jolly Jim turned me on to. He schooled me that only real men can handle Cubans, so I thought I'd jump on the bandwagon. Although, I'm not exactly impressing anybody here at the Duck. The clientele generally consists of unkempt old men who neglect the fundamentals of general hygiene.

I take my stogie to the smoking area out front and puff away into the world. I often gaze at people in public and analyze all the different faces and mannerisms. It's interesting to me because a person's face can tell a billion different tales. I've read many books about Leonardo Da Vinci and found out he used to do the same thing if he got stuck with a painting. He'd go out to public gatherings and watch people go about their business for hours and often returned with a better sense of clarity when outlining a particular face. I guess the reason I find myself staring at people is because my life is so monotonous, it's a good way to escape.

As I lean against the side puffing away, four overly-excited alpha males approach me from the street.

"Alright, mate," says a slick, Danny Zuko lookalike with a funny accent. "Is that a real Cuban you got there?"

"Sure is," I reply, trying not to choke.

He returns with more lingo like *"wicked, mate, awesome"* and asks where I got it because they're celebrating. I kind of figured that as this animated posse are dressed like a boyband who's about to shoot their first video.

"What's the occasion?"

"Archie here is getting married!" says the blonde kid putting his arm around Danny Zuko.

"Ahhh, well congratulations, Mr. Archie. You're in for a wild ride. You see, marriage is one of life's true blessings."

"Yeah, right!" snickers one of the others.

I go on informing them I've been married nearly twenty years and give them a little synopsis of the ups and downs in the real world along with a little joke to finish: "just the other day I asked her if she still fantasizes about me. She told me *'yes, all the time'* — about me taking out the trash, mowing the lawn, doing the dishes…"

This gets a laugh from the posse.

"Where are you guys from?"

"Australia," they say in perfect unison.

"Ahhh, *Down-Under*. Cool. What brings you to this neck of the woods?"

Archie informs me he met a local gal online and it was love at first sight.

"Well, that makes perfect geographical sense now doesn't it? Anyway, my friend who owns this bar sells Cubans on the down-low, they are illegal after all. If you guys want you can come in with me and I'll hook you up so you can celebrate in style."

They seem very pleased with my proposition saying words like *"bloody cracking, fella"* so I extinguish the butt and lead them inside.

As I escort my bandwagon of merry men into my dingy bar, the old-timers ogle us like the Four Horseman and JJ Dillon entered the building.

"Mitch, my man," I hurl to my royal barman, "let me get five shots of…" I turn to Archie and ask him what's his poison.

He looks indecisive and tells me to surprise him.

"Come on, Archie, it's *your* world, we're all just living in it. Right, boys?"

They laugh and do hi-fives all around. I didn't think that was particularly funny — guess they've been Americanized.

"Wait a minute," I turn back to Mitch. "Hit us with some Alabama Swirlies."

"What's an Alabama Swirly?" says the other dark-haired guy (to which I realize there's a pair of twins in this bunch).

"Holy shit, I just noticed you two are twins! You'll have to excuse me, I've been drinking all day. Anyway, you don't need to know what's in an Alabama Swirly, you just need to know they:

A: Blow your head off.

B: Taste delicious. And

C: Blow your freaking head off in case you forgot *A*!"

They chuckle as I turn once again to Mitch who's also enjoying my show. "And five Cubans too, Mr. Mitch." I drunkenly hold out four fingers for some silly reason.

"You got it, Bobby," Mitch responds as he makes up these deadly orange shots with a swirl of whipped cream.

"Ahh, so your name is Bobby, I was just about to ask you that," says the bleach blonde. "I'm Reko, you've met Archie of course," who hi-fives me on cue. "And the infamous twins are Tony and Tom."

I shake all hands cordially as the shots arrive.

"Hallelujah. The shots are here! Gentlemen, a toast." I stand on a rickety bar stool and address my crowd like I'm Dr. Martin Luther King: "To Archie, and my new Aussie posse. May you have a long and fruitful marriage. You see, marriage is full of arguments, cellulite, grey hairs, screaming kids and annual sex if you're lucky. But you have all that ahead of you so don't listen to an asshole like me, you'll find all this stuff out for yourself."

They once again snicker in unison.

"In all seriousness, Archie: your marriage will be exactly how you decide it to be. No bullshit—man to man. It really is as simple as that. Everything is a choice, you can choose to have an amazing marriage or you can choose to neglect it after it's reached its apex and you become complacent. The choice is always yours. Sometimes, I forget that myself..." I look at the floor dwelling on what I just said until I catch myself and snap out of it. "To Archie!"

I come down and clang glasses with them and guzzle our creamy liqueur in unison. Mitch then asks how I'm paying for the cigars.

"Put them on my tab," I say, wiping my lips. "They're a gift to my new mates from the southern hem."

"We can't let you pay for the cigars, Bobby," says the groom.

"Hey, don't worry about it, it will be my honor, boys."

He tells me that's awfully generous and asks what my plans are tonight.

"Well, you're looking at it."

"Like hell you are. We can't let you spend a Saturday night in here; it smells of stale beer and sweaty feet. You're coming with us!"

"What are you talking about? I'm not even slightly in your age bracket. I have well over fifteen years on you guys."

"So bloody what! You are by far the coolest Yank we've met over here, and besides, do you really want to stay in this place, or join us in our limo to a strip club?"

"Limo? Strip club?" I grin. "Which one are you going to?"

"The Lococabana," says Tony (at least I think it's him).

"I've never heard of it."

They tell me it's a new Latino strip club on the outskirts of the city. This excites me as you probably figured.

"How the hell can I say no to that proposition?" I say rubbing my hands together.

"Exactly, you can't!" says Archie.

"But I can't go there dressed like this, you look like a modern day 'N Sync, while I look like I just came from Home Depot."

The defiant groom informs me their limo is picking them up at a sports bar down the street in about an hour, so we can swing by my place to can change real quick.

"No can do. I had a major blow-up with the wife earlier so I can't go back there." I ponder for a split-sec… Light bulb! "Wait a minute, my work! I always keep a spare suit at work in case of emergencies! And this is an emergency, is it not?"

"Sure is," they agree.

"Gentlemen, I believe our planets are aligned. I have no choice but to join you for a night of decadence at this exotic dance club that you speak of. We should drink to this." I turn to Mitch. "Mitch, my man, another round of Alabamas, pronto!"

CHAPTER 24

An hour and change later and I find myself cruising in the back of a limo with these rowdy bunch of Aussies, sipping clear liquor and shouting out the window at anything with an ass. These guys are great, I love hanging with the younger generation, it brings the youngster out in me. Plus the fact they are Australian is even better.

They seem outright happier than the average American that I see. Granted they're in vacation mode and are extra excited to be on a bachelor party but I can tell they're naturally happy people. They aren't hung up on money or status like us insatiable Americans. They haven't once bragged about material bullshit like BMWs or Rolex watches or anything, they seem to brag about being home by three to watch the cricket.

The limo ride was short and sweet (yet we still manage to devour a bottle of Cîroc) while I thoroughly enjoyed a long, in-depth conversation with the twins about their painting and decorating business. I didn't have to fake interest at all, they're so down to Earth and genuine which is such a breath of fresh air.

We deploy into the titty bar in style like John Travolta and crew in *Saturday Night Fever* as we head straight for the bar to get our drink on. This club has an interesting mix of high rollers making it rain for the cock-teasers on the main stage, and shady characters spanking strippers' asses as they walk past. Usually I'd be self-conscious hanging out with a bunch of guys about eighteen years my junior but I'm too intoxicated to really care.

The first thing on my agenda is to sneak off to the bathroom to powder my nose. I didn't mention anything about sniffing coke to these cool cats and don't want to be the guy who influences them to join my decadent ways. Now, if they had asked me about scoring some drugs, maybe I would have let them dip into my baggy or maybe I would have lied and said I'm the wrong guy to be asking. I don't know. One thing I do know is these kids are diamonds and come from good families who have instilled ethics and morals in them. They are anything but corrupt seeds, and I certainly don't want to be their corrupter even though this is a bachelor party and anything goes.

I often think if Cam hadn't have been so insistent that night at the Blackout, I would never have even tried coke and wouldn't have spent God knows how much money on it throughout the year. Sometimes I lay in bed mad at him for putting me onto this shit, but then I conclude that I'm the one choosing to do it because I like it. Anyone who tells you they don't like doing recreational drugs, but continues to do them over and over is an outright liar. They are doing it *because* they like it. They may rationalize or make excuses all day long as to why they repeatedly do it, but at the end of the day, they like that high feeling that the drug gives them and it helps them escape from their stresses, plain and simple. And I'm no different, I love the Superstar Billy Graham feeling that coke gives me, plus I know I can stop any time I want.

After my incognito little pit-stop at the washroom I strut through the club like Rick Martel eyeing everybody and embracing the vibe. All I want to do now is drink, drink and drink. I need to show this whole club I can keep up with these whipper-snappers so I order a bottle of Belvedere to our table and introduce some shot games that I did back in college.

I'm like a machine chugging one after the other, nobody can touch me in this group of rookies as I have more intestinal fortitude than Gorilla Monsoon. Although, I have two clear advantages over these boys:

1: My big fat belly, which allows me to out-drink practically anyone who's slimmer, and;

2: My bag of sniff that balances out my increasingly intoxicated levels. These kids don't have a chance, this fight is fixed.

"Is this a fucking party or what, Bobby?" Reko shouts over the loud hip-hop music.

I wholeheartedly agree and grab two beers off the table and chug them simultaneously as they *wooooo* me on.

Why must I always go further than everybody? Maybe I do have a problem? Or maybe it's a personality flaw? Or am I cursed with the deadly sins of greed, gluttony and sloth? These are the bizarre thoughts that enter my mind when inebriated. It's the devil and angel chirping in my God damn ears and won't shut the fuck up.

All rational sense goes out the window when I'm in one of these moods and I just want to hit it to the max until I blackout. I do this in other areas too — when I used to train at the gym I'd work out until I nearly puked. When I eat, I notoriously do it like I'm at an all-you-can-eat buffet until I can barely breathe.

With sniffing coke, I'm never satisfied; I just keep wanting to get higher and higher and higher. And with prostitutes, I just want to keep fucking and fucking and then do another and another to feel that sense of power and glory.

"These girls here are the crème-da-la-crème, huh, Bobby?" says Reko.

"Yes, sir. Think I'm gonna become a regular." I raise my glass and form a huddle with the boys. "Are you guys loving this shit?"

"Fucking right, mate!" Archie shouts. "This is the buck of all buck nights!"

"I don't know what the hell that means but I like it. Hey before I forget, I must warn you about something before you get married, Archie."

"What's that, mate?"

"Do you know what food makes women stop giving blow jobs…?"

"I dunno, Bobby?"

"Wedding cake!"

Everyone laughs.

It's funny, two hours ago I was sat in the Duck lonely and depressed, listening to old man Sam ramble on and on about the Russians being the first to send monkeys into space, and now I'm popping bottles while curvaceous women with no clothes on shake their ass right in front of my face! It doesn't get better than this.

CHAPTER 25

I enjoyed every single second in the club with the boys. Hours flew by like minutes as the night got crazier and more out of control. I paid a ridiculous amount of money in the VIP room for a smoking hot exotic dancer who told me she hailed from the Amazon rainforest. She was so forward about what I could or could not do to her in private. In fact, there was no *could nots,* I could basically do anything I wanted if I waved enough dead presidents in her face, including hitting it raw. I couldn't believe it. She didn't care about a condom or not, she just charged more for going raw, so of course, I paid it and had her bent over in the full nelson like the Warlord, making her scream *"PAPI!"* to the high heavens.

The Brazilian girls are something else; they have a lot less rules than the American and Asian hoes. I've been fucking prostitutes for many months and some won't even suck you off without wearing a condom, but the Brazilians don't care about any of that; anything goes.

Thirty minutes later I reloaded and had two of them swallowing my DNA. Freaking amazing! Best bachelor party ever, especially since I didn't technically know the guys. The whole night was just nonstop drinking, sniffing and fucking — full tilt, and plenty of boogie.

That was until the club closed.

The Aussie boys are long gone and somehow I've ended up at a seedy after party with some wanna-be gangster motherfuckers who use the *N-word* so much you'd think it was their Christian name. There's a mini-mountain of uncut cocaine on the glass table, next to a semi-automatic with a banana clip. Surprisingly I don't feel any threat of danger, which is probably the drugs making me impervious. All that's concerning me is how the hell did I get here and do I even know any of these people?

"Go ahead, Bobby, dip in," says a do-rag wearing black dude next to me on the couch.

I literally have no idea who he is.

100

"I'm sorry, man, how do you know my name?"

This makes him crack up laughing.

"Damn you fucked up more than I thought. Who do you thang'k drove your drunk ass here from the club?"

I have zero recollection but don't want to seem stupid.

"Oh yeah. My bad. I am kinda fucked up. What's ya name again?"

"Sly."

"Sly, that's right, now I remember."

I'm winging it, to say the least and look around thinking *what the hell am I doing here...*

"It's all good, man. Here, take a blast, this will clear your head up real nice." He passes me a crusty dollar bill.

I lean into the glass table and sniff a quick line in two seconds flat. The buzz is strong but something is different about it though, it has a unique aftertaste that I can't quite put my finger on...

"Wow, this is some high powered stuff, Sly. It's different from anything I've had before. Where did you get it?"

"I got connections, G. This Fishscale shit is the shit. It's hella different to all the other shit out there."

"Cool. I might have to holla at you for a hook-up."

"No doubt. I got you, my nigga."

He gives me a fist-bump as I lean back on the couch and ask him what kind of business he's involved in.

"I'm a salesman," he says, exhaling a blunt.

"No way. Me too."

"Fo' real? What do you sell, G?"

"Beds and mattresses. I run a little store on LeBelle. How about you?"

"Home protection."

"Oh, like security systems? ADT?"

"Shit no, nigga," he scoffs. "I sling guns." He grabs the gun from the table and waves it in the air. "I got guns, mad fucking guns, son! Some new, some got dirt on 'em but so what, they still work like new, ya-know-whud-I'm-sayin'?"

"Got it. Sounds like you have a strong business acumen." I start to feel dizzy and a tad sick and tell him I need to hit the head.

"Fo' sure, it's down the hall, second on the right."

I excuse myself and vacate through a throng of shiesty individuals and find my way to the bathroom upstairs. I'm the whitest motherfucker in this entire place by far. I probably stand out like Colonel Sanders at a Wu-Tang Clan concert. Why the fuck would I mention business acumens to that guy? He's not a fucking bank manager! Get a grip, you fuckhead!

I splash some water on my drugged up face but it doesn't work. I think I've got to wave the white flag. My vision is blurry, my equilibrium is not equal and my tank is well and truly on empty. I need to just rest my eyes for a sec...

CHAPTER 26

Hazy head, blurry vision, mental fog, all-around disorientation. Hmmm, okay what's going on? You know that moment when you wake up clueless to what, where, how, why and when? Well, that's what's taking place at this very moment. My head feels like it's been rammed into an exposed turnbuckle.

It takes me a while to gather my senses and ask myself the question: where the hell am I? I soon realize that I'm sprawled out on a hardwood floor with an achy neck, throbbing ear and have the worst case of cottonmouth in the history of cottoned mouths. My white shirt looks like a damn wash detergent commercial where they smear it with mustard, red wine and gravy. I probably have all seven colors of the rainbow on this damn thing. And one stain that stands out is red. I hope to God it's ketchup! What the fuck is going on?

I check my vital organs in case I've been shot, stabbed or beaten like the Big Boss Man when Nailz broke out of prison, but luckily my body is fine on the outside. Everything is just aching like a motherfucker on the inside but it doesn't take a genius to figure out where that came from. Ugh, welcome to the hangover from hell!

Sunlight beams into the room making me grimace as I rise off the floor and check my reflection: Unshaven, triple chin, blotchy skin, stanky yellow teeth, messy hair, bloodshot eyes, droopy flab. I am undoubtedly an absolute fucking disgrace. In fact, the word *disgrace* is not accurate enough, I'm a fucking abysmal humiliation of a human being. I'm somebody's husband and father for God's sake! When am I gonna grow the fuck up?

I slap myself out of embarrassment and enter into shame. Now the tears start to fall. It's as if all the emotions that I've suppressed for years have just smashed into me like a battering ram.

I can't go on like this…

I have to quickly snap out of this weak, disempowering state, I might be in danger. I'm not sure if this is the same place with the black guys and guns. It's just some random dump with crap everywhere.

103

I check my pockets: no phone, no keys, no wallet, no cash. No fucking way! This cannot be happening to me right now!

The place is pretty small so it doesn't take me long to bumrush the whole apartment, turning sofas, draws and anything else in my way upside down to retain my possessions. I ransack the entire place in a fit of extreme rage and find diddly-fucking-squat, just a trashed shit-hole with empty beer bottles and broken glass. Not a human in sight. I can't believe I've been fucking robbed! I bet it was those motherfuckers from last night!

I peek out the window to see a dilapidated neighborhood that I don't recognize at all. Thank God it's daytime. I have no choice but to abort from this cesspool and get myself into safety. Sometimes you gotta cut your losses and run.

I cover my multi-colored shirt with my blue blazer and stomp down the sidewalk like Psycho Sid. It's relatively quiet upon the horizon, kids from mixed ethnic backgrounds are playing in the street and a few bums are scattered around the alleyways amongst discarded diapers and tin cans. I can feel the eyeballs glued on me as I trample through the filthy streets. Guess they aren't used to an overweight, angry white man in a suit steaming through their hood but I pay them no mind, I have to keep moving and sweat the drugs and other toxins out my body. I'd kill for a cold bottle of water right now.

I march for blocks having no idea where I'm going, this is all foreign territory to me and I think it's best I don't ask for directions as I want to be as incognito as possible.

Things look different in this part of town, it's hard to explain. It's not just the grimy conditions, things just look odd and alien over here, I can't quite put my finger on it. It's probably the drugs fucking with my head. I figure I'll soon hit an intersection that I recognize and work out a route from there.

Fifteen minutes of haphazard navigation goes by and I don't hit an intersection but do find a park. A hood park, but still an okay place to rest for five minutes with minimal danger (at least I hope). And there's a water fountain upon the horizon, thank God. It looks almost like an oasis. I don't care if the water comes out brown; anything will do to soothe my unbearable cottonmouth.

As I come closer my lips start to pucker from anticipation like when the ice-cream man hits the block. I press the button but nothing comes out. Are you freaking kidding me?! The fucking thing is broken! Of course, it's broken! The one and only time I ever need a motherfucking water fountain and it has to be broken.

I let out the appropriate profanities and park myself on a bench, out of breath, hot, sticky and thirsty. I place my head in my hands and just want to explode.

"Are you alright, mister?" chirps a sweet voice.

I look up to see an adorable little black girl a few years older than Max, who's wearing the jazziest looking big boots I've ever seen.

"I've been better."

"You don't look too good."

"I neither look nor feel good, little lady."

"Are you sick?"

"Sick in the head, I think."

"That's a shame. You should get a remedy and you'll be all fixed up."

"I don't think there's a remedy for my sickness."

"CONRAD can help you," she glees. "Ask CONRAD for a remedy."

"CONRAD?"

"Ya know, *CONRAD.*"

"I'm sorry I don't follow. Who's CONRAD?"

She starts to laugh.

"What's so funny?"

"CONRAD...on your Fuji?"

I have no clue what the hell she's talking about.

"Don't worry, I'll help you out." She reaches into her pocket and pulls out an electronic gadget that's about the size of a pack of cigarettes. Then she somehow stretches it to the size of an iPad. Incredible; a stretchable computer tablet type thing. I've never seen one of these before.

"What is that?"

She looks at me innocently and simply tells me it's a Fuji.

"Fuji?"

"Yeah."

"Isn't that a fruit?"

She speaks directly into the device telling CONRAD to identify symptoms and hands it to me.

"What do I do?"

"Blow into the hole for three seconds."

"What? Why?"

"It will help you."

I really don't know what's going on but decide to go along with this innocent little darling and blow into the device. A green light flashes then it speaks with a robotic southern accent telling me my body temperature is high, my blood sugar is low and my immune system is weak.

"How on earth did it know all that?"

She looks at me bemused and tells me CONRAD knows everything. "Haven't you used him on your phone before?"

"This thing is a phone?" I say, rubbing my eyes.

"A Fuji is a lot more than just a phone, mister, my whole world is inside this; Facebook, Snapchat, Foxy, I use it to do all my homework and I can play Rock-Paper-Scissors with anybody in all fifty-three states on here."

As the screen bleeps, she walks me through the instructions placing my finger on the screen for the Remedy Suggestions. It responds within seconds:

"Remedy Suggestion; One point five gallons of Alkaline water, pH nine point five. Vitamins A, C and E. Avoid caffeine, sugar, aspartame. Closest pharmacy zero point seven miles south on Franklin BLVD. Would you like to place an order, Mr. Jannetty?"

"Holy shit," I say before apologizing for my French. "How could it possibly know my name?"

"It scanned your fingerprint, silly."

"That's amazing! Who invented this?"

"Beats me. Hit the YES button and you can go to the pharmacy over there and you'll be all fixed up. It's not far to walk and it's a beautiful day, don't you think?"

"A-huh…" I'm so taken aback by this angelic little sweetheart. "What's your name, angel?"

She tells me it's Leah as I hit the YES button.

"Well, Leah, I can't thank you enough. Your parents have done a marvelous job raising you."

She thanks me and says she better be going, then shrinks the device back down to its original size and slides it in her pocket.

"Hope you get well, mister."

She clicks a button on her funny-looking boots and four tiny wheels extend out the bottom like landing wheels on a plane, transforming them into roller boots before skating away. That was pretty cool. How come Max hasn't pestered me for a pair of these? She'd be in heaven.

I exit the park and proceed down the street, still not entirely sure where I'm going. The houses are becoming nicer now, less ghetto at least.

As I keep moving I soon notice more odd things again, like cars driving past that I've never seen before, they look so new and cutting edge. I'm not a car guy but I tend to notice models I've never seen before. It isn't a mere few either, it's a plethora of vehicles that I just don't recognize which is rather weird. And other things too; the street lights are different in this part of town, they are shaped like Raiden's hat in Mortal Kombat, and the white lines that separate the lanes are fluorescent over here. I've never seen that before. Hmmm…whatever, who cares? I just need water and tablets for my head as quick as possible.

CHAPTER 27

I arrive at the pharmacy in hopes they'll take pity on me without ID, money or credit cards.

Immediately upon arrival, I'm assaulted by the fluorescent lights burning their way into my exposed retinas. I might have to put shades on just to walk around this bitch. It's quite unlike anything I've seen before, it seems to have two separate sections under one roof. The first has a corporate feel like a CVS or Walgreens with it's strategically placed quick-fix remedies and salted snacks available everywhere, but across the other side has a totally different identity. Wind chimes, Himalayan salt lamps and incense sticks adorn the new-age section, along with portraits of the Buddha and Indian folk music playing softly in the background. Funny.

I grab a bottle of water and go straight to the first human I spot behind the counter; a big jolly man with a clown-like grin and rosy red cheeks.

"Hello, sir, welcome to Wendy's Wellness Center and Pharmacy. How may we serve you today?" His voice is like a warm sounding cyborg, let's see if I can win him over.

"I'm having a really bad day," I say with my go-to puppy dog look of sympathy. "I'm in a huge jam. I'm stranded out here with no phone, no cash, no ID or credit cards and I have the worst hangover imaginable. Is there any way you can help me out? I just need a little water and something for my head if that's not too much to ask."

The fat man's grin doesn't budge but his forehead frowns a tad as if what I said didn't compute.

"I'm sorry to hear of your situation, sir, but I see you still have your fingers intact."

Now I'm the one grinning and frowning. What the hell is he talking about? He gestures to a computerized cube on the counter labeled FIT.

"What's this?" I ask.

He chuckles a little and motions for me to do something with it. I question him again as I have no clue.

"You're kidding, right?"

I feel like slapping that silly grin right off his fat fucking face! I'm too hungover for this shit. "What is it? What do you want me to do?"

"I'm sorry, sir." His demeanor changes as he's noticed how vexed I'm getting. "You are having a bad day. Press your index finger on the top of the cube."

I follow suit then this cube device thing starts talking back: *"Welcome, Mr. Jannetty. Your remedies are ready for pick up. Press YES to accept the charges."*

I zone-out while hitting the YES button.

A bag suddenly pops out some kind of shoot underneath the counter which the clerk hands to me. "Here are your supplies, sir, and I have just what you need for a hangover. Come with me."

He leads me through the store towards the far end.

"Wait a minute; what's in this bag and where are we going?"

"You'll see." He leads me through the heavily lit, corporate section until we reach the opposite end of the building where it's all zen, spiritual and weird. A gleaming, thirty-something chick with broad shoulders and big guns is stood next to some kind of strange machine with hoses attached from the wall.

"Kirstin here runs our in-store oxygen bar," he turns to her. "Mr. Jannetty is suffering with dire hangover symptoms."

"I think we can take care of that," she says with a cute squeaky dialect. "Hi, I'm Stepps. Have you heard of TT Oxygen before?"

"No I haven't, and I've never heard anybody called Stepps before either. Listen, I'm extremely hungover so the only bars I like are the ones that serve Stella Artois. What are you guys trying to pitch over here?"

"You said you're feeling bad, right?" intervenes the jolly fellow. "Pure oxygen is what you need. Headache, muscle ache, fatigue, and alcohol toxins, all will cease after just fifteen minutes from this miraculous technology."

I gaze at him like he's lost his mind. "Look, man, I just need water and some Tylenol and I'm good to go."

Both he and the young lady burst into laughter.

"Oh, Mr. Jannetty that's a good one. *Tylenol.* I haven't heard that in years. Allow me to demonstrate…"

He goes on to show me the torpedo-shaped oxygen device with its long, thin tubes attached to the wall and recites a bunch of science on how it will rejuvenate my polluted system. "Bottom line: you'll feel like a million bucks."

I look at him once again like he's from Mars and remark that this is such a strange way to get rid of a hangover.

"Think about it like this; how long can humans go without food? Months, agreed? How long can we go without water? Days, technically. But how long can we go without air? Seconds. This is what your body needs to eliminate the parasites and rejuvenate your cells, but I must get back to the front. Kirstin here will take excellent care of you." He pats me on the shoulder and leaves me befuddled with the busty lady.

"Sorry, so what's your name again? Kirstin or Stepps?"

"Kirstin Stepps," she answers, bubbly. "Stepps is my last name. Most my friends call me that or Dub-Stepps, like a nickname."

"That's quite an unusual name."

"Yeah, my family is of German descent so of course, I hate baseball, but I was raised in California so I love the Eagles."

None of what she said made sense so I feel the need to point that out. "Errr, what you said made no sense at all."

"Ha! That's what everybody tells me," she relishes before handing me an oxygen pamphlet. "So, if you're hungover this will help tremendously. When I first saw it I was thrown off too, but he's right, when you breathe in pure oxygen you'll feel replenished like never before and there's no charge if your hangover still remains."

I take a second to ponder. This is nuts, but my head is pounding like I've been hit by Hacksaw Jim Duggan's Two-by-Four. "You know what, Miss — screw it, I'll give it a go."

"Cool. Just sit over here and make yourself comfortable, you might want to take your blazer off and I'll hook you right up."

I take off my blazer, totally forgetting about my multi-colored shirt underneath.

"Oh wow. Your shirt looks like it's had quite an adventure. Here, take it off and I'll fix it up."

Embarrassment sets in. "I can't take it off; you'll see my man-boobs."

"Oh, Mr. Jannetty, it's okay, it will literally take ten seconds, nobody will see."

"I think this shirt has gone to the point of no return, I'll just throw it out when I get home."

"Oh, I don't think that will be necessary. Trust me."

I reluctantly oblige and remove my shirt, leaving me exposed like a blubbery beached whale. She grabs a yellow spray bottle from a nearby shelf and tells me to hold it nice and straight.

"Are you sure this will work?"

"Prepare to be wowed…"

She blankets the shirt in about five seconds dissolving every stain like magic before my eyes, leaving nothing but a perfectly crisp shirt smelling lemony fresh.

"Holy shit, that's incredible! What is that stuff?"

"I guess you haven't seen the infomercials for Wipeout. Their slogan is: *'Any stain, anywhere, every time!'* Cool stuff, don't you think?"

I nod in agreement and slip my flab back into this perfectly scented article then place myself at the oxygen bar. "The inventors must be damn billionaires."

"I wouldn't doubt it. So do you need any water or anything before we start?"

I tell her I would kill for some water and rummage through the bag to find a fancy glass bottle labeled Super-Alkaline H2O. I unscrew the lid and start guzzling like Stone Cold with a Steveweiser. It's the most refreshing water I've ever tasted and feels like a disco in my mouth. I consume the whole quart in no time and feel oh so hydrated.

"Wow, you were real thirsty," she says discarding the bottle. "Let's get you hooked up."

And so it begins. It doesn't take long for me to feel the effects as the fresh, crisp air circulates my respiratory system. After just a few minutes my headache dissipates as does my diabolical hangover fog. I keep breathing deeply feeling so pure and cleansed, it's incredible. It's like I'm up in the Rockies breathing fresh mountain air. It's the best natural high I've ever felt!

When you sniff cocaine you get an immediate buzz which you think is pleasurable but once it wears off you chastise yourself because you know it's a deadly addictive poison, but despite all that you crave more and thus do more. This natural high is a million times better than any drug that I've ever experimented with. I can literally feel the toxins exhaling from my body like a demon leaving the possessed.

The fifteen minutes flies by quicker than a Demolition squash match, which is unfortunate because I want more. Stepps and her distracting cleavage unhooks the things around my nose as I tell her like a true convert how phenomenal and clear-headed I feel.

"I'm not the type of person to say I told you so, but…" she smiles knowing she was right on the money.

I grab my stuff and head to the front where the jolly fellow resides. "Hey, man, what can I say, that was a phenomenal experience. I feel like a whole new Bobby."

"It's a remarkable machine. What's even more incredible is the human body itself. When your cells are exposed to a pure oxygenated environment, they replenish, rejuvenate and heal, and that my friend is what's truly incredible."

This guy is a smart cookie and obviously in-the-know. I ask him for more of that delicious water for the road.

"Here you go," he says, handing it to me. "You just have to imprint your finger on here again and hit YES to accept the charges."

"The charges," I contemplate. "Hold on: I can buy anything in here and all I have to do is press my finger on that screen and the money gets deducted from my account?"

"Right," he replies as if he's conversing with a third-grader. "Have you honestly never used one before? They've been out for years."

"No, never. I love the idea though; I guess it minimizes credit card fraud and things like that."

"Agreed. Have you been living in a foreign country or something?"

I tell him I've lived here all my life and press why he asked that.

"Because these FIT devices are in every store, restaurant, gas station, even street fairs have them. How have you not seen one before?"

I really don't know how to answer that, so that's what I tell him. I also inform him I've never set up my fingerprints with my bank, so how could it possibly take money from my account.

"You must have done it with your phone in the past. Your transaction went through perfectly."

"Well, happy days then." I scratch my head before realizing I should buy more stuff.

"You know what's funny? I was speaking to a customer the other day who told me she's never seen an episode of *The Simpsons*! Not even one. I found that almost unfathomable."

"Now that is strange. Love that Homer," I quickly hunt for more supplies, grabbing a ham and cheese footlong, two big bags of Doritos (cool ranch and nacho cheese), and a Milky Way before returning to the counter. "Listen, I know I told you I've lived here my whole life but I have to admit, I have no idea where we are. I'm trying to get back to Mayfield."

"That's quite a way across town. We're like twenty-five minutes from there."

"Shit. I don't have my car with me."

"Oh, well, you're a long walk from there," he says as I pay for the new items with my index finger. "It went through again, Mr. Jannetty, and these things are nearly impossible to scam unless you cut off somebody's finger like that guy did in Fort Lauderdale. Everything is tickety-boo. Be well."

I thank him and exit with my bagged goods. The first thing on the agenda is to wolf down this big sandwich.

I park myself at a nearby bus stop a few seats away from a raggedy bum who's bent over talking to his blistered feet. I get an awful whiff of his unsanitary aroma and shun away from him hoping he won't strike up a conversation with me.

"Excuse me, buddy," he grunts while I pretend not to notice and start shoveling bread into my gullet. "Could I get some of that sandwich? I haven't eaten in a long time and I'm homeless."

My wishful thinking obviously didn't materialize. I don't really want to face him because it will probably put me off my food.

"I can't," I answer with a mouth full of cheese. "I haven't eaten in a long time and I could eat a pregnant horse right now."

"Ahh, man. Could you at least loan me five bucks for the bus? Please, friend, I'm trying to get home."

As I turn to face him I catch an awful whiff of booze, cigarettes and other foul carcinogens transpiring out of him.

"*Loan*…that's original. Anyway, you just said you're homeless, now you trying to get home. Nice try."

He pleads saying he's staying in a shelter downtown.

"Anyway, five dollars, are you kidding me? I thought the bus was like a dollar-fifty. Stop trying to hustle me."

"I ain't hustling you. You know damn well the bus ain't been a dollar-fifty in years."

"That's where you're wrong. I haven't been on a bus since Dino Bravo was the world's strongest man. Besides, I couldn't give you anything if I wanted to—which I don't—because like you, I have no money. I'm only sitting here trying to eat this sandwich in peace but somebody's ruining that, aren't they?"

"Would it be too much to ask that you pay my fare when the bus arrives? Please, sir?"

"I just told you, I got no money. What are you, deaf?"

"But, sir, you don't need no money. You pay with your finger."

"What are you talking about?" I frown.

"You use your finger to pay on the machine."

"Wait a minute; they have them things on the bus too?"

"Yeah."

"Since when?"

"Like forever, man."

"Interesting," I say, finishing off the sloppy sandwich and start munching the nacho cheese Doritos. It then dawns on me to question him on why doesn't he use his finger when the bus arrives.

"I've been homeless for eleven years. They cut off my bank account. I lost everything."

"Eleven years…" I turn to him and let my remark hang. "And what have you been doing for the past eleven years?"

"I've been in the streets," he shrugs.

"And what have you been doing in the streets? In fact, don't answer because I already know." Here comes my unapologetic rant that I must have said to a hundred bums alike. "I'm willing to bet that what you've been doing in the streets is drinking, smoking and begging hard-working citizens out of their money. Correct?"

He remains silent confirming what I already know so I glare deep into his crusty eyes and press that I'm dead right.

Again he doesn't answer, he just remains silent and embraces in a little shame.

"I asked you a question and if you want me to pay your fucking fare I expect an honest response. Do you beg people for money to buy booze and smokes? Just be straight up with me, no bullshit."

"Yeah…" he sheepishly replies looking down at his disheveled, unsanitary feet.

"So here's my point; your little sob story is not gonna work on me, buster. Life deals bad hands to everybody, not just you. The difference is when life dealt you a few bad hands, you folded like a cheap fucking suit and gave up like the loser you are."

I turn away and chomp into my chips as the bus approaches us.

"Having said that, I would like to thank you for the information because I would have never considered getting the bus." I turn back to him. "But I can't pay your fare because I'll be rewarding bad behavior, and that, my friend, goes against my ethics." I grab the brown bag and hop on the bus.

The bus driver informs me the ETA to my neck of the woods is thirty-seven minutes. I pay the five-dollar fare with my finger (guess the bum wasn't lying after all) and head to the back and start munching my Milky Way. Acid reflux soon burns my chest along with the appropriate expletives for not getting tablets at the pharmacy. Oh well, I'll survive.

It's been so long since I've been on a bus, I'm actually impressed how clean and professional it is. I can't believe they have mini touch screens to stream videos or play games on like an airplane. I thought buses were full of bums, lowlifes and transvestites with Hepatitis C squashed next to you. This is not the case at all. There's an abundance of space and most of the passengers are frail senior citizens keeping themselves to themselves. It's funny how the mind builds up false perceptions on things you know little about.

As I gaze out the window I notice more things in this part of town that are strangely different. There seems to be a lot of flashing ads on buildings, cars, motorcycles, even baby strollers — I've never seen that before, it's quite over-the-top. And police cars have an unfamiliar design over here too, they look more like armored military vehicles, all black and bulky like they could ram through a wall. What is this martial law? Something doesn't seem right and I can't blame it on my hangover because that has completely evaporated. My mind and body feel amazing after that oxygen session but something definitely feels amiss.

CHAPTER 28

The bus arrives on the outskirts of my neighborhood thirty-seven minutes to the dot. Even though it's my day off I need to pop into work and change my clothes, plus I'll get one of my staff to make a phony vouch for me in case Earthquake starts prying with questions. I'll concoct a credible and dastardly alibi soon when I put my mind to it, after all, I'm the master of deceit and having a third party testimonial only makes it all the more convincing. The principle of *Social Proof* is one of the highest forms of influence; it's gotten me out of a million jams over the years.

I walk north on LaBelle and soon notice things looking strangely different. Stores are here that I've never seen before. I know this boulevard like the back of my hand and have to do a double-take. What the hell is going on? *3D Printing* the flashing sign reads on a jazzy looking store that I walk past. What on Earth? What happened to the hardware store?

I pass another storefront and read the window display: *Hydroponic Heaven! Grow your own garden in four to six weeks in any season!* Yeah right.

Finally, I arrive at my store's vicinity except there's a problem: it isn't here. I know this is the building, it clearly says 10304 but I've never heard of this Nutty Butty place before. My store has been turned into a fucking fast food joint! What the fuck? This doesn't make sense...

Despite the delicious smell, I'm irate and have to see what the hell is going on.

I enter the building and scan the surroundings, trying to gather my confused thoughts. This is so bizarre. I know one hundred percent that this is the building I've worked in for the past near-decade but now it's become a stupid peanut butter and jelly sandwich place. I can't explain it. I receive a weird sense of nostalgia even though I was here yesterday to change my clothes while the Aussie boys waited in the limo. This is beyond strange.

The decor is now red and brown and the layout is quite unorthodox for this kind of operation. It isn't a bakery and it certainly isn't a Starbucks or Dunkin' Donuts, this is way more suave and systematic.

The patrons seem to be minding their own business playing with their personal devices so the place is pretty quiet except for a giant projector broadcasting the news.

I approach a pimple-faced teenager working the counter. "Hello, sir," he greets. "Welcome to Nutty Butty, the world's nuttiest peanut butter and jelly distribution outlet. You'll be nutty about our butty!"

What a ridiculous tag line, I think as I place my brown paper bag down on the counter. "Hi. I need to double-check something; is this one-o-three-o-four LaBelle Boulevard?"

"That's correct, sir."

"I don't understand what's going on. What happened to Box Spring Boogie?"

"Box Spring Boogie? I'm sorry I've never heard of it."

"It's a mattress store that I've worked at for nine years at this very address."

"Right here?"

"Yes, right here."

"Are you sure, sir?"

I tell him with great conviction I'm absolutely positive.

The kid just gawks at me and clearly doesn't know how to respond. "I'm sorry I can't help you. Would you like to try our new Nutty Butty sugar-free, aspartame-free, gluten-free, non-GMO, bio-wich?"

"No, I don't! I want you to give me some straight answers!"

Looking clueless he suggests to get the manager. Probably a good idea.

About a minute later an overweight Afro-American manager with thick cornrows dangling from her yellow Nutty Butty baseball cap asks how can she help me.

"I want to know what the hell is going on here," I squawk. "When did this company take over this building?"

"I'm sorry, sir, I really don't know that information."

Her deadpan look irritates the fuck out of me. I don't feel that she cares for my plight. Probably thinks I'm a weirdo that's wandered in off the street. She goes on to inform me the Nutty Butty franchise has been around for five years and she's been at this location for three. I tell her that's impossible but it falls on deaf ears.

"There must be some confusion that I can't help with right now and I have to get back. Can I offer you a complimentary Nutty Butty Supreme? It's a special kind of sandwich that will leave you mesmerized."

"My whole career has gone down the tubes and you want to offer me a free sandwich?"

"Yes," she says with a ludicrous grin on her funny fucking face. I can't help but laugh at the sheer audacity of the proposition; after all, this is not exactly her fault.

"You know what, fuck it. I will have the biggest, fattest freaking sandwich you have, ma'am."

Sixty seconds later the divine smelling sandwich is handed to me creating more salivation than Pavlov's dogs. I take a seat and unwrap the warm bundle of carbs in an almost pornographic fashion as the delicious oil and fat seep out the focaccia bread. This is definitely my type of artery-clogging sandwich. I get comfortable and tuck right in while racking my brain with this whole situation.

As the hot, sticky, peanut butter sticks to the roof of my mouth I turn to the projection unit to a news feature that catches my attention:

"The revolutionary form of transportation is finally operational from west to east!" The piece was delivered by an enthused news anchor that looks like a runway model. I watch with intrigue. It's something called the Hyperloop where passengers sit inside a pressurized capsule (that looks like a giant bullet) and are strapped in like a rollercoaster. The capsule sits inside a thin duct above ground where it's blasted by air pressure with speeds of over six hundred miles per hour.

"What the?"

"Now you can travel from LA to New York in an hour and a half and it's all powered by solar!" The lady finishes her segment and goes to commercial.

This is freaking unbelievable! I turn to a fellow patron who's about my age and has a truck driver look about him.

"Hey, man," I say, wiping my mouth, "what do you think of that Hyperloop thing? LA to New York in an hour and a half? Hard to believe don't you think?"

"I've traveled on it a bunch of times," he replies in-between chewing. "It's pretty rad."

"How come? She said it only just opened."

"It's LA to New York which has just opened now they've finished laying the ducting. I used to live in LA for years so I regularly traveled from there to San-Fran on the Hyperloop. They were the first two destinations to have it."

"No shit, huh. How long did it take?"

"Twenty-eight minutes. It's like going on a Six Flags ride that lasts thirty minutes instead of two and you end up in a different city."

"That's amazing. I don't know how I've never heard of it before."

"I'm surprised. It's been out on the west coast for years. When they lay the ducts around the whole country they will put about seventy-five percent of the airline companies out of business, I guarantee." He wipes his lips free of peanut butter and screws up his napkin. "The only times we'll need to fly will be if we want to leave the country excluding Alaska and Hawaii obviously. It's a faster, cheaper, greener and safer way to travel; it's even crash and earthquake-proof. And it's more fun traveling six hundred miles an hour through a giant circular duct."

"I can imagine," I look on as he rises out his seat.

"Good talking to you, bro. I gotta hit the road."

"Truck driver?"

He swings his head back around. "Truck driver? You're asking me if I'm a damn truck driver?" His eyes turn malign and pierce me.

"Errr, yeah…"

"Pleeze!" he snarls before marching away.

What was that about? Whatever. I better get moving too and face Earthquake's deadly wrath. I argue with her all the time so one more night of drunken belligerence won't make much difference, at least I can only hope.

CHAPTER 29

As the oily sandwich plays havoc in my belly I arrive outside my house still without an alibi. Fuck it, I'll just call it in the ring and come up with something on the fly. It's time to shit my pants and dive in.

Or maybe not, as it appears the front door is locked. Typical! It's never locked. That's weird. I guess I'll have to try knocking.

Nothing.

"Come on, Sherri! Since when do you lock the door? I know you're mad at me but be reasonable. This is *my* house remember…"

I thought I'd try the sympathetic angle.

I knock again.

Still nothing.

I go around the side and notice something odd. We have a small brown gate but this is a tall black gate that is also locked. What the hell? I go back to the front and realize my front door is different too. How did I not notice this a minute ago? This door is white, not brown, but this is definitely my house. I don't understand.

I knock again in a more inpatient fashion and hear noises inside.

The door opens just a crack by a teenage boy with blonde curly hair who's either stoned, paranoid or has just woken up, (or probably all three).

"Who the hell are you?" I scoff, "And what are you doing in my house?"

"Bro, what are you talking about?" replies this yahoo surfer dude in between yawning.

"Shall I repeat myself?" feeling my blood starting to boil. "Who the fuck are you and what the hell are you doing in my house?!"

He wipes the sleep out his eyes and echos back to me saying his name is Taylor, and what the hell am I doing on his property.

"*Your* property?" I frown.

"Okay *our* property, my mom has owned this house for years."

"That's impossible!"

"Errr no it's not," he says standing his ground.

"How many years?"

He tells me they've been here for nearly seven years, so I ask him is this some kind of fucking joke.

"What's so strange about that?"

"Because this is *my* house! I was here less than twenty-four hours ago. I left in the afternoon, got shit-faced, then woke up across town with all my possessions missing, and now you're telling me this has been your family's house for seven years. That, my friend, is what's so strange!"

He squints like he doesn't believe me and looks me up and down. "I know what's going on here. You're trying to punk me, ain't ya? Did Cory put you up to this? That's it, isn't it? *Cory.* Very funny, mister! Where's the hidden camera at?"

He pokes his head a little more out the door and scans the perimeter looking everywhere, even in the sky.

"I don't know any Cory! This is not a joke. Hey, man, stop looking around. I'm serious."

"Look, dude, we had band practice late last night, I went to bed and now you woke me up with this shit. I know somebody put you up to this! So long, weirdo!" He closes the door in my face.

I pound against the wood telling him I haven't finished talking to him but he doesn't bite and informs me if I don't leave now he'll notify the cops.

I decide to obey and regroup on the curb. This is the most bizarre day I've ever encountered…

I grab the Super Alkaline H2O from the bag and take a healthy guzzle. As I finish chugging the expiration date catches my eye: *'Best Before Sept. 2031.'* I drop the bottle in utter shock and watch it smash into pieces on the sidewalk. 2031! What the fuck?! I grab the cool ranch bag of Doritos and search for the expiration date: *'Best Before June. 2031.'* There's no fucking way! The vitamin bottle says the same thing. Am I in the future? It can't be… Is this why everything is so different now? What the fuck?

I need to talk to that kid again, so I march back down the drive and knock in a more civilized manner.

"Look, man," I hear through the door, "this is your last chance before I hit the crisis button and the cops will come take you away."

"I'm not here for trouble. I just have a couple more questions and I'll leave in peace, I promise."

It works. He opens the door with less paranoia and tells me to make it quick.

"You've been here seven years, right? What year did you move in?"

"2023."

"2023? The year two thousand, twenty-three?"

"That's right, we left Seattle in 2023 and been here ever since."

"How old are you?"

"Sixteen."

"When's your bornday?"

"July fifth."

"What year?"

"2014."

"If you were born in 2014, that would make you six."

"Six?" he laughs. "Do I look like I'm six, dude? I celebrated my sixteenth like three months ago."

"What's today's date?

"October eighteenth, I think."

"October eighteenth... That's the day after Max's bornday..." I mutter to myself.

"Satisfied now?"

"What year?" I turn back to him.

"Come on, man. Stop playing."

"What year?"

"2030," he says exhaustedly.

"How can it be 2030?"

"What are you talking about, man? You been smoking 'dat bomb shit? That sticky-icky?"

"I assure you I have not. Let me see your ID card?"

"My ID *card*?" he laughs. "What are you, a caveman?"

"What?"

"Look, if I can prove my identity will you go away?"

"Yes."

"Hold on."

He walks away and grabs a device that looks just like the little girl's in the park. He stretches it out and scans his finger in the middle of the screen. What follows on the screen is everything about this kid: name, address, D.O.B. even his favorite football team—the Seahawks.

"There you go, mister: name, age, address."

I freeze in my stance, realizing all this must be true. I'm bewildered and silent for a moment letting it sink in.

"Can you please GOOGLE the current date on that thing too?"

"GOOGLE?" he smirks. "GOOGLE is as dead as the Toronto Raptors. It's all about CONRAD."

"CONRAD is a search engine?"

"What are you, high? I don't know how you old folks functioned before him," he shakes his head. "CONRAD is like God, bro. We worship him like Haile Selassie. He's the reason Siri, Alexa, Watson and Jon-Jon all went to virtual hell. Ask him anything and this dude has the answer." He puts the device close to his mouth and asks CONRAD for today's date.

"Today is Friday, October 18, 2030," says the machine with the same robotic southern twang that I heard in the park.

Holy motherfucking shit. This explains all this weird shit going on.

"Okay, I believe you. I just have one last question; do you remember the people who your parents bought this house from all those years ago?"

"Jeez, dude, I really don't. I was like nine when we moved in. I gotta go. Good luck."

He politely closes the door as I fall to my knees in confusion.

I sit back on the street curb and stare at the Doritos packet. How could it possibly be ten years into the future? I'm completely dumbfounded. How can I go out, get shit faced and then wake up exactly ten years in the fucking future wearing the same clothes? It makes no sense. It's not like I've been in a coma for ten years because you can't just wake up and start walking around normally. The body takes time to adjust like the Bride in *Kill Bill*. Plus I woke up in that ghetto apartment not a hospital and I look and feel exactly the same, I certainly haven't aged ten years overnight.

Wait a minute; does this mean there's another me? Is that how I've been able to spend money using my fingerprint? I must have been spending money from my future self's account. This is some *Twilight Zone* shit…

"Mr. J?" says a faint voice from behind.

I turn around to see a girl carrying a school bag.

"Oh my God!" she lights up. "How are you?"

"Who are you? And how do you know my name?"

"Mr. Jannetty it's me, Julie… Julie Barnett."

I look at her dumbfounded.

"I used to play with Max when we were kids."

"Holy shit! Cowboy Bruce's Julie?" I stand up.

"Yeah, it's me," she almost blushes. "Haven't seen you guys in forever."

"I can't believe you're all grown up now, Julie. I remember you being so little like it was yesterday."

She smiles and tells me I look great and her parents haven't aged as gracefully as I. "So how's Max doing? It's a real shame our friendship kind of drifted when you guys moved away."

I know I'll have to wing it from now on so I tell her Max is doing fine and ask how old is she now.

"Just turned eighteen. I'm exactly one month older than Max if you can remember. How was her bornday? I guess you guys celebrated yesterday, right?"

I remain vague by saying it was a quiet celebration.

"So what are you doing around here, now you blew up and all?"

Blew up? What could she mean by that? Once again I wing it by avoiding the specifics and deflect with a question: "Do you remember what part of town we moved to?"

"Of course, Montclair, I'm still totally well-jell."

"We live in Montclair? Holy shit."

"Are you still in the same house?"

"Ahhh yep, the same house in Montclair." I nod. "Hey, do you remember where I worked on LaBelle? Box Spring Boogie."

"Yeah I remember, who could forget that funny old man who used to dance around excited all the time."

"That's right. Do you know what happened to it? It's a peanut butter and jelly place now."

"Didn't they move over to the plaza downtown? The one off Cooke Street."

"The big plaza downtown? Chess Plaza?"

"Yeah, I'm pretty sure that's the one." Her funky watch bleeps and says *"Julie, it's time to feed Fred."*

"Oh, snap, you watch just spoke."

"Shucks, I gotta run and feed Fred."

"Fred?"

"Our pet armadillo and I gotta walk him too. It's been lovely seeing you again, Mr. J."

We say our goodbyes and head in opposite directions. I once again trance-out with a million freaking thoughts rushing through my mind: What shall I do now? Shall I try and track down the other version of me? Is there really another version of me out there? A fifty-one year old version of me living in the most prestigious part of the city...

I wonder what the other me is like? I must be rich living in Montclair. Am I still with Sherri? Is she still fat? What does Max look like now she's eighteen? Is this some kind of *Back to the Future* type shit? I haven't seen any flying cars or Hover Boards yet. How any of this is even possible is beyond me...

My mind is overloaded, I need to get a grip and figure out what the hell to do.

CHAPTER 30

I figure the best thing to do is go to the new Box Spring Boogie to try and shed some light on this madness. As I walk down the street towards the bus stop that I'm guessing goes downtown, I'm approached by a petite fella who's overall style looks as if it's directly patterned after Irwin R. Schyster — slick hair, reading glasses with a white shirt and suspenders to boot.

"Hello, friend, I'm Barry Bockwinkel with the Lidgard & Bratley Campaign. In a nutshell, our mission is aimed towards helping people in the community who have stumbled upon hard times…"

I drift into a daze. I'm patient but not that patient, I have to intervene.

"—Hey, bud, spare the pitch, alright. I've gotta figure out which bus goes downtown."

"I can help you with that. You need to stand over there and take bus 302 south. I rode the bus for many years when I was in the struggle."

"Oh, thanks, I'm kind of glad you approached me after all," I say almost apologetically. "Tell you what, I'll let you pitch your company's agenda in twenty-five words or less. Go."

"Alrighty. We're asking for donations that will go towards those who are less fortunate…"

As he re-pitches I trance-out again as I often do when people babble on. I stare at this guy's name badge and get a strange sense of déjà vu…

Five seconds later it hits me. This is the homeless guy I cursed out for being a worthless, piece of shit, bum. *Barry Bockwinkel!* I'll never forget that name because it reminded me of old Nick from Minnesota. I interrupt him before his twenty-five words are up.

"Holy shit, it's you!"

"Excuse me?"

"You! The homeless guy. It's you!"

"I'm sorry, sir?"

I tell him he approached me in this very neighborhood months ago and begged me for change until I cursed him out.

He looks back a little startled and tells me he thinks I've confused him with someone else. "But it's funny you said that because I actually was homeless, but that was over ten years ago."

"Of course, you're right. It was ten years ago. I meant it *feels* like months ago, I have a pretty good memory."

He looks puzzled and asks me if I'm sure.

"When I say *cursed*, I mean I *really* cursed you out. I said you were a piece-of-shit bum that's a disgrace to yourself, to America, and probably more than that."

"Holy moly, you're right!" he joys. "I remember you! You have an impeccable memory, sir. I can't believe it."

I feel appropriately awkward as you can imagine. It's almost like running into an old bully from school that you haven't seen in years and he tries being nice to you out of sheer guilt. I attempt to muster some kind of apology but nothing comes out so he takes the stage.

"You know, that day was a huge turning point for me. I was pretty upset with what you said, not from the profanity, more from the truth. I'd been deluding myself for years in the streets, trying to escape my problems. You were right; I was an absolute disgrace to society.

"So that day I wandered into the library like I usually did when it was cold, but instead of just sitting there feeling sorry for myself I noticed a big, glitzy book on the table called *Your Life Can Be Fantastic Too*. As I started to read it struck something within me."

A warm emotional glow lights up his face as he continues his story. "It was filled with inspiring stories about turning tragedy to triumph and how anyone can turn their life around so it changed me from feeling down in the dumps. I read the whole thing from cover to cover in about four hours and was vibrating from my excitement.

"I asked the librarian if they had any more books from these authors, but they didn't. In fact, their names weren't even registered in the library's database and had no ticket inside. That's when I got the heebie-jeebies. I took it as a sign from above it was left on that table for me, because what is the likelihood of that very book being there when it didn't even belong to any library in the county? I figured it has to stay with me so I took it to my shack and reread it over and over like it was my bible."

He then goes on to say he got hooked on philosophy and started reading more inspirational books. "Many were personal development ones, others were biographies about great people who'd lived inspiring lives; people who were once down but determined to turn their life around. I got so inspired by books I became a glutton. I devoured book after book because I had a lot of time on my hands and I started to believe in myself again. With each book, I started to gain confidence and I soon quit smoking, drinking and doing drugs. Books became my new high! Within four months, I had a job, an apartment and a new circle of friends. And I've never stopped reading, I continue to read inspiring books today—I still can't get enough."

This guy finally takes a breath from his rant. It was a good rant, however.

I'm in shock to be quite frank and struggle to look him in the eye. "Well, my friend. I'm glad my words had that effect on you initially."

"Sir, you have no idea. That was the day the seed was planted which ultimately turned my life around. I didn't know it at the time, but it led me to an insatiable drive that I've never lost since that first life-changing book by Nik and Eva Speakman and it's all because of you telling me what I needed to hear."

It's a touching moment as this guy has completely changed from how I remember him. He's so cheery and upbeat and filled with gratitude. I still can't believe what I'm witnessing. "It's great that you interpreted my message in the correct and positive way, Barry. You turned it into drive instead of feeling sorry for yourself. I'm real proud of you, my friend."

He thanks me and loosens up a little, then asks if I would be interested in making a small donation to the cause.

"I would if I had any cash on me."

"Cash? Ha! Nobody uses cash anymore unless you're dealing with drug dealers or farmer's markets. We have FIT."

"FIT?"

"Yeah: *Finger Identification Technology,*" he says pulling out the little cube device that's becoming familiar to me now.

"Oh, that thing. Well, usually I wouldn't, but seeing that I changed your life and all, I'll be delighted to donate."

He beams with joy as he guides me through the onscreen instructions and then thanks me three times for my donation.

"Wait a second, I keep spending money with my finger, but how am I supposed to know how much I have in my account?"

"Just check your account balance on your Fuji."

"I don't have a Fuji."

"You don't? How come?"

"I lost all my possessions last night."

"Oh, sorry to hear that. Just go to a bank to check your balance."

"But I don't have my card or ID."

He chuckles again and tells me I can access my account with my finger.

"There's a bank right across the street."

He gives me a hug and thanks me again before we go our separate ways. I immediately ponder on what just happened. I must have cursed out hundreds of bums, beggars, charity collectors and the like but never have I heard a story like this. Finally, somebody actually listened to my message and did something with it. I'm kinda feeling pretty good about myself right now.

I cross the street and approach a bank I've never heard of: Babylon Bank. It's slickly designed, shaped like a dome with stained glass windows covering the building. Must be a biblical reference, or stained glass windows have become in vogue for businesses of the future.

I use the machine outside and press my fingerprint on the FIT thing. It identifies me and grants me access to my account right away. Wasting no time I hit the balance inquiry option and wait… Ticktock-ticktock-ticktock…

The suspense is over. The numbers hit the screen. Oh my fucking God! I think I'm about to have a heart attack! I can't believe the digits and decimals before my eyes. I knew this has to be a weird dream or something because this is just unfathomable. Whatever it is, I don't want it to end. I want to cum in my pants!

The precise digits displayed are: $5,436,212,27. Nearly five and a half million fucking dollars! Un-freaking-believable! How can this be? Fuck it, I better take advantage before this wet dream comes to an end.

I withdraw four thousand dollars for shits and giggles, stuffing two grand in each pocket (next to the hardest erection I've ever had), and mosey on down the street like one happy chappy.

CHAPTER 31

I depart from the bus beaming like I'm on cloud nine, saying hi to anybody and everybody walking the downtown streets. They sure do dress differently in the future, giant hats and baggy garments seem to be in vogue right now.

I make my way to the plaza where Box Spring Boogie now resides and scope it out immediately. It's much bigger than my store on LaBelle and looks like it's full of bells and whistles with promo signs and *'1 Day Special'* banners sprawled across the bay windows in giant bold lettering. Too overkill in my opinion. It must be twice the size though and seems more high end at this location; I guess David stepped up his game (assuming he's still around). I don't think that fun-loving old bastard will ever retire and is probably in better health than me.

As I stand outside the store staring, anxiety assaults my mind from not knowing what to do. I keep contemplating what I'm supposed to say when I'm in there. I have no proper strategy or plan of attack, just paralysis from analysis. Hmmm. Maybe I should have a couple of drinks to loosen me up and rethink my approach, and there just happens to be a bar across the street. Yeah, that sounds plausible, plus I'm getting thirsty again.

I pull up a high stool by the bar and get lost in all the sports mania. They have everything from NFL helmets molded to the walls to framed throwbacks autographed by the stars who sported them. It's a testosterone rich jock haven that probably serves green eggs and ham. Fuck it, a shot and a beer will hopefully get my juices flowing, plus I feel the need to celebrate that I'm a fucking millionaire!

I scan the horizon and spot a little barman in the background preoccupied with slicing lemons. Damn, he's tiny; a bona fide midget who's like four-foot-two and dressed as an Irish Leprechaun. How cool? I'm pretty sure he hasn't noticed me so I turn my attention to one of the plasmas that droop from the ceilings. They're the clearest I've ever seen, I can literally see teeny beads of sweat on the NBA player's faces like they're right next to me.

Then TMZ flashes a tease about an upcoming DocuDrama on Dr. Bill. The voice-over says Dr. Bill has been clinically diagnosed as insane and has been admitted into a mental hospital. Wow. Looks like that guy really lost it.

Unfortunately, there's nobody here at the bar to talk to and the little barman is now reading his magazine and still hasn't noticed me. Instead of getting annoyed like I usually would, I break my frustration by reminding myself that I'm a fucking millionaire and feel the thick wads of cash next to my aroused dick.

I summon the little guy to come over as I'm now getting thirsty for some adult beverages.

"Sorry, bro," he says, walking over. "I didn't see you,"

"No worries. I'm Bobby."

"Fink. Pleased to meet you."

We shake hands which feels like I'm greeting an infant. They are about the same size as my eight year old daughter's.

"Fink? I have to say that's quite an unusual name."

He tells me he was named after the late great orator: H. Finkel. "In here I'm the guy everyone seems to divulge their problems to so they've nicknamed me Fink 'The Shrink.'"

"Ha! Brilliant on so many levels! Fink, I'm in a tantalizing mood for a beer and a shot of Fireball, despite the fact I know how early it is."

"Hey, man, I don't judge, I just serve. We haven't served Fireball in a long time. Ever tried a Texas Tornado?"

"Can't say that I have. What's in it?"

"More like what isn't in it?" he says, raising his fluffy eyebrows. "Trust me, it's a winner."

I tell him it sounds good and rub my hands together. I also tell him to pour himself one although I don't want to be a bad influence.

"Fuck it, the weekend's nearly here. I'm in." He pours the beer first which I almost snatch from his tiny digits then watch him make up a couple of turquoise shots with white smoke escaping out the top. They look deadly. "Salud."

We cheers it up and knock them back.

I shiver from the burning sensation at the back of my throat and remark that he wasn't lying. "Woowee that hit the spot!" I cough. "Hey, I just saw this thing on TV about Dr. Bill in a mental asylum. Did you hear about that?"

"Oh yeah, everybody's been talking about it for a while now. I never did like that fat phony fuck."

"I second the notion," raising my glass. "Do you know what happened?"

"Well, apparently behind the scenes there were all kinds of rumor and innuendo floating around. Several interns reported about his abusive actions, things like if his coffee wasn't exactly the way he liked it, he'd verbally assault them until they got it just right. And if that wasn't bad enough he'd grope them and insinuate sexual advances behind closed doors."

"That's crazy. What a pervy prima-donna."

"I know right. So this one particular intern decided she'd had enough and devised a plan to set him up by stashing a hidden camera in his office. When he made a pass at her, she flirted back and played along — tongue kissing and whatnot."

"No way!" I blurt. "All on camera? He's married, right?"

"Yep, and it gets better. Get this: she told him she had a fetish for licking maple syrup off guy's bodies and he was all for it. He's a freak ya know."

I erupt with laughter and can't stop for the life of me. This is unbelievably good. Fink goes on to tell me the intern grabbed a bottle of syrup and ordered him to strip. "Then rubbed it over his hairy, rippled body as he laid spreadeagled on his desk."

I continue laughing interrupting his flow of the story.

"I must have seen it twenty times. It was so funny to see her licking his moobs and then wack him off with a bottle of Hungry Jack syrup."

"No fucking way!" I gasp.

"It became the viral of all virals because the next day she sold the footage to the highest media bidder—getting about four hundred grand for it before they leaked it out."

I continue to laugh and tell him I freaking love shit like this.

"She became an overnight sensation and went on all the talk shows," he continues. "She got invited to pose nude for *Playboy* and to do porn, she even got offered to endorse that brand of maple syrup with a sister product named Horny Jack. She was a smart MoFo that carefully calculated everything which created a media bidding war. Not bad for an intern that worked for free."

"Kudos to her," I say raising my glass. "So what happened to the mad doctor?"

He tells me they canned him from the network which wrecked him emotionally. Then many other staff and interns came forward to report his groping and verbal abuse. "His wife and kids disowned him, severing all ties, leaving him in a deep, dark depression. He wouldn't leave his house for months and gained a ton of weight. We started hearing funny stories of him eating churros dipped in whipped cream and gulping giant whiskey flavored milkshakes for breakfast. He just went insane, man, hitting rock bottom."
I sip more beer and marvel how he knows all these details.

"That's funny, I was just going to ask you how the hell haven't you heard about this?"

"Actually…" I say trying to think of some plausible excuse. "I've been living in the Amazon jungle with no TV or internet."

"No shit, huh? Well, my friend, I'm kind of in the opposite boat. I'm just like the gossip girls. I love reading trashy tabloid magazines about celebrities and scandals, especially when it's quiet at work. It makes the day go faster and gives me a good conversation starter with the chicks."

"Chicks…" I chuckle. "Can I ask you a straight-up question, Fink?"

"Sure," he says as he cleans a set of perfectly fine wine glasses just for something to do.

"Do you get a lot of chicks being…" I hesitate in coming up with the correct phrase.

"—A bartender or a midget?"

I choke on my beer as his reply catches me off-guard. "I didn't think it was politically correct saying *midget*. I thought the term was *little person.*"

"Fuck that, man. *Little person* sounds so condescending to me. I'm a *midget* and I'm a proud motherfucking *midget*. There's nothing *little* about me! I've got a huge schlong for one thing!"

I interrupt once again with boisterous laughter. This guy is brilliant.

"I'm not even kidding, my dick looks like Dr. Bill's bald head."

I interrupt him again with a hi-five and calm my laughter down. "Ya know I always wondered when you guys decided you didn't like to be called *midgets* anymore, was there like a big meeting held with five hundred midgets to vote for a name change?"

"Shit, if there was I sure didn't get the memo. The term doesn't bother me in the slightest because I don't see it as derogatory, it's all a mindset. And it's the same with chicks, as a midget bartender I do very well with the ladies because I have the biggest advantage over my peers."

"How so? I thought you'd have the biggest disadvantage over them being a midget."

"That's *little person* thinking. Fuck that! And don't get me wrong, I used to be like that for years. My childhood was a nightmare; everybody made fun of me all the time. I hated it. I hated school. I hated my parents and brothers who are all regular size humans. I hated all the girls for rejecting me. I hated the fucking world. I couldn't muster up any courage to even speak to girls until I was about nineteen."

His state has changed significantly, he's reliving his juvenile pain all over again. It's written all over his little features.

"Then one day everything changed." He goes on to tell me his mother found out about a guy in Chicago who was worse off than him by tenfold. He was born with a debilitating rare bone condition which left him even smaller than the average midget. His bones were so fragile if he coughed he could crack a rib, if he sneezed he could crack several ribs and would be hospitalized for weeks. He's never weighed more than eighty pounds and was confined to a wheelchair for his entire life. "Most people would think he had no hope, no future and permanently depressed — not so. He became one of the top therapists in Chicago, people came to see him from around the world with their *'problems'* and soon came to realize their problems aren't ever going to be as bad as Dr. Sean Stephenson."

"Wow."

"And he was a killer with the chicks and even did speeches about how to be confident with the opposite sex."

"No kidding?"

"Yeap. It's such a shame he died so young—at forty, his work touched me beyond belief. He was a true master of the art of *reframing* where you take something negative and turn it into a positive by changing the frame of reference. After studying his legendary book *Get Off Your But,* I made a deal with myself that this is how I'm gonna live my life. I don't see a shy little person in the mirror anymore, I see a fucking big dicked adonis!"

Of course, I pipe up laughing again. This guy is so captivating, I could listen to him all day.

"So when the chicks come in here wanting to have fun, I schmooze them with my wit and it totally blows their mind. Plus they think I'm adorable dressed as a leprechaun because I am."

I can't deny, I think I have a man-crush on Fink 'The Shrink', he's that charismatic. "Well, Mr. Fink, you've certainly blown my mind. I think you should be the one teaching seminars and workshops about how to be confident. You'd be great at it."

"Bro, that's the next step. I've been told that a few times and now I'm thoroughly studying it as a profession. I'm reading everything by Owen Cook, Von Markovik, Double D, and Neil Strauss of course. Then I wanna branch out into other fields like Wayne Dyer and Jack Benza, and inspire people with my words because the suicide rates for midgets have always been high throughout history. It's so sad because many don't realize how special and unique they are."

"Jeez, I never knew that about midgets. I thought the high rates of suicides were from prison guards, air traffic controllers and Olive Garden employees."

"Yeah, it's quite common in the midget community. It's so sad that anyone would take their own life because we're all blessed to have won that big swimming race against astronomical odds in the first place. Most people forget the truth that we're here for a divine purpose, and if everybody reminded themselves just how special they are we wouldn't be witnessing any suicides or depressions throughout the world."

"Hear-hear," I say, finishing my beer. "Well said."

"Sorry, that was a bit of a soapbox. Let's do another Tornado. This one's on me."

"I'm all in, brother."

He pours a couple more shots and raises his glass. "To the fallen midgets of yesteryear: Rest In Paradise."

I follow suit and clink glasses again. "Fink, this has been an incredible confabulation between us, I'd love to swing by again sometime."

"Absolutely. It's been a pleasure. Let me get the bill."

I tell him to forget the bill and go old-school by pulling out a crispy hundred with JFK on the back and plop it on the bar. "Keep the change."

CHAPTER 32

I make my way across the street feeling more confident even though talking about midgets, Dr. Bill, and maple syrup have technically done nothing to help me form a game plan. Those drinks have certainly loosened me up though.

I enter the new Box Spring Boogie and wander around taking in everything — the water beds, the futons and the funky crystal lighting that dangles from the high ceilings. After some quick observations, I come to the conclusion they are basically the same looking beds that I used to sell, although I'm sure the quality has improved like most things do with technological advantages.

I spot a well-dressed salesman with Wolverine-like muttonchops and cool designer stubble on his chinny-chin-chin. I decide to eavesdrop as he carefully stealths towards an old lady hovering around a Serta Deluxe queen.

"She's a beauty, isn't she?" he says approaching from behind. "The Deluxe is one of our top sellers."

"I've been keeping my eye on this one for a while."

"Hold on a second," he points to her, "I thought I recognized you! Aren't you that new sensation that's taken Hollywood by storm?"

I giggle at his cheese. This lady is about sixty-five and dressed like she's off to feed the ducks in the park. She takes the bait, hook, line and sinker.

"I can't believe a big movie star has walked into our store."

"Oh, stop it!" she blushes.

"I'm sorry, I'm just so star-struck! Anyway if you're interested in this particular bed I should tell you this is actually the last one we have left."

"It is?"

"Yes, ma'am, these puppies have been flying out the door, so if I was you, I wouldn't dawdle around too much. And seeing that it's you — if you take it at this price, I'll even throw in a velour comforter set that will leave you snug-as-a-bug-in-a-rug."

"Hmmm…" she ponders.

"I shouldn't tell you this because of customer confidentiality regulations but…" he lowers his voice, leaning in, "a young couple about twenty minutes ago were very interested and went to the bank to see if they can borrow a little credit so they can get it at this great price."

"Those sons-of-bitches! They can't take the last one! I'll pay for it right now."

She means business and without hesitation opens up her handbag. It's such a great feeling when you win them over and they practically beg you to take their money. Winning feels good.

"Fabulous! Let's step into the closing office over here and I'll have my associate Betty take care of the details and whatnot. I can't wait to see your famous autograph."

This smooth-talking son-of-gun leads her arm-in-arm to the office in such a graceful manner it's an art to watch. I have to hand it to him, he has a way with words—the type of guy I'd hire in a second.

He withdraws from the office with a spring in his step so I collar him.

"Hey, man, nice close," I wink. "You hit her with three of the most influential principles: *liking, social proof,* and my personal favorite: *scarcity.* Or should I say *'artificial' scarcity.*"

After swallowing my statement, his face resembles a magician whose whole repertoire has been exposed. "Let me guess," he pauses "you're in sales."

"Bingo. Matter of fact, I used to manage this place when it was over on LaBelle."

"Really? That was some time ago, right?"

I keep it vague by saying I guess so and move into formal introductions. He is Shawn the assistant manager, then I ask him if David's around.

"No. Haven't you heard the news about him?"

"No. What?"

He skirts around the specifics and basically tells me David's very ill and on his last legs.

"Oh no. Do we know what's wrong?"

"It's some kind of rare disorder and he's in and out of consciousness day-to-day."

"Fuck! This is bad. I have to see him. Where can I find him?"

He tells me he's at Calaway hospital on Hayes Street, a place I'm familiar with and calls me a cab after I inform him about my situation.

I mill around a little longer observing more beds and soon spot another senior citizen lingering near a Sleepeezee King and get the urge to strike up a conversation.

"I think you should get it."

"You do?" she turns around. "Do you work here?"

"I used to at the old location."

"Oh. Are you still in this business?"

"I don't know…"

She shoots me a rather funny look and presses how I don't know. She has a point. That must have sounded pretty strange.

"Let's just say I'm into bigger and better things now but I can't share the specifics or I might have to put you in the Sharpshooter," I smile. "So this Sleepeezee is the créme-de-la-créme in the mattress world, and at this price, it's a no-brainer. In fact, it's the biggest no-brainer in the history of civilization. Two months ago the price was much higher, so if you're interested…" I lower my voice as if I'm about to tell her something secret, "a friend of mine works here and if you want I can tell him you're my favorite aunt and he'll probably cut you a deal, but you have to take it right away."

"You could do that for me?" she glees.

"Sure. You have no idea how this bed will change your life. You'll sleep better and function throughout the day in a much more effective state, all because of the supreme ingredients that are carefully crafted into the fabrics of this Sleepeezee."

"Ingredients?"

"Yeah, that's what we in the biz call the intricate fabrics, layers and upholstery that go into such a high-quality mattress…" The super-salesman in me is back and right on cue here comes Shawn. "Shawn, my man, I believe this fabulous freebird is ready to take this bad-boy home, as long as you promise to give her a great deal like you would to a family member."

Admiring my setup, Shawn tags in and takes it from here. "Why, thank you, Bobby. Do come in again soon," he winks. We are speaking the salesman's code. He locks her arm-in-arm like his last victim and then turns back to me. "And your cab will be right out front. See you next time."

I give him the thumbs up and stroll towards the exit. Yep, even in the future, I've still got it. Winning feels good!

CHAPTER 33

"How you doin', brother?" hurls a raspy voice behind the wheel.

"I'm having a very strange, bizarre day, my friend," I say stepping inside the taxi and instruct him to take me to the hospital.

My judgmental interpretation of this dude is a rough, gruff, gnarly type meathead, rocking everything NYC. This cab could pass as a memorabilia store on wheels as it's covered in Knicks stickers, Jets logos, a miniature Stanley Cup mounted on the dash, and a D-Fence shaped air-freshener dangling from the rear-view — you've gotta love it (he couldn't be any more of a stereotype if he tried).

"And how about you, Joey?" I say, spotting his name from the computer screen at the front.

"Living the dream, son." His accent is so thick like he's just arrived from the Bronx. "Hey, talk about a bizarre turnaround in the game last night. Did you see that shit?"

"Baseball?" I say transfixed out the window.

"Baseball is for steers and queers, I can't stand that faggoty-ass game! As far as I'm concerned anybody that watches baseball is a straight-up fucking herb."

Damn, this guy is intense. You'd think he was European talking ill about baseball like that. "Why don't you tell me how you really feel?"

"Don't get me started now," he sips his big coffee as we turn a corner.

"You know you're wearing a Yankees cap?" I smirk.

"You don't have to like the game to sport the gear. I'm repping NY hard out here, boy. Besides, it helps block out the sun."

I resist pointing out he's wearing the cap backward as I marvel at the new downtown skyline.

"Anyway, I'm talking about the man's game. The game that's only built for modern-day gladiators."

"Ballet?" I tease. "Let me guess; you mean smash-mouth football?"

"Way-da-go, Einstein! Are you a fan?"

I tell him hell yeah but I've been out the loop for a while.

"Ahh, man, let me fill you in from last night," he says as we hit a little gridlock. "So the Jets were down thirty-eight—zip to the Jammers at the half. I mean, we were getting killed."

"The Jammers?" I question as I roll down the window like a hound dog searching for fresh air.

"Ya know, the Jammers. The Alabama Jammers."

"Oh, okay."

"But when the second half got underway the Jets looked like a whole new team. It was unbelievable. Marino was just slinging napalms like bang-bang-bang—connecting with everybody. Like four different receivers scored in the third alone. It was freaking insane, bro!"

"Marino?"

"Yeah, Marino the QB."

"Marino? Wait a minute, is he related to Dan?"

Joey responds confused as if I asked a ridiculous question. "Are you fucking kidding me, man?"

Fuck! Again I have to think of a valid excuse for my ignorance. This is becoming an annoying theme. "Bro, I told you I'm out the loop. I admit I have no idea."

"You're seriously telling me you haven't heard about baby Marino?" he dips in and out lanes picking up more speed.

"Nah, man," I shake my head and gaze out the window again. He drives very aggressively and so close to the curb that he nearly hits a cyclist riding alongside—he sure is living up to the stereotype of an impatient New York cabbie.

"Unbelievable! You must have been living on Pluto or something not to hear about this."

"If you must know, Joey, I've been living in Shaolin for the last ten years and haven't been following any sports."

"Shaolin? Staten Island?"

"Nah, Shaolin, China."

"Oh, you mean the *real* Shaolin. What the fuck you been doing over there?"

"It doesn't matter, now get back to Marino!" I jest, acting all east coast. "You're killing me over here."

"You caught me off guard, son. See, I'm from Staten Island and the slang term for the Island is *Shaolin*."

"Joey, we're gonna be at the hospital soon, bro," I smirk as we come down Williamson which is pretty close to our destination.

"Alright, alright. It's so funny you ain't heard this 'cause it's old news now. It was huge when this kid first came on the scene in college," he gulps more coffee and makes that annoying afterward sound. "At KU a few years ago there was this kid called Starks who started making noise, putting up star-like numbers. But nobody really knew his background or nuttin', he was like an enigma, always shying away from the media and stuff.

"But soon enough he became the hottest college quarterback in the country breaking records at Kentucky, getting all the attention and notoriety. And then the truth came out about this mystery kid." He takes another large gulp of coffee from his flask (probably just to keep me in suspense, the fucker). "Dan Marino has a bunch of kids with his wife, you knew that much, right?"

"Yeah, I knew that."

"Well, it turned out that *Dirty Dan* had more than one love child. First, a girl that everybody knew about, and then a boy with another broad which was kept top secret until he became a superstar in college. Everybody loved the story that this mystery kid Starks was really a Marino, so instead of shying away he eventually embraced it and became the hottest commodity entering the draft."

"Wow, so Marino's kid is a star in the NFL now?"

"A *star?!*" he almost chokes. "He's a fucking wizard! In the five years he's been in the league he's led the Jets to three back to back titles, along with a couple of MVPs to boot!"

"Get the fuck outta here! The New York Jets are the champs right now? Man, that's unbelievable!"

"Three-time Super Bowl champs, my friend," he gloats flashing three digits— each sporting an imitation Super Bowl ring as we come to a stoplight. "The franchise got completely turned around since Vaynerchuk took over and built them up from scratch."

"Who?"

"Gary V, the billionaire internet mogul. He's the best owner in sports bar none. I can't believe you never knew any of this. Don't you got the internet in the Shaolin Temple?"

"No internet in the Temple!" I snap, fucking with him. "So what happened in last night's game?"

"Well, like I said, the Jets were getting killed by halftime, and then we came out with a completely different mindset led by Marino. They turned it on and laid the hammer down beating the Jammers 45—41 all in the second half and on the road too! It was un-freaking-believable."

I tell him I'll have to catch the replay as we pull up to the hospital and then take a second to contemplate on reality: the New York Jets are the three-time champs! Not in my wildest dreams…

"Here we are, Mr. Shaolin. That will be thirty-six beans. Press here." He hands me the little finger payment thing.

Thirty-six bucks? Damn, that's a lot of scratch for such a short ride, but this is the future with inflation and everything. Anyway, who cares? I'm a multimillionaire, apparently.

I pay with my thumb and thank him as I open the door.

"So I gotta ask, what were you doing in Shaolin? I never heard anybody going out there to live."

I have to think quickly. "I studied Tiger Style Kung-Fu with the Wu-Tang Clan. Protect your neck, son!"

CHAPTER 34

I've always loathed hospitals and try my best to avoid sick people at all costs. I can't think of a worse place to spend time in than a hospital waiting room. When I was a kid I'd sit there observing obese patients stuffing their faces at the vending machines and get transfixed on their bellies like I had X-ray vision and it would make me cringe. *"How could you do that in a place like this?"* is what I wanted to say but never did out loud.

I'd also think why would they put vending machines in here for sick people to be tempted instead of having healthy foods that could help them get better? Then I'd see patients outside smoking cigarettes in their hospital gown (sometimes with an IV attached) and wonder why doesn't a nurse or doctor stop or at least advise them. At school, if we did something wrong, the teachers would put us right back in line, but as an adult, you could be as sick as a dog but still continue to eat junk and smoke without any guidance or—

"Do you need any assistance, sir?" a friendly nurse breaks my inner rant as I wander aimlessly around the lobby.

"Ahh yeah, I do actually. I'm here to visit my friend David Gordy. Do you know where I can find him?"

"No," she says all straight-faced. "There's approximately eight hundred patients in here, sir. You need to go to the front desk, they'll be able to look him up on the system and point you in the right direction, okay?"

She pats me on the shoulder and leaves me feeling like a retard. I can't believe I asked her that. That's like flying to LA and asking a random person in the street if they know Johnny from Hollywood. What a moron.

Despite my disdain for hospitals, this place looks pretty professional and immaculately clean. I don't feel the threat of diseases floating through the air as I observe the staff mill around in a somewhat organized, yet chaotic fashion.

The lady at the front desk helps me with the whereabouts of my man David so I ascend in the elevator to the seventh floor and gather my thoughts. I'm facing the same problem as before: what am I supposed to say to him? I'll have to figure it out on the fly, assuming he's even conscious.

I find his room and peep through the window, it's filled with flowers, fruit, books, magazines, plus a Playboy calendar on the wall—old dirty bastard. I quietly let myself in, only to see him passed out with drool leaking out the side of his mouth. His face looks basically the same as when I last saw him, although his former tanned complexion is more Casper the Ghost and his hair is now pure white like the late-great Freddie Blassie.

"David? Are you awake?"

His eyes begin to flicker open. He looks so frail and helpless, the complete opposite of the man I know.

"Bobby, my boy," he responds a little disoriented. "What happened? You're all chubby again."

"Errr yeah…" is about all I can muster.

"You've fallen back into your old ways. I've gotta say, I'm disappointed." He makes grunting noises as he stretches and twists his neck. "Anyway, who am I to talk? I'm hardly the poster boy for healthy living anymore, but I'm glad you're here especially after all that stuff that came between us. You're a real man being here, I want you to know that."

Stuff that came between us? What could that be? Knowing zilch about what he's talking about I know I'll have to wing it again.

"I'll always be here for you, boss."

I used to never call any of my bosses *'boss'* because I always felt I was the boss of myself and my world. Nobody tells me what to do. David, however, earned that from me because he's so much more than somebody I work for.

He tells me that means a lot and opens his arms for a big hug.

We embrace and do some general chit-chatting before he asks me how's business. Once again, I'm clueless and have to segue.

"Everything's fine but forget me for a minute, I'm here to see about you. What did the doctors say?"

As the words eject from my mouth, the look on his face change to a man with zero hope. It's painful to witness.

"They've told me straight-up, I don't have much time left. I have something called Mesothelioma, and if that ain't enough I got Pulmonary Fibrosis thrown in the mix. I've been hit with a devastating one-two punch that I can't get up from."

I don't verbally respond, or should I say I can't verbally respond. I merely caress him and gently stroke his Freddie Blassie mane.

"This is the first time in my life I can't turn it around. I've lost all hope…"

"Come on, boss. Since when do you believe what doctors say? They're wrong all the time, you know that. You're a fighter. You'll bounce back."

"I don't see it, Bobby, the reality is bleak. They don't even give me green bananas anymore," he starts to cough. "Listen, it's very serendipitous you came here today, I've got something I must tell you."

"I'm all ears, boss."

"Pay attention like your life depends on it. I need to tell you about the most terrifying emotion in the world…" He takes his time sitting up, composing himself. "As I've been cooped up in this God damn room for weeks I've done a lot of reflecting on my life and legacy. Even though I've had an incredible life and achieved many great things, there's an unforgivable amount I still didn't do."

This makes me frown and really gets my attention.

"That emotion, Bobby is *regret.*"

His eyes become sharp and congruent. I've never seen him this serious before, it's as if his soul is opening up.

"Regret?" Regret over what I can only guess.

"Regret is haunting me right now. It's eating me alive," he starts to well up. "I've missed out on so much throughout my life, and there is no legitimate or rational explanation at all. Just fucking lame excuses! It all comes down to I simply wasn't focused, disciplined or dedicated enough. I allowed myself to get easily distracted from my ambition and my mission, and now, Bobby it's absolutely killing me."

He shakes his head while I try to add something positive but can't.

"I keep playing the '*I wish I coulda or shoulda*' scenario over and over and it's overwhelming me. I can't sleep, I can barely eat and just feel immobilized. This pang in my gut is ten times worse than the actual diseases I've got."

He starts to weep badly. I'm on the edge of tears too and still don't know what to say. I've never seen him like this. All I can think of is making him look at the other end of the spectrum.

"Come on, David that's crazy. You've had a life that most people would dream of."

My comforting words have little or no effect, he just lays there and continues to sob saying he didn't do enough meaningful things. This situation reminds me of Leonardo da Vinci oddly enough. Apparently, Leonardo spent his final moments apologizing and repenting to God about not doing enough with his life or fulfilling his potential, which is crazy if you think about all the inventions and paintings and thousands of other things that that genius left behind. Leonardo had the highest of high standards and was way ahead of his time, but in his final moments, he thought he could have done a lot more with his time on Earth. Now David, who has lived a remarkable life in his own right, is having similar feelings and it's absolutely wrecking him at this very moment.

As he continues to cry, I'm still left unable to respond — comforting people on their deathbed is not exactly my forte.

"Promise me, Bobby, you'll never live with regret for the rest of your days. You must take immaculate care of your health, that's number one, both you and your family. Drink water and wheatgrass constantly, and have fresh vegetables every single day. You can't go on poisoning yourself with shitty fast-foods because you will significantly shorten your life. Understood?"

"I know. You're right," I say, avoiding eye contact.

"And do everything you set out to achieve by making clear, defined goals centered around growing and giving and spend time every day moving towards them. Don't distract yourself with TV because you're too tired to work on your passions. Fuck fatigue! Remember, TV stands for *Time Vanished*, so make sure you don't piss away any single moment of your precious life! Scarcity is real and it's so scary when there's no time left!" He smacks his fist into his hand to make his point. "Please heed this and never take anything for granted again! Remember what I always told you: you must wrench the neck of life and squeeze out every last fucking drop!"

His passion for what he believes in hasn't changed one iota. Even on his deathbed, he can move people to tears.

For a brief moment, I trance-out, pondering on my recent ills. What an abysmal pig of a human being I have become. I've practically wasted an entire year on drugs, excessive drinking and of course, prostitutes. Not to mention turning into a fucking sloth and satiating myself with food. All of this with absolutely no regard to my health and family. I wonder if I'm even still with Sherri today? If she had any sense she would have left me a long time ago. When I really focus on all the debauchery I've caused, it's absolutely sickening. David is right on the money, I just can't do this anymore.

"I promise, David, I will change. I won't take anything for granted again."

That was tough for me to say, but it had to be said because I meant it.

"Do you really mean it or are you just telling me what I wanna hear?"

This motherfucker always knows how to close me.

"Are you a man of your word?" he presses.

"Listen to me, David, I mean it, seriously. You've touched me. I too hate feeling regret."

"Are you gonna lose that horrendous belly and get healthy and back in shape?"

"Yes!"

"Good, Bobby, good. It's time to stop messing around with your most precious gift: your health, and start living free from toxins. Remember, if Man makes it, don't eat it. If it's been grown from Mother Earth then it's usually a good sign that it's healthy." He starts coughing again and continues for what seems like hours. He thoroughly goes over all his philosophy, his values, beliefs and ambitions like he's a professional self-help speaker or more accurately an evangelist.

My original strategy of trying to shed some light on how the hell I've mysteriously appeared ten years in the future has been totally swayed, but instead I receive a remarkable gift from a man I have the utmost respect for. I can only pray he miraculously fights back and somehow kicks his disease's ass.

CHAPTER 35

I check into a fancy hotel and order some lavish room service. I figure what's a few hundred on a room when you've got millions in the bank. Unfortunately, they don't have any ulcer pills or antacids so I'll have to tackle my shrimp and lobster (with a side salad) without them. Instead of pigging out like I usually would, I hear David's voice circulating in my head and eat properly and composed, making me feel somewhat proud.

Hours go by and I'm still racking my brain, going around and around deciphering what my next move will be. How am I supposed to track my future-self down, and if I do, what am I supposed to say: *'Hi I'm you from ten years ago, do you wanna hang out and go bowling?'* And how are Sherri and Max going to react to all this?

Generally, when I'm in a quagmire and can't see a way out, I get frustrated and use food as my go-to method of breaking my stressed state. Ironically after all that sagacity with David, I unconsciously order a sticky toffee pudding from room service and before I know it, there's a knock at the door. Damn, talk about efficiency.

"Room service," says a horse-faced young bellboy with rosy red cheeks like Brother Love.

As I let him inside it now occurs to me I can get a second opinion from this bellhop boy. I'm too damn introverted and need another party to vent to instead of going around in circles with myself. Even though this kid must be nineteen at the most, I figure it can't hurt to ask for his opinion.

"What's your name, son?" I say, inviting him in.

He tells me it's Victor as he puts down the dessert and makes himself comfy on the cream sofa.

"Victor, I need your opinion and advice if you'll be so gracious."

"Okay…" He looks a little confused and for good reason, I'm not even sure where I'm going with this.

"Don't worry, I'm not a weirdo. And I'm not stingy, I'll tip you for your time."

"That's okay. What is it you need help with, sir?"

"Victor, I don't know how to quite say this..." I'm hesitating. Too much going on inside my fucking head. "I'm in a strange situation at the moment and erm..." I hope he doesn't think I'm a sicko that wants to sodomize him or something. I just told him I'm not a weirdo but this must seem kind of strange. "Have you ever been in a situation where you don't know what angle or approach to take?"

"I guess..." he shrugs.

There's no way I'm going to tell him I've mysteriously appeared here from ten years ago. He would probably be on the floor laughing or call the men in white coats and fishnets. I have to get creative.

I keep thinking of that scene in *Back to the Future III* where Doc tells Clara that he's from 1985 and he now must return back to the future. If you recall, she chews him out and calls him a liar because she can't possibly fathom his story. I always thought Doc was a fool for taking that approach because you have to think of the other person's point of view in a situation like that. How is someone from 1885 going to feasibly believe he's from the future with no evidence or proof? He should have just taken her for a ride on the Hover Board then showed her the DeLorean and said: *'get in, baby, we're going back to the future!'*

"Okay, here's the bottom line," I continue, "I'm stuck and I need help. I need to contact someone very close to me but it's not very likely this person will understand the situation I'm in."

"What situation is that?"

"That's the problem, I can't tell you or anybody else."

He mulls it over for a moment. "It's kinda hard to get help if you can't explain what's going on."

I take on board what he said. It's a good point.

"Okay let's try a different approach: If you needed to tell somebody the truth even if that person will not believe you in a million years; how would you go about it?" Finally, I'm making some kind of sense.

"That's easy, you should just come out and tell the truth. It may be awkward or hard to comprehend or whatever, but if the truth is what this person must hear then you should tell them regardless. That's what I would do."

"That's actually pretty good, Victor." I give him a thumbs up. "The direct approach. I should have thought that myself."

"I read a lot of *Vogue*," he says drily.

I chuckle as that remark catches me off base.

"The truth shall set you free."

Now he's getting cocky. I tell him his parents brought him up very well, and I shall now set him free.

"Glad I could be of some help, sir. Good luck." He stands up and motions to leave.

"Oh, Victor, you're forgetting something…" I pull out a crispy Kennedy that still has that fresh bank smell and hand it to the happy camper.

He exits the suite leaving me with my unresolved issue and my unresolved dessert. I pick up this mouth-watering sticky treat and hold it close to my mouth but suddenly become conscious of David delivering those majestic words that touched me so deeply. By forming a powerful image of him watching me it breaks me from *pig-out mode* making me realize I don't even want it. I emphatically throw it in the trash and you know what? It feels fucking great like I've conquered something monumental. Now all I have to do is keep this up for the rest of my life.

CHAPTER 36

After hours of racking my brain, pacing up and down and talking to an empty room, I've hit a wall. I'm so tired of over-analyzing everything in my incessant fucking mind that the time has come to act. Victor was right all along to be direct. I have to call up my future self and come right out with the truth and hope to hell he doesn't freak out.

I stare at the hotel phone for a while and finally summon the courage to dial my cell phone and pray it's still the same number after all these years. I can't see why not, I've had the same number for about twenty years when cell phones were the new craze.

Okay, here we go… I dial and shit my pants. It rings.

"Hello?" answers a voice who sounds like me, at least I think…

"Hello, is this Bobby Jannetty?"

"Bobby Jannetty…? Bobby is dead."

"What?!" I gasp as my heart sinks.

"Relax, I'm talking in the metaphorical sense. I am the artist formally known as Bobby. Now everybody calls me JJ."

JJ? This completely throws me. Nobody calls me JJ.

"Is this Robert James Jannetty?" I double-check just to make sure. "Son of Terry and Jeanie Jannetty?"

"Yes. And who am I speaking to?"

This has to be me. What the hell is he playing at?

"Okay," I continue (still shitting my pants), "I want you to brace yourself as I have something inconceivable to tell you…"

"Who is this?" he says, I mean *other me* says.

"Bobby, this is going to sound ridiculous and unbelievable and—"

"Before you continue, who am I speaking to?"

"That's what I'm trying to tell you. This is gonna sound like a prank or something but I have to just come right out and say it."

"What? What do you have to tell me?"

He's beginning to sound a little agitated, I need to get to the point and quick. "Bobby, I am you. I am Robert James Jannetty..."

"What?"

"I am you, Bobby. I was born December 21st, 1978. My sister, Luna was born, October 26th, 1985. My daughter Maxine was born—"

"What are you talking about? And why are you reeling off my family's info?"

"Because I am you, Bobby. Well, I'm the younger you. You are fifty-one, right? Fifty-two in December?"

"Yes, that's correct."

"Well, I'm you but I'm forty-one."

"What the hell are you talking about?!"

I can feel older me getting tense again on the other end of the phone.

"I told you it sounds crazy, but I don't know any other way to explain it. I'm the younger version of you."

An awkward silence ensues.

"I don't know what kind of coke or crack you are smoking, mister, but don't call here again trying to punk me. Bye!"

The phone cuts off at the other end. Shit, I had a feeling that might happen. I would definitely do the same if somebody called me out-the-blue spieling the same story. I can't let it phase me though. I have to be flexible, like when I was a cold caller so I hit the redial and it picks up.

"Bobby, please don't hang up! I have to prove it to you—"

"Listen, whoever you are, you're obviously some crackpot with a lot of time on your hands. All the information about me and my family are very easily attained from social media so you can just ride away on whatever donkey you rode in on. So long, jackass!"

"—Ask me something that only you would know, like something from our childhood."

"Sorry, dude. I'm not playing your silly games. You can't close a closer. Don't call again."

He hangs up.

Motherfucker! Okay, it's time to bring the big guns out. The closer is about to get closed.

I dial again...

Fuck, it went straight to voice-mail. Okay, here goes:

"Listen, Bobby, let me prove this is not a scam or hoax: In eleventh-grade cooking class you got red-headed Chantel to spike your stew with her period blood then served it to the evil Mrs. Kandetzke as revenge for those two months of detention. Your idols consist of Leonardo da Vinci, Thomas Edison and Ric Flair, in fact, you watch Flair promos whenever you need to get fired up before a meeting.

"You jerk off over muscle porn instead of satisfying your wife Sherri who you met at McSweet's frat party when you were nineteen. At the beginning of 2020 you secretly started sniffing coke with Cameron Glynn and then went completely off the rail with prostitutes, especially Asian ones and began a life of deceit that nobody knows about. Oh, and if you check your bank account you'll see that I've been spending your money all over town: the pharmacy, the bus, the taxi, the hotel, and let's not forget the four thousand dollars I withdrew from Babylon Bank on Griffin BLVD. And how did I do that? Because we're the same person with the same fingerprints. So stop fucking around and call me back. I'm at the downtown Marriott, room 806!"

I hang up and sprawl on the bed like a starfish.

It doesn't take long until the phone rings.

"I just checked my bank transactions," other me says. "What the hell is going on? How do you know all that stuff? Are you trying to blackmail me?"

"No! I need your help. I don't know what the fuck is going on but I'm trapped here in the future."

He becomes confused and tries to extract details of how, but of course, I don't know how the hell to answer.

"Look, I don't get it either, but I'm here. Do you remember Max's eighth bornday party where you got shitfaced and destroyed the bouncy house?"

"Of course. I was a drunken embarrassment."

"Yes, you were. And only I would know exactly what happened afterward, wouldn't I? You got wasted with some Australian kids having a bachelor party, fucked a couple of skanky Brazilian strippers and ended up in some ghetto motherfucker's apartment with Fishscale and guns."

"Yeah, I remember. That was when I hit rock bottom."

"Exactly! And that's the last thing I remember. Then I woke up and somehow it's exactly ten years in the future. So you think *you're* confused, how the hell do you think *I* feel? I have absolutely no explanation whatsoever!"

"Okay, we've gotta meet face to face and quick. Do not under any circumstances talk to anybody else about this and never talk over the phone. The government could be listening in. Grab your things, go downstairs, pay in cash when you check out and hop in a taxi to my place so we can get you off the grid."

"What about Max and Sherri? What are we supposed to tell them?"

"It''s not a big concern right now."

"What do you mean *not a big concern?* How can you say that?"

Wesley Thomas

"I'll tell you everything as soon as you're here, just get here quick!"

CHAPTER 37

I pull up in a cab outside an incredible house in the affluent suburb Montclair. It's more of a mini-mansion to be precise. I have to stop and just take this in for a moment. I take a deep breath of anxiety riddled fall air and just stare at the architecture. It looks Spanish or Italian maybe, with red and orange mismatched bricks and a turret directly in the middle that stands oh so grandiose. Incredible!

I finally muster up the courage to walk up the long cobbled drive in complete awe at everything. The grounds are immaculately groomed like a professional golf course, the windows are rainbow colored stained glass which looks cool as shit, and the whole house is lit up like Disney World on New Year's Eve — talk about a Magic Kingdom! It almost brings a tear to my eye that somehow I've accumulated this kind of wealth. Lord knows how the hell this came to be, I just hope it's all legit.

I can't wait to hear how it all went down, but of course, fear and apprehension hits me like a motherfucker and takes over my whole body. It's hard to explain what's going on through my head. Uncertainty I guess. I mean, I'm here to meet *me*, an aged fifty-one version of me. This is some freaky shit.

As I approach the oval archway I become even more arrested with fear, like the way cold-callers get from knocking on their first door of the day. I'm on the brink of chickening out and running away but pull myself together and ring the bell.

The door slowly swings open.

"Bobby?" I say to the figure lurking in the doorway.

Silence.

We just stare at each other like a couple of ice statues. He looks just as flabbergasted as me.

"Technically, yes. He is I and I am him but I now go by JJ."

"Oh my God, look at you!" I say completely bowled-over.

I can't believe it, I'm staring at an older me. This is fucking freaky to witness. He looks so much better than me in every area. For starters, he must be a hundred and fifty pounds thinner, I kid you not. He's got great skin, great hair and no double chin that I have. How on Earth could this be? We don't even look remotely alike but I know it's me staring back. This totally reminds me of that TV show *The Biggest Loser* where, on the season finale the new slim person crashes through an old life-size photograph of their old fat self, except this is not a photograph; he is right in front of me. I must have invested a lot of loot on liposuction to achieve something this remarkable.

"I'm speechless. You look tremendous!"

"And you look hideous, bloated and out of shape." An awkward stillness ensues. "I thought I killed you."

"What?"

"Just looking at you makes me sick to my stomach."

He's certainly pulling no punches. I don't know how to react.

"You better come inside…"

He leads me through this spectacular house which I have no time to take in and soon find ourselves in his office. It appears to be more of a man cave, as the walls are covered with pictures, posters, decals and stickers of all my passions and pop culture — movies, wrestlers, inventors, superheroes, athletes and musicians (with an Elvis section of course). I freaking love it! It's so me!

He walks around his large, oak desk that looks like a lot of stuff goes down behind—if I only knew what business I'm involved in. Whatever it is, I'm fucking killing it. This place is lush with a capital L!

"Let's get a few things straight," he says as we sit. "First of all, you are *Bobby*. I am *JJ*. After I cut out excessive drinking, drugs, hookers and all my other deadly sins, I decided that was it for Bobby, he had to go. So I killed him… That's right, I fucking killed him!"

I sit back staying mute as this hits home with me.

"I made a complete one-eighty and reinvented myself as JJ, kind of like Sting when he changed his gimmick from the bleached blonde babyface to the Crow."

I'm tickled at his wrestling analogy and feel compelled to compliment him on it.

"Bobby is who you are: the fat, out-of-control piece of shit that abuses himself with food, drink and drugs, while JJ walks a righteous path of health, family, success and adventure. Understand?"

"But why JJ? Why not BJ?"

"As much as I used to like the name *Bobby*, I had to kill him and resurrect myself as James Jannetty esquire. Besides, *BJ* reminds me too much of the word *blowjob*."

"Right," I smirk looking up at the spectacular Venetian plastered ceiling. "I've gotta know how you earned all this? How come you're mega-rich? What business

are you in? How did you get so thin? Liposuction? Plastic surgery? And your hair—
"

"Whoa whoa whoa, time-out. You need to shaddup and listen!"

He's very assertive, to say the least. I get the message and sit back as he tells me everything will come in due time.

"Here's what I meant when I said looking at you makes me sick to my stomach: it's because it reminds me of when I hit rock bottom. Ten years is a long freaking time and as far as I'm concerned, that version of me is dead and buried. You see, whatever's going on here, whether you're spontaneously trapped in a parallel universe, or you came here in a souped-up DeLorean with an in-built flux capacitor, something divine or omnipresent is definitely going on. It's too much of a coincidence that my ten year anniversary of being clean from cheating, drugs, food binges and excessive alcohol is today and here you are magically appearing in front of me."

"You don't drink anymore?"

"I still have a beer or a glass of wine once in a blue moon but it's rare. It's too much of a distraction from my purpose. I certainly don't go to excess with anything anymore because I'm a professional now, and I can't let anything sway me from that."

"Professional what?" I press.

"Again you're jumping the gun, Bobby, we'll get to that. Right now you just need to know that I'm a completely different version of you. You have no idea how my life has been altered in the last ten years so I feel the need to enlighten you with my knowledge, wisdom and understanding."

I think he's right, this guy doesn't resemble me at all. "I'm starting to doubt whether we're the same person."

"Oh we're not the same person, Bobby, we just have the same DNA. But you will change when you heed what I'm going to teach you." He stares back at me, judging me with his inquisitive eyes (at least that's what I think). "Are you ready for change, or do you want to carry on fucking around, wasting your life at the Duck Dive, with beer, wine and swine?"

"Swine?"

"Yes, swine is not divine, Bobby. The pig is an ill descendant of a bunch of shit you don't want to know. Do your research and you'll discover that it's part cat, part rat, and the rest dog. Not the most cleansing thing you want to be ingesting into your digestive system."

I come back with a defensive rebuttal but my efforts are futile as he adamantly pins me in a corner like a master debater.

"And you wonder why your stomach is giving you hell every day. It just can't digest all that dead animal flesh, so I have to teach you some fundamental health principles which are absolutely paramount, but also, we have to work on your psychology. You see, ninety percent of change is upstairs in your head, only ten percent is the actual mechanics, so I'm gonna ask you again: are you ready for a transformation? A breakthrough? A reinvention?"

I openly admit that I need this bad and plead that I'll do anything.

"Good," he says. "You didn't hesitate and you seem congruent. You just passed the first test." He twiddles his hands together behind his desk like an evil James Bond villain. "You are in desperate need of wisdom, Bobby, so I want to overwhelm you with a crash course on the most important areas in life. I have to download what's in my head and upload it to yours. Total immersion, understand?"

I shoot back with an emphatic YES before telling him I'd be a fool not to listen. "I mean, look at all the wealth I've accumulated—I mean *you've* created."

"That's right, Bobby, *I've* accumulated, not you. You haven't accumulated shit except a lot of fat and a lot of debt from ignorance, negligence, greed and stupidity. For you to acquire this kind of wealth you have to change your whole mentality." He pauses to drink some strange looking green liquid. "Look at you; a fat fucking disgrace! If somebody walked in here they probably wouldn't even think we're related. True wealth, Bobby, is optimal health, not material bullshit like BMWs, 4D TV's and J-Dongles."

"J-what?"

—He grabs an expensive looking vase off his desk and hurls it across the room, scaring me shitless as it smashes into smithereens on the door. "That thing cost like seven grand but it doesn't mean anything to me. It's just a stupid inanimate object, understand?"

"Errr yeah…" This guy's a fucking psycho!

"Wealth starts up here," he taps the side of his temple. "I've played the game that you're about to play, Bobby, so I'm about to give you an incredible anticipatorial advantage—"

"Is that even a word?"

"Yes! Don't interrupt me. I'm gonna give you a step by step strategy of winning. This is your time to shine if you want it badly enough. The only question is are you gonna give it your all and become a legend like Mr. Perfect? Or are you gonna not believe in yourself and be a flop like the Red Rooster?"

"Ha. Nice analogy once again."

"I know, I'm full of them," he smiles in an oh-so cocky fashion and guzzles about a half quart of that green murky liquid down his neck. I have a sneaky feeling it's that swamp juice stuff that David tried to turn me onto way-back-when.

"Anyway, I digress, we need to switch gears and talk about what's most important which is *health*. I've been studying health like a deranged madman for the past decade; Bernie Siegel, Robert Young, Max Gerson, Deepak Chopra, authors like that. When you take the time to study the science of the human body, you will come to the conclusion that you and I aren't even the same person, at least on the molecular level. Every four days a human being gets a new stomach lining. Your outer layer of skin; the epidermis replaces itself every thirty-five days. You are given a new liver every six weeks, and our entire skeletal structures are regenerated every three months. Even the brain replaces itself every two months, and overall, the entire human body, right down to the last atom, is replaced every five to seven years. Incredible stuff, right? Every year we become new versions of ourselves, literally."

I sit back and agree that's pretty interesting.

"Interesting is an understatement. I personally think our bodies are the most splendiferous structures on the face of this earth. Most of us, however, take this wealth for granted, and some even abuse it with hard narcotics and frosted cinnamon swirls."

I avoid direct eye contact knowing that was a subliminal dart towards me.

"So what you're looking at is the 2030 version of JJ, who's got his shit together because he became serious and driven. What I'm looking at is the 2020, out of date, unambitious, fat, lazy, selfish version of Bobby James Jannetty. Get it?"

I nod and humbly admit I do.

"I actually think of it as literal, not metaphorical when it comes to transformation. We can literally become a different version of ourselves with new empowering beliefs if we want it badly enough. I need to know are you ready to leave that old lifestyle behind? Because that coke-sniffing, alcohol-abusing, wife cheating, fucking piece of shit has been dead inside me for ten years now, but he's still inside you, isn't he?"

"To be perfectly honest, he is," I answer in a rather meek fashion.

He challenges me again by asking if I definitely want to change.

"I do because if I don't then I know what kind of path I'll be heading down."

"And what path is that, Bobby? Let's elaborate by going down that path right now."

I look up to the ceiling once again and take my time in answering. I form a clear picture of the destructive path I'll be heading down if I carry on living recklessly like Jake 'The Snake' in the early nineties. "The path of destruction."

"That's right, Bobby, what else?"

"A broken marriage."

"That's right" he nods. "What else?"

"A deadbeat father."

"Exactly. What else?"

"Becoming obese."

"Agreed. What else?"

"Being broke from squandering my money."

"One hundred percent correct. Come on, what else?"

"The path of ill health."

"Hmmm," he nods. "Correct. What else will happen?"

"Death," I say solemnly.

That last one was hard to accept but I have to face up to it. I guess this is the point he's trying to make.

"Every one of them is right on the money, Bobby. If you carry on messing around with drugs then you already know your destiny, don't you?"

I nod like a naughty schoolboy who's been caught smoking behind the dumpsters.

"But you look unsure like you still want to continue that late-night drinking lifestyle."

"Look, man," I defend, "this is just a shock to me as it is you. I haven't had time to really process this."

"Well, it's time to start processing because if you don't change from your deceitful life of debauchery then you'll fucking destroy yourself and never get to live this extravagant life that I enjoy. *Capiche?*"

I look down and tell him all this stuff is hard because everything is so new.

"Think about it; the recollection you have of collapsing the bouncy house and getting wasted with the Australians must be like a distant memory in the back of your mind, isn't it?"

"It sure is. And that's where I like to keep it."

"Right. But for me, that incident happened last freaking night. Twenty-four hours ago I was popping bottles in a titty bar and banging Brazilian strippers in the VIP room."

"It's crazy, I know."

"But when I woke up in that rundown apartment and looked in the mirror I felt absolutely disgraced with myself, so I know, without a shadow of a doubt I must change. Maybe that's how this whole time warp thing came about?"

"I think so too," he adds. "And you know damn well if you don't change right now, you're heading down a deadly path and early death. It's just that simple."

"You're absolutely right. There's no two ways about it."

"We'll cover drugs more thoroughly another time. For now, we need to start with the most important area in life: *health…*"

He continues preaching a plethora of health principles and fitness regiments for about an hour and a half straight. He has a step by step methodology down to a meticulous science. He's done his homework and certainly walks his talk, that's for sure.

It's late now and my head is starting to spin, and worst of all he doesn't mention anything about how he made all his money which is what I'm really waiting for. He did reveal that Sherri took Max to Hawaii for a week to celebrate her bornday in style, which is one less thing to worry about. The only thing I squeezed out of him is what went down between him and David eight years ago, which was so unexpected I'm still having trouble processing it.

Fatigue is setting in as I nod along with whatever he says.

"You look tired, Bobby. Maybe this is enough of me orating to you for one night. I'll show you to a guest room and we'll pick this up in the morning. Tomorrow will be the first day of the rest of your life, as clichéd as that may sound."

"Music to my ears."

As we leave the office and ascend the spiral staircase, I turn to him.

"So I've got to ask you the million-dollar question one more time: how on Earth did I, or you accumulate all this wealth? It's killing me because I know damn well you ain't working as a mattress store manager to make this kind of bank."

"All in due time, Bobby. All in due time…"

CHAPTER 38

I sleep like a baby through the night and wake up thinking it was probably just a strange dream. I check my surroundings and evidently, it's not. I stretch out in this oh so comfy bed, marveling at a chandelier that looks like it's made from pure crystal. Wow. I can certainly get used to this. I still can't believe I'm in a freaking mini-mansion that one day I'm gonna own. Despite a mild stomach pang, I spring out of bed as if I've been given a new lease in life, like Jim Hellwig going from the Dingo Warrior to the Ultimate Warrior. I can barely contain my enthusiasm.

"Bobby, baby, you're up!" hurls a vivacious JJ, stirring something in a big pan as I glide into the kitchen. "I'm having a blast cooking us breakfast. It's been a little while since I've done this, that's for sure." He goes on to inform me that his chef normally makes the meals, but he's told him and the other house staff to take a little sabbatical for the time being.

I wipe the morning crusties from my eyes and try to comprehend that one day I'm actually gonna have staff waiting on me. Fucking surreal.

The kitchen, like everything else here, is top-notch — giant double fridge, shining marble unit and a slick, dome-shaped device attached to the faucet that I'm guessing is some kind of water filter.

"That thing you're looking at is a medical-grade water ionizer that I had imported from Okinawa. You didn't think we're gonna make soup with tap water did you?"

I tell him the thought hadn't crossed my mind. Man, he and I are a million miles from each other. I'm not even slightly like him.

"Hope you're ready for spinach soup," he says, throwing in some herbs.

"Spinach?" I say, losing all enthusiasm. "Have you turned into David or something?"

"Well, he was a huge inspiration for me starting out, but I live by my own code now."

"So I guess pancakes and maple syrup are out of the question?"

"There you go, Bobby, with your short term thinking. Don't you remember talking about turning over a new leaf last night?"

"Yeah," I reply feebly.

"You've gotta kill that little devil chirping in your ear or you'll be heading down that decadent path of destruction that we talked about. Just remember that the little things add up over the long haul — small leaks sink the ship. Let me elaborate:" he clears his throat like he's about to deliver a speech. "Ladies and gentlemen of the jury, allow me to demonstrate what happens if one indulges in pancakes and syrup, sausage and swine compounded over time: Please examine exhibit A:" he lifts my shirt, exposing my fat belly. "Cholesterol rising, artery-clogging, obesity epidemics that are plaguing our country and most of the industrialized nations. What we have here, ladies and gentlemen is a direct path to some of the top killers in the US of A today: heart disease, over-acidification, cardiac arrest and a plethora of other symptomologies. What we really have here is a walking heart attack. If we don't do the little things now, they soon become the big things and the next thing you know, you're fucking dead."

His passionate words feel like a stake in my heart in front of a judge and jury that don't even exist. He lets go of my shirt and continues his performance:

"However, ladies and gentlemen, if we incorporate fresh vegetables, sprouts and low sugar fruits and other alkalinizing food and beverages into our lifestyle then we can reap rewards like this," he lifts up his shirt to reveal a very impressive abdomen, especially for someone of fifty-one. "Case closed."

"Very nice, JJ." I bow down to his greatness.

"Seriously though, we hear stories all the time where someone looks perfectly okay on the outside and—BAM—they drop dead on a tennis court at forty-six. It's all because they made poor health choices every day like eating a hearty breakfast or grabbing a quick-fix at McDonald's, which, if done consistently over time will result in arteriosclerosis, heart attacks, strokes, clogged colon and many, many more preventable diseases. That's why I take this so seriously because negligence can take your fucking life!"

Damn, he's good. I can't argue with that and tell him I'm willing to give this a shot.

"Whoa whoa, Bobby, *'willing to give it a shot?'* That shit ain't gonna fly around here, buster. That's pussy talk and won't get you anywhere! This is not some silly little dilly-dally program. This is self-mastery! This is total immersion! This is about improving every aspect about you, especially what you put in your body. You see, I invented this motherfucker JJ that you see before you. I had to construct him from the ground up after I hit rock bottom and totally changed everything in my life that wasn't serving me. It's imperative that you take absolute care of yourself or you won't have the energy to create a legacy."

Shit, that was powerful. I feel like I've been hit with a haymaker because he's a hundred percent correct. I'm never gonna achieve anything major if I continue the way I've been going.

"If you start your day by stuffing your gullet with nasty-ass Red Velvet Pop-Tarts then you're fighting an uphill battle from the jump. I've had such a big advantage over basically all the people I've worked with in the last ten years because I avoid foods that enervate me. Instead, I choose foods that give me the best return in energy and zest. Since I made that switch I've been like the Energizer Bunny, and combine that with my passion, my drive, my mentality, I feel fucking unstoppable! That's how I accumulated all my wealth."

"It is?"

"I thought that would get your attention. Every time you're about to eat, simply ask yourself this question: Is this going to give me enervation or energization?"

He spits words with more passion and assertiveness than a damn self-help guru. I wonder though, is he just making words up?

"Bobby pay attention! You're drifting off. You need to take this in."

I snap out of my head and look lively as he continues:

"I've only been able to out-work people because I have the energy to burn the midnight oil from eating the highest quality foods. Most people become exhausted by the early afternoon and can't focus until they have their next Starbucks or Marlboro. It's pathetic. It just comes from ignorance and a sheep-like mentality. You know some people actually wake up tired, even after eight or nine hours of freaking sleep! Can you believe that? How embarrassing?"

"I can relate." I humbly respond.

"So none of this candy ass *I'm willing to give it a shot'* shit. This is total fucking immersion!" He slams his fist on the table. "You need to learn a little psychology 101."

I sit at the breakfast bar while he grabs a pair of large mugs with Luke and Butch from the Bushwhackers on the side before returning to the pan.

"Your brain might tell you ahead of time that drinking spinach soup is gross because you're not used to it and if my memory serves me correctly, you and vegetables are mortal enemies, right?"

"Hundred percent," I nod.

He comes close and sits down with me.

"Okay, here's what I want you to do: close your eyes and think of your favorite food like a Big Mac or Mac 'N Cheese or whatever. Have you got it?"

"Let's go with something sweet like a chocolate gateau."

"Perfect. Now tell me, Bobby, where is the picture of the gateau in your minds-eye? Is it close or far away?"

"It's close."

"Is it in color or black and white?"

"Color."

"Is it in the top, middle or bottom of your minds-eye?"

"The middle."

"Is it to the left, the right or the middle?"

"Slightly left."

"Okay. Is it focused or unfocused? Clear or fuzzy?"

"It's very clear and focused."

"Okay great. Now open your eyes a second, Bobby and look over at the pan of soup. When you taste it do you think you'll love it or hate it?"

"Honestly I don't think I'll like it. The smell, for one thing is vile."

"I thought you'd say that," he says. "This is what we need to change. Close your eyes again."

I follow suit.

"Picture the soup in your minds-eye again and tell me, is it close or far away?"

"It's far."

"How far?"

"Like ten feet."

"Is it in color or black and white?"

"Black and white."

"Is it clear or fuzzy?"

"It's fuzzy, not clear at all."

"Is it in the top, middle or bottom?"

"The bottom."

"Is it to the left, right or central?"

"It's far to the right."

"Okay. Now keeping your eyes closed have you realized that they are basically all opposite to the gateau?"

"Yes."

"So all we need to do is match them right now. Now go back to the black and white picture of the soup."

"Okay I'm there," I say picturing it.

"Add color to the picture and make the green soup your favorite shade of green."

"Okay. I did that."

"Bring the picture of the soup exactly where the gateau is, meaning in the middle and slightly to the left."

"Okay. Done."

"Make the picture clear, focused and sexy."

"Alright, did that."

"And also make the smell of the soup the most attractive smell possible and take a big whiff right now."

I inhale deeply expanding my lungs while thinking of the divine smell of barbecued chicken.

"And allow these changes to lock in your subconscious mind now."

Something strange goes on in my brain, at least I think.

"So, Bobby, how do you feel about having some soup?"

"It's really weird. I actually feel good about it."

"Smell the soup aroma once again and make it smell so pleasant and desirable that you can't wait to drink it."

"It's funny, it doesn't smell bad at all now."

I open my eyes to a smiling JJ.

"Pretty cool, huh? All we did in a matter of minutes is elicit two things: one thing you like, and one thing you don't like, and we simply matched the thing you don't like to the positions and colors of what you do like."

I tell him I'm very impressed as he decants the soup into the Bushwhacker mugs.

"Where on Earth did you learn that?"

"It's a fascinating offshoot of psychology called Neuro-Linguistic Programming developed by a couple of geniuses from California."

We each grab a mug and toast to health, wealth and prosperity.

"Oh my God, this soup is delicious! What did you do to my brain?"

"Just a little NLP, I told you you'd love it."

"You're a smart MoFo, JJ. Does everyone in the future know this new NLP stuff?"

He sips more soup and chuckles. "NLP has been around since the 1970s. Even today it's still kind of an underground movement. I've studied a bunch of different forms of psychology, and NLP is still right up there with the best."

"Ahhh, so that's how you've become mega-rich. You play with people's minds."

"No-no, you're way off. I study it because psychology and behaviorism are fascinating subjects to me."

"Well, I'm not gonna stop bugging you. Come on, man, spill the beans: how did you get so rich?"

"I told you last night I'll tell you when the time is right. Will you shaddup and enjoy your soup."

"Fair enough. I'll just sneak through the house looking for clues when you're not around."

"Very funny."

"So why are we drinking the soup out of a mug and not from a bowl with bread?"

"Bread is just yeasty sludge which festers in your gut providing little or no energy. I avoid starchy crap most of the time. When soup is blended into a liquid it takes zero toll on your digestive system, unlike the Standard American Diet or *SAD* as I like to call it. We must avoid foods that take away more energy than they provide."

He certainly knows his stuff. Maybe the future me is a motivational guru for Weight Watchers or something.

"Anyway, enough talk, it's time for conditioning." He stands up. "Come on, let's go."

"Go where?"

"We're going to slay the beast inside you."

"Okay? But where are we going?"

"You wouldn't want to ruin the element of surprise now, would you? Come on, chop-chop."

CHAPTER 39

JJ takes the wheel of his slick, diamond-shaped Mercedes, I can't even describe all the state-of-the-art gidgets and gadgets inside, too overwhelming. Instead, my eyes dart to the beautiful neighborhood of Montclair. Big, colorful houses with souped-up sports cars are all the eye can see within this gated community. Haven't got a clue where he's taking me and I don't care as I'm thoroughly enjoying the cruise.

I can't believe I'm actually gonna live like this, I'm so pumped. I must follow his teachings and heed every single thing that comes out his mouth and try not to second-guess or question him—after all, that would be second-guessing myself. He is my Bobby 'The Brain.'

We swing by a couple of stores to pick up some necessities and so I can change from my tired suit into a more comfortable outfit: Puma sweats, dark glasses and a baseball cap before hitting the country roads to the middle of bumfuck nowhere. All of this to decrease the odds of somebody noticing our similarities. He keeps telling me if a cop or fed agent found out we are the same person with the exact same fingerprints, they'd take us both away.

Luckily we don't look at all alike considering the circumstances. To start with, we calculate that I'm a hundred and seventy-nine pounds heavier than he, which is over double his mass, as he's at an impressive one-six-five. Our hair is totally different as well; he's got that Big Daddy Cool '95 look going on, while I look more like a modern-day Brutus 'The Barber' Beefcake. Our voices though are pretty similar, so he decides we will play the role of cousins when we interact amongst others. I choose Randy as my alias as it's a cool sounding name, plus I'm a huge fan of the legendary Macho Man from the golden era of wrestling.

I soon find out his love and passion for wrestling from yesteryear is as strong at fifty-one as mine at forty-one. I knew I'd never grow up. He informs me, however, that the WWE has gone massively downhill ever since Vince McMahon—

"And here we are," says JJ, pulling up outside a factory in the middle of a farm.

I snap out of my wrestling shit and think what the fuck are we doing here. Something is rotten in Rotterdam.

Wait-a-sec... it's not a factory at all. It's a fucking slaughterhouse!

"Slaughterhouse?" I snap. "Please don't tell me we're going to a slaughterhouse?"

"No, *you're* going to a slaughterhouse."

"But why?"

"You know why, Bobby."

"Errr, no I don't."

"We're going to look at the whole picture and take a journey into the animal kingdom — from eating grass in a meadow to becoming a Texas BBQ, from clucking in the barn to deep-fried buffalo wings, and we're going to examine 'the protein myth' so you become very conscious of eating dead animal flesh." He pauses and waves his right index in my face. "You've been digging your own grave with your teeth and you'll have a cardiac arrest if you don't control your addiction to meat."

"Meat?"

"Yes, meat and all the other bullshit you shovel into your gullet. Yeah, that's right, I remember how sick I used to be. You have no idea how bad the accumulation of meat is to your body."

I fight back, pleading my case saying eating lean meat is good for you.

"Come on, Bobby, it's time to wake up! Where the fuck do you think those stomach ulcers came from? I've been observing you grimacing. You still have an ulcer, don't you?"

"Yeah," I say rubbing my belly. "It's killing me because I haven't taken my pills for nearly two days now. Shit, we should have picked some up at the store."

"Well, instead of popping those tablets that society sold you on, I know with one hundred percent certainty the cause of your ulcers."

"So do I, it's my stress."

"Well, stress is a contributing factor, but it's the damn meat that's been playing hell with your insides."

I find that pretty difficult to believe and again put up a fight.

"I'm dead certain on this. The dead pig, the dead cow, the dead birds just sit there decomposing in your gut. Jimmy Dean is not your fucking friend, Bobby."

With a mournful look on my face, I ask him if he's trying to make me cry with all this shit.

"I'm trying to get you to walk a new path. We have all been told a big lie; human beings are not primarily designed to eat meat, our teeth and digestive tract are similar to the frugivores of the world. And the molecules inside our blood match the chlorophyll of plants."

"Chloro what?"

"Chlorophyll is like the blood of the plant and it's perfectly compatible with your digestive tract. How many times do you hear people having stomach upsets or ulcers from eating vibrant fresh vegetables? It just doesn't happen. And think about this: there's never been a case in medical history throughout the world where a pathologist has cut open a corpse and said '*look what caused this person to have clogged arteries, diabetes or a heart attack — it was those damn vegetables that got him! It wasn't all those Whoppers and fries, and steaks and shakes, it was the damn broccoli and tofu that ruined his health!*'"

I snicker and obviously get the point as he continues his rap:

"You haven't been educated properly about what's correct to put inside you. That's why after going from doctor to doctor about my stomach problems it was David of all people who schooled me to the truth. I stopped eating meat and eliminated other poisons like dairy, sugar and a few other things, and within forty days no more ulcers, no more upset stomach pangs and no more pills!"

"Really?"

"Yes fucking really. You think I'm lying to you?"

"No. I just still can't believe *meat* was the cause."

"It was the biggest cause, and I can say that with absolute certainty, so you better take this shit seriously! You're a walking heart attack weighing nearly three-fifty, you have to get serious and make health your number one value in life.

"Just think of the process of how to make sausages for instance: the pig is bred or *imprisoned* in horrendous environments. He rolls around in his own feces, injected with growth hormones, and gets fattened up with poor quality food including dead animals from roadkill. Then he gets strung upside down and savagely brutalized, his insides get ripped out, chopped up, stuffed in plastic and sent to the supermarket where they advertise pork as '*lean meat / high protein / low fat*' so the consumer thinks swine is good for them. It's time to stop being so fucking naïve to these marketing tactics and wake the fuck up!"

This is not what I want to hear and he picks up on it.

"Look, Bobby, we both know how much you love cold cuts, street meat and dirty water dogs, but once you become educated how the foul fowl is killed and how they treat the animals you'll develop new beliefs, so think of this as liberation, not deprivation."

"This is too extreme and over-the-top," I protest. "Eating meat can't be that bad for you. Don't you miss it at all?"

"Nope. When I switched my diet ten years ago, my energy levels went through the roof because meat fatigues humans as it takes forever to digest. When you see with your own two eyes undigested steaks bigger than blocks of cheese come out of you after a colonic hydrotherapy treatment, you'll say *'fuck putting this shit in my body!'*"

I take a deep sigh. Puns aside, this is not easy for me to digest. But I have no choice but to go along no matter how overzealous I think it is.

"I'm telling you, man, once you feel this good you'll never go back. This isn't a sad day, it's enlightenment!"

"Enlightenment?"

"Precisely. Now let's go get enlightened!"

CHAPTER 40

It turns out JJ had previously arranged a tour for me around this slaughterhouse. What a setup! And this motherfucker knows the staff on a first-name basis so I get the impression this is not his first rodeo.

We walk through the dull, narrow corridors hearing nothing but loud machinery coming from the far end. The staff milling around look like they have ice water in their veins, they're just stone cold and somber, with about as much emotion as a Milk Dud. They remind me of the staff at funeral homes; bleakness and gloom radiating out of them like an awful stench. I guess in both cases, being surrounded by death and dead bodies have that effect on some people. I seriously want to get out of here as the feeling of nausea in the pit of my stomach is making this whole situation unbearable.

One thing I've always hated is animal cruelty. If I saw someone abusing a cat or a dog I'd get in their face and chew them out. I once stepped in when I witnessed some asshole kick his dog in the middle of the street, so I intervened and we started duking it out like 'Rowdy' Roddy Piper and Greg Valentine. I managed to deck the guy but then his fucking dog came at me protecting his master. Oh, the irony. I guess I never saw eating meat as an act of cruelty. Now we're getting closer I'm completely freaked, I might puke before we get in there just from the putrid smell.

We arrive outside what appears to be the main room, the chubby supervisor who acts as our tour guide leads the way. His name ironically is Bob:

"Here we are, boys; The Killing Room," says fat Bob, adjusting his tie.

"Bob, why don't you walk us through what goes on behind those doors," instructs JJ.

"Alrighty. This is the stage where the cows enter from the outside and form a line on the moving belt. They get motioned forward until the machine flips them upside down and leads them towards the serrated blade."

"And what does the serrated blade do?" asks JJ.

"It severs their neck," Bob says expressionlessly.

"It severs their neck…" repeats JJ letting it hang. "Is that the moment when you hear the cow screaming for her life?"

He's definitely trying to add drama to this situation, Hollywood motherfucker.

"Yup," Bob says with that deadpan voice of his. "but she soon goes real quiet."

"Is that because her insides have been savagely gutted out and she bleeds to death?"

"Basically, yup."

"Are you listening to this, Randy?" JJ says turning to me.

Unfortunately, I am but don't want to respond.

"Bob, can we get Randy up, close and personal to this process, so he can really take it in?"

"Sure. Follow me."

"Wait a minute" I turn to JJ. "You're not coming with us?"

"Hell no! I did it years ago and the images are still deeply ingrained in my psyche. It's all for you."

"Oh, God."

"Why do you think you're here? It's abysmally disturbing to watch a helpless animal strung upside down, fighting for her life and squealing in terror before a big machine lacerates her in such a gruesome and violent fashion. You will never be the same after you watch how inhumane it is to make the product we call beef. This is the quickest, most powerful way you're going to change. It will be an experience you'll never forget."

The mental images I concoct actually make me upchuck a little but I can't throw up in the presence of others, so I hold it in. It's obvious to them how frightened I must look as I'm doing a poor job trying to conceal it.

"You should be scared," continues JJ, "and the next time you get the urge to tuck into some deep-fried chitterlings you'll be spoiled by these images for the rest of your life!" He turns to Bob. "Bob the clock is ticking, take Randy into *The Killing Room* and give him the twenty-minute show; no pauses, no intermissions, no ear protection and no turning away—"

"No ear protection?" I interrupt. "It's loud as hell in there."

"Fuck ear protection! You need to hear the cows scream and witness this barbaric ordeal over and over for it to become ingrained in your nervous system. By turning away or blocking out the sounds you're not going to be as deeply affected."

My fight or flight instincts kick-in, sending my pulse and blood pressure through the roof so I take deep diaphragmatic yoga breaths in an effort to calm myself down. JJ picks up on this and softens his tone a little as he tells me Bob will be with me the whole time and he'll be right outside observing through the window.

I look back at my future self, unable to speak for a minute. I merely nod and look off to the distance wishing I was in a happy place, and can't resist calling him a diabolical madman.

"I'm more of a diabolical genius to be precise. Bob knows all the people I've brought here over the years, and I can proudly say not one person has ever eaten meat since. We can't argue with results, now can we?"

"No, sir," Bob replies as he turns to me. "Come on, son, let's get this over with. It's nearly lunchtime."

Bob leads me through the double doors (which is actually labeled *The Killing Room*) while the loud machine noises is enough to make my eardrums explode. But the sound is not the worst thing; it's the feeling in my gut. I get an immediate sense of torture, mutilation and horror all wrapped up together like an evil plague—creating a heightened state of awareness. I'm waiting for Bob to say something like: *'Welcome to the House of Pain.'*

He gets me into position so I have a front-row view to witness the slaughtering of helpless cattle.

"Okay, son," he shouts over the machinery, "he wants you to stand here and just take it all in."

I nod solemnly and observe the surroundings. There's a long conveyor belt in the shape of an S coming from a square hatch on the far side. I can only assume this is where the cows enter before their life comes to a gruesome end.

Bob clearly notices the devastation plastered on my face and pats my back to console me. "It will all be over soon, son. The sooner we start, the sooner y'all can go home." He pats again and gives the thumbs up to his staff.

I grimly stare at the plastic blinds where the hatch is and upchuck in my mouth again. It reminds me of baggage claim at the airport oddly enough. The anticipation is killing me, death is definitely in the air.

"Can I ask you a question, Bob?"

"Shoot."

"Do you eat meat?"

"Sure, I love this shit."

"Oh, yeah?"

"You won't find too many vegetarians working in a slaughterhouse, kid," he snickers. "Let's get this show on the road, I'm getting hungry."

I mini puke again but conceal it and swallow it down. I can't go through with this and just want to run away.

I attempt to talk, trying to muster some words—any words to comfort myself while Bob is in the exact same state. Guess it's just another day at the office for him.

"In about thirty seconds the cows will enter through the blinds on the belt one by one... Hey," he smiles, "that sounds a little like that old nursery rhyme, don't it? '*The animals came in one by one, hoorah, hoorah! The animals came in one by one, HOORAH, HOORAH!*'"

I can't believe this sick fucker is singing nursery rhymes in a situation like this. What a fucking schizo!

A loud buzzer goes off.

Oh, God! I can't take this. I really want to run the fuck away. I'm finding it very hard to keep still in the same spot so I fidget around like I have ants in my pants, dreading the inevitable.

The first cow enters through the plastic blinds, being moved at a slow pace on the conveyor belt. She is locked in by a large metal railing to keep her from moving around before she reaches the ascending ramp.

"See the ramp, Randy?"

"A-huh."

"We call that *The Stairway to Heaven*..." He crudely starts laughing then continues humming that fucking nursery rhyme. I'm so tempted to punch this motherfucker out. This is not a time to be joking around!

I watch the poor, defenseless animal look around with panic and trepidation as she ascends the ramp. She is absolutely petrified and wriggles around to try and break free but to no avail. I feel so sorry for her, trapped and helpless in her very last moments on Earth. The machine that's hooked to her legs flips her upside down where she squeals for her very life right in front of my eyes. The squealing sound is absolutely horrific as she wriggles and swings again but nothing at all will free her.

"Oh, God!"

The big serrated knife attached from the machine severs her throat quickly which makes me turn away. Bob forces my head back, making me see the blood gushing from her jugular. This is so fucking appalling!

"No turning away, that's the deal," he says breaking his humming.

This is fucking intense!

The squealing stops but the silence is deafening. Her life has been ripped out of her. In a matter of moments, she's transformed into a bloody corpse. I look down at my knees shaking until he reminds me again to resume watching. As the loose skin of the bloody, dead carcass dangles along the belt the next cow enters.

I witness the second cow go through the same horrific process; trapped, helpless and squealing as she's flipped upside down before the big knife slits her tender throat. Blood is everywhere and this sick fucker is still humming that fucking nursery rhyme! This is a million times worse than any horror movie I've ever seen because that's all fiction and fantasy. This is reality that's live in front of my face. My future self is crazy for making me do this. I'm not too sure how much of this I can take and I've only witnessed two slaughters.

"The next one should be here by now," he looks at his watch. "I don't know what the holdup is."

I stare at the plastic blinds praying there's no more, like they've run out of cow. But I know this is wishful thinking, there's always more cow. I just need a feeling of hope to get me through this savage ordeal.

The loud buzzer goes off again.

Oh God, here she comes.

The third cow comes down the narrow conveyor belt, screaming and wriggling for her life as the giant knife slits her throat spraying blood everywhere. This is getting too much. I resist turning away and watch more terror as instructed. I'm not much of a crier but I can't hold the tears now, this is just exorbitantly gruesome being this close to a live killing zone.

I'm continually forced to watch five more murders and it does not get any easier in the slightest. It was the longest twenty minutes of my life but it's over now so I wipe away my tears and pull myself together the best I can. I certainly get the point my sick future self is trying to make. If I even think of eating a quarter pounder with cheese I'd throw up at the sheer notion.

I'm still in tears as Bob leads me out to JJ who asks how it went. What a stupid fucking question.

"It was fucking devastating," I wipe my face again.

"I'm sure it was. And like I told you earlier; what eating meat does for your insides and digestive tract is so horrendous as well. So when somebody starts waffling on about *'lean meat this'*, and *'high protein that'* you now know all the myths and truths about eating dead animal flesh. It's fucking insane, isn't it?"

I wholeheartedly agree by nodding while avoiding eye contact.

"Come on, Randy, let's get out of this wretched, Pinacoteca of death. No offense, Bob."

"None taken," Bob shrugs.

"Bob, we're all done here, thanks for the tour," JJ says shaking his hand. "We're gonna head back into the city."

"You should check out the new Rib Shack off Robinson, we supply their meat."

Bob grins all goofy like. JJ and I do not.

"Real funny, Bob. Here's a little something so you can buy your wife a real pretty dress." JJ hands Bob a couple of bills of high denomination.

"Shit, I wouldn't buy that corn fed mule a damn TV dinner. But one thing I do know—I'm gonna get tanked tonight!"

CHAPTER 41

An eerie silence envelops JJ's fancy car as we flee the dirt roads and head towards the city. We're now going to pick up some health supplements for my stomach and wheatgrass powder that *'I now must incorporate into my diet.'*

I stare out the window in a deep trance as those nauseating images keep playing over and over in my mind, making me queasy. That inhumane experience has been branded in my brain without a doubt.

"Look, man," says JJ breaking the lumbering silence, "all I did was expose you to the truth. By avoiding meat, your ulcers, abdominal pains and digestive disorders will all vanish in due time because we've now dealt with the *cause*. I'm telling you, the upside versus the downside ain't even in the same league, that's why I had to put you through that grisly ordeal. You have to admit it was effective."

"Yeah. Effective, horrifying, detrimental and a million other disturbing elements that will haunt me for the rest of my days."

"I'm glad because the best way to train our nervous system is through intense neuro-associative experiences."

"What was that?"

"It's just a fancy expression for training your nervous system through powerful associations. I'll get into the real science of it another time."

I don't respond, I merely gaze out the window at the trees and wildlife, still shell-shocked from the blood splattering.

We pull up outside a little strip of retail outlets and eateries on Riperton BLVD but the parking situation is difficult so we try around back and manage to find a spot near an adjacent alley. As we step out I notice a little cockroach crawling into my path along the loose cement.

"Ugh, I hate these damn things!" and without hesitation, I squish it with my shoe.

"What the fuck is wrong with you!" snaps JJ.

"What?"

He's super pissed. His eyes have turned blood red and demands to know why I did that.

"I hate all bugs. They're gross."

My innocent defense does not go down well as he proceeds to chew me out for about six straight minutes (I kid you not), making me feel about as small as the damn cockroach I just squashed. He tells me he's disgusted by my actions and goes on and on about karma and living righteously and treating all things with love, respect and compassion.

This whole thing has caught me completely off guard, I don't get what all the fuss is about. "What's the big deal? Why are you so vexed over this?"

"You senselessly murdered one of the universe's divine creatures all because you think they are gross! Did you not just learn anything about the killing of innocent animals?"

He gets all up in my face, spitting words like The Iron Sheik. I'm kinda scared.

"I seriously can't believe you did that!"

"It's just a bug, bro." I defend. "It ain't that deep."

"It *is* that deep, asshole! I'm embarrassed that I used to be like that. You've just reminded me of what a filthy rotten scoundrel I once was."

I put my defense up once again telling him it's just intuition.

"You need to kill that erroneous belief right now, mister! We're all equal on this planet. You have no right to take the life of any creature that poses no threat to you! Every being on this Earth has a purpose or it wouldn't be here, got it?"

"I guess so."

"You guess so?"

"I got it-I got it. Can we move on please?"

He blows me off, still visibly upset as we cut through the alley as a shortcut to the health store. Waiting strategically at the top is a bum in raggedy clothes, scraggly hair, rubbery skin and an unkempt beard that could double as a bird's nest. He's a dead ringer for Nick Nolte from that infamous mug shot in the early millennium. The smell of BO and St. Ides gets stronger and stronger as we have no choice but to cross his path to get to our destination.

"Excuse me, gentlemen," he initiates, "by any chance could you help out a poor old man get something to eat?"

"Listen up, buster," I hurl, "we ain't falling for that old—"

"I got this," says JJ, taking over. "That's no way to talk to such a pleasant peasant." He turns to the bum and asks him his name.

"Koko."

"Greetings, Koko, I am JJ, this is Randy. How long have you been in the streets, my friend?"

"Years."

"How many years?"

"I don't know, 'bout sixteen, seventeen."

"How old are you?"

"Fifty-nine."

"Hmmm. Fifty-nine years young and you've been in the streets for about seventeen years. That's a long time, isn't it? Let me ask you a very important question—perhaps the most important question you'll ever be asked," JJ clears his throat. "Have you found an opportunity or business plan, or put together any kind of financial projections that if you implemented with diligence and persistence it could take care of you and your family for the rest of your days?"

"Huh?" is all Koko can respond. He looks gone-out. I don't blame him, that shit went over my head too.

"Let me restate. Have you found a financial opportunity that if you put your whole self into it, it would take care of you and your family for the rest of your life?"

"I ain't got no family, they abandoned me."

"I'm sorry to hear that, Koko. Now let me ask perhaps the second most important question you might ever be asked: Are you taking an allocated amount of time each day to look for such an opportunity that could set you free of this way of life?"

I can tell my future self's bizarre style of questioning has gone straight over the bum once again. Koko simply shakes his head.

"Hmmm, interesting. Two of the most important questions that you might ever be asked and you answered no to both of them." JJ turns to me. "That's quite extraordinary isn't it, Randy?"

I too am puzzled, but don't show it on my face. I just go along with him.

"What you're doing is backward, instead of begging for change from others you should be begging yourself to change your life. Are you not tired of begging people for money after seventeen years?"

"But this is all I know."

"Don't you realize your business strategy is never going to work?"

Koko questions what he means by *business strategy*.

"Yes, begging for change in the streets is your current business strategy, is it not? And here's why I believe it's flawed: you're begging to get food, right?"

"Yeah," Koko nods in an unconvincing manner.

"I'm sure some of the time you do buy food. But be honest, most of the time when you get money off people you go buy beer, don't you? I can smell it on your breath. And judging from your yellow-stained fingers you smoke cigarettes too, don't you?"

"A-huh," Koko replies in a kind of shameful tone.

JJ then asks why would a man of so little means do such a thing if money is so scarce.

"I like beer," shrugs Koko.

"So your current business strategy is to beg for money in the streets to scrape enough together to smoke and drink for free, then wake up the next day and repeat the cycle all over again? Do you see how flawed and depleting that is, Koko?"

It looks like JJ's philosophical tirade is having an effect; I see it in the bum's face.

"I'm going to ask you again: are you sick of living this lifestyle?"

"Yeah, but what else am I supposed to do?"

JJ smiles and tells him today's his lucky day because he's in the presence of greatness, which startles the raggedy bum. "I'm not saying that to be a swell guy, and I'm not saying that because we're better or above you, I'm just conveying a fact. And I think you too can become great if you apply some simple principles. Do you believe in destiny, Koko?"

Koko shrugs, looking gone-out again.

"Well, I do. And I know without a shadow of a doubt I can help you."

He stares back at JJ and asks him how.

"We'll get to that in a minute, I just need to know with a hundred percent certainty are you ready for a change?"

"Yeah," he says incongruently.

"You don't sound very convincing, Koko."

"But I don't know how you're going to help me."

"What if I was to tell you we run a rehabilitation program that helps homeless people get back into society. Would that interest you?"

"Yeah..." he nods, looking somewhat convinced.

"And what if I was to tell you I'll go out on a limb and personally sponsor you so you too can completely turn your life around. Would that interest you?"

"Most definitely, sir!"

"Just take a moment and imagine your life completely changing because you finally had enough of this horrendous way of living. Do it right now and imagine your old life back. Does that excite you when you picture it?"

"Absolutely."

"You're not just saying that?"

"No, sir."

"See, I was once down and nearly out, maybe not on your level but I was a broken man at the lowest of the low, so I know you can turn it around if you demand yourself to change and never look back."

Koko looks up with a glimmer in his eyes and admits that he needs help to escape from this way of life.

"Okay, two things right off the bat: first, no more begging for beer or cigarettes. Those things are a great waste of health, wealth and time; three important commodities that you so desperately need. You use that money that you would have spent on beer and smokes and buy some clean clothes. Go to the thrift store if that's all you can afford. And bathe yourself regularly with soap and water, it's fundamental."

I observe this bum take in what JJ said about general hygiene and see the wheels turning in his head like he's had a revelation — this is fascinating.

"Then comes education," JJ continues. "I want you to find a library and read three amazing books. Two are classics from a long time ago: *Think and Grow Rich* by Napoleon Hill. This book will blow you away, and you must follow all the exercises down to the latter. Then *Unlimited Power* by Anthony Robbins which is an absolute must-read for everyone. It will get you so pumped you won't be able to contain your passion for life. And lastly a newer book: *Fresh Flowers* by WJT which will leave you mesmerized, that's all I'm going to say. These three books will completely change your outlook on life and you'll start to believe in yourself again. How do you feel about reading three books that will absolutely change your life if you put in the work and apply the principles?"

"I used to love reading back in the day. Haven't read a book in years."

"Then today is the day you get back in the game. Knowledge, plus action equals power. A good book is like a treasure, if you want to discover where the gold is then you have to put in the time to search." JJ pulls out a business card and starts writing on the back. "So that's all you have to do to get started: no beer, no smoking, get some clean clothes, bathe regularly and read three books. Can you handle that?"

"Okay. But then what?"

"Then you give me a call." JJ goes to hand him the card but does a takeaway. "You call me on this number and I'm going to diligently quiz you on those books. If you pass my test over the phone, I will give you the address to my foundation and personally sponsor you for enrollment. But, and it's a big *but*, Koko, if I meet you again and you are unwashed, unkempt and stinking of beer and cigarettes, then I will turn my back on you because you didn't heed what I told you and you only get one chance, just like in life. Does this sound fair or are you just wasting our precious time?"

"No, sir. I'll do it, I promise!"

JJ seems satisfied and tells him to take copious notes because he will be quizzed and hands him the card for real this time. "The quicker you clean up, the quicker you'll regain your life, so clean yourself up *today*, go to the thrift store *today* and start studying one of those books *TODAY*. Got it?"

"Yes, sir!" says the bum staring at the business card.

"It was a pleasure being in your presence, Koko. Maybe the universe brought us together at this exact time as a form of divine intervention, who knows? Randy and I need to be moving along now. *May The Force Be With You.*"

We start walking away.

"Thank you, sir. I won't let you down."

JJ stops and turns around.

"It's not about letting *me* down, it's about letting *YOU* down. You've been letting yourself down for seventeen years, so it's time for a change NOW! You have to be dead fucking serious if you want your life to take a complete one-eighty. So I'm gonna ask you one more time: are you dead fucking serious about this?"

"Yes."

"Make a pledge then. Say: *'I am done with this way of life!'*"

"I am done with this way of life!" Koko repeats.

"Come on, man, I'm not convinced. Say it louder and demand that you must change!"

"I am done with this way of life! I must change!"

"One more time, Koko, let it out with even more passion!"

"I'M FED UP OF THIS BULLSHIT!! I MUST CHANGE NOW!!"

Koko is vibrating. He looks like he just left a religious tabernacle in Arkansas. Maybe his devils got exorcised?

JJ and I turn to each other and nod in unison.

"That's more like it, Koko, you just passed the real congruency test. Now you're truly ready for change. Sometimes we need to be little effervescent to relight our fires."

"I feel pretty good," Koko smiles.

"Of course you do. When you live in perfect harmony with your goals and ambitions, life becomes so beautiful. Imagine if you fired yourself up like this every day. Imagine if you lived with so much passion you could barely contain yourself. Imagine if every day you wrenched the neck of life and squeezed out every last fucking drop!" JJ's intensity has risen to Brian Pillman like levels, looking almost creepy and sadistic as he grills Koko chin to chin. "Your life would be legendary, would it not?"

"You're right!" Koko says taking a step back to breathe a little. "I can't settle for living like this ever again! I'm gonna do it, you watch, sir. I'm done with this street life!"

His state has gone from doom and gloom to excitement and hope in under five minutes. What the hell have I just witnessed?

"There you go, Koko, now go prove it to yourself. Your new life starts now. Go!"

Koko darts away like a man on a mission.

"*Wrench the neck of life and squeeze out every last drop,*" I quote to my crazy other self as we resume walking. "You got that from—"

"David. Absolutely. It's the best thing he ever taught me. When you live in a driven, purposeful state, you become unstoppable. I cannot live any other way and soon you won't either."

"Well, you definitely got through to that guy."

"I got amped at the end there because I know he can change his ways. We have to be direct, passionate and sometimes aggressive when you're dealing with transformation, there's no time for namby-pamby bullshit. Time will tell if he's really serious about changing his life. Action is the ultimate measuring stick. And that goes for you too: I can school you with life-changing strategies and health principles but if you're not driven to put the work in then you'll go back to the old ways because it's easy and convenient."

I take on board his wise words as we turn the corner and arrive at the health store.

CHAPTER 42

The store was a quick grab and go deal—in and out like a robbery, then JJ arranged a training session with his PT at a local park in Montclair. Of course, this is with no prior warning or heads-up—he likes to keep me on my toes I guess. And after being influenced to take holistic remedies (including that dark green swamp juice that David used to drink), my stomach pangs minimized greatly. The juice tastes like cold green tea so it isn't so bad. He informed me this stuff will change me from the inside out, which is probably true because I kept running to the bathroom every twenty minutes.

I get dropped off in the midst of Hathaway Park amongst the upper echelons of the community; over here it's nothing but convertible Jags and elephant cars (the two-seater sports cars with the trunk in the front). The trainer dude, Tommy, is a beast — a 5'6" blonde stud that has quad muscles like tree trunks and shoulders that look as if they've been molded from clay. He could pass for a Venice Beach poster boy and has the most immaculate pearly whites I've ever seen.

"So, Randy," he says as we arrive at the footpath surrounding the lake, "we're going to start with a nice power-walk around the park to get the blood pumping before we flex the guns," he smiles boastfully, flashing those flawless teeth that seem to glisten in the sunshine.

"Coolio," I say as we begin the march.

"I'm going to be very direct with you — you're struggling with control. But the good news is it's not complicated, so let's start with the number one rule you'll ever need to know to lose weight, and it's so simple you would think it's a joke."

"I'm all ears, brother."

"If you think about it, it's just common sense and having some patience because weight loss or gaining muscle is never an overnight thing. I once worked with a lady from Long Island that weighed herself three times a day and it would drive her crazy when the scales wouldn't move. That, my friend, is not being intelligent."

I smirk, thinking even I know that is moronic.

"We all get the body we deserve. How to get yourself in optimal condition is to simply burn more calories than you consume every single day and you will eventually reach your ideal weight. It's easy if you consistently eat the right foods and stay active, it's a lot harder if you eat the wrong foods and don't move around much. That's all you have to remember. Period. End of story."

"But if I do that all the time aren't I just depriving myself of my favorite treats like Laffy Taffy and Dominos Pizza?"

"Dominos?" he laughs. "What year are you living in? They went out of business years ago, dude."

"Get the fuck out of here? Dominos? That's impossible."

"It's been years, bro. You didn't notice?"

Of course, I'm completely shocked by this. He informs me they got permanently shut down for serving pigeon meat in their pies and claiming it was ostrich.

"Gross!" I say, disheartened from the news. "So how do you do it, Tommy? What's your secret to avoiding bad foods and staying motivated to exercise?"

"There are no *secrets*, just drive and hard work. I had to earn this."

"You definitely look like you put in the work. I'm in complete envy of your physique, you're built like Lex Luger in his prime."

He thanks me for the compliment and flashes that million-dollar smile again — he's an orthodontist's dream, this guy. "There's no such thing as 'instant weight-loss' despite what those imbeciles on late-night TV tell you about some magic bullet or pill. They're just trying to sell you a fad."

"You have no idea how many times I've fallen for that shit," I say, sipping more swamp juice, getting somewhat accustomed to it. "And when it didn't work I'd just give up and become frustrated."

"Hey, we've all been there. You won't need to pay attention to that crap anymore. JJ's gonna give you a few books that will build a good foundational philosophy. Books like *The pH Miracle* by Robert Young, and *I Like It Raw* by Robert Diggs — simple programs to follow by eating the highest quality, mineral-rich foods. Plus incorporating alkaline fluids to get your body back in balance."

"You mean like this green drink?"

"Correct. This is your new best friend that never leaves your sight." He pauses and takes a large swig then asks how do I and JJ know each other.

Oh shit, here we go again, just stay in character, Randy. "We actually go way back, but I won't bore you with the details. I was completely shocked by his radical transformation though, he didn't use to be like that back in the day."

"How so?"

"He was as big as me about ten years ago. Even bigger than Fat Elvis. He used to eat deep-fried Belgian waffles for breakfast and Ding Dong sandwiches for brunch."

"Jeez," he grimaces. "I had no idea. Now you've seen how far he's come, if he can do it, you can do it."

I turn to him and agree wholeheartedly. "If I hadn't seen him face to face I would never have believed it in my wildest dreams. I mean, this guy was a complete slob; he once drunkenly stumbled into a supermarket and ate fourteen yogurts back to back and wandered out without paying."

"Are you serious?" he laughs as we turn the bend around the lake.

"Hundred percent."

"Funny. So, I'm curious, when's the last time you trained on a regular basis?"

"Not since *WrestleMania XVIII*, so I'm totally out the loop. How often do you work out?"

"I do some form of training for the body and the mind every single day. Every morning I start by reading philosophy for thirty minutes, it helps keep my mind clear. Then I jump on a rebounder for twenty minutes which gets me focused and centered for the day ahead. I can't imagine living any other way."

"You do it every day? Don't you get bored or tired?"

"Every day without question," he says congruently. "You've been neglecting exercise for some time and it's obvious why. One of the key aspects of becoming fit is to make the ritual of exercising fun and pleasurable. The pump, after all, is an amazing natural high. Conversely, if you loathe the idea of exercising you're setting yourself up to lose from the get-go because who wants to do something they hate every day?"

"Makes sense. So how can I make myself like it again, like back in my college days?"

"Well, what's the difference between now and back then?"

"I don't know. I was a kid with a lot of energy. Plus I was surrounded by jock roommates so we all lifted together."

As we come to another bend he tells me he wants me to think of my excess pounds in a different way. "Those rolls of fat are nothing but a result, what I want to know is how you produced that result?"

I frown and ask him what he means exactly.

He repeats by asking if he wanted to achieve the exact same result, what would he have to do specifically. "Once we figure out your behavioral pattern, all we have to do is do the opposite pattern and you'll get the opposite result. Get it?"

"I think so," I mutter, not fully understanding where he's going.

He tells me to not overthink this and just walk him through a day in the life of my typical eating patterns which led me to destination lard-ville. "And remember, be very specific, I need to know everything that passes your lips in an average day, so don't hold anything back."

I take a deep breath thinking *oh boy, here we go* and let loose. "Okay. On a typical day, I'll wake up to my morning coffee."

"Just coffee or do you add to it? Remember don't leave anything out."

"Coffee with four sugars and a dollop of butter."

He grimaces and asks do I really put butter in my morning coffee.

"I prefer it to cream but sometimes have both," I shrug. "Then I'll usually have four large pancakes with syrup and four rashers of Canadian bacon with three fried eggs, ketchup and spicy mayo. For lunch, I basically have wings or a burger and fries or BBQ ribs—those types of power-lunches, ya know. In between lunch and dinner, I might snack on a couple of things like Snickers or Twix, or some Beef Jerky and Gummy Worms with either a Sprite or 7 Up." I pause my recital as I'm starting to salivate but he notions to carry on. "For dinner, I'll usually have a large T-Bone with potatoes and veg or a chicken primavera with Cheez Whiz and diced ham. I'll then chase that up with Toffee flavored Häagen-Dazs or a Godiva chocolate mousse and oh, I almost forgot, that will be alongside four cans of Michelob ULTRA at home—I usually drink light beer because it's less calories. And if I go to the Duck there will be about another four to six beers added to the mix with a pizza to go. Or if I skip that I might top the night off with a peanut butter and jelly sandwich with a glass of milk before bed. It's the child in me..."

Perplexed would be an understatement to describe the look on Tommy's face. "That would be a typical day, would it?"

"Pretty much, yeah. Give or take a few Gummy Worms."

He lets out a sigh and tells me this is worse than he thought and asks if I do any kind of exercise. I tell him I don't other than walking to work and the bar.

He looks back gritting his teeth and asks how long have I been living like this.

"Years. I'm forty-one and haven't been in good shape since about twenty-four. When I left college it kind of went downhill from there."

"*It* went downhill, or *you* went downhill?"

"You're right, 'I' went downhill."

"Correct. There is no 'it.' It's YOU that makes yourself eat all that crap and when you compound it over seventeen years, can you see how you've produced this result right here?" he points to my belly again. There's only two reasons why we eat: physical hunger or emotional hunger. Do you think what you just described was your body physically craving all that crap or emotionally craving all that crap?"

"Emotionally obviously."

"Right. And how's that working out for you?"

"It's not working out well at all."

"Correct again. So now you can see how and why you produced the result of three hundred and forty-five pounds — you're emotionally eating, which never satisfies you. You don't emotionally put beer, milk, wine or Pepsi into your car every day because they're the wrong fuels, it's the same with you. Is this making sense?"

"Yeah."

"You see, Randy, you were given the greatest gift of all: life. A healthy life, but you're digging your own grave with a knife and fork. It must be hell to try to function with all that extra weight. I can see how labored your breathing is just from a few minutes of walking."

"It really is hard work every day," I shamefully admit. "And it's gotten worse over time."

"*It?*" he challenges and stops to emphasize my mistake.

"Sorry. *I've* gotten worse."

"Yes, that *it* shit has got to go." We park ourselves on a bench. "I want you to take a second to elaborate how you've gotten worse over time, so you get fully associated to the pains you've caused from your deadly eating patterns."

This makes me stop a minute to really think, and again he insists that I be detailed and specific, so I compose myself and don't hold anything back.

"I get headaches throughout the day and often have itching sensations all over my skin, and most nights I wake up with night-sweats, finding it difficult to get off to sleep. My stomach and intestines constantly are upset and struggle to digest a good meal — probably 'cause of the peptic ulcer I've developed. I get either cold sweats or hot flashes out of nowhere and often feel faint so I have to nap until it goes away…"

He looks on, trying to keep a poker face, but I know what he must be thinking.

"… I often forget things and get temperamental from sugar highs and carb crashes but still add sugar or hot-sauce to everything. I get restless at work, I can't concentrate or work under pressure or make important decisions. And I get depressed very easily, constantly worrying about things I never used to and lose my temper at the drop of a hat. Every day seems to be an emotional rollercoaster, especially with my wife… I don't know how the hell I ended up like this."

I look down at my feet, feeling peak levels of disgust. I had to let it out. These built-up feelings that I never talk to anyone about have weighed on me for so long. I'm not sure how I just did that. I never talk to others how I feel, I've always thought it was weak or girly.

Tommy once again has that WTF look plastered across his chiseled features and remains in silence, wanting me to embrace my pain no doubt.

"I wish I'd never gotten like this in the first place. I can't handle it any longer."

"I'm glad you feel it," he stands over me, "because you need to use it as motivation to say *never again!* Our bodies are our vehicles so we must feed them with the highest quality fuels. It's easy and convenient to comfort ourselves with junk food but it's a silly way to deal with emotions because it makes everything so much worse."

"You're right, Tommy. You're so right. I'm sick of this shit and can't go on any longer!"

"Finally I'm seeing some passion and fire from you, Randy. Me giving you information is not gonna help very much, you need a radical shift in physiology! Are you ready to change or are you gonna go back to your Twinkies and Cheez Whiz when times get tough?"

"No," I snap. "I'm ready!"

"Are you sure?"

"I've never been so sure in my life! I'm at the end of my rope."

"That's all I needed to hear. Follow me."

CHAPTER 43

Tommy and I descend to the bowels of the house where JJ's home gym is situated. Like his office it has a man-cave vibe; the walls are covered with framed pictures of muscled-up legends like Tom Platz, Lou Ferrigno, Arnold Schwarzenegger and Jimmy 'Superfly' Snuka. He even has a life-sized bronze statue of Jack LaLanne. It's obvious the man is a serious student of fitness.

"Wow. This must have cost thousands to deck out," I say, marveling at all the equipment that sparkles like it's brand new.

"Yeah, it's pretty state-of-the-art." Tommy leads me to the ab corner where we sit on a couple of exercise balls. "Have you ever wondered why some people have the drive to shape their bodies the way they desire and others don't?"

"I guess."

"Would you like to know?"

"Sure."

He begins telling me that people who never get off track with their weight simply have higher standards than those who become out of shape "and it's usually because they link a lot of pain and embarrassment to looking dumpy. So it's not so much that health is driving them, it's more vanity. Ask a guy why he just did two hundred sit-ups, is it because he wants to live until eighty-five or to look ripped on the beach?"

"Right," I chuckle, getting the obvious point.

"*Vanity* all too often gets mixed up with *narcissism*—which is the bad guy—so in my opinion vanity is a good trait to adopt because it motivates us to stay in shape and live healthier."

"So is that what drives you? Your vainness?"

"To a degree, yes. I certainly love myself, make no mistake about it, but I'm a bit of a rare breed because of my...how can I put it? My childhood—let's just say."

"Can I ask what happened or am I being too nosy?"

"Well, I usually keep the bad old days to myself, but after you opened up with all your personal shit I feel obliged to do the same because you might learn

189

something."

He starts his story saying he was born with a rare blood disorder called sickle-cell anemia which is a lot more prevalent in afro-Americans and Latinos. "I'm one of the few Caucasians that have it and let me tell you, it's no picnic having constant muscle fatigue and all-around physical suffering. And if that wasn't enough I contracted a rare throat disease when I was eight which nearly took my life. The doctors weren't sure how to heal me so they opened me up for exploratory surgery where they found multiple cancerous polyps. By the time I left ninth grade I'd been through seventeen throat operations."

As he speaks my eyes wander towards his neck region—noticing the scars masked by a killer beach tan.

"Throughout my adolescence, I was hit with asthma problems, respiratory disorders, eczema and rashes. I would have spazzing-out fits and have to see doctor after doctor who all disagreed which medication I should take. I was more chemically imbalanced throughout junior high than Black Sabbath in their heyday and was forced to see a therapist." He takes a moment and looks off into the distance, going right back to his pain. "Man, I used to hate seeing that guy so much, I'd turn psycho in his office. I'd cry, shout, mess up his desk or sometimes I'd whip out my dick and start peeing on his couch so I'd get kicked out."

"That's intense. Was he a bad guy or something?"

"Actually no, he was just trying to help. It wasn't so much him; I hated the situation I was in. I hated being sick. I hated being forced to see a shrink when I knew there was nothing wrong with my personality. I wanted to be normal like my friends but the drugs made me constantly sick. Some days I didn't even want to get out of bed so I took it out on him and my parents and anybody else who tried to help."

The ambiance in here has completely flipped. Sorrow and empathy have filled the room as I can only imagine what pain he's been through.

"Looks like you turned out pretty good, my friend, but how did you turn everything around?"

He clears his throat and looks directly into his reflection off the mirrored walls. "One day I got dragged to a lecture by a nutritionist at our high school who lo-and-behold told me the formula to completely save my health. What he said struck a chord with me, I became obsessed. His words became my mantra. And bear in mind I was at the end of my rope, in fact, in the months leading up to this I had actually set a goal to save twenty-five dollars per month so I could buy a gun and take my life before graduation."

He takes a moment as you'd expect, on the verge of choking up, but recomposes himself and sits upright. "I found out I could get my hands on a gun for two hundred and fifty bucks," his voice begins to crack. "As soon as I saved enough, I was gonna end all my pain and misery without hesitation." He pauses, exhaling deeply like he's practicing Lamaze and stares again at his reflection in the mirror. "Do you know how much money I had saved up in my shoebox?"

I shake my head.

"Two hundred and twenty-five dollars. I was nine days away until my monthly allowance came in and I'd been counting down the days so I could end it all."

It almost feels like the afflicted little boy is in the room with me right now. Tommy's eyes well up like he's eaten too much wasabi as he continues his painful recollection:

"But I came home that night so happy to have heard this revelation. It seemed like all the pain went away. And then I remembered the shoebox under my bed and started weeping uncontrollably. First out of dismay but then out of elation because I knew with this new foundational principle, I could use that money to restore my health."

"This is real deep, man. So what was this big revelation in that guy's speech?"

"I remember like it was yesterday! He said: *'It matters not, your conditions. If you obey nature's laws, you can be born again and completely restore your health.'* You might be thinking that's a pretty trivial statement, Randy, but to me, it meant the world. All throughout my adolescence I'd been treated for sickness and disease with drugs, but nobody up until that point had explained to me what the root cause of all my ailments was. That was the day I realized my cause. It was all the crap I was putting in my body that prevented me from healing — Gatorade, TruMoo, Little Debbie's, Big Al's, Crunch 'n Munch and the rest of that garbage! It was like I was once blind but now I see. None of what I was eating was natural from Mother Earth; they were all Man-made and laced with sugar which is a deadly poison that's more addictive than cocaine."

"It is?"

"Sucrose, my friend, is deadly with a capital D. It's in over ninety percent of the products at supermarkets. They're putting it in everything to keep us sick and addicted. It's real scary shit. You have to read Russell Simmons' new book *Def, Dumb and Blind* about how the government laces our foods with chemicals to keep us sick so we're dependent on their drugs and healthcare."

"Shit, is that true?"

"Yeap. The truth is grimmer than Grimsby."

"Where?"

"It's not important." He jumps off the exercise ball and loosens up stretching. "After I made the switch my whole life turned around! Within three months of eating Mother Nature's food and weaning off my medications, I became born again! Not in the religious way, I mean my body rejuvenated and my strength reached levels I've never dreamed of."

And with that, he gives me a front-row seat to the gun show. His flexed pythons are more impressive than the late-great British Bulldog's.

"Whoa!"

"Fast forward to today: I'm as strong as Shane Ox, I take no medications whatsoever and I've reversed all those symptoms and even eliminated my sickle-cell *dis-ease.*"

"Amazing!"

"All that shit you're consuming on a regular basis will ruin your health unless we do something about it now and you have to be deadly serious! You have no idea how lucky you are. You've been given everything but you're throwing it all away over some silly emotional eating patterns and shit!"

His evaluation hurts but it's what I need to hear—can't keep burying my head in the sand. "I agree, Tommy. It's ridiculous."

"*It's* ridiculous?"

Shit, he caught me again.

"You mean *you're* ridiculous, Randy," he snaps, becoming rather animated. "Your problem is you don't give yourself enough pain when you gain weight, you accept it and then ignore it, then it becomes worse down the line. Don't you wish you nipped it in the bud when you hit fifteen pounds overweight instead of becoming this big?"

"Of course."

"So why didn't you?"

I remain mute and look away knowing he's pinned me in a corner.

"You allowed yourself to become distracted on the most important thing in your life. If you don't make health your number one importance then you're not fit to live, that's why you need a radical shift in physiology to ensure this will never happen again! Does that make sense?"

"It does, but haven't you got any secrets to put me on the fast track?"

"There you go again! There is no fucking secrets, man! You got yourself in this mess, only you can get yourself out! You need to man-up and take back control and stop making fucking excuses! Agreed?"

I nod.

"Are you ready?"

I nod again.

"I said *are you fucking ready?!*"

"Yes!" I retort with more conviction. Tommy seems to have morphed into a drill sergeant in the last two minutes.

"Stand up!"

I quickly obey. His eyes have become dark, almost menacing as he grills me chin to chin.

"Take off your clothes."

"What?"

"You heard me. I want you to strip off every single article of clothing right this second."

I stall and defend that he's lost his mind and demand to know why.

"You'll see why in a minute."

"Boxers too?"

"Yep, boxers and all. And don't worry, I'm not some kind of wacko."

I stare back thinking he is some kind of wacko and try to reason why I won't do it.

"Yes, you will, motherfucker! What's the big deal? Pretend we're teammates in a locker room."

"But I'm embarrassed."

"That's the fucking point, bro. Trust me; there's a method to my madness. Take it all off right now, sweetheart."

I begrudgingly obey and take off my T-shirt, shorts, sneakers, socks and yes, my fucking boxer shorts in front of a man I just met about forty-five minutes ago.

"Remember what I said: we all get the body we deserve. This is your fault and only you can change it."

I get the message loud and clear while I try my best to cover my bits.

"Okay," he points. "Look in the mirror and tell me what you see."

This is so embarrassing! I can't believe I'm actually naked in front of this guy. "I'm not going through with this ridicule!" I try and walk away but he adamantly stops me and repeats the question. "What kind of exercise is this, you fucking schizo?!"

"Stop questioning me and just tell me exactly what you see."

"Why do you keep asking me that?" I say exhaustedly. "I see me!"

"So what do you see?"

I come to the conclusion that this motherfucker is not gonna let up so I let out a long, frustrated sigh and focus on all my rolls of flab, my Jabba the Hutt-like neck, my love-handles, my chunky thighs and my shriveled dick, (it's cold in here). "What do you want me to say, Tommy? I see a fucking pig."

"You see a fucking pig. What else, Randy?"

"I see years of sloth and gluttony."

"What else?"

"Man boobs."

"What else?"

"A fat belly."

"Okay. What else?"

"I see a man who's lost his standards."

"Correct. What else do you see, Randy?"

"A hideous, selfish beast."

"Alright, what else?"

"A fat fucking slob!"

"What else?"

"A fat fucking fuck."

"Now, turn around and look at the back of you. What do you see?"

I comply with this madness and tell him I see a fat ass.

"What else?"

"Love-handles."

"What else do you see?"

"I'm just disgusted with myself."

"Okay, turn around. What do you see?"

"I can't live like this any longer." I turn back around.

"Hallelujah! That's the answer I've been waiting for. Do you really mean it?" He walks off to the side and grabs a backpack.

"I most definitely do, Tommy."

"What happens if you get stressed out? Will you look for some shitty foods to comfort you?"

"No. Not anymore. I can't. I just can't."

He unzips the backpack to reveal its contents. It's filled to the brim with about fifty candy bars. He's got everything in there; Mars Bar, Reese's Pieces, Boost, Clark Bar, Hersey's pretzels, Twizzlers, even a Golden Pyramid which I've never heard of before. He unwraps a Mars and sticks it in my face.

"You need to get this in your freaking head, Randy! These sugary, chocolate-deaths will create all this excess fat and sludge that's plaguing your body! Do you want to continue sludging through life like you have been for years?"

"No, I can't."

"Are you sure?" he says sticking the chocolate in my face again.

"No!" I swat it away and tell him I don't want it.

"These foods create this result," he points to my flab as I stare in the mirror. "You're fully aware of this now, aren't you?"

"Yes."

"Do you ever want to put your body through all this turmoil again? All for a little sugar high?"

"No!"

"Do you ever want to go through this kind of embarrassment ever again?"

"No, I certainly do not!"

"From this day forth, what are your new beliefs about nutrition and lifestyle?"

"I must eat foods that genuinely support me. No comfort foods, because they don't actually comfort me, they just make me fatter."

"—Which makes you more uncomfortable in the long run. Good, you're finally getting it. But just in case you're full of shit…" he pulls out his Fuji from the backpack and starts snapping pics of me.

What the fuck!? "Hey, what are you doing?" I say, covering my bits. "I didn't consent to this. Stop right now!"

He blatantly ignores me and continues snapping away from every angle. "I'm gonna post these bad boys online for everyone to see if I find out you've gone back to your old ways. So you better take this fucking seriously, Mr. Peewee!"

"Don't you dare!"

"Oh, I dare. So you better be serious, dude!"

"I am! Can I please put my clothes on now?"

"Are you a man of your word that will commit to this way of living from this day forth?"

"Yes."

"I can't hear you! Say it like you've got a pair!"

"YES!"

"Say it again!"

"YES!!"

"Are you gonna follow through or become distracted and make excuses?"

"No!" I say, getting more jazzed and scared. "I can do this! I can absolutely do this!"

"How are you gonna succeed?"

"All I have to do is burn more calories than I consume every single day, never getting off track and no more emotional eating."

"Spoken like a true disciple," he hi-fives me. "You were listening after all. See how simple it can be? I believe it was Einstein that said *genius is making complex ideas simple, not making simple ideas complex* and he was one smart MoFo." He pauses, flashing a cheesy smile. "I think we've just had a breakthrough, my friend."

I agree, feeling a little déjà vu. What he just did to me was like what JJ did with Koko a few hours ago. Trippy.

We remain standing in an awkward silence.

"Can I put my clothes on now?"

"Yes, you may. It's time to pump iron."

CHAPTER 44

After the eye-opening session with Tommy and a plant-based protein shake, I spend the next twenty minutes mesmerized with JJ's state-of-the-art refrigerator. Like the Smart-Phone somebody has invented the Smart-Fridge which logs all your items along with the remaining quantities. For instance; if you are down to the last few slices of bread, or low on milk, it automatically places an order via the internet and within minutes your favorite brand of bread or milk is delivered to your door by a drone so you never go without. It's direct-to-consumer commerce, eliminating the middle man. Freaking fascinating stuff. (Although I should be more specific, there is no bread or milk in JJ's fridge, more like seaweed, alfalfa sprouts and kale smoothies).

Now I have about fifteen apparent minutes before JJ returns home, so I decide to be dastardly like the Repo Man and sneak around the house for clues about my future self's business. Scandalous I know, but it's killing me how I've earned all this wealth. I just have to know.

As I stroll through my dream house like a kid in a candy store, I'm suddenly hit with thoughts of Max and Sherri. This is the first occurrence I've really had to focus on them. I miss them dearly and feel awful about all the foul shit I've done behind Sherri's back. I wish I could just turn back the clock and retract it all. Half of me wants to see pictures and videos of them from the past ten years, but the other half can't handle it. I don't think I'm ready to see pictures of an eighteen year old Max, she's still an eight year old little princess to me, so I'm actually glad they're in Honolulu for the time being.

I ascend the majestic spiral staircase and enter JJ's master bedroom. Wow! It's stunning like Sable in '97. The bed, for one thing, is something I've never felt before; it's so incredibly soft and is shaped like a cloud. I dig underneath and find the brand label: *Cloud Nine*, oh how fitting. What a cool design, a bed that feels like you're floating on a cloud. These were not out in my day, unfortunately; I would have sold these bad boys like hotcakes.

There's an en-suite bathroom with 'his' and 'hers' showers, as well as twin walk-in closets like you see in the mafia movies. A book by the nightlight catches my eye, and upon further inspection, it seems to be some kind of diary or journal. Since when do I write in a journal? That's something little girls do when going through puberty.

I thumb through it recognizing my writing style — scribbled and messy but I can understand it (it is me after all). I start at the beginning of January and see written goals for the forthcoming year: *Reduce body fat 3%, grow the foundation 17% (minimum), soft launch Z Cube Pro by July* and a few more things that I don't really understand.

Then I find detailed notes of books and bios he's studied. He's obviously gone through a plethora of them because there are writings about Zen and Buddhism, detailed notes about Berry Gordy, Robert Rodriguez, Elon Musk, Richard Bandler, Alexander Graham Bell, DJ Davidson, Paul Heyman, Jim Rohn and Tupac Shakur. What am I, a fucking librarian? *MKD merger meeting, Four Seasons, Dubai. Wrap party, Lady Luck, Monaco.* What does any of this even mean?

It looks like JJ has a more exciting and productive life in one year than me in the last twenty. I still can't believe this is how I'm going to live. All this information doesn't give me any insight into what I do as a profession. Shit, I have to abort as I hear the door opening downstairs. I place the journal down exactly where I found it and dart out to the landing area and spot JJ entering the house.

"Hey there," I hurl from above.

"Bobby, what are you up to? Snooping around?"

"No-no, don't be silly. I've never been up here and wanted to see the views of the city since you haven't given me a proper tour yet."

"Fair enough, it's very not bad, isn't it? Overlooking Hathaway Park."

"Pretty extravagant."

"Meet me in my office in two minutes. I have something for you." He walks away.

Shit! Mission unsuccessful.

JJ sits me down in his man-cave office while pouring two wheatgrass smoothies and asks me how the training session went—quizzing me in great detail about all the powerful wisdom I took away. I tell him my health absolutely has to come first, I cannot be blind to it ever again because my life is on the line (while leaving out the naked part).

"It was something I'll definitely never forget," I conclude. "So how do you two know each other?"

"I conducted some business with his father who's a savvy businessman and one of the original angel investors in the automated haulage revolution."

"The what?"

"Oh sorry, I keep forgetting. Have you noticed something about trucks these days?"

"Trucks? Errr, not really. Was I supposed to?"

"You've never noticed anything about the drivers?"

"No."

"Trucks have the ability to drive themselves now."

"Really? All trucks?"

"Most of 'em."

This catches me off guard, but what's new.

"How do they do it?"

"It's like autopilot on a plane, in a nutshell. Robots basically."

"Robot truck drivers? Wow…"

"Yep, that's how it is now. They don't sleep, they don't eat, they don't need time off to take the kids to Daytona for spring break."

"Kind of spooky if you ask me. Do they ever crash?"

"Never, although one Robot recently got caught for being too oiled up at the wheel."

I roll my eyes and realize that's why that guy at the peanut butter and jelly place said what he said. He tries asking more about the session but I deflect.

"When are you gonna answer some of my questions, Mr. JJ? Are you going to let me in on how the hell you, I, whoever, made all this money? I've been racking my brain forever, so you need to stop torturing me. Please." I wonder if he'll finally bite. "Come on, man, out with it."

He remains silent. I can't read if he's going to crack or if he's just taking his time answering.

"Look, Bobby, I know it must be killing you trying to figure it out, so I'll let you in on a couple of things. I've been debating back and forth on exactly what to say to you because knowing too much about your future could be destructive like Doc said in *Back to the Future*."

Another *Back to the Future* reference, really? "Are you gonna tell me, or not?"

"Okay." He leans in. "I'm an inventor."

"Really? Holy shit! Seriously, an inventor?"

"Yep, I'm an inventor and product designer now." He leans back in his chair, slurping his greens through a straw.

"Holy motherfucking shit!" I laugh, not quite knowing how to digest this.

"Yep. I design, innovate and invent things useful for Man."

I'm speechless, but only for a second.

"I'm an inventor! I mean, we're inventors! This is unbelievable! I always wanted to be one but I never took my ideas seriously enough."

"Well, Bobby, that is about to change. You will pursue that dream you've had in that head of yours since you were a little boy and it will lead to all this," he motions to the palace we're encased in.

My inner thoughts race at light speed now. I bliss out for a second and do a poor job of suppressing my enthusiasm. This is so surreal. I can't believe I'm going to make it as an inventor!

"When you start taking yourself seriously, Bobby, and never squander the all-important commodity of time, that's when your whole life will change. You can decide right now to change, or you can wait for life to change you, it's up to you. And it's the same with other key areas of life like health; you can get your ass up every morning and work out, or you can carry on eating Slim Jims or Oreo milkshakes for breakfast and reap those results." He points at my love-handles.

"We live in a world of sowing and reaping, for you to evolve into JJ you have to do all the little insurmountable things even when you don't feel like it, even when it hurts, even when you're too tired and so on. By doing all the so called *little things* over and over you inevitably reap the big rewards."

I nod along.

"But don't get it twisted, it's not an over-night thing. It takes years of study, thought and practice, just like anything of great importance. There's no such thing as an overnight athlete. There's no such thing as an overnight musician. There's no such thing as an overnight artist, entrepreneur, inventor, doctor, teacher, or healer, we could go on and on. Each one of these individuals had to discipline themselves through thousands of hours of diligent practice and repetition when nobody was watching and then suddenly when preparation meets opportunity: BOOM! They blow up. That's when people label them an overnight sensation."

He's making sense, no doubt about it but I want him to get specific and ask him directly what I invented.

"That, Bobby, I cannot reveal. Yes, I told you I'm an inventor but no, I'm not telling you about any of my inventions or designs because that would be cheating. I'd be robbing you from the sheer pleasure of coming up with something brilliant and then acting upon it. When you have that Eureka moment, it will be one of the most amazing feelings you'll ever have."

I get where he's coming from logically, but his caginess only makes things worse as it feels like one big tease. "Great, torture me even more. Tell me I'm an outstanding inventor but don't tell me about any of my inventions."

"I have to. It would be wrong, unethical and cheating which wouldn't make you grow as a man. Imagine if Thomas Edison invented a time machine as his last invention and he took a trip back to visit his younger self when he was just starting out and said: *'This is a light bulb, let me show you how it works so I can save you thousands of hours of hard work, diligence and persistence.'* What he'd be doing is robbing his younger self of the process, the growth, the formula, the excitement, the creativity. The journey of going through all the blood, sweat and tears and then coming out on top is what will give you the most growth and satisfaction."

He pauses briefly to let it sink in and sips his green smoothie.

"What if George Lucas traveled back in time to the seventies and handed a younger George the original scripts for Star Wars and said: *'Here take these to the studios, they're going to be the biggest blockbuster trilogy of all time and change the world!'* I bet he would feel like a fraud or a cheater because he never sat down and created that amazing mythology. He would feel like a charlatan, don't you think?"

I have to agree. Stingy motherfucker. But I'd still love to know.

"Being handed a winning lottery ticket will only lead to unworthiness, inner conflict and feeling like a fraud and by the way, what happens to most people who win big in the lottery? They notoriously squander the money, get divorced, alienate their friends and feel like they're being judged by everyone, ending up worse than before they won the damn money. How sad? Nobody is given an owner's manual for the brain, so we're all here on this Earth trying to figure it out for ourselves, but that's the fun part, especially with inventions because you're creating something tangible from an intangible thought. So there's no way I can allow you to cheat ahead of time, you have to earn this shit, that's how you develop balls the size of grapefruits and a dick bigger than Lord Alfred Hayes."

"Haha, you're nuts."

"So the moral of the story is don't be like Biff Tannen; he too tried to cheat himself into wealth with *Grey's Sports Almanac* and that's exactly what you're doing by asking me about my inventions. Your time will come, be patient."

"I get it, I get it." I laugh.

"You like that, huh? Well, since you mysteriously appeared in my life I've been thinking a lot about *Back to the Future* as a reference and guidance. I think I know why you're here, and I think you can figure it out too, but in the meantime let's not over-analyze anything. Just know that you're on the right path and all things will come together whenever the universe decides."

"Fair enough."

"Having said all that I should tell you Hover Boards have been out on the market for some time now, matter-of-fact, I have a couple in the garage..."

My fucking jaw drops.

"Shall we take them out for a float and grab some food?"

CHAPTER 45

JJ and I enter the Chill Grill, a laid-back trendy hotspot with high-quality edibles and a fun ambiance. It's only six-thirty and already this place has a fair number of patrons enjoying the scene; some play what looks like a virtual game of chess, others play Jenga, while a bunch of college kids congregate around a stretched pool table. We came early to beat the rush and, in case you're wondering, no we did not ride Hover Boards here, it was a fucking rib, that motherfucker, I can't believe I fell for it!

We are shown to our seats by the host who hands us a couple of electronic menus, which to me, look like iPads.

"These menus are a bit state-of-the-art, aren't they?" I say as we get acquainted in our seats.

"That they are," says JJ, playing with his Fuji. "You select the items you want, then hit the submit button which sends your order directly to the kitchen. It cuts out fifty percent of the server's job, if not more."

"What if I want to ask questions about a certain dish?"

"Of course you can still ask a server or you can click on the item and it will show you a little video about the ingredients, how it's made, how they prepare it and whatnot."

"Pretty slick. So, shall we order some coffee to start?"

"Errr, no!" snarls JJ as if I said something blasphemous.

I ask if he drinks coffee anymore, but I think I know the answer.

"Absolutely not. Caffeine is a highly addictive neurotoxin. When you learn the truth about the ills of caffeine it freaks you out and makes you never want to touch it again."

"So no coffee at all? Not even in the morning?"

"Not ever. Remember, I was heavily into drugs and caffeine was my first drug of the day. I had to eliminate it and replace that warm feeling, so soup is the way I always start my day."

"Don't you get tired of soup every morning?"

"Not at all, it keeps me souped-up," he winks and waffles on about the infinite variety of soups that can be made.

"What about decaf? Still a no go?"

"Don't get me started. It's not at all good for us, too acidic. Plus it's a diuretic which basically means for every cup of coffee you drink, your body gets dehydrated the equivalent of four cups of water, so it has to work much harder to function. The more you drink, the more acidic and depleted you get."

JJ's Fuji rings (thank god) while I scan the menu. He tells me he has to duck out for twenty minutes and handle something.

"Just order a starter while I'm gone and we'll order the main when I'm back. You know what you're doing, right?"

"Yeah, I'm pretty sure I can order food in a grill."

He shoots me a sarcastic look and hands me a fifty-dollar bill with Barack Obama on the back telling me to leave a tip before the meal.

"Wait a minute; people in the future tip before the meal?"

"No. Just me. The word tip is actually an acronym: To Insure Promptness. When you leave a nice cash tip up front, your server will treat you as if you're Jerry Lawler himself."

"Pretty smart."

"Right, I gotta go. Remember: food is fuel, only order something that cleanses you, not clogs you. See you soon, Randy Savage."

As JJ slithers away I scroll the E-menu and make a conscious effort to skip over all the naughty items before I start picturing how delicious they'll be melting in my mouth. This is the new me, and I have to be serious about what I put in.

I order *The Big Daddy* — an avocado salad with all the trimmings and soon get lost in the funky decor. They have electronic art spread across the walls that morphs into different pictures every minute like the way those electronic billboards do. Pretty cool.

I then catch a glimpse of the TV by the bar where a big text flashes at the bottom saying Justin Bieber is running for prime minister of Canada, followed by a news montage of him looking all grown up in a suit. *No freaking way!* This must be a publicity stunt. I feel the need to flag a waitress down and one just happens to be passing by.

"Hi," says the freckled-face server who looks to be in her early-to-mid-twenties. "Can I help you?"

"Yes. How's your day going?"

"Errr, so so."

"Just so so?"

She goes on to say she had a customer earlier who drove her up the wall. "Plus everybody seems to be stingy today. Do you need help with something?"

"Yes, but not about the food, I wanted to ask about Justin Bieber."

"Justin Bieber?" she questions as confusion swarms those big blue eyes.

"Surely that little douche-bag can't be running for prime minister? What's the world coming to?"

"I know, right. I guess after his singing and acting career took a nose dive he's trying to regain the spotlight somehow."

We talk about Bieber-Prime-Minister-Fever a little while longer as well as his robot monkey that never leaves his side before switching to this funky cafe.

"I really like the vibe here, it's my first time."

"We're delighted to have you."

"I'm Bobby. Oops…" I catch myself. "I mean Randy, my name is Randy." I chuckle to deflect my faux-pas.

She looks a little confused but shrugs it off. "Pleased to meet you, I'm Arnold."

"Your name is Arnold?"

"Yes, Arnold is my last name, and that's what I like to be called."

"That's funny. I met a girl yesterday who also liked to be addressed by her last name. Is there a trend going on where girls are ditching their first names or something?"

She tells me she hates her Christian name and under no circumstances will she reveal it. This, of course, makes me want to know it more.

"It can't be that bad, surely. It's Beatrice, right?" I smile. "No? Is it Leyva?"

"Listen, Bobby or, Randy or whatever the heck your name is, even if you guessed it correctly I still wouldn't tell you, that's how much I loathe it."

I back down and ask her to join me for a minute. "You look like you could use a break."

As she sits I ask what was the problem with the customer.

"You're not gonna believe this but I'll tell you anyway: This nimrod comes in and orders a deep dish mushroom pizza which is priced at eighteen ninety-nine. After he'd finished eating he tells me he'd calculated that each slice costs two dollars and thirty-seven point five cents, but because he left two slices, he wanted the bill reduced by four dollars and seventy-five cents."

"Are you serious?!"

"I said the same thing. He was such a weirdo and looked like a lonely mathematics teacher."

"He must have been Jewish."

My remark makes us both chuckle then I ask did she get the manager.

"I couldn't be bothered with confrontation; I just deducted the bill and moved on. I didn't want to go back near that guy, he was wearing a dusty old anorak that kept making me sneeze."

"What an oddball." I then inform her my wife used to be a server and would occasionally complain to me about people leaving shabby tips until I taught her some of my master-sales-tactics to increase her yield.

"Did it work?"

"Of course. Once I trained her to go the extra mile and do what the other servers did not, her tips went through the roof. But anyway, I actually did want to ask you what's good here that's healthy? I can't have anything naughty, I've started a new diet, or should I say *lifestyle* to shed some pounds."

"Hey, I know how that is. I was a yo-yo dieter in my teens."

"Really? You look pretty fab right now, Arnold."

"I guess. This might sound embarrassing but in my high school days I used to binge-eat and throw it back up."

She looks on with a little shame, which makes me wonder why she just opened up like that.

I inform her my cousin Tania did that back in the day, I never have understood why anybody would do that. It didn't make any sense to me.

"Yeah, I have to agree, it doesn't make sense at all."

"I'm curious why did you do it back then?"

"At the time I was in the cheerleading squad and was under a lot of pressure to stay slim so I started doing it little by little but then it became like a normal routine. I'd do it on Fridays which was Pizza Day, then on Saturdays after the game, and then, of course, Sundays to finish off the weekend at Arby's. Soon it became an everyday thing to deal with my insecurities, but it just made everything worse especially when I started involuntarily upchucking food in front of people."

"Did any of your friends know your secret?"

"God no. I never told a soul. Not even my mom, I was way too embarrassed."

"Hmmm. I'm curious, why did you just tell me?"

"Well, I'm over it now, this was a long time ago. I'm a bit more open with things these days."

"Except with your first name."

"Exactly," she smirks.

"So why did you tell me?"

"I don't know… Probably because we don't know each other so there's no risk of anybody finding out. I'm usually way more open with strangers than I am with my friends. Plus you're easy to talk to, I mean, you flagged me down to talk about Justin Bieber."

We both chuckle again before I ask how she stopped her bulimic behavior.

"It just got too embarrassing spontaneously upchucking food in front of my friends, so I knew it had to stop. Then I watched a documentary about what happens if you continue doing it. First comes the constant upchucking of food because you can't hold anything down, then you start to throw up blood. Then if you continue, it strips your enamel away and you can lose your teeth."

"Jeez."

"I know, right? Then you stop getting your period, and if you carry on it will eventually ruin your uterus and you can't have a baby."

"Wow. So you did not want to carry on down that road and forced yourself to quit, right?"

"Basically, yeah. And I started eating fresh, whole foods again so I didn't have any guilt after I ate, and I avoided Pizza Hut at all costs."

"Interesting. I used to binge on pizza and beer, but only throw up when I had too many IPAs."

"I think everybody has done that."

We share a laugh again and reach a little moment of silence, but not an awkward one. I thank her for opening up and say our former versions of ourselves are actually somewhat similar. "I used to binge-eat as a stupid way to deal with my emotions, and like you, it just made everything worse. But I cannot continue going down that path any longer because my future will be well-and-truly ruined. You've just reaffirmed that for me and I want to thank you, Arnold."

Those big blue eyes light up as she accepts my compliment. I then pull out a fifty and lay it on the table.

"What's this for?"

"It's your tip."

"But I haven't even brought your food yet."

"I know, but once I found out what the word TIP stood for, I've been tipping this way ever since."

"What does it stand for?"

"To Insure Promptness."

"Oh. I did not know that."

"Most people don't," I wink.

She reaches over to claim the crispy Barack, but I retract it to mess with her. "There is something I do want from you, Miss Arnold."

A little look of despair spreads across her face.

"Your name of course."

She gives me a look like *you asshole* and pleads does she have to. I nod knowing I have her locked in like the Figure Four. She mulls it over and eventually gives in like I knew she would. The Million Dollar Man was right: *Everybody's got a price!*

"Alright. For this kind of tip, I'll spill the beans, but you have to promise to keep it top secret, okay?"

"My lips are sealed."

She leans in and lowers her voice. "My name is Dawn."

"That's it? That's not so hideous, I thought you'd say Leanne or Nicola or something."

"I hated it ever since school. They used to call me *Crack of Dawn* or *Porn Dawn*, or a million other sexual innuendos."

"Too funny, but hey, it could be worse; you could have been called Waylene Wienerschnitzel."

CHAPTER 46

I'm a genius! I'm a fucking genius!

These are the first thoughts that enter my incessant mind as I awaken in JJ's lavish guest room. I can hardly contain my enthusiasm.

I've just been assaulted by a phenomenal idea for an invention: *Ice-cream drones*. With this being the future I think it's totally doable. Here's the rundown: Say you're walking down the street and you suddenly get hit with an overwhelming craving for a mint choc-chip cone; what do you do? Answer: you get on your Fuji and place an order, and within minutes your ice-cream or ice-creams are flown inside a temperature-controlled box to your exact location by drones. It's like Uber but way better! I have to go pitch this to JJ! I just hope nobody else has thought of it already.

I bounce out of bed, put on a guest robe and descend the spiral stairway. It's really started to hit me now; *I am a successful inventor*. I've been waiting my whole life for this! The loser in me is officially dead, I feel like a giant has been awoken within!

I smell soup (surprise surprise) seeping through the kitchen door, and observe JJ at the blender.

"Good morning, Bobby. I've made a big batch of divine alkaline in my new Vitamix Supreme. I'm telling you, man, I haven't lost my touch one iota. I just love cooking up some marvelous shit to make your mouth water."

He's so buzzing this early in the morning, and takes a large guzzle of the thin green liquid and makes that satisfied *ahhh* sound people make when sipping coffee.

"Man, this is good stuff, today I threw in broccoli, avocado, seaweed, dill weed, Udos 369 oil and pulverized that shit to a pulp. Your energy will go through the roof, so get it while it's warm."

I comply and pour myself a large mug and join him at the breakfast bar.

"Bobby, your mission momentarily is to go to the store and get yourself some golfing attire. Should only take you thirty minutes or so, and to save time, change at the store and head right back here because you and I are going somewhere special."

"Let me guess — we're going golfing this morning?"

"Nope."

"Then why do you want me to purchase golfing apparel and remain in it?"

"Because we're going to play golf this afternoon. This morning we have something else going on and time is a critical factor."

"Fair enough," I stand up. "And would one be kind enough to enlighten me as to where we're going this morning?"

"One is not inclined," he mimics. "One doesn't want to ruin the element of surprise."

"Touché."

He tells me to take the Benz, where the on-screen computer will guide me to the best pro-shop in town on Womack Ave.

"I know how to get to Womack. I've lived in this city my whole life as well, ya know. But wait a minute: you trust me with one of your fancy cars?"

"Yeah. If you trash it, I have others."

"Can't argue with that. Where're the keys?"

"Keys? Keys are a thing of the past like Twitter, the Tennessee Titans and genetically modified mayonnaise. Place your finger on the little scanner next to the door handle to unlock it. You'll be fine, it's idiot-proof."

"Welcome to Tee Time!" says a radiant little sales lady before I've even gotten through the door. "What brought you into our store today?"

"The Mercedes," I wink. "I'm here to acquire some attire for eighteen holes. Do you have any big enough to fit a waistline of a Typhoon?"

She looks back at me with a funny face, obviously confused.

"I just mean I need a golfing outfit for a frame such as this one," motioning to my big-bellied self.

"Ah. Right this way," she leads.

As we stroll through the spacious, high-end pro shop, we make formal introductions and chitchat about Tiger Woods' new wife (you aren't going to believe who it is) then she fills me in on the current PGA champion, along with his love for the fast life and gangster shit. It appears golf has become thugged out in 2030.

"Is Joan your first name, or last name?"

"First, of course."

"Just checking. So, Joanie, on the drive over here a remarkable idea for an invention came into my head, my second of the day as a matter of fact. I'm on fire,

I'm telling ya."

"You are?" she plays along.

"I feel like Lanny Poffo! I want to run it by you, alright? Listen up: With so many things being electronic and connected to the web these days I just came up with: *The Smart-Surfboard!* A surfboard that has a built-in screen hooked up to the web where you can check your email, check your messages, search CONRAD and whatnot. And here's the tag-line: *Surf the Net While You Surf the Ocean...*"

Silence.

She's either weirded out because I'm bouncing off the walls or she hates my brilliant idea and doesn't know what to say. All she can muster is *Errr.*

"You know what, Joanie, no need to answer. Your look has told me enough."

"Yeah, it's pretty terrible."

"Whatever, ideas are a dime a dozen," I shrug. "So, Joanie, I desperately need your help. We need to make chicken salad out of chicken shit."

She laughs, shaking her head.

"What I mean is I need your help to make me look good on the green and spare no expense. Show me your finest golfing attire available, please."

"Are you always like this?" she asks as we maneuver to the luxury section.

"Actually no. But I certainly plan to be on fire from now on. You see, I woke up this morning with two things on my mind, *Ice Cream Delivery Drones* and dinosaurs. Do you ever think about dinosaurs, Joanie?"

"Dinosaurs?"

"Yes."

"No, I can't say that I do."

"Well, did you know that dinosaurs lived on this Earth for about a hundred and seventy-five million years until a big meteor wiped them all out and then humans miraculously came along about sixty-five million years later? You know what all this means don't you?"

"What?"

"That it's our time to shine. The dinosaur era has gone with the wind, so you and I, Joanie have the opportunity and the obligation to live our lives to the fullest before we get wiped out by a colossal meteorite or eaten by an evil race of mutant Giraffes."

She laughs once again as we arrive at the section. "I have to say this is one of the most unusual conversations I've had in a long time."

"Interesting. I like your vibe, Joanie, so I'm gonna make you an offer you can't refuse. Whatever they're paying you I'll double it, all I want is for you to follow me around all day and laugh at my silly jokes."

"Done."

"We'll be like Joanie and Chachi all over again!"

"Who?"

"It doesn't matter. Anyway, I'm on a time constraint, we have to get moving and pick out the very best garments regardless of expense. I'm trusting you to turn me from a Bam Bam Big to the Heartbreak Kid."

She laughs again, but I seriously doubt she gets my silly wrestling reference.

"And there's a nice tip if you pull this off within ten minutes. Show me the double XLs!"

CHAPTER 47

I could so get used to this — cruising behind the wheel of a mayonnaise colored Benz, flaunting expensive golf attire as old-school WWF entrance themes blare out the speakers. Needless to say, heads turn in my direction amongst the hustle and bustle of downtown. Talk about utopia. I feel like the heavyweight champ!

After scooping up JJ in his flashy orange and blue golfing apparel he reclaims the wheel and takes me for a drive without revealing what, where or why (surprise, surprise). We end up down some beaten up back roads which I don't recognize but I refrain from being like an impatient child asking repetitive questions about where are we going and are we there yet? I have to be laid back and nonchalant.

Then it hits me that we're in the southside. It was a shit-hole in my time and looks even worse now. We park up in this ghetto parking lot where all I see is hoopties with big, over-the-top rims and a tall, chubby, security guard who looks a little like Barry White.

"Okay, time-out," I crack. "What the hell are we doing in Holloway? It's a danger zone out here!" (so much for being nonchalant).

He blatantly ignores me as he hunts for something in the glove compartment.

"Are you telling me the southside has been cleaned up now?"

"Nope."

"Then what the hell are we doing in the hood?"

"Relax. Obviously, I'm not gonna come around here when the sun goes down, but it's the AM so we have nothing to worry about."

I have to repeat by demanding to know why we're here in the first place.

"All will be understood in a few minutes." And with that, JJ presses a secret button underneath the steering wheel and out emerges a Sig Sauer from the middle console like a James Bond car. He grabs it and inspects the magazine.

"What the fuck, JJ, a gun? What the hell is going on?!"

"Even though it's extremely unlikely we'll need it, better to have a gun and not need it than to need a gun and not have it. You know how the old saying goes."

I'm completely baffled by this and feel compelled to ask him again why we're here.

"Look, you're sounding like a broken MP3 right now. Trust that I know what I'm doing! I'm Mr. Miyagi, you're Danielsan, got it?" He gets out, conceals the gun in his checkered golf pants and marches forward.

I follow suit and catch up to him by the security guard who's sat at his post eating fried chicken.

"Brother-man," he pulls out a fifty. "Here's for the parking and a little something extra if you promise to watch my baby while we're gone."

This pleases Barry White very much as he expresses his gratitude, "Y'all too kind, mister. Y'all want some fried chicken?"

"Thank you," declines JJ. "We're good."

"You, sho?" he munches. "It's Popeyes, man. It's sooo gud it makes ya eyeballs pop, that's why they be callin' it Pop-eyes."

We're now deep in the projects amongst the burnt-out buildings and bums sleeping in doorways. The liquor store across the street has about twelve shyster-looking dudes loitering outside drinking forty-ounce beers and it's barely ten in the morning. I can only imagine what these people are thinking of two white boys rolling up in their hood in a souped-up mayonnaise-Benz, rocking flashy golf attire. This is a weird situation.

"Errr, JJ, those people are looking at us…"

Instead of answering me he pulls out his Fuji and places a call as we stop outside a dilapidated building. "KK, we're here. Be outside the spot in two minutes."

He kills the call and puts away his Fuji.

"Okay, I think now's the time to inform me what the hell we're doing here."

"You're right, it is. I'm gonna talk fast so you better listen fast because this is important." He clears his throat. "Many people over the years have told me they're going to change their lives and get off drugs. Now, even though they were probably sincere in the moment, those demons usually end up influencing them into having one more line, one more time. Guess what? It's never one more time. That's how addiction works and so they wake up five years later and their life has gone down the drain because they let drugs become the dominant factor in their life."

I try to interject but he cuts me off and continues steamrolling.

"I know this is new to you, I get that, and I know you told me you will never go back to that destructive lifestyle, but I can't be that naïve with you, Bobby. I've done it before with other people and some of them are no longer here. One of my biggest problems in the past was taking people's word as their bond and it's come back to haunt me in so many ways; in business, in relationships, at the foundation and so on. You are here today, to experience all this hell to ensure that you'll never go back."

"By hanging out in the ghetto?"

"By watching how people who choose to fuck around with drugs for years end up," he says adamantly.

"But these people aren't indulging in the same drugs or lifestyle as me. Nor are they anything like me, so how can I relate to this?"

"Don't be so naïve, Bobby. You went from having just a few beers a few nights per week to a six-pack every night. Then you added cocaine into the mix which rapidly increased, not to mention hookers, erratic spending, pills and using excessive amounts of food like a drug." He punches his fist into his hand and becomes more animated. "This could totally happen to you so don't take this fucking lightly!"

He's more fired up now, while I remain frozen like Sub-Zero. He has a point, I have to admit.

"Have you ever looked at a homeless person sleeping in the street and wondered how the hell they ended up there?" he goes on. "I've interviewed hundreds of them and let me tell you; I've come to the conclusion that drugs play the biggest part in every single case with very few exceptions. And by the way, not only hard drugs but alcohol which is arguably one of the hardest and most deadly drugs. It has ruined so many 'normal people' and turned them into street beggars because they fell into the addiction trap. You're here today, Bobby, because you're at a fork in the road."

I plead that I'll never go back, I've completely changed for good, but he doesn't buy it and looks back with malevolence.

"Bobby, as much as I want to believe you, it's backfired on me so many times in the past. You have to just trust that I know what I'm doing because I've played the game before. I'm ten years older and wiser than you, so I know exactly what it's like to be in your shoes."

As I take in his point of view, an impeccably dressed brother-man struts up to us from the street.

"Whud-up, JJ! Come show a brother some love."

They embrace like the close friends I can only presume they are.

"Keith, I want you to meet my cousin Randy," says JJ.

"What's crackin', fam? They call me Kool Keith." He leans in to give me a dap. "Dammnn, look at you dressed like a couple of skittles. I can't front though, you be cooler than a motherfuckin' polar bear's toenails."

We all chuckle at his silliness.

"Like Elvis in '68," JJ plays along. He then asks Keith to inform me about what his life was like four years ago before he enrolled in JJ's program.

"Are you sure, man? I was kinda fucked up back in the day."

JJ nods and gives him the floor.

"Alright." Keith takes a breath and turns to me. "Back then, man, I was just a lost soul with no sense, no purpose, no direction. Before Kool Keith, nigga's around the way called me Ketamine Keith. I was always fucking with Ket or that Amphet which sent a nigga crazy, ya know. I always strived to be an uppity negro, but we were bummy, all of us, dirty niggas. We had two bunk-beds b'tween eleven niggas. It be Survivor Series fo' real out here, man, and back then I'd do any-motherfuckin'-thang to make a dollar. I was on some '*By Any Means Necessary*' shit, without thinking 'bout the repercussions — jostling, boosting, Three-card Molly, stealin', slingin', you name it, I dun did it..." He stares off into the distance looking ashamed. "Man, I was such a dirty, rotten, scoundrel-ass-nigga, I once ran up in the church and robbed the preacher for the offering..."

Sheesh is the only word I can muster as a car slowly drives past us. Needless to say, all eyes are on us from the passers-by — two white men dressed in colorful golf attire and one jiving black dude who appears so slick, he's probably got a doctrine in style. We must stand out like a dildo in a bingo hall.

"Here's the mentality of nigga's in the hood, right," he continues his rap, "picture a bunch of pigeons in a coop — they all family who love each other, right? But when you throw 'em crumbs, they all scramble and do anythang including kill each other just to get a crumb. That's exactly what's going on every day in these streets, dawg."

"Tell him about...ya know," instructs JJ.

"I was just about to jump on that, J." He turns back to me. "The only way out the hood was to hustle my way out, at least that's what I thought. I knew I couldn't buy a Lexus Coupe with no damn coupon so I started strategizing ways to make it big like Ricky Ross. I wanted to be different from other niggas so I started with books. Ever heard of *The Psychology of Selling* by...what's his name..."

"Brian Tracy," I say helping him out. "Of course, it's a classic in the sales industry."

"Right. I studied that shit and applied it to the drug game. I could have wrote my own shit called *The Psychology of Selling Drugs*. I became totally obsessed with product and distribution — product/distribution, product/distribution, product/distribution. That's all that went through my head like a motherfuckin' 2Pac hook. I kept reading corporate America business books and applied key principles to the drug game, especially *flexibility* because the market is always changing. If there was no money selling weed, then I'd sell dope, if there was no money selling dope, then I'd sell coke, if there was no money selling coke, then I'd sell X, and if niggas didn't cop the X then I'd sling techs."

"I guess you had to do what you had to do."

"That was my whole mentality back then, dawg; I didn't care about what it was doing to my people in the community," he pauses. "But I fucked up when I started getting high on my own supply, which is the cardinal motherfuckin' sin in the drug game. That's when my life really spiraled outta control and I started stealin' again."

"And what changed?" interjects JJ. "What was the major turning point that shifted you?"

"Niggas were getting three strikes and I ain't talking about bowling. That shit scared me to motherfuckin' death. The rest of my friends were either dead or in hood-rehab, so I knew I'd have to change or I'd end up just like them. That's when it really hit me I had to turn my life around or I would have offed myself with a nine-milly or took wild pharmaceuticals like Milli Vanilli. That's how low I was…" He breaks. "That was the moment it became a MUST to me. No more SHOULD shit, it was a motherfuckin' MUST."

"Then what happened?" asks JJ.

"I took motherfuckin' action! I found out about your shit and I got my ass enrolled. And I'll never forget your first speech that really hit home, Double J. That shit you said about straightening your life out struck a chord with a nigga and got me all emotional and shit. I never dun seen a white man care so much about strangers—mostly black strangers in the hood. It made me think differently about other races and hooked me to get involved with the movement. And since that day, I've never looked back and it's all thanks to you, my man." He reaches out for a pound.

"No-no, it wasn't down to me, I was just a catalyst. It was down to you making a decision to change your life and never reneging on that decision. The foundation is just a vehicle. You're the one who's responsible for all the changes up here," JJ points to his head, "and thus, Kool Keith was born."

"I guess you're right. Damn, I am responsible, ain't I? But I gotta give you mad props too, son. It's KK and JJ forever as far as I'm concerned."

"You better believe it and, Randy," JJ says, turning to me, "he's the coolest MoFo you'll ever meet, I'm telling you. He's like the black Fonze."

"He ain't lying. I'm so bad I make happiness sad."

We all share a laugh. This dude is crazy.

JJ suggests that we enter the crack-house to see if we can find any lost souls.

"Shit, man, we in the right place. Let's go check it out and see what we can find. And don't worry, dawgs, ain't nobody gonna fuck with us."

I ask with great caution how can he be so sure.

"Because me and the goons have an understanding, we speak the same language, ya dig? Come on, let's boogie."

CHAPTER 48

JJ and I follow Kool Keith into the grimy, abandoned building, carefully dodging broken glass, bird shit and a plethora of discarded junk in our path. As the door swings open the awful stench of urine and lord knows what else violently assaults our nasal cavities. Strangely, this doesn't faze the both of them while I'm on the verge of puking and plead to go back. But my begging is in vain so I man up and sidestep more smelly filth as we make our way through the building.

In the far corner, we spot a middle-aged black man curled up in a pissy yellow sleeping bag amongst heaps of old magazines. I'm pretty sure he isn't asleep because he's wriggling around like a worm while clutching a wine bottle.

"Damn, this cat's back again?" says Keith. "We go way back, me and this guy."

"Oh yeah?" says JJ.

"He was the kingpin back in the day."

"A drug kingpin?" I ask.

"Nah, he was the *man* at The Lucky Strike—the best I'd ever seen. We used to call him *The Street Sweeper* because he hit nothing but strikes and spares every time. And this dude was immaculate, from his outfits to his whips—even his bowling ball seemed to glisten like cubic zirconia."

"And now he's ended up here," remarks JJ. "What a travesty."

"True that. This dude had it all together, he'd have more exotic birds than a motherfuckin' rainforest. Let's go holla at him real quick."

Kool Keith glides towards the corner while we linger cautiously behind.

"Burt. What's crackalackin', my brother? Haven't seen you in a minute."

Burt's crusty eyes come to life and suspiciously gaze in our direction. "Keith?" he frowns as a butt-end dangles from his ashy lips.

"Don't you know anything about those damn cigarettes, dawg? The *Man* wants to hook you with his poisons as a way of controlling the black race! It ain't nuttin' but euthanasia. You better quit bullshitting yourself, nigga!"

Kool Keith's passionate credo goes in one ear and out the other as he remains transfixed at us white boys. "Who are these people you with?"

"These are my friends."

"Friends? I've never dun seen you with these friends before. Are you Five-O?" he says directly at JJ and I.

"Do they look like Five-O, man?" returns Keith. "They about to be screamin' *FOUR*, not *Five-O*."

"So what are you, their bag-boy? What you doing with a couple of golfers, man?" The bum turns his head and hocks a loogie off to the side like the classy guy he is.

"These are some good friends of mine and I'd appreciate a little hospitality. JJ here has a foundation that changes people's lives and shit. He has a lot of great knowledge, wisdom and understandin' that will help your raggedy-ass if you just listen for a minute."

"Whut he gonna do? Teach me how to swing a nine?"

JJ interjects by asking Burt in a somewhat elegant manner if he could ask him a few questions about living in the streets.

"I thought you had all the wisdom and understanding, Mr. golf man? I ain't interested in parlaying with your caddy-shack-ass. I got all the wisdom and understanding I need right here." Burt grabs his bottle of cherry wine and slurps a healthy amount with it dribbling out the side of his mouth.

Keith tries reasoning with him, going back and forth until JJ comes up with the bright idea to offer him some fried chicken from the place across the street. It works beautifully. Burt perks up like he's just downed three shots of 5-hour ENERGY.

"Shit, Mr. golf man, why didn't you say? I'll give you white folks anything you want for some Popeyes biscuits and gravy..." he lets his request hang, "...and a Diet Coke."

JJ pulls out a fifty and asks Keith to do the food run then asks Burt how he ended up here.

"I wasn't always like this." He sits up against the corner. "I was a high roller back in the day: Hair tight, swagger right, manicures and pedicures was like a weekly routine. Life was fly back then, man. Shit... I'd walk down the street in the softest minks and the shiniest gators with my pockets looking like they got appendicitis..." His mood brightens a little from a trip down memory lane as he lights a half-smoked cigarette.

"What did you do back then for work?"

He tells us he used to sell knives door to door, and he was the hottest salesman *they ever dun seen.*

"Get outta here. You?"

"Shit, yeah. Ever heard of Ginsu knives? I used to sell those thangs by the truckload. I had my whole shit down and everythang, the loot kept pouring in like a slot machine."

He puffs away on his butt and plows on about his boss used to tell him he had a special gift to fire everybody up to sell knives. "I didn't care what their background was, I just wanted money-hungry cats on my team. We were straight-commission-niggas, so it be impossible to say no, ya-know-whud-I'm-sayin'?"

"How did it come to an end if things were so good back then?"

"The leeches and snakes came out the woodwork. I used to take care of all the tabs when we hung out at the club. I was running around with people I thought were my friends but turned out to be fugazi. They didn't like me; they liked the nigga with the Afro-American Express." He continues puffing away on the butt revealing he felt unworthy of all his material possessions. "How could I cruise down the block in a Range Rover, flossing like a motherfuckin' dentist, while these nigga's be starving in the hood? That's like dangling that shit in they face!"

He looks torn as he coughs up another loogie and hacks it right in front of us which makes me cringe.

"I felt like everybody be judging a nigga," he continues, "so I began to squander all my shit and eventually stopped going to work. Then I started doing all kinds of wild pharmaceuticals and believe me, it didn't take long for the money to dry up. And when the skrilla was gone, nigga's scattered like roaches."

He takes a swig from his cherry wine, throws away his cigarette and stares off into the distance.

"What happened next?"

"I stayed intoxicated for as long as I can remember and got caught slipping. Everybody knew my fur game was off the chain — nigga's used to call my closet the *Pet Cemetery* and one night they raided my whole shit. They be so cold those crackhead niggas, they even took my Christmas sweater my grandmomma made before she passed."

He takes another healthy guzzle of wine as he clutches the bottle tight like he's trying to strangle it. "I lost everythang. My girl, my friends, my job, my house, my family, all gone, and they blackballed a nigga. When I eventually tried to get myself back on my feet, they wouldn't have nuttin' to do with me, even though I could smoke anybody on the whole roster."

He takes another swig and regurgitates more phlegm. "I'd be out there selling them shits right now if they give a nigga a chance."

You can see the major conflict written all over his face. It's obvious to me he's bitter and angry because he knows he's better than this. To see such a vast amount of homelessness in such a rich nation is one of the saddest things about our country in my opinion. This is the first time I've actually taken the time to listen how somebody ended up like this.

"Well," says JJ. "Why don't you pull yourself up by your boots and apply for another sales position and relaunch your career? You have a gift don't you, Burt?"

"Ain't nobody gonna hire an old, down-and-out bummy-ass-nigga. I always end up right back in the gutter like a motherfuckin' bowling pin." Burt's depression is pretty ingrained. It's like an awful funk radiating out of him. He looks back at the floor and comments that he's broken and there ain't no hope.

JJ steps closer and changes his demeanor to that of an authority figure. "Here's how I see it; you're just not looking at this situation the right way. Let me give you an analogy." He pulls out a fifty-dollar bill and asks does he want it.

"Shit yeah, nigga!" Burt lights up. "What the fuck you thank?"

"How about now?" JJ rips it a little and crumples it up. "Do you still want it?"

"Shit, that don't matter to me, I'll take it."

"How about now?" JJ throws it on the floor, spits and tramples on it before looking back at Burt. "How about now? Do you still want it?"

Burt doesn't look fazed. "It don't bother me. Give it here."

"It doesn't bother you that's it's been spat, torn and stomped on?"

"Shit, man, you could wipe your ass with that shit and I'll still take it."

"But why would you take it after all what it's been through?" asks JJ.

"Because, man, fifty bucks is fifty bucks."

"So what you're saying is; it doesn't matter that it's damaged because the value is still the same, right?"

Burt nods, remaining transfixed with the bill on the floor.

"Well, that's exactly how I feel about you, Burt. You may have been hurt, damaged and shitted on like you said, but your value in life is the same as before. There's a champion inside you, we just need to bring him out again, my brother."

After more ping-ponging back and forth with Burt being skeptical about JJ having ulterior motives, JJ wins the conversation by being more assertive and congruent—convincing him to at least try his rehabilitation program. It's been said when two people have a debate the person with the most certainty and the most conviction wins. Also, JJ had the added leverage of the fried chicken and threatened to take it away when Burt was on the fence.

"So," continues JJ, "are you willing to put in the work and get cleaned up at our program and in return, you'll not only get food, clothing and shelter, you'll regain *you* in the process?"

"Shit, man, where do I sign?"

"This is an opportunity to get your life back and it can start right now. And I really do mean right now. We are willing to drive you to the foundation this very minute, but I need to know are you willing to commit yourself a hundred percent to turning your life around?"

"Yes, sir!"

"Well then, get up off the floor, put that wine down and come this way. We have a van waiting for you with your Popeyes in the back."

Burt suddenly springs into action, grabs his meager possessions and follows us out the grotty building.

Out in the street, we see Kool Keith with his charismatic smile behind the wheel of a white van. "Hold on a second," Burt drops his stuff on the floor and runs back in the building, soon returning with the crumpled up fifty. "Shit, you better believe I ain't forgetting 'bout this. You boys must think I'm crazy." Then climbs in the back, immediately digging into the bucket of chicken as Keith peels off.

"I wonder how he's gonna take it when he realizes it's vegan chicken?" he smiles. "Did you see that, Bobby? I really want you to get a sense of what it's like to lose everything because of drugs and irresponsible behavior. Anybody can turn their life around, some just need a little help and motivation, that's why I formed the foundation."

Before I can interrogate, JJ saves me the trouble and elaborates about this foundation he keeps alluding to. "We reach out to the people who society has forgotten about; the outcasts, the downtrodden and offer them guidance and direction. The problems that I've seen throughout the ghettos in this country is when you live in a poor neighborhood, the only schools available are poor ones. When you have poor schools, you have poor teachers. When you have poor teachers, you get a poor education. When you get a poor education you'll most likely end up in a poor paying job. And that poor-paying job only enables you to live in a poor neighborhood. It's a vicious cycle that unfortunately traps so many generations in poor communities, so we developed a foundation that takes people from poverty to prosperity. We teach them the fundamentals of living a righteous life—and that's not a religious connotation, *righteous* just means living a life that's right for the individual."

"Makes sense. Sounds pretty incredible."

"I like to think so. After years of trial and error, we've now got an impeccable step by step system down to a syntactical science. It's a beautiful thing to watch. We first teach the basics like cleanliness and general hygiene, that's essential. Then we get them involved with the community, helping others, helping kids, instilling discipline in them military-style, and then of course education. Nourishing their minds with life-changing wisdom and testing them vigorously. When they graduate they are like a whole new person. Then we help them find a place to live, get back to employment and loads of other good stuff.

"But anyway, Bobby, let's not get off base, you're here today to learn. I don't give people free handouts, that's stupid. Any rich fuck can walk around the projects handing out hundred-dollar bills like Ted DiBiase and they're just gonna say *thank you, sucker,* then go off to buy Thunderbird and Newports. We don't give out fish, we help people become fishermen. That's what we're all about: teaching them how to help themselves back into society."

"It sounds very moralistic, to say the least." I have to admit I'm very impressed with my future self's ideology.

"And now you've seen my technique. It took me a while to get it down, but we figured seduce them with free food and lure them in with a free ride. That's what seems to work best. All we have to do is get them there and stick with the program if they do their life will be forever changed for the greater good."

"It almost seems like a form of ethical bribery."

"Hey, call it what you want, but it's effective. I come around the southside one Sunday a month with Kool Keith for a couple of hours to interact with the people. We simply listen to their stories and present them with an opportunity to get their lives back together. And because of that, we influence a large percentage of new enrollments every month because it's much more powerful than some generic ad campaign on the web. Not too many homeless folks spend a lot of time on the internet, you see."

"I can believe that."

"So before we go off to the green, let's see if we can influence a few more lives, and when you hear their stories about losing everything you'll start to see patterns. You'll notice the common denominator in about ninety-five percent of cases is *drugs.* Their whole downfall was putting drugs as their highest priority and it ruined everything. It's so sad. By getting to know these people it will make you re-evaluate the choices you've made recently and I guarantee this will be an experience you'll never forget…"

And he was right. It was another experience I'll truly never forget.

One lady told us that she sold her dog just to get high. Instead of buying food and diapers for her newborn, she'd buy crack-cocaine. This got me on the brink of tears, especially when she told me they took her daughter away for eight years while denying the freedom to see her. I thought my drug abuse was bad in recent months, but I cannot ever imagine having my daughter taken away because of drugs.

Another man told me and I quote: *"Dope, no doubt, is the biggest pimp in the history of the world because if you allow yourself to get hooked on dope, you become its prostitute—you become its ho. That's exactly what happened to me. I'm a ho to this motherfucking crack pipe and I cannot stop.*"

I'd never thought about it like that. It was so touching, to say the least, but the sad thing was we couldn't convince him to put the pipe down and join the program so he ran off to score more.

One guy called Fester told us he did so much speedballing over the years, the accumulated effect had permanently altered his brain chemistry so he can no longer control his bodily functions. And to prove it he lifted up his trouser leg to reveal shit smeared all around his ankles. It seriously was one of the nastiest and saddest things I've ever witnessed. He kept pleading and begging money for beer because he said it helps numb the pain, but JJ didn't give in, instead, he gave him food, recited some inspirational words and off in the van he went.

We went around about seven or eight more people using the same exact system — Kool Keith breaks the ice with ebonics and criminal slang, then JJ asks them the same routine questions basically. Then offers them food, sells them on changing their life with the help of his program and Keith drives them away in the van. They're a perfect tag-team like Hawk and Animal and have their technique down to a T.

There's no way in a million years would I think I'd form some kind of homeless rehabilitation program and actually spend time every month talking to the bums in the slums while packing a gun. Thank God we didn't have to use it. My future self really is a diabolical genius who seems to get off on helping people change for the greater good. I have a long way to go if I'm going to become him.

CHAPTER 49

We haul ass in the Benz to the country club as we're a little late from talking to so many street people. To see the homeless so down and out on everything but yet still scrape enough money together to buy drugs, alcohol and cigarettes (which are all drugs I know) is such a travesty. It hardly makes me a damn saint, but still, I can never go back to my old destructive ways. No fucking way.

Anyway, I have to switch gears and get into character as we're off for a round of golf with some of JJ's associates.

"When's the last time you've been on the green, Bobby?"

"It's been years," I say with a slight frown. "You should know that."

"What do you mean by that?"

"What do you mean, *what do I mean?* I'm you, you dingbat?"

"Like I've told you," explains JJ, "I do my best to block out a lot of my ill past until you showed up, so my memory of those days are hazy at best. Oh, and that reminds me; if they ask you a lot of personal questions about how we know each other, just keep it brief. Remember they've never known me as Bobby, only JJ, so let's stick to the script, *Randy.*"

We soon arrive at the club of all country clubs and merge into a little gridlock of cars who have pulled up at the same time. I take the opportunity to observe the pristine, well-manicured greenery and upscale clubhouse. Complete awe would be an understatement. It's funny; thirty minutes ago we were in a foul, stenchy, rat-infested crack-house, now we're at what has to be the hottest club in the city.

"This is the hottest club in the city," says JJ, right on cue, "so be on your best behavior. You're going to get some key insights and maybe some life lessons from two of my closest kindred spirits."

"Kindred spirits?"

"Yup. These two have both defied the odds and are living proof that anybody can overcome anything. You're gonna love it."

We enter the spectacular lobby that houses the biggest, most majestic chandelier I've ever seen from the Venetian plastered ceiling. Many heads turn in our direction, or more precisely towards JJ's direction. Well-wishers wish him well and shake his hand as if President Jack Tunney just entered the building. He's the man around here without a doubt.

After all the hoopla, we fetch our clubs to the golf buggies where JJ introduces me to his people. First, Kerry; a six-foot-two stocky brute with hands like Big John Studd. He's a southern boy that has that stereotypical jock vibe about him, like a grown-up version of A.C. Slater. Then, Charlene X, a petite young lady rocking a pink, Chanel golfing outfit, with large Bret Hart style sunglasses that are too big for her face. She looks very comfortable around all this testosterone as we shake hands and get acquainted.

We drive out to the green in two parties as the buggies are only seated for two. I'm paired with Kerry, riding shotgun who tells me how much he likes my name *Raaandy* with his deep southern drawl, and seems to be very much drawn to the sky.

"Man, there ain't a cloud up there," he says, inhaling a healthy dose of autumn air. "It don't git much more perfect than this."

I too admire the picturesque horizon as we approach the first hole. "So glad it ain't raining. It would have ruined today if it had."

"I once read when I was a little boy that when it rains it means God's crying, so I too ain't much a fan of the rain."

I do my best to hold in my laughter as I can't say I share that belief.

"Looks like we have to wait a few minutes for the folk in front," he continues. "That's aah-ite, it's gud sometimes to just kick back n' observe Mother Nature's beauty."

There's a party of six in front of us, so we pull up to the side as they prepare to tee-off.

"Do y'all read much, Raaandy?"

I have to come clean by telling him I don't. "In all honesty, I don't make it a high priority and make excuses like I haven't got the time."

"My uncle Jimmy once told me if you only had time for a meal or a chapter you shud skip the meal. N' most books now be available in audio, so you can read with your ears while you're traveling, exercising or doing the dishes."

"You're right. I've never listened to an audiobook before, I must get into that."

"You gotta. Audiobooks are the best! It's like having a complete stranger read you a bedtime story for like eight hours n' you don't even have to be in bed!"

"I've gotta admit, Kerry, I took you for more of a jock than a bookworm."

"Is it that obvious?" he smiles, putting his sunglasses on. "Yeah ever since I was a young-un growin' up I had two major obsessions in life: football n' the solar system."

"The solar system? That kinda threw me off."

"You n' err'body else. I grew up in a little place near Round Rock, Texas where there ain't much going on. In fact, the only thing on the agenda throughout the entire town is football, football, football. Friday it's high school football, Saturday it's college, n' Sunday it's the pros. You don't hear guys talking about Saturn n' Uranus where I come from, just Tight Ends n' Cheerleaders…"

I chuckle at his delivery. He's quirky with a capital Q. "Sports and the solar system. You gotta love it!"

"Dang right! They were my escape cuz we were the dirt po' family in our community. We'd have to wait until the supermarkets closed so we cud get the produce that they were 'bout to throw out for free. Collard greens were called *collard browns* in our house cuz that's all we cud git, n' we'd go on midnight dumpster dives at Dunkkkin's just to get some leftover Munchkkkins."

Damn, all these people I keep meeting seem to have grown up so hard. Makes me realize how easy I had it in my youth.

"Sounds like it was tough for you guys back then."

"Raaandy, you don't even know the half, my brother. I wanted more than anything to become a star Running Back or an Astronaut. Err'body used to laugh at that cuz we were the po'est of the po' so they had already labeled me a loser that could never escape to 'nother world. Sum times I believed them n' wilded out. I once stole a crate offa back of a truck n' ran into the woods. Me n' my brother Lance got so excited when we opened it, it wassa case a honey. We never had honey befo' so guess what we did?"

"What?"

"We drank all twelve jars between us, one after the other."

I scrunch up my face and can only imagine that nasty shit.

"I had OD like symptoms afterwards, fo' real. Hallucinations, the shakes and throwing up all day. It was real bad. I couldn't even look at honey fo' 'bout twenny years."

He shivers a little as he recalls that incident which spreads to me like an infectious yawn. I then segue the conversation by asking if he played football growing up.

"Sure thing. About eighteen seasons ago—in ninth grade, I tried out for the team…" he pauses, "but received the most devastating news I cud ever imagine."

"What?"

"Coach told me I was too weak, I was too skinny n' too small to ever play football on a competitive level, so I should just stick to my planets n' stuff. Those were his words; I remember it like it wer yesterday."

"What a dick."

"It absolutely ruined me, Raaandy, I was utterly pulverized. Football was my life, my number one obsession, but I was such a disproportioned kid from all that junk we ate growing up. I worked-out I had three hundred n' twelve days 'til next season so I made a pledge to do whatever it took to get in condition n' prove that egg-sucking son-of-a-bitch wrong."

He's getting all pumped up now like he's back there again. It's clear that pain was his primary motivation, I've seen it in others over many times. "Rejection can fuck you up or drive you."

"Dang straight. I was 5'7 back then n' knew I couldn't grow upwards by choice, so I set out to grow sideways. I lifted weights with all the might n' force in the world, knowing not only am I gonna make the team, I'm gonna be the best dang player they ever seen. I was militant, guzzling raw eggs every morning like Rocky, n' eating grilled flamingo burgers six times a week to keep me lean. I didn't even have one piece of cake on my bornday cuz I didn't want anything slowing me down. I wanted to be an impeccable physical specimen n' become like gold-dust for the team."

"The wrestler?"

"No. Like actual *gold-dust*. Like being so valuable they cud never let me go. By the time next season came 'round I was seven inches taller, forty-seven pounds heavier, n' one mean son-of-a-gun. I wanted the opponents to fear me in every possible way so they couldn't function as a unit, and went on to smash all the high school records."

"That's pretty remarkable. There was nothing stopping you."

"Right. My hunger n' drive was unmatched. I was so devastated from being rejected by Coach Tolos that I used it as my fuel. You might actually say being rejected was the best thing that ever happened to me cuz it made me out-work err'body else. I wasn't just in competition with our opponents, I was in competition with my teammates too, cuz I knew I'd be damn near suicidal if somebody took my spot."

"You sound like you were one hell of a player."

"I was 'cuz I demanded nothing else. My rookie year of college was the same, the NFL scouts were all over me, so I couldn't let anything get in the way of me making it to the big leagues so I could buy Momma her pig farm that she always dreamed 'bout."

"That's pretty sweet of you. Did you make it to the big time?"

He shoots me a look of disdain and says, "I would have if it wasn't for this," and reaches down to the lower part of his left leg and detaches it like a robot. I shudder at his exposed nub of skin just hanging there, then he hands me the leg to examine.

"God, it looks so freaking real. What's this made of and what the hell happened?"

He tells me his leg is the result of the miracle of modern technology. "It's easier to put together than a dang protein shake blender."

"You're not a cyborg surrounded by living tissue are you?"

He laughs while reattaching it and reveals that he skidded under a mack truck while making a sharp turn on his motorcycle—completely crushing his leg and inches away from killing him.

"Oh my god!"

"It was totally my fault — I got distracted by a redhead at a bus stop."

"No way!"

"Changed my entire destiny in a single second, ruining my whole NFL career before it had even begun."

I look on thinking what a travesty and ask him how he took it.

"I just denied it thinking it was sum kinda baaad dream." He sits up. "Then I fell into a pit of depression n' mourning n' feeling sorry for myself. I never did drugs because I knew they were baaad, but I did everything else like lying, cheating, stealing n' was so ashamed that I could no longer get Momma her pig farm."

"Did you have to resort to working a regular job or something?"

"Eventually after they dun fixed me up. I ended up helping Daddy at his fumigation bizness. I hated it. I never worked a 'job' job in my life. I was a football star, my destiny wasn't supposed to be getting up at dawn to kill rodents just to make enough bread to drive a used pickup. I cudn't take it, I went from living the *American Dream,* to living a nightmare... I actually did have nightmares 'bout all the rats I killed coming back to life and nibbling my gud leg off."

His bizarre haunting of rats oddly inspires a great idea for a fumigation company in me — instead of using poisonous gas to kill pests; why not use a gas that sedates them for a few hours so they can be hauled off and freed into the woods (or wherever rats and rodents live) where they can enjoy the rest of their natural life... Maybe I could pitch this to his dad?

"That's pretty deep," I say, snapping out of my brilliance. "So how did you overcome your depression?"

"One day I just flipped, I cudn't take it no longer. I declared that this must change n' I must be the one to change it, so I went right back to the solar system. I became very at peace after studying the planets n' stars n' the galaxy n' all that other celestial gud shit which lead me to form my own company: *Supercluster.*"

"Interesting," I say, noticing the people in front have finally moved on. "Hey, looks like we're up."

We step out the buggy, grab our drivers and walk to the teeing off area. I notice him walking perfectly for a man with a fake leg.

"Be my guest, Raaandy, y'all go first."

I step up and hit a horrible shot that veers off to the left. "Ah shit, I hooked it."

"Y'all get the hang of it," he steps into position. "It's all about concentration and focus."

BANG.

He hits a terrific shot down the middle of the fairway. "Owee, momma, I hit that son-of-a-bitch gud."

"So how did learning about the planets help you change?" I ask as we hop back in the buggy and depart.

"Have y'all ever taken the time to study the *Cosmos*, Raaandy?"

"Negative. I know a little about the universe as a whole and enjoy those shows on the Discovery channel, but never studied it at any great length."

"When you take the time to study the *Observable Universe,* y'all can't help being fascinated. It made me so clear-headed n' really put things into perspective about what life's about."

"What is life about?" I echo, putting him on the spot.

"Life is a blessing n' a gift my friend. We're all on this Earth to contribute to one another in a positive way for the betterment of the planet. It's when you lose perspective of the truth, you become discombobulated with reality. Real talk."

"Pretty good philosophy," I step out the buggy and hit my ball once again like an amateur.

"Yes, sir, it is. I live every day in accordance with my life's highest goals," he says as I hop back in the buggy and take off. "And if I get off track I remind myself we're living in a perfectly organized galaxy n' everything happens for a reason."

It's quite fascinating to observe this jacked-up jock from Texas come out with such an interesting philosophy and angle of life. We step out the buggy once again and Kerry lines up to swing.

"Yup, when people ask me what kinda business I'm involved in, I just say *celestial navigation.* Even though it ain't technically true, it sounds pretty rad. One thing that is true: I'm blessed to be living the life that I've designed, I may-a had a few bumps in the road but I cudn't be happier with the path I'm on."

BOOM.

Once again he hits his ball with awesome power and precision.

"Sometimes I lose perspective of that." I say soberly, "My identity, my path, myself. I feel that I've spent the past year or so going through a mid-life crisis."

"I think we've all felt like that at sum point, Raaandy. The old me used to get so stressed 'bout everything, if I went to Jack in the Box and they forgot to put the dang pickles on my sourdough, I'd become enraged n' cuss a hella storm."

"I can certainly relate to that," I say as we approach my ball in the rough.

"But after studying our *milky way*, I just think what's the point of getting all stressed over extra cheese n' Jalapeños. We're only on this little planet fo' 'bout thirty-one thousand days anyway, so all that stuff is insignificant when you look at the big picture."

"True that," I swing. I'm getting better.

"My friends noticed my spiritual awakening too. I became more centered n' calm. I had to walk away from Daddy's company n' move on. I'm way too spiritual to commit genocide on termites n' cockroaches now. They're Earthlings after all."

"Hmmm." I nod and go into a little trance again as we stride along the fairway.

"Yep, now I actually have a small ant farm n' nurture my little critters every day. I feel like God to my six-legged blessings cuz if you think 'bout it, I am. If I wanted to I could poison them, crush them, burn them, flood them, infect them with pestilence. I could put rival insects in there to create a war or a gecko in there to eat them up in a matta of minutes. I cud literally create an ant Sodom and Gomorrah if I wanted to, but I ain't no dang Neo-Nazi. Instead, I choose to nurture them, love them, whisper sweet nothings in their ears. I provide them with resources to create their very own Ant Rapture — I kinda like having power over this little race of ants. Every morning I stare at them thinking I wonder what they think of me, do they worship me as their Lord n' Savior?"

"When you put it like that, I think you are their God," I pat his back. "Would you class yourself as a religious man?"

"Well, Raaandy," he adjusts his collar. "My religion is very simple: *happiness*."

"Wow. That's probably the best answer I've ever heard," I say as we arrive at his ball.

"My whole philosophy is helping others reach their goals and ambitions in life—including ants. A wise man once told me: *'if you help enough people get what they want; you'll get exactly what you want'*. It don't git any better than that now does it?"

He wallops his ball once again perfectly towards the flag and hollers. "Boy, I'm on fire today! Wooooo!"

CHAPTER 50

After an interesting and insightful nine-hole beat down courtesy of big Kerry, we switch it up. I'm now paired with Charlene X who rides the passenger seat as the gleaming sun reflects off her 'Hitman' style sunglasses.

"How did you get on with JJ?" I ask as we drive towards the tenth hole.

"Beat him like a piñata," she responds all cool and nonchalant.

"Oh boy, what have I got myself into? Are you a pro or something?"

"No, but I have a pretty good sense for golf. I decided years ago to get good at it, so I did."

"That simple, eh?"

She tells me it was simple. "It wasn't easy, but it was simple. So I'm assuming JJ hasn't told you much about me."

"Yeah, not really. He kept it pretty brief about both of you, he likes to keep me on my toes I guess. I had no idea I was about to play golf with a one-legged man, who, by the way, wiped the floor with me."

We arrive at the hole where I offer her to go first. She takes her time going to the back where the clubs are and starts meticulously feeling the driver heads before selecting one.

"Are you okay?" I ask, sensing something odd.

"He didn't tell you, did he?"

"Tell me what?"

"Wow, I know you said he kept it brief, but I didn't think you meant that brief."

"What are you talking about?"

"I'm blind."

"You're blind?" I say, completely taken aback.

"Yes. I'm surprised you never noticed."

"Well, I wasn't paying that much attention when we met earlier. I did notice those enormous sunglasses though."

She smiles and agrees that they're pretty big.

"Wait a minute, how do you play golf if you're blind?"

"I just need help getting lined up. Once I'm there, I'm good."

"I've gotta say, I'm shocked and impressed that you can play. Did you really beat JJ, or was that a joke?"

"No, I whooped him. I usually win unless he plays a trick by positioning me in the wrong direction."

"Ha. I guess you have to totally trust the person you're playing with."

"A-huh. Just don't ask me to drive the buggy."

I laugh again at her dry wit then lead her to the teeing area, plant her ball and set her in the correct position. "You're all set. Good luck."

"Thanks for the guidance, Randy, but…" she wallops her ball perfectly like a blind, white, female version of Tiger Woods, "…I don't believe in luck. I believe in probability."

"Wait a minute, are you guys yanking my chain? First, he sets me up with a one-legged dude who kicked my ass, now a blind gal that's even better. Come on, let me see those eyes."

"Trust me; you don't want to see underneath these glasses."

"Sorry. Had to ask."

I line up and hit my shot, not a bad one, but no way near as good as hers then we hop back in and take off.

"I couldn't imagine being born blind and not knowing what yellow polka dots look like. Can I ask what happened? Were you born that way? Or did you have an accident? Or am I being too prying?"

"No, it's okay. I think I should illuminate you with my story. It is a little heavy though."

I tell her it's perfectly okay if she doesn't want to as I've heard some pretty heavy stories this morning.

"Well," she hesitates. "I think I should just come out and say it: Stop the buggy a sec."

I comply by pulling up to the side and kill the engine.

"I wasn't born blind; I grew up a very normal girl, in Normalville, USA."

"I've heard of that place," I wink before realizing it's pointless to wink at a blind chick. "I, however, grew up in Abnormalville where we believed in Santa Claus and WWF wrestling."

"Ignorance is bliss, my friend—at least in that context. Yep, I was just a regular little girl with dreams of growing up to be an archaeologist or an entrepreneur."

I chuckle at the dissimilarities and ask her if she could have only chosen one back then, which would it have been.

"Entrepreneur. I had a major passion for business from a young age and was always thinking outside the box. When I'd receive a bornday gift I'd always ask for the receipt, then I'd take it back for a refund and buy it back when it was on sale and save the profit. Then I'd invest the profits into a second bike, so I had one to ride and one to rent."

"Interesting," I muse. "How old were you when you started thinking like this?"

"About eleven."

"Eleven? Wow. When I was eleven, I was transfixed with video games and Dusty Rhodes, which is why I always wanted to be a dreamer. Sounds like you were brought up in a pretty smart family."

"Well, yes and no," she dithers. "When I was nineteen, my whole world changed…"

I notice an obvious change in physiology, she's a tad uneasy, her breathing is heavier and her face has gone milky-white like she's about to reveal something big. I resist intervening and give her space to take her time before continuing.

"It was a Saturday night, my parents were out while I stayed in to watch the season finale of *Mormon Mob Wives*."

"*Mormon Mob Wives?*" I chuckle.

"It's embarrassing I know."

I tell her I've never seen it, but it sounds bad-ass.

"It was so bad it actually was good," she smirks. "Any-hoo, as I'm sat alone watching *MMW*, out the blue — blackness…"

"Blackness?"

"Everything went black. I got knocked out, that's the last thing I remember."

"What the hell happened?"

"I learned after the fact a man snuck into the house and smothered me with a chloroform-soaked sponge."

"Holy shit!" I did not see that coming.

"I was then dragged unconsciously into my parents' bedroom and violated…"

I can't respond, just aghast with emotion. This takes me completely by surprise. *Oh my God* are the only words I can muster.

"Yep," she says softly.

"This is one of the worst things I've heard in my life. I don't know what to say."

"It's okay. JJ told me to tell you my story so you can learn."

"Well I don't know what I'm learning other than the world is a sick fucking place."

"That is one way of looking at it. He was my uncle after all."

"What!?" I say with more astonishment than a Jerry Springer guest who just found out his fiancée is a bisexual martian.

"Yeah. He knew I was alone that night and entered with his key. And the idea of using chloroform was so I couldn't witness anything, but it was obvious and didn't take the police long to extract a confession out of him after they found the sponge that he used. He actually used a SpongeBob and didn't even clean it or throw it away, the moron. He was pretty deranged, I think he wanted to get caught."

"Jeeze, this is heavy."

"And the chloroform was so strong when he smothered me it burnt my retinas and permanently blinded me."

I study her face thinking this is the craziest story I've ever heard. "I'm surprised how you're telling me this in such a calm and collective manner. Shouldn't you be flooded with tears right now?"

"Not really, I have no eyes."

"You know what I mean, you don't seem deeply emotional."

"I'm done with all that. If I do that then I give him the satisfaction and power. Besides, this happened when I was nineteen. I'm twenty-six now so I've moved on."

"You were raped and blinded by your uncle and you've *moved on*?" I can't believe my freaking ears.

"I had to or I would have gone stark raving mad. I just had to forgive him."

"You actually forgave him?"

"It was the only way to let go. I had to change my whole outlook on the situation. See, he was abused as a child, so he later took it out on a few unlucky people. I was just in the wrong place at the wrong time. He only acted the way he did because he's never been loved the way he wanted to be loved."

I remain in silence trying to digest this sick shit. My jaw is basically wide open and I think she can sense it.

"Are you alright?" she asks.

"I'm okay; you just sound so at peace with this."

"Have you not read anything by Louise Hay?"

"No, I haven't," I say gawking back at her like *what the fuck?*

"She wrote a classic, *You Can Heal Your Life*, you should check it out."

"Wait a minute, how do you read?"

"Audiobooks, duh! The bottom line is: forgiveness is a gift you give yourself. It took me a while to get that, but once I did, it was like a grand awakening."

"I think you're my new personal hero, Charlene."

"Oh stop, I just learned this stuff from the right sources like Lou Hay and Oprah Win. She too was violated by a family member when she was young."

"I never knew that."

"Yep. I've studied a lot about self-healing. In fact, that quote about forgiveness I actually learned from the speaker we're going to see tonight."

"What speaker?"

"JJ didn't tell you?"

"No. Like I said, he doesn't tell me much."

"Oh, oops. Well, we're all going to see a very gifted speaker tonight. I guess he'll fill you in later."

"I think you should be the one on a stage, Charlene."

"I'm flattered by the compliment. I've been very fortunate to learn a lot of amazing methods for self-healing, one of the most important principles is: it's not our *conditions*, but rather our *decisions* that shape us. Once I saw that I'm choosing to be a *victim* instead of a *victor*, that's when I was open to healing."

"So you've totally forgiven your uncle and moved on with no resentment today?"

"Yes, but make no mistake, it wasn't overnight. One thing I did do back then was change my last name because he's my dad's brother so we shared the same surname. I was ashamed to be affiliated with the name *Winnan*, and I would not answer to it, so I legally changed it to X."

I ask her why X, as it seems like an odd last name.

"It's symbolic like I crossed *Winnan* out my vocabulary. But today, I don't mind hearing it; it's just a name as far as I'm concerned. If I start to feel resentment towards him again, then he's won and I've lost, so I refuse to let him rent space in my mind again. I'm a grown woman that's in complete control of how I interpret any situation in my life, if I ever lose touch of that then I'm the idiot for not being resourceful. Emotions don't just happen, we're totally in control of them."

I nod in agreement (forgetting she's blind) and once again drift away in my mind as I occasionally do.

"If you have low self-esteem then *you* can change it. If somebody is feeling lonely, depressed, hopeless or helpless or anything else, it always can be turned around if they get creative and resourceful enough. And there's never a lack of resources, only a lack of *resourcefulness*."

"That's powerful. I've gotta say I'm in complete awe how you can take a major pain and use it as strength. You are the real deal, Charline X."

"Thank you. I've come to believe that pain is a part of life, it happens to everybody on both minor and major scales, but *suffering* is a choice. There was a time in my life when I was choosing to suffer, but now I choose not to because what's the point in that? Life's too short."

I take in what she says with the utmost respect while looking around at the perfectly manicured greenery. "What can I say? I'm absolutely speechless in your presence, Miss X. Whoever this speaker is tonight, I bet he has nothing on you."

"Stop it" she smiles. "I'm in a good place now. Anyway, I think it's time for another whooping. Fire this puppy back up and move over, I'll drive."

CHAPTER 51

After a shit, shower and shave back at the crib, JJ and I are decked out in our Sunday best about to head out the door.

"Check this out, Bobby, you've gotta see this." JJ stretches his Fuji, to show me a picture of a strange-looking oblong item that I couldn't guess for the life of me what it's supposed to be.

"It's a new product by Hustler which is about to hit the market."

"Hustler, the porno people?" I question.

"Yeah, they've gotten into the children's toy market."

"Please don't tell me what I think you're saying…children's *toys?*"

"No, you dingbat. Not *'toy'* toys. This is a children's toy."

"A children's toy made by sick-ass Larry Flynt?"

"What's wrong with you? How the hell are they gonna market sex toys to kids?"

I'm not even going to answer that. I just look at him weirdly.

"Besides, Larry Flynt died a long time ago."

"Oh yeah? How did he pass?"

"He was having an affair with a floozy that modeled for his magazine until his wife snapped one night and sought revenge."

Of course, I'm a sucker for the celeb gossip and asked what did she do.

"She tailed his limo to Mulholland Drive where he'd always park up and fuck overlooking LA, then she rammed into the limo with her Hummer with so much force that it careened off the edge right down the canyon."

"Holy shit, that's crazy!"

"Luckily the limo driver was smoking a cigarette outside or he too would have rode the canyon."

"Jesus."

"Nuts, huh? Anyway, check this out: I'd love to tell you I invented this but I didn't. It's made from a new form of polypropylene which enables the plastic to bend in a unique—"

BEEP-BEEP honks an SUV, pulling into the driveway.

"Never mind, I'll show you later."

"Cool." I grab my jacket. "So why are we taking a car service tonight? It's not like we're going to be drinking."

"I anticipate it's gonna be a long night, so it's more convenient to Uber in style."

"Fair enough. Hey, one thing that just struck me: if your life is so incredible and everything seems to be in perfect harmony; why do you still go to seminars and workshops? I mean, don't you know all this stuff by now?"

JJ looks back at me as if I asked a novel question. "First of all, I'd never be so naïve to say my life is in perfect harmony, or I know it all. Far from it. It's about the journey, the process, the growth, not the actual end goal. Constantly growing in life is an addiction in itself, at least for me. What personal development is for the mind, exercise is for the body. You don't go to the gym a couple of times and say to yourself *'now I'm fit for life'*. It's a continuing process of conditioning."

"Good point," I say as we step out into the oval archway. While JJ locks the door with the electronic keypad I suddenly spot a cockroach crawling near my feet. "Ahhh! A roach!"

My immediate intuition is to pile drive it into the ground.

"—Whoa-whoa-whoa, don't you do that, Bobby!"

I catch myself from stomping it, then it scatters away.

"You're right, I can't kill that little bug now, it's a creature of the universe."

"A *divine* creature of the universe," he adds. "They have just enough reason and purpose to be on this Earth as us."

We turn our heads to see the driver witnessing our exchange by the SUV.

"Evening, gentlemen," he says as he opens the back door with a slight weirded-out expression.

I can only wonder what he thought of that.

"How's the world treating ya?" says a zesty JJ from the back seat. "Or should I say how are you treating the world?"

"Nothing new to be honest."

Our driver looks like a bit of a man-boy: forty-five going on eighteen, I'm guessing. He's unshaven, hiding his hair in a baseball cap and wearing a *Mr. Lazy* T-shirt from *The Mr. Men* line (talk about an '80s throwback).

"Just a different day from the last," he pulls out onto the road.

"I'm JJ, this is Randy. What's your name, my friend?"

"Adams. Terry Adams."

"Pleased to meet you, Mr. Adams."

He tells us to call him Terry or Tez but JJ insists on nicknaming him T-Bone.

"I'm curious, T-Bone, what do you like about this job?"

"Not much to be honest," he says picking up speed. "I just drive around the city, fighting the damn traffic."

"Do you like meeting new people?"

"Most passengers rarely bother talking to me. They just sit in the back playing with their Fujis."

"Well, even though we've only got a relatively short drive together, I bet we can have some fun and learn something valuable from one another."

"Oh yeah?"

"Absolutely. I learn from everybody. I love sitting next to elderly people on a plane because they've played the game before, so I know I can take away some great wisdom from them. So tell me, T-Bone; what's going on in your world? Where are you in this stage of life?"

"There's not much going on with me. I don't exactly live an exciting lifestyle, shall we say."

"Come on, you can do better than that."

"I don't really talk about myself all that much. I'm not very good at socializing."

"Nonsense, I bet you're just a little introverted that's all. I used to be the same way."

"You don't seem like the introverted type."

"Au contraire. Randy here can vouch for that. I used to be so stuck in my head. I'd shut my office door for hours because I didn't want to deal with any humans."

"Really?"

"Yeah. So let's try this again; what's exciting in your life right now?"

"I live a boring life. I don't have much money and don't have a lot of free time, so there's not a lot of excitement going on."

"Oh come on, T-Bone, that's twice now. I'm not gonna give up on you that easy," he teases. He then reaches into the front and starts poking his ribs. "Come on, T-Bone, don't make me prod you all the way downtown."

He lightens up and smiles. "Hmmm, let me see... Well, I just celebrated my fortieth bornday last week."

"There you go. How was it?" asks JJ as he discontinues his childlike prodding and sits back with me.

"It was a huge disappointment. Many of my so-called friends didn't show up or even notify me for that matter, so I ended up canceling and went bowling alone."

An awkward silence envelops the vehicle while we're halted at a red. JJ and I look at each other gritting our teeth.

"I couldn't afford to do anything fun or travel anywhere nice. Everything's so expensive these days. There's nothing to do in this town when you're struggling to get by."

"Just because you're not living the lavish life like Murphy Levesque doesn't mean there's nothing to do, you just have to get a little creative."

"I guess I'm not a very creative person."

"You don't have to be. It's simple. Most people forget the very basics about the world they're living in. We all live in a very rich world and I'm not talking about excessive wealth, I'm talking about regular people with regular means. Every day we live in a utopia that our ancestors could never dream of. Today we can travel such vast distances in hours instead of weeks for relatively little money. We drive on roads we didn't construct, with automobiles we didn't design, video chat to people anywhere around the globe for free thanks to the World Wide Web.

"We can watch news, sports, entertainment from all over the world on a plethora of different devices or we can go to the movie theatre and watch a five hundred million dollar film for a few mere dollars just so we can be entertained for a couple of hours." JJ takes a break after his rant and turns to me smiling. "Or something like that anyway."

The driver looks provoked as the light goes green. "When you put it like that, you're right. I've never taken time to really notice that."

"Believe me, T-Bone, I used to suffer from the same thing, as did Randy here."

"A hundred percent," I chime in. "I used to moan at everything because nothing would go my way."

"I hear that," says T-Bone as he bolts through a yellow light. "So let me turn the tables on you; what's going on tonight with you guys? You're dressed all fancy and seem fired up."

"We're going to a speech by a phenomenal speaker from across the pond who's become a good friend of mine over the years. You can't help but feel juiced after one of his talks."

"What does he speak about?"

"Addiction is tonight's theme, however, it's a lot more than just that. He goes over many things that you can apply in life, so it's more of a personal development theme."

"Sounds interesting actually…like something I need. To be honest, I've never read a self-help book or been to a seminar. Maybe I should look into the PD movement because I've been feeling down lately, especially since hitting forty. It's silly if you think about it because it's just another bornday with a zero on the end."

"I think we all have a little uncertainty when the first digit of our age changes," remarks JJ. "It's somewhat natural."

"*Uncertainty*, that's an interesting word. Every morning now I wake up thinking *is this all there is to life?* I'm forty fucking years old, no wife, no kids, barely any money, living in a tiny, shared apartment next to a run-down fricking bowling alley. I have nothing going for me and don't know where I'm heading. I just feel like I should have tried harder by this stage."

I can tell that that statement took a lot for T-Bone to vent. I notice his breathing is more elevated as he merges into traffic.

"And forgive me for cursing, I'm sorry."

"Cursing is fine. It's good to not hold anything back. We curse all the motherfucking time."

"Fucking aye," I add.

"Here's what I'm thinking, you're just in a funk at the moment and have no vision of an exciting future for yourself because you're caught up in making a living instead of designing a life."

"Story of my life," T-Bone agrees as we come to another red.

"I was in a funk at one point in my life too, it can happen to the best of us."

"I guess."

"You work for yourself, don't you T-Bone? There's no actual boss with Uber."

"Right."

"Then, why don't you join us? This guy might just change your life, you never know."

"Oh come on. Change my whole life from one speech? Pleeze."

"Hey don't doubt the power of the universe, man. He might say that one thing which plants something inside you which leads you down an entirely new destination."

"But how are you even gonna get me in? Do you have a spare ticket or something?"

"I'll take care of it. I got you," says JJ as we pull off again.

"But I can't go dressed in shorts and a T-shirt. You guys are dressed to the nines."

"No problem," JJ blows it off and seems to have everything figured out. "I know a great clothes store around the corner from the venue."

"Oh, I can't afford any new clothes, sir. I'm strapped."

"Hey, don't worry about it, it's my treat. This is how much I value you joining us tonight. Tonight could be your date with fate, even though you don't have an addiction. The most common addiction throughout the world is people being addicted to their problems, so I know you'll benefit a great deal."

As we come to a stop sign T-Bone turns around to face us and says he can't possibly accept a new outfit.

"I insist, it's totally fine, plus I know the owner who always hooks me up, so you're coming." JJ looks at his stylish watch. "But shit, I think they close soon so you better step on it and make a left on Troutman two streets down."

I clock eyes with T-Bone off the rear-view and notice his features change. He's touched.

"I can't believe how nice you are to me."

"T-Bone it will be my pleasure. Now time is-a-tickin'— hit the gas!"

CHAPTER 52

"Fuck the law of probability! Come on, everybody, say it with me!"

The crowd in this mini auditorium are jazzed from this zany looking English fella who sports a nice tan, tinted Gucci frames and a dark suit like the *Blues Brothers*. He's only been on stage for a few minutes and already has everybody buzzing like we're at a *Sunday Night Slam* show.

"FUCK THE LAW OF PROBABILITY!" repeats the raucous crowd.

Our posse has front-row seats thanks to JJ, who is seated to my left, along with Kerry and T-Bone (in his dapper new outfit), and Charlene X to my right.

"When you are told *relapsing is part of recovery*, or *you have a ninety-two percent chance of failure*, it's not a fact, it's just somebody's silly opinion which has absolutely no merit because you can defy the odds and create your own destiny. Anybody can free themselves from an addiction or unwanted behaviors and you can do it immediately if you get all your beliefs in proper alignment!

"So tonight's talk is simply about questioning any beliefs that are holding you back and eliminating any fears about making a change. Does that sound good to you?"

This goes over well with the crowd as they clap in approval.

"Allow me to give you a little background on what I used to believe and how I used to live back in the late nineties before I started to question what I put in my body. I used to wake up and pour copious amounts of coffee down my throat every single morning. What is coffee? A deadly neurotoxin and highly addictive drug; caffeine. Then I'd fire up a thin little cylinder of finely cut tobacco and purposefully inhale hundreds of poisons and carcinogens thinking this was a great way to start the day.

"Then I'd heat bread in a toaster and spread thick globes of Lurpak butter along with even thicker globes of marmalade. What is butter? Nothing but condensed milk and pus that's been crudely extracted from an animal that's not at all designed for human consumption. And what is marmalade by the way? Artificially flavored crap that has zero nutritional value and is so loaded with sugar which is another addictive drug called sucrose. Think about it, guys, it wasn't even 8 AM and I'd already had three highly addictive drugs to start my day; caffeine, nicotine and sucrose, plus casein that's found in the butter which is a food additive that wreaks havoc in the body and is linked to several forms of cancer! Real smart, wasn't I?

"If I didn't have toast I might have had cereal which is nothing but starchy carbs drowned in more cows milk that breaks down into more sugar. Or if I didn't have that I may have had eggs and bacon for breakfast. What is an egg? An embryo before it has formed or a chicken's menstrual cycle as some people have labeled it. Pretty delicious, huh? And what is bacon? A small strip of a dead pig that used to be living and breathing in its own filth — now we're really getting started, aren't we?"

The audience snickers.

"So throughout the day I'd ingest more dead animals, drink more coffee and energy drinks—which are nothing but carbonated sugar and caffeine giving me the illusion of a boost in energy. I'd smoke more cigarettes and sometimes 'treat' myself to a chocolate bar. What is chocolate? More condensed milk, more sugar, along with another drug called theobromine that's contained in chocolate so we keep coming back for more. And if it was a weekend there would be a lot more poison added to the mix which I think you can work out for yourselves.

"Now, the reason why I tell you this is because you probably know someone like the younger me, and I'm not saying by any stretch you have to stop consuming any of these things. All I'm saying is once I started to question everything I was putting into my body I became open to change.

"Once I realized the caffeine was giving me awful headaches a few hours after my first coffee I stopped drinking it and they went away. Once I realized the butter, chocolate and milk were giving me terrible allergies like sneezing uncontrollably and so much mucus that I couldn't clearly breathe it was easy to stop consuming them and all the symptoms went away.

"When I realized all that dead animal flesh and all the sugary shit were playing havoc in my body and robbing my energy, I researched better alternatives and it was very easy to make changes. And once I started to feel the horrendous coughing and wheezing in my lungs I put the cigarettes down without going through any depravity at all because I started to really value my health. And you can too if you so desire. Does that sound cool to you guys?"

More applause hail from the audience.

"And the same is true of recreational drugs. If you've come to a point in your life where you're sick of feeling like hell from all the poisons you are ingesting then get excited that you're ready to make a decision to change. That word *decision,* by the way, is very interesting in its root because it's actually related to the word *incision,* which obviously means *to cut.* So when you make a real decision you literally cut off any other possibilities, thus—never go back on your word.

"Every single one of you in this room has the capability to make a decision to become free of anything that's bothering you—so why wait? Why not make that all-important decision right now, tonight, so you get your life back to its proper destination or destiny."

The audience responds with more clapping and merriment. This guy has a lot of fire and spunk which is resinating with everyone.

"Have you ever gotten so pissed off with something and said: '*that's it! No more! Never again! I'm done!'* and never gone back to it? Raise your hand and say *YO!*"

"YO!" is yelled by many of us in the audience at near-deafening levels.

"That was the day you made a real decision and stuck to it. The good news is you don't have to wait for life to change you after years of hardship; you can literally make a decision right now regardless of your background, your religion, your past, your socioeconomic status, your environment or anything else and walk out of those doors a free person. The million-dollar question then is *how?* How can we change a behavior that we've struggled with for years and ensure it sticks for the long term?"

He pauses from his rhetorical question and lets it hang.

"Many people who struggle with addictions think because they've indulged in drugs for years, it's too hard to live any other way. That, ladies and gentlemen, is an incredibly disempowering belief. Remember: the past does not have to dictate the future! Just because you've had problems with drugs before, it doesn't mean you have to carry on living that way. Millions of people from all walks of life have been in the same or worse position as you, and they overcame their problems and went on to live a happy existence and there's absolutely no reason why every single one of you cannot either."

As he continues his piece, he jumps off the stage and lingers amongst the crowd.

"Invariably, at this point, someone in the audience will tell me they're different, they can't change because they come from an abusive family, or their life is hell because they don't have any money or their spouse has left them or whatever-whatever. Think, deep down what's preventing you from making the decision to eliminate an addiction or get in shape, or overcome a depression—whatever the case may be, and write it down. What has been holding you back up until now? Take two or three minutes and do this please."

Shit, I think he just listed everything I need to change about myself...

He hops back on stage while everybody starts writing on their fancy stretched out Fuji things. I'm one of the few old-schoolers with a pad and pen so I jot down my lame excuses and stare at them for a minute. My hateful eight looks like this:

1. *I'm too big to shed all this weight.*
2. *I always go back on my word.*
3. *I haven't got what it takes.*
4. *I get distracted and overwhelmed too easily.*
5. *I'm a failure at everything, so why even try?*
6. *It's just too hard to change.*
7. *I never follow through on anything.*
8. *Why even try? I always end up sabotaging myself.*

As I stare at the paper, I see how these destructive excuses have completely stopped me from improving myself, (and the sad thing is I could go on and on if I wanted to).

"Once you know what's been stopping you," the speaker continues, "you'll start associating pain to them and be in a better position to figure out a solution. Demand from yourself that these erroneous beliefs will never hold you back again because you can overcome anything. *Anything?* Yes, anything! In fact, let's say this all together: *I can overcome anything!*"

"I CAN OVERCOME ANYTHING!" the crowd hurls.

"That's right. You can overcome *anything* including substance abuse or an abusive relationship or anything else. So thank anyone from your past that may have done you ill, because they've shaped you into the person you are today. Even if you don't feel like forgiving them, do it for yourself so all your resentment goes and you can move on with your life. Always remember; forgiveness is a gift you give yourself."

I turn to Charlene who gives me a little wink as the speaker moves on.

"Our brains are fundamentally hardwired for pleasure and to avoid pain, we all know this, but some of us forget the obvious, so I quickly want to take you through an exercise I call the *Best Case Scenario* to drive home a point about drugs and what they truly mean when you look at the big picture.

"Just for a minute, I want you to close your eyes and imagine everything in your life as perfect as can be. You are working in your dream career, with a dream income, you live in your dream house, in a dream location, you have a dream spouse or dream lover…or both…"

The audience chuckles.

"And you have perfect kids if you want them too. Everything in your life is as perfect as can be, and you are just so high on life you cannot wait to jump out of bed everyday… Do you all have the picture? If so, say *YO!*"

The crowd responds with more "YOs."

"Good. Now as you come back from your utopia, raise your hand if doing copious amounts of drugs and binge-drinking for five straight days was in the picture…"

Nobody raises their hands.

"… Look around, not one person in this room has raised their hands when thinking about their perfect reality. Drugs weren't in the picture. Isn't that interesting, ladies and gentlemen? So maybe instead of putting our focus into *not doing drugs* or *resisting temptations* every day, maybe we should focus on making our life a masterpiece that you dreamed about. Maybe we should put our energies into creating a phenomenal career, attracting the perfect mate, raising a healthy family, creating a legacy and maybe, just maybe, you'll be so happy and high on life that your so-called *'drug addiction'* will cease. How cool does that sound?"

The audience agrees.

"When you live your life exactly the way you've designed it, you'll be so fulfilled and excited that no drug or anything else will take you away from that. So please never think you're powerless against an addiction and just have to manage it for the rest of your life — simply look at it as the truth: Drugs are designed to trap and addict you so you become dependent. And why do they want you to be dependent on their product? That's right, to make themselves rich, of course. From Pablo Escobar to Starbucks to the Marlboro Man and everyone in between — if you're being sold a drug which doesn't benefit you in any way, you can take your power back and break free any time you choose. Once you see drugs as a trap and a scam to get your money you'll never be suckered into them again."

That's powerful, I contemplate. I've never thought about it like that: *I fell into a trap which never helped with anything. No matter how high I got I still felt empty because I knew it wasn't the real me.* I need to write this down…

"People only do excessive amounts of drugs to temporarily escape from emotional pain, but obviously it never works because it cannot heal the cause. As soon as the drug wears off, they start to focus on the pain again. Anybody who does a particular drug over and over has the illusion that it's pleasurable, but think carefully about this: do drugs really give you pleasure? Can anybody answer that?"

A man in the second row raises his hand. "I can honestly say I like getting high. I love taking drugs, that's my problem."

"First of all, thanks for your honesty," returns the speaker. "Let's analyze this by doing another closed-eye exercise, not just for you, sir, for all of you. He clears his throat: "Everybody close your eyes and imagine you're in an empty room. Inside the room is basically nothing, no computers, no tablets, no Fujis, no Bobulators, no friends, no communication to the outside world. No books, no magazines, no games and yes, no pornography…"

This gets a little laugh from the audience.

"And no windows or furniture except a chair and a table. And on this table I want you to imagine a very large quantity of your favorite drug. If it's cocaine imagine a big mountain of it on the table. If it's pills imagine dozens and dozens of them right in front of you. If your vice is alcohol put umpteen bottles of your favorite tipple on the table — you get the picture. Now, imagine you're locked in this four-cornered room for a fortnight…"

"What's a fortnight?" I whisper to JJ, breaking from the exercise.

"Two weeks."

"Oh. Damn British." I close my eyes again.

"You have absolutely nothing to do in this room except your favorite drug, and you can do as much of this substance as you like. Imagine getting really, really high for days and days—getting all drugged out worse than Max and Bobby Sheen. Take your time and think about this for a minute…

"Now, open your eyes and raise your hand if you think this scenario is your idea of fun, happiness or bliss."

I turn around to see that nobody in the crowd has raised their hand.

"Think about it; you can do as much drugs as you want for free for two weeks but you're completely shut off from the outside world. Who here thinks that would be a form of extreme pleasure?"

Again, nobody raises their hands at all.

"Who thinks this would help with any of your problems?"

Nothing from the audience.

"And, sir," he directs to the man in the second row, "did that seem like a great form of pleasure for you?"

"Not at all," he answers honestly.

"I thought so. So when you really think about the truth, drugs aren't a genuine source of pleasure. When you properly analyze them, they're just forms of distraction that chemically alter your brain. It's never the drug that gives you the pleasure, it's all the other things that you do in an exhilarated state, like connecting with friends, meeting new people, dancing to music, attracting a mate or going on wild adventures in hip places like Las Vegas or Skegness — those are the *real* pleasures."

Many of us nod along knowing he's absolutely right.

"Pleasure and pain drive all human behavior, ladies and gentlemen because our brains are hardwired that way to ensure our survival. Why some people become addicted is simply because they are under the impression—or illusion as I like to say, that the drug is a good way to escape from some form of pain or a good way to get immediate pleasure, that's what hooks them.

"So if your way of dealing with life's problems is doing copious amounts of drugs, I've got news for you: It never fucking works! It's an un-winnable game, my friends because drugs are designed to trap you. When you get high all that happens is you distract yourself for a short period, but it soon returns because you never eliminated the true cause of the problem. Eliminate the cause and the effect will cease."

Some food for thought right there. I think a light bulb just went off above my head as he writes on a big electronic board and stays on this part for another twenty minutes.

After a short intermission, he's back on stage.

"Raise your hand if you know someone who's died from a drug overdose or drug-related death."

The entire audience raises their hands including the speaker.

"Just like I thought, one hundred percent of us have lost somebody because they chose to partake in excessive amounts of drugs. This is why we have to get serious because your life is at stake. If you slip up by telling yourself *just one more hit* then that one more hit could be the fatal one which takes you out, just like Janis Joplin, ODB, River Phoenix, Rick James, Marilyn Monroe, Sid Vicious, David Ruffin, Jim Morrison and an uncountable amount of others around the world, including your late friends."

As he pauses to let us take it in JJ turns to me and whispers "And let's not forget all those wrestlers that passed from drug-related causes: Brian Pillman, Crush, Luna Vachon, Curt Hennig, Sherri Martel…"

"Agreed," I add. "Not forgetting Matt Borne, Bam Bam Bigelow, Chyna, Miss Elisabeth and the rest of 'em. It's such a travesty."

"What legacy are you going to leave behind?" continues the speaker. "If you think about it, it's not going to be very long until you become worm food, especially if you're going to abuse drugs, so this might sound a little morbid but I want to ask you another question: Do you ever think about death?"

Talk about a state change, the whole room has turned eerie-like. I notice many people looking tense now. I personally try to not to focus on the big D, it freaks me out too much.

"I want to jump into another closed-eye process called the *Worst Case Scenario*. Close your eyes and imagine leaving here tonight and doing exorbitant amounts of your favorite drug or drugs… Really think about going for it full-on— getting so high like you're at a bachelor party or something…"

I follow suit and form a clear image of booze and powder like I'm back with

Cam.

"Now imagine after hours of drug abuse something goes severely wrong. See the images in your mind and make it very rich and graphic. See yourself struggling for your life from a drug that did not sit well in your body. Think about being rushed to the hospital, with your family in the waiting room praying that the doctors can save you... But unfortunately, they can't because you over-indulged and your body couldn't take it... Now imagine the looks on your families' faces when the doctor informs them they couldn't save you. It's official, you are dead..."

You can cut the tension in this room with a knife. This is majorly intense.

"See your parents, your siblings, your kids, your partner, and your friends crying their eyes out uncontrollably from your passing. Get a vivid image of them being devastated that you passed away, and feel it in your body now..."

Weeping and crying emerge from all parts of the auditorium.

"Now imagine your funeral. Everybody is crying as they take one last look at your face in the coffin as they say their goodbyes. Take time to picture this..."

"Now, as they lower your casket into an open grave, feel that horrendous feeling of your legacy being cut short from a stupid fucking drug. Feel the devastation, the sorrow, the stupidity, the regret, all in your body right now..."

More moans and wailing emerge from the crowd.

"Picture your life as the ultimate travesty, the ultimate regret, all because you continued to mess around abusing drugs and feel it deep in your soul..."

"Now, fast forward and imagine life going on now you've left this earth...Imagine somebody else driving your car, somebody else doing your job, somebody else living in your home, somebody else eating your food, somebody else watching your TV, somebody else sleeping in your bed, somebody else fucking your partner, somebody else raising your kids and feel these intense feelings throughout your whole body.

"Really feel what it will be like if you're gone and forgotten from this earth because you fell into the drug trap... When you start to focus on that as your future (as you come back and open your eyes) I want to ask you: is it worth it?"

Wow, that little mind-trip was effective. I saw my life ending from too much coke and it was sickening to see Max and Sherri crying by my hospital bed. He's right, it's just not worth it when you fully associate to the consequences of drugs.

I look around to see many people teary-eyed and emotional. Just when you think he's going to stop, he goes a few steps further.

A short while later and we've come to the end. He's back on stage wrapping things up.

"I'm going to finish with perhaps the most important thing I've said all night, so please listen carefully: You have your whole life in front of you, and I want you to think of it as a book full of empty pages. You're the writer who gets to write that book. You write that book with every choice you make. If you decide you're here on this planet for a purpose, a reason, and to do great things, then that will be the book you will write. If you decide you're a loser who just plods through life depressed and chemically addicted then that will be the book you will write.

"When you walk out those doors, there are only two paths to walk: the path of drug addiction or the path of freedom. Which path are you going to walk and how bad do you want it? Your destiny is entirely up to you. Are you going to become a *warning* to others how not to live life, or are you going to be a great *example* to others on how to live happy, healthy and righteously?

"Victim or victor? Addiction or freedom? Warning or example? Loser or winner?"

You can feel the emotion in the room once again, he's pulling on our heartstrings, it's powerful.

"I'm not here to call you out or tell you what book you should write, I'm just here to tell you, you can write whatever you want. The choice is entirely yours…"

The emotional audience reacts solemnly.

"Ladies and gentlemen, I am Thomas Wesley, it has been my honor, my pleasure and my privilege to speak to you this evening. Thank you from the bottom of my heart. Good night."

CHAPTER 53

It's now 23:34 and I'm spent. That was an intense three and a half hours even though it was supposed to be two. I guess that guy got in the zone and lost track of time.

There were moments during the exercises that I felt like I was in suspended animation; particularly my regrets of abusing food, booze, drugs and prostitutes. It struck a chord with me — all that pain I've inflicted on myself and others, and that's what hurts the most. Regret is a bitch like what David said on his deathbed, so I cannot ever go back to my former way of dealing with emotional shit by sticking my head in the sand, hoping everything will turn out okay. Living a life of lies and deceit will only bring me pain—pain that I'll always have to live with.

JJ introduced me to the speaker before we left. Despite being surrounded by a swarm of fans he gave me his undivided attention for about a minute so I took the opportunity to reveal something very personal that I've never divulged to anyone (including you fuckers). After I'd finished my ramble he told me straight up I over-analyze things and I'm trying too hard to be perfect when it's just not necessary. This floored me because he's right on the money, I over-think things all the time but how the hell he knew that after meeting me for about sixty-seconds is incredible. The man is brilliant.

My body may be physically spent, but my brain feels electrified. I find myself reflecting next to JJ in the backseat of the SUV, as a revitalized T-Bone takes the wheel.

We've only been driving a few minutes and have come to a stop. I thought we were heading home but we appear to be outside a hospital.

"Thanks, T-Bone, it's been an illuminating night," says JJ as he opens the door.

T-Bone agrees and thanks him. "You were right, it was truly life-changing. I feel like I've had a breakthrough."

"I do too. Stay in touch, my friend."

JJ attempts to exit the vehicle but I interrupt him. "Ahhh, what are we doing here?"

"The night is still young, young Randy. Follow me."

"You mean we aren't going home?"

"Not yet."

"But why a hospital?"

"You'll see. Come on," he insists as he exits the Uber.

I don't want to argue, I'm too tired for that. I just want to sleep but have no choice but to go with the flow.

JJ doesn't even wait for me; he just shoots off towards the entrance like a man on a mission.

After a quick elevator ride to floor negative three, JJ exits like he knows where he's heading. I trail behind noticing a sign with an arrow pointing left to a department I want no part in. If he's taking me where I think he's taking me I'll fucking freak. Of course, when there's a 50/50 chance of going one way or the other, it's always the other. JJ swings left leaving me no choice but to confront him.

"Please don't tell me we're going to a morgue," I hurl, catching up to him.

He says nothing but his looks have given him away.

"You're fucking kidding me, JJ. Why?"

No answer.

"Wait a second. Stop!"

Surprisingly he obeys, giving me a glimmer of hope.

"Let me say this in plain English: What exactly are we doing here? Of all the places, why a God damn morgue?"

"We're here to meet Percy," he smiles with a ridiculous grin.

"Percy? You've arranged to meet someone at nearly midnight in a morgue?"

"Correct-a-mondo. Besides, what we're doing is not exactly kosher, so what better time than the graveyard shift. No pun intended."

He tries to walk away but I'm adamant in stopping him.

"Whoa-whoa-whoa, time-out!" I stand my ground. "You have to tell me or I'm not coming."

"Look, Bobby, you enjoyed the speech tonight, right?"

"Yeah."

"You got a lot of valuable information."

"Yes."

"And all those exercises we went through, you got some powerful insights, correct?"

"Yes, he was quite brilliant, will you please get to the point?"

"Even though I do believe you, I have to give you a little caveat: I've watched people from all walks of life over the last ten years who've been recommended life-changing books, life-changing rehab programs, life-changing seminars.

"At first they get all pumped up with excitement and tell me they're going to follow through. They tell me they're going to stop smoking, they tell me they're going to lose weight, going to get off drugs, going to get their life on track, etcetera, etcetera; and I believed them because they seemed sincere. However, after some observation down the line, I found many of them just lost interest or didn't take it seriously. With you, Bobby, I can't take any chances, if you want to change you have to be committed and you have to be dead fucking serious."

He squares up to me eye to eye. His light-hearted demeanor has instantly morphed into seriousness.

"You've been ruining your fucking life for the past year with drugs and you've told me that will never happen again. You've told me your mind has been made up and your decision is final. I get that, but I still can't take any chances. Not with you."

I can't resist fighting back but my efforts are futile as he overbears me with his dominance.

"We are here, Bobby, to get a crystal clear vision at what your destiny is going to be if you renege on your decision. We're here to kill any demons that may still be lurking in your brain telling you *just one more line, one more time.* Understand?"

"But I already—"

"Ah-ah-ah, no *buts*! Haven't you learned anything from me yet? Jeez, you really have trust issues, don't you?"

"Yeah, I do. We're about to go into a fucking morgue!"

"That's right, we are. It's time to meet Percy."

We walk through another corridor and are greeted outside an office by a little old man who looks like Mr. Magoo. His crusty face and squinted eyes have definitely been around the block. If I were to take a stab in the dark at his chronological age I would have to say eighty-nine.

"Percy," JJ shakes his hand, "it's been way too long. How the devil are you? Thanks for doing this by the way."

"Ahhh, don't mention it, nothing much goes on here at this hour. I get a lot of time to just sit back, play cards and watch *Cheerleaders Gone Wild.*" His voice is a dead ringer for Lawrence Tierney; real gravelly like he smokes Dutch Masters on the regular. "It's funny, in all the years I've worked around dead bodies, tonight is the first time I've wondered if maggots get drunk when they bury alcoholics." He lets out an almost evil, gruff laugh and turns to me. "This will be an eye-opening experience for your friend here. I'm Percy, pleased to meet you."

"Randy," we shake hands. "I'm a little freaked to be quite frank."

"Percy, will you please brief Randy to why I arranged this late-night meeting?"

"Certainly. We are going to take a trip into the world of death. To really understand life, you first must understand death…" he pauses for a spooky silence. "Gentlemen, follow me."

He spins around and descends the adjacent steps at the speed of a lame tortoise. To make things even spookier the lighting is poor and crackly, I feel like I'm about to be led into Stu Hart's dungeon.

Before opening the door, Percy stops and turns to me. "Randy, when we get inside just remain pretty silent, let whatever feelings arise and marinate inside you. Your instincts will serve as your guide and any feelings you want to express is best to be done afterward. I'm going to show you three recently deceased bodies, or *fresh flesh* as I call them, all dead from drug overdoses."

"And as you observe them," adds JJ, "something will click inside you that you'll never forget."

They both ogle me like I'm the Elephant Man and I don't like it. "I'm not at all comfortable with this, I mean, we're gonna be in there with the defunct. I don't know how you can do this every day as a job."

"You get used to it when you become a veteran of this business. When I started out it was a different ball game altogether, nothing could have prepared me for what I saw on my first day."

Feeling curious, I have to ask what happened.

"They had me examine a young man called Junebug who walked into a McDonald's with his sister, then out of nowhere — BAM; he took a pump action-slug, point blank to the chest from a case of mistaken identity. The poor kid was only nineteen and all he wanted was a damn Happy Meal for his little sister." He shakes his head looking down at the checkered floor. "They had me assisting my boss opening up his chest on my very first day. I'll never forget his vital organs dangling from a thread like in the movie *Saw XII*. I couldn't eat ribs for a year."

I turn to JJ like *Did he really just fucking say that?* I wish I never asked him what happened now. None of this is helping at all.

"So what you're feeling is perfectly normal. Let's get this show on the road."

A great chill shudders through my bones upon entering, not just from this cold habitat but because of the fact I'm in a room surrounded by dead bodies confined in large steel drawers. I stare at the unapologetic iron containers knowing what's inside and feel an eerie presence so strong that it's palpable. Being surrounded by death has that immediate effect on me. I never did like the sight of blood and can never understand why people gawk when they see a car crash or dead animal at the side of the road. The ghostly feeling gets worse, circulating throughout my body like a virus. I notice my breathing getting elevated and he hasn't even opened any drawers yet, I guess it's the fear of anticipation that's messing with me.

JJ hovers behind at a fair distance while I'm about to be up, close and personal with the defunct as Percy pulls open the first drawer.

I take deep breaths as a vain attempt to calm myself down as he slowly unzips the body bag and force myself to stare at the Latino lady's pale naked body, it looks like her life has been drained out of her. So young, so innocent looking. What's hard to swallow is there's no person here, there's a body but no life is left in it. It's just emptiness. This is fucking freaky.

I remain as quiet as I can, shivering over her lifeless face wishing I could do something to bring her back. My nervous system feels like it's got a bad case of the DTs despite not touching a drop of booze last night.

He zips her back up, closes the drawer then leads us to the next one and asks if I'm ready. Even though I'm not, I nod and let out a long exhalation of anxiety. My heart is pumping out my chest like a canon, I can literally hear it echo off the walls as he opens the next draw.

This guido looking teenager looks so tragic lying there with his tongue sticking out like a dead deer. He had his whole life ahead of him and now it's gone because of drugs. Again I'm hit with that feeling of emptiness: there's no one here, just a stiff, colorless corpse that soon will be returned to the Earth. These people weighed the same amount as when they were alive, but whatever they were—the essence of who they truly were—is no longer present. When death occurs there's no question what's missing is the intangible, weightless identity, that essence of life some call spirit.

A tear trickles from my eye as he closes the drawer and moves onto the next.

"You okay, kid?" Percy gravels.

"No, but just do it," I reply wanting this to be over as soon as possible.

I can barely look at the next man's face, it's even pastier than the Latino girl's. His mustache has a touch of frost on it which freaks me out for some reason. I force myself again to stare at his cold, anemic face completely devoid of life.

It's clearly obvious to me now that we are not our bodies, they are just a vehicle that houses us while we enjoy the privilege of this thing called *life*. I can't take much more of this. It's too overwhelming being around lifeless bodies. I'm well aware that these awful images will be ingrained in my psyche from now on, which is what my diabolical future-self wants.

As Percy closes the last drawer I let out a huge sigh of relief while my body is still physically shaking. Any more of that and I probably would have fainted.

"It's all over now," he says looking me up and down. "You alright?"

I lean up against the wall with my head in my hands and don't bother answering.

"Percy, would you mind stepping out for a minute?" asks JJ.

"Sure, I'll go grab me a coffee. Just remember kid: we are not human beings having a spiritual experience, we are spiritual beings having a human experience. I'll leave you with that." He waddles out the door.

"There's one last experience you must go through," says JJ.

This gets my attention. I raise my head out of my hands and question him on what exactly.

"This is probably going to throw you off, Bobby, but remember; there's a method to my madness."

"Just spit it out so we can go home to bed."

"You're spending the night here."

"What? Where?"

"Here."

"Here? Where? In this hospital?"

"In here," he says as he opens an empty drawer.

His request hits me like a rude awakening. This has to be a sick fucking joke, but after a little back and forth along with his best efforts of reassurance it's not a joke at all.

"You want me to spend the night in this freezing room with all these dead bodies? Are you fucking nuts?!"

"You have to trust me on this."

I'm still having trouble digesting this shit and tell him this is fucking insanity!

"Bobby, I have calculated everything down to an exact science."

"Well, I'm not doing it! It's too spooky and insane to sleep in a container designed for dead people!"

"Everything I'm asking of you, I've been through myself, so I know what I'm talking about. Besides it's actually quite snug once you get used to it."

His light-hearted remark does nothing to ease my tension=filled state. I'm way too vexed to even reply to his ridiculousness so I shun away before I blow up.

"Do you trust me?"

I remain silent.

"Do you trust me?" he repeats more emphatically.

"Yes."

"Do you respect me?"

"Yes."

"Do you value my knowledge and wisdom?"

"Yes." (He's using an old sales tactic called *the yes ladder* as a way to pin me into a corner and it's fucking working).

"Do you believe I'm doing this for the greater good?"

"Yes."

"Do you believe I'm doing this for your wellbeing?"

"Yes."

"Do you want to live my lifestyle?"

"Yes!"

"Healthy?"

"Yes!"

"Happy?"

"Yes!"

"Affluent?"

"Yes!"

"Successful?"

"Yes!"

"Driven?"

"Yes!"

"Ambitious?"

"Yes!"

"Are you gonna truly commit to changing your life?"

"Yes!!"

"Good. Man up and get in the fucking drawer!"

CHAPTER 54

Regardless of being physically exhausted, I lay in this morgue drawer as stiff as the bodies I just witnessed. It's freezing in here and that stingy motherfucker didn't even give me a blanket. Snug my ass! If it gets any colder I might become a corpse myself. JJ did, however, give me a special pill that sustains your body at the correct temperature to prevent hypothermia. It was invented for Eskimos and Canadians apparently.

About ten minutes have passed and I'm still scared to death. I'm doubting if I can make it through the night. I just lay here numb, staring at the cold, shiny metal unable to sleep. Seeing the young men and women who have been taken from this earth because of drugs is literally sickening. I know with absolute certainty I will never touch drugs again.

I try my best to change my focus, but it doesn't help, it just switches one pain to another. I'm totally and utterly overwhelmed with emotion from these past few days, and it's weighing on me heavily. Sweat accumulates my upper neck region regardless of this cold habitat.

I'm paranoid that I'm unworthy of my future self's life. It's just so foreign to me. I mean, his place is a palace. His guest room alone must have cost tens of thousands to kit out. Hell, his kitchen probably cost more than my whole house. And his body: I still can't imagine getting in that kind of shape despite the fact I know he is me. When someone else loses a lot of weight I always think I could never achieve that, but even with him being the future me, I still can't picture having a body like that, it's just too hard to accept.

Tears come in droves like I've been rejected from life itself. I'm not sure if I'm cut out for this…

I begin to toss and turn as more images come flooding back. The image of David's last moments still wrecks me because he was so full of life and truly lived it to the max. Him wallowing on his deathbed will act as a stark reminder to live life to the fullest and never take anything for granted, or I too will have major regrets when I'm old and wrinkly.

Then images of slaughtered animals creep into my head. It was so horrendous to watch them squeal as they fought and struggled before their throats were severed open so they can be made into a Sloppy Joe. I can't ever support eating meat again because this inhumane process has woken me up. Every time I see meat now I'm completely repulsed.

I continue to sob.

Then the images of all the people I used to refer as *bums* shoots into my mind, the ones I met in the streets like Barry Bockwinkel and Koko, to the ones Kool Keith exposed me to like Burt and Fester. Can you imagine doing so many drugs you can no longer control your bodily functions? The lessons I took away are absolutely priceless and will act as a jarring reminder to never squander my precious life. How could I have ever called them *bums?* Most are just lost souls with no direction but all I ever did was overbear them like a big fat angry bully. I can't be like that anymore. I'm going to speak to them with courtesy and respect and help guide them from now on.

Then, Fink 'The Shrink' pops into my head. Here's a guy born a midget who must have gone through hell growing up being teased at school and looked at like an oddity, but today he has more happiness and confidence than about ninety-five percent of the population. Extraordinary human being!

Then Tommy; he overcame unbelievable health challenges and chronic diseases but healed himself through a sound diet and healthy lifestyle. And with a body like Ricky 'The Dragon' Steamboat he's become a leading example of what's possible. What a guy!

And finally, Kerry and Charlene X come into play. For Kerry to have been maimed from a horrendous accident that ended his football career and left him disabled, then turned it all around, formed a successful company and lives every day with such gratitude and fulfillment is truly incredible. And for Charlene to have been blinded and raped by her uncle but refuses to hang on to any pain from the past, instead she became a leading business lady in her community. She's a monumental success without a shadow of a doubt.

I will never forget these priceless lessons and every time I'm faced with a so-called 'problem' all I need to do is think at least I'm not a one-legged, blind, diseased riddled midget that's been raped by my uncle!

CHAPTER 55

My eyes begin to flicker as I slowly awaken from my slumber. I'm pretty fuzzy and disoriented so it takes me a while to gather my senses. I almost feel like I've been asleep for days. I notice a little drool coming out the side of my mouth and I'm having trouble breathing through my congested nose. Hmmm, okay…something feels odd.

I feel the need to stretch for a second as I'm as stiff as a board and soon observe sunlight seeping into the room.

What the hell?

I rub my watery eyes to clear my vision and look around. Holy motherfucking shit, I'm back here in this shit-hole ghetto house again! It looks exactly the same as before — beer-stained floors, smashed bottles and all-around uncleanliness and filth. I can't freaking believe it. What the hell is going on?

I stand up and stretch out again, cracking my stiff joints, and notice a multitude of stains on my white shirt just like before. Okay, is this some kind of Groundhog Day shit or what?

I rush to the bathroom, avoiding broken glass, spilled beer and God knows what else on this filthy floor and check my reflection. Ugh, my ELF looks so rough and rugged and my suit looks like it's been through a Royal Rumble. I'm just a hot mess, with a large emphasis on the word *mess*.

I gaze out the window to observe the surroundings and of course, it's the hood. A group of boisterous kids play in the street (including some without shoes), old men are sat in their porches babbling away to each other, while dogs run carelessly around the roads without human supervision. Nothing looks or feels different now. The cars and houses all look normal, there's nothing futuristic anymore. Hmmm, does this mean I'm back in my time?

A wave of emotions hits me like a lightning bolt.

I get it now. This is my time to change! My chance to put things right and follow the path of my future self instead of living like a selfish, out-of-control swine. I'm on my own now, but know what I have to do! There's no time to waste; I have to get back to my family!

I pull my head together and check my pockets; surprise-surprise: no wallet, no cash, no keys, no phone. Fuck it, it's pointless getting upset again, there's nothing I can do about it, I've gotta get home.

I button up my blazer and exit to the street. I need to get into familiar territory so I head the same way I did before (at least I think I do).

I then spot a taxi coming my way, thank God. I'll just pay when I get home assuming home is still home. Luckily the cab isn't occupied so I flag it down and jump right in.

"Oh, how excited am I to see you, my lovely," I say to the redheaded doll-face behind the wheel.

"Ditto, where have you been all my life? You seem awfully happy today."

"Well, my dear, what can I say; I woke up this morning with both my legs and both my eyes perfectly intact. I have no diseases, I've never been raped, pillaged or plundered and I'm not a four foot four midget."

She laughs probably thinking I'm a bonafide weirdo.

"I would class that as a great way to start the day, wouldn't you?"

"Pretty bizarre philosophy. I'm Peggy and where are we going to, Mr. Excitement?"

"Mayfield."

"That's a bit of a trip across town."

"I know right, but what am I supposed to do, skip all the way home?" I smile as she pulls off. "Hey, Miss Peggy, let me ask you something which may come across a little strange."

"Stranger than the shit you said a minute ago? Oh, now I can't wait."

"Well, maybe not that strange, just a simple request: can you tell me the exact day, month and year, please?"

She asks if this is some kind of test or something.

"I assure you, it's not. I have no ulterior motives, so no need to be all nervous up there." I catch her smiling in the rearview.

"I'm not nervous, you just threw me off. I'm pretty sure I can flawlessly recite that information."

"Well, then let's hear it and maybe this will earn you a little extra tip assuming you get me there safely with both my legs intact."

"Deal. Are you ready?"

"Oh, I'm ready, Peggy Sue." I start patting the back of the headrest doing a mock drum roll.

"Okay. It is Sunday, October, eighteenth, two thousand and—"

BEEP!

Some crazed driver in a black van comes out of nowhere, completely cutting us off and nearly causing a pile-up. Luckily her super-hero like reflexes save us as she swerves out of harm's way.

"WATCH WHERE YOU'RE GOING, JACKASS!" shouts my frantic driver beeping the horn again.

I start to laugh as we resume driving which bemuses her, to say the least. I reveal that I love the word *jackass* and crack up every time I hear it.

"We nearly get involved in a bad auto-wreck and you start laughing? Man, you are positive!"

"Guess I am." I shrug.

She ogles me in the rearview and tells me in all my years of driving a cab I'm one of the zaniest fellas she's ever met.

"Well, recently I've decided to not let things bother me anymore. You see, I was a loser in my former life and used to have reoccurring nightmares about failing at everything and dying with my music inside me."

"You're a musician?"

"Certainly not, I don't even sing in the shower. I mean it in the metaphorical sense."

She nods but not convincingly.

"I mean, we all have something inside us, a purpose, a hunger, a passion that we yearn to put out into the universe. The sad thing is very few actually do. Most just plod along in life and have major regrets right until their final moments and then die with their music still inside them."

This makes her ponder as he hit a little gridlock.

"And that, Peggie, scares me more than anything so I've made the decision to live my life exactly how I want to before I too am eaten by worms."

"I've gotta be honest, I can't remember the last time I met somebody who talks like you."

"Something amazing happened to me recently that has..." I try to think of the right way to word it, "...lit a fire under my ass."

"Really?"

"Oh yeah."

Of course, she proceeds in wanting to know everything.

"It's so unbelievable that I can't share it with you or anyone, unfortunately."

"Ahhh, man, please."

I shake my head.

"What a gyp. You got me all intrigued now."

"I'm sorry, Peggy, I can't. I mean, I know we've known each other a long time and all, but I really can't."

"Fair enough."

We turn a corner and come to a red.

"Just think of it like asking a professional wrestler to break Kayfabe."

"Huh?"

"Oh sorry, let me rephrase the analogy: think of it like asking a magician on how he does his tricks; once you know it, it can ruin the fun. Sometimes it's better not to know."

"I guess," she says as we pull off again.

"Do you know any magicians, Peggy?"

"No, I can't say that I do."

"Me neither. Do you believe in magic?"

"Yeah, I think so. Do you?"

"Yeah, I think I do too."

"So what's your name? I forgot to ask."

"Bobby," I say automatically before catching myself. "My friends, though, call me JJ…"

CHAPTER 56

I arrive home to a locked house with no cars or humans in sight. Probably a good thing because my stained shirt and overall horrendous appearance will not go down well. I'm a big believer in stashing an emergency key in the back yard for situations like this, unlike my parents who were always too paranoid that a stranger would find it and rob the place without technically breaking and entering. Luckily I've never been that paranoid.

I retrieve the key from my secret hideout behind the tree, enter through the rear, then pay for the cab with some loose cash that I grab from my bedroom draw. The house is exactly as I remember it; too much clutter and hoarded junk along with Max's toys slung everywhere — I think it's safe to say I'm home.

After a much-needed power-shower, I hear noises from below and can barely contain myself. I rush downstairs dripping wet, sporting nothing but my JYD beach towel and approach a sight for sore eyes known as my wife. She unloads a couple of shopping bags onto the counter in the kitchen as I scurry up to her from behind.

"Hey, pumpkin-head."

I startle her as she spins around and move in for a hug. It doesn't work. She's understandably resistant and rejects my embracing arms. It's okay, damage control is my area of expertise.

"Listen, before you say anything I know you're mad at me, and you have every right to be. I've been a disgrace—"

"A disgrace? A disgrace would be the understatement of the millennium, Bobby. Do you even remember yesterday? You ruined the entire party because once again you drank too much! You humiliated everybody! Poor Max will be the laughing stock of the school now."

It's so nice just to hear her voice even though it's in a vicious and indignant tone.

"You're right, you're right, you're right, and for that, I must apologize. In fact, there's a lot more than just yesterday that I need to apologize for." I get down on one knee with the towel luckily still holding in place. "Listen. Over the past few months, I've been a wretched swine of a human being. I've been a candidate for the world's worst husband, no doubt. I've neglected you and treated you like shit, I've neglected Max, I've neglected work, I've neglected my health with food, alcohol and even something else…"

"What are you talking about?"

I take a deep breath, shit myself and dive right in. "Can you remember when I told you I felt like I was going through a midlife crisis and didn't know where I was going in life?"

"Yeah, I remember."

"I felt deeply ashamed and embarrassed and didn't want to bring you down with my problems, so I went into a shell for a while. Let me tell you; it had nothing to do with you, it was all me thinking the grass is greener on the other side of the fence."

This is hard for me to come clean like this, it's something I've ever done before. I become a little mushy while thinking of the best way to convey what's coming next. "So one night Cam gave me some coke for a little fun, and ever since then I developed a taste for it. It took a life of its own and really got out of control which explains all the late nights I've been having."

"Cocaine, Bobby? Are you freaking kidding me?"

"It's true. I'm absolutely appalled at myself and I'm sorry again for the shit I've put you through. It was a foolish way to try and escape my depression, instead of stepping up and facing it like a man." I stand back up, towering over her perplexed face. "Ever since I lost my status as a realtor and accepted a job that was beneath me I've never been the same. That's when the depression really started to manifest, which led me down my path of self-destruction, and worst of all: the path of being a bad husband and father, and for that, I beg for your forgiveness."

I take a little five-second pause to let her digest my sins but must continue before she takes it in a different direction.

"None of that shit was the real me, Sherri, it was just some bullshit escapism and being too cowardly to face my problems. The real me doesn't settle for less. The real me gives it my all. The real me cherishes every single moment because we only get one shot at life. And the real me is a great freaking husband, father and human being." I tear up. "There's a good person inside me, Sherri, I just selfishly locked him away for too long, but I've awakened him now!"

She starts to well up too as she leans against the counter for balance. "Oh, Bobby, come here."

We embrace in perhaps the best hug of our entire marriage, at least the most emotional. Her warm hands grip around my slippery back and feel so comforting like she's my protector. It's such a sweet moment and is long overdue and I, quite frankly, don't want it to end.

"From this day forth you will see a new me! I've had a revelation!"

"A revelation?" she questions as I break the hug and look deep into those exquisite moist eyes.

"Yes! My depression has completely cleared up, one hundred percent. No out-of-control drinking, no more drugs, no more abusing myself with shitty foods! I'll never be that piece of shit husband ever again, I swear to you on my soul."

She stands all teary-eyed and tells me she can't remember the last time I opened up like this.

"You mark my words, Sherri, I'm gonna get back in shape, and I'm gonna go all-in on my mission and ambition! And I guarantee our marriage will be legendary!"

We hug again. Oh, the sweet feeling of forgiveness. We embrace tighter than two Eskimos in an igloo until I break it telling her there's one thing I need. "No more Bobby, okay? Bobby is dead."

"Come again?"

"From this day forth I will no longer be referred to as Bobby."

Obviously confused she just stands there mute wanting me to elaborate.

"Look, I know it sounds a little strange but I cannot and will not live as Bobby any longer, and I'm deadly serious about that."

"What are you talking about?" Her forehead tightens with more confusion until I finally let on what I mean exactly.

"*Bobby* reminds me too much of the person I used to be. I'm not into dwelling on the past anymore; I'm about reinventing myself for the future and working towards a legacy to be proud of."

"Okay…?"

"From this day forth I want you to refer to me as JJ."

"*JJ?*"

"Yes, James Jannetty, but JJ sounds cooler. Your husband JJ is the most incredible husband you can ever dream of. I know it sounds strange but I can't go on as Bobby. He reminds me too much of the guy I don't want to be anymore, so I've buried him and reinvented myself."

"Are you still on drugs?"

"Very funny. It's strange I know, because you've always known me as Bobby, but I really don't like that guy anymore, and I will not answer to that name. Think of it like Rocky Maivia reinventing himself as The Rock."

"Again with your stupid wrestling."

"Okay, how about this: Bobby was a caterpillar who has evolved into a butterfly called JJ. Are you cool with that?"

"When did you decide this?"

"When I woke up this morning. I just can't be that guy anymore."

I pause to study her face. I think she finally gets that I'm serious and accepts me. Overwhelmed with joy I embrace her once again and tell her it's time to celebrate with Max.

"She's across the street with Julie."

"Well let's go get our little dynamite kid and celebrate her bornday properly."

"Alright, Mr. JJ, but just one thing."

"What?"

"Put some clothes on first."

"Ah yes, clothes. I got so excited, I forgot I wasn't wearing any."

I waste no time and hustle up the stairs. In a fit of excitement, I rush too quickly across the landing and slip on the wooden floor — hitting the deck like Cactus Jack taking a bump off the top rope. I start laughing uncontrollably as I lay on the floor like a dead fish, despite being in pain.

As I look up at the light bulb dangling from the ceiling, I calm my silly laughter down and just stare, drifting off in my mind. I forget about my pain and feel a sense of tranquillity, almost like I'm floating on a cloud... Cloud Nine...

A remarkable idea for an invention hits me like a ton of bricks. I can't believe nobody has ever thought of this before! Talk about the elusive obvious! I get a full-on, clear image of my brilliance almost like it's being channeled into me from the Divine. This is literally a light bulb moment, my Eureka, my Flux Capacitor. If I can pull this off, it will be absolutely phenomenal and it would be extremely beneficial for Mankind! I can't believe it came from my freaking brain! This is definitely something I can patent, put together and get out to the world. I feel it in my bones!

"Wooohooo!"

I gotta draw the designs out right now!

Acknowledgements

I want to thank everybody who supported and inspired me over the years while putting this project together. Victoria Midgley. David Tasker. Daniel Davidson. Kristin Stepp. Laura Kandetzke. Lisa Walker. Jenette "Gillette" Litvin. Karl & Clare Pearson. Anna "Molly" Barley. Jim Rohn. Trista St. Mary. Andrea Fenton. Lee Gorman. Tom Platz. Sarah Bester. Nicola Arnold. Eric "BananaMan" Bochniarz. David Rayner. Dave Winter. Liam Sweet. Richard Waltz. Robert Rodriguez. Gigi Rodriguez. Jilly "Belligerent Beanz" Gehring. Tony Robbins. "Jolly" Jim O'Sullivan. David "Stubsy" Abbott. Steve Martin. Lisa Boothby. Aimee Arnold. Jordan Belfort. Ric Flair. Matt Groening. Joey Traeger. Bobbie & Jeff Thomas. Terry & Jeanie Wykes. Ben Tombs aka "The Foundation." Taylor Dillion. Gav Conlan. Iain Oaten. Bobsy Alltoft. Sean Conroy. Matty "Tony" Stark. Simon "No Pie Si" Lidgard. Adam Bratley. Simon Tasker. Conrad Thompson. Bruce Prichard. Jim Cornette. Stephen & Gemma King. Jason Bacon. Richard "Tricky" Bacon. James Young. Matthew Pattinson. Ian Bacon aka "The Solution." Robert Zemeckis. Dennis "Ghostface Killah" Coles. Robert "The Rza" Diggs. Shyheim Franklin. Nathan Wrigley. Josh Chesler. Paul Dean. Zoe Gilbertson. Mike Gilbertson aka "The Junkyard Dog." Tom & Jemma Lister. Jack Benza. Barry Foy. Neil Strauss. Erik Von Markovik. QT. Vinnie Mack. Tania Leyva. Gary Vaynerchuk. Deirdre Colgan. Sean Stephenson. Richard Bandler. Jake Roberts. Vijay Paltoo. And my sister from the same Mister: Melissa Shaw, and anybody else who I may have missed.

CPSIA information can be obtained
at www.ICGtesting.com
Printed in the USA
LVHW030702160321
681657LV00009B/86